THE THIRTY-THIRD HOUR

ALSO BY MITCHELL CHEFITZ

The Seventh Telling

THE
THIRTY-THIRD
HOUR

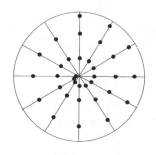

MITCHELL CHEFITZ

St. Martin's Press
New York

www.stmartins.com

Library of Congress Cataloging-in-Publication Data

Chefitz, Mitchell.
The thirty-third hour / Mitchell Chefitz.—1st ed.
p.   cm.
ISBN 0-312-27758-X
1. Family—Religious aspects—Judaism—Fiction. 2. Jews—Florida—Miami—Fiction. 3. Jewish
educators—Fiction. 4. Miami (Fla.)—Fiction. 5. Rabbis—Fiction. I. Title: 33rd hour. II. Title.
PS3553.H34873 T48   2002
813'.6—dc21   2001041979

First Edition: January 2002

10 9 8 7 6 5 4 3 2 1

In memory of George

Introduction

"So, what is real, and what isn't?" Is every novelist hounded by such questions?

In the introduction to *The Seventh Telling*, the precursor to this volume, I cautioned the reader not to confuse me with Moshe Katan, being neither so competent nor so terrible as he appears to be. In truth, I am far more like Stephanie, who chafes against the limitations of the Lurianic Kabbalah. But neither Moshe nor Stephanie is in any way real. The teaching of the Kabbalah, however, is.

The Thirty-third Hour is also a teaching tale. As the discipline of the Kabbalah in *The Seventh Telling* is genuine, so is the teaching of Torah (Scripture) in *The Thirty-third Hour*.

The family learning program described has been ongoing in Miami for twenty years. Anyone who has participated in the Sunday morning Family Bayt Midrash (house of study) will recognize the programs. But another caution: please do not attempt to identify the participants, because they spring entirely from the imagination.

The real students, those children who matured through the process of the Bayt Midrash, are far more wonderful than any of those sketched in these pages. They learned from an early age to argue words of Torah with adults. Their opinions were cherished whenever spoken. They became confident in their expression and have carried that confidence through bar / bat mitzvah into the world. If I should write of the accomplishments of these students, I would be accused of fiction, so I write a novel instead.

· · ·

My wife, Walli, has been involved in the development of this sequel from its earliest stages. If St. Martin's Press has provided the checks that have sustained me through this work, Walli has provided the balance. Some years ago we walked through the streets of Coconut Grove and imagined the paths of Arthur, Charlotte, Brenda, and Daniel. A rabbi and his wife. Temptation and redemption. None of it real. Patterned after no one and no institution in particular. Fiction, but still a reflection from beyond denominational boundaries to blend with the visions of others who are speculating upon the shape of religious community in this new paradigm.

I also benefit from a professional team that must be the envy of every writer: my agent, Natasha Kern; my writing coach, Lesley Kellas Payne; my editor at St. Martin's, Michael Denneny; and his assistant, Christina Prestia, who manages to juggle a dozen projects at a time and keep them all, miraculously, in the air.

There is no glossary to this work, no appendix to anticipate and answer your questions. A Web site is a far more versatile tool for such a task: www.mitchellchefitz.com will provide you a vehicle for feedback. I will be as responsive as time permits, posting programs and reading group guides to meet the needs of those who desire to continue learning.

—MITCHELL CHEFITZ

THE THIRTY-THIRD HOUR

CHAPTER 1

SUNDAY, 12:05 A.M.

Just after midnight, as Saturday became the Sunday of Memorial Day weekend, Rabbi Arthur Greenberg parked in the space reserved for him alongside Temple Emet, the largest Liberal Jewish congregation in greater Miami. If the broad and elegant facade of the sanctuary did not testify to that, surely the number of reserved spaces under the canopy did. His space first, then those of the two assistant rabbis, the cantor, the cantorial assistant, the executive director, the assistant director, and still more beyond that. He closed the door of his Oldsmobile gently so as not to disturb the neighbor to the south. The plans for the new buildings were before the zoning board. There were enough problems with the neighbors to the north without inviting additional complaints.

Two years it had taken him to coax, cajole, commit the leadership of the temple to the building campaign, and now the whole project was in doubt. Zoning and funding, so necessary if the day school was to expand. Outmoded classrooms and not enough of them. The weekend religious school so large it demanded double sessions Saturday and Sunday. Eight hundred more families since the last structure had been dedicated. Even the sanctuary, sumptuous as it was, still not large enough to contain the entire congregation on the High Holidays. The time had come to build. He had everything almost in place. So close, but all so fragile. One scandal and the zoning and funding would come to an end.

Zoning and funding. The words echoed through the numbness. Weddings did this, every time. Alcohol, loud music, and the constant need to smile at banal conversation he couldn't hear from across the table. The Grand Bay or Signature Gardens, it was always the same.

1

Only midnight, and he was so tired. With a scandal about to ignite, he knew he would not be able to sleep, so he had dropped Charlotte at the house and in his tuxedo proceeded, half awake, into the night.

Arthur entered the sanctuary building through the side door, the one by the kitchen the caterers used. He answered the beeps of the security pad with what he hoped to be the current code. Please, he prayed, eyes braced closed lest the alarm go off. The executive director, paranoid since the desecration, changed the numbers every month. Would he have to explain to the Miami police once again he was the rabbi, not a neo-Nazi intent on spraying swastikas on the synagogue walls?

Blessed silence.

Another pad gained him direct access to his study. Not much of a secret that, the year of his birth entered backward, 7491.

An extension of the sanctuary roof sloped down through the long room into the exterior wall. Charlotte had done her best to atone for the sins with antiques and oriental carpets, but the ceiling and the cinder block wall, punctuated by stained plastic panes, were too much to overcome.

Was it because of those windows he wanted the new sanctuary? The windows were a crime, atrocious. Long ago he had begged the board for funds to replace them. It was not only a matter of the two that penetrated his study, but the twenty that scarred the southern wall. No, if it were a matter of vanity, he would have moved for the new building years before. There was a greater need now that commanded it, the need for adequate classrooms, for space to assemble for a single service on Rosh Hashanah, for an entire community together on Yom Kippur to stand in unison for Kol Nidre. Repeating the service left a foul taste in his mouth, but the distaste for the congregants was the balagan, the traffic confusion between the sessions as families rushed to leave and arrive. He had a vision: a larger sanctuary, a single service for the entire community, a smooth-flowing traffic pattern. The board was sold.

It was all true, every argument, every justification. But Arthur heard the echo of a deeper argument, the decades-old advice of his mentor, Rabbi Howard Lowenstein, of blessed memory, who had stood in the pulpit in Cleveland unscathed for forty years. "You will have doubts," Howard had advised the young Arthur. "When in doubt, build. The community will gather around a new building. If you perceive a weakness, a vacuum, if there is dissension, discord, build. It doesn't matter what. Just build. Nature abhors a vacuum. Build into it. A structure, an edifice. Attach names to it, and the people will come."

Had Howard really said that, or was Arthur confusing it with something he had heard in a movie? No matter. The classrooms were needed. The larger sanctuary, needed. But at the same time Howard's advice was solid. There was dissension in the ranks, grumbling about the program with little notion of how to make change, a vacuum of leadership. Arthur would create space to fill the vacuum.

With the lights toned down, the study was bearable, stained glass and cinder block notwithstanding, but Arthur needed light to clear the fog in his head. Caffeine was no longer available to him, by doctor's orders. Light was all he had.

With one hand he undid his bow tie and stuffed it into the breast pocket of his tuxedo jacket. The jacket he removed and hung in the closet next to his robes. He had a dozen, eight black for use on the Sabbath, four white for the Holy Days. He had never discarded a robe. He collected them, a history of his rabbinate, most in mothballs, the camphor vaguely odorous through plastic covers. Only the newest two, one black, one white, had the three stripes on each arm that marked the honorary doctorate bestowed upon him the year before by the seminary. The wedding couple had requested he not wear a robe, only the tuxedo. More and more he was hearing such a request. It used to be . . . He suspended the thought. No use considering what used to be.

He removed his ten-commandment cufflinks, put them in his right pocket, and groped for his keys. They weren't there. The keys were always in his right trouser pocket, wallet in his left. The french-cuff sleeves, linkless, sagged limp below his wrists. "Damn," he said aloud, not knowing the target of the epithet, only his need to express it. He rolled the cuffs up to his elbows, tracked back across the floor, found the keys on the carpet, by the closet. He didn't remember dropping them.

A key only he possessed unlocked the private filing cabinet. There was one more file to redeem, one that always remained behind lock and key, but he needed it now. Distasteful as it was, he would read it again. That file joined a stack of tapes, papers, a journal on his desk. He had a lot of work ahead of him and then a decision to make concerning a charge against a colleague. More than a matter of ethics, a criminal charge. With all the resultant publicity, a likely end to the zoning and funding.

The tapes and documents were unsettling, not only because of their nature and threat but by their very essence. Arthur was accustomed to a clean desk at the end of every day. He should have been a lawyer, he thought, as he did every time his work seemed unbearable. He placed his Montblanc pen by a fresh legal pad and considered where in the stack he should begin.

"Brenda," he said aloud. "It begins and ends with Brenda."

Nathan Karman had brought Brenda to Arthur eighteen years before.

Nathan and Arthur had played tennis and golf together at the club. Nathan was the attorney one consulted for zoning, the man of influence one consulted for funding. He knew what could be done and how.

He was divorced from his first wife before Arthur arrived in Miami. Brenda was to be his second. "She is not Jewish," Nathan said, "but she is very spiritual. She wants to convert."

Spiritual maybe, beautiful certainly. Twenty, maybe thirty years Nathan's junior, no secret the motivation for their relationship.

"I want to know something about Judaism," Brenda said, "and then I'll make a decision whether or not I want to convert." The words were empty, her direction already set. Such was the price she was willing to pay for status and security.

"She's what I always dreamed of," Nathan confided in the cart on the course. Blond and blue eyed, she reminded Arthur that he too had once entertained such dreams. He had outgrown them, but his friend had not.

Charlotte asked Arthur about the direction he would take in Brenda's instruction. Brenda was not a candidate for the conversion course. As the intended of a friend, she warranted personal coaching from the senior rabbi. He said he would begin with the story of Avishag, the young beauty obtained to warm the aging King David in his bed. "Don't you dare," Charlotte said, throwing a pillow at him. "Besides, you don't have to be so young or so beautiful to keep a bed warm." There was benefit from being around Nathan and Brenda in the excitement of their romance. Arthur and Charlotte made the most of it.

The wedding was a big affair at the Eden Roc. Charlotte took Brenda under her wing, and the two couples became a foursome for tennis, bridge, and dinner in the Gables.

After five years of trying, Brenda was pregnant and more beautiful than ever. Only her belly grew. It seemed but days after Daniel was born she was back in her bikini by the pool at the club. Daniel seemed fine at first, no

4

hint of any difficulty, but toward the end of the first year they began to make the round of doctors to find a name for what they knew to be wrong.

Nathan died at tennis. He won the set and lost his life, gone before help could arrive. Arthur and Charlotte did what they could for Brenda. She was consolable, left with ample means to provide for herself and her son.

Charlotte was more patient with Brenda than Arthur was. Without Nathan, Arthur had no reason to maintain the relationship, but Charlotte insisted for the sake of the son. A saint, Arthur's wife. He was not worthy of her, the thought no mere formulation. He knew it to be true. Her patience so far exceeded his, she was willing to put up even with him. He told her so every time he slipped beneath what he construed to be her measure. She shook her head, and he laughed, both expressions of love.

Some years after Nathan died, Brenda had come to see the rabbi, not Arthur but the rabbi. She came to his study in the synagogue, not to his home. She settled into the sofa across the coffee table from the rabbi in his wing chair.

"I need to consult with you about something," she began. Arthur waited for her to become comfortable. "It's about men," she said, "married men. Mostly it's the married men who make the passes. The single men don't— it's because of Daniel, I guess. But he doesn't keep the married men away. I must send out some signal that attracts them. Some are members of the temple." She named the names.

Arthur pretended astonishment to be polite. This was no great revelation. Brenda bragged of her men to Charlotte, those who wanted her, those who got her. Arthur heard similar stories from other sources. Once she thought a man might leave his wife. He did, for someone else. Brenda was vicious for weeks following. Still Charlotte put up with her. Brenda was like another daughter. To Charlotte, not to Arthur.

"Something in her childhood," Charlotte the social worker explained. She never ventured quite what but said, "It either turns them away from sex or turns them onto sex, rarely anything between. It's probably better this way. But their interest is in unavailable men, so you'd better be careful, darling."

Brenda's list became a litany, a veritable slate of officers for the next Board of Trustees. "I don't know what to do about it," Brenda went on. "If this is what the leadership of a synagogue is like, I don't know that I want to be a part of a synagogue anymore. I don't know that I want to be Jewish anymore, Rabbi. Arthur. I don't know what I want. No, I do know. I want

5

something spiritual. I want a religion that points toward God. I want to be able to ask God questions. I have a lot of questions. I don't know that I expect answers, but I want to be around people who are asking questions. I don't mean to hurt you, Arthur, but I haven't found that here. I haven't found that in Judaism."

Arthur defended his faith, made his suggestions. There were different expressions of spirituality, he explained. Not all involved prayer and talking to God. Social action and righteous deeds were a form of doing God's work and filled one with a sense of divine purpose. He suggested participation in the temple committee that cared for the homeless or work with Habitat for Humanity, a Christian program that nonetheless had a tie to the temple. That seemed to hold Brenda a while. She remained Jewish and continued her affiliation even after Turin came to town and opened his Institute for Jewish Spiritual Experience.

Rafael Turin had Orthodox ordination, *smichah* from a yeshivah in Jerusalem. For a decade he had taught Talmud and Zohar at a school in Safed. Some leaders of the Jewish Federation, the secular organization that funneled resources to the Jewish agencies of greater Miami, frustrated that less than twenty percent of the Jewish population of Dade County had any involvement with a synagogue, had invited him to Miami to attract those who might otherwise leave for alien disciplines. With such endorsement it would have been difficult to refuse him entry into the rabbinic association, but Turin made the rounds anyway, to assure colleagues his Institute would in no way compete with the standing synagogues. His intention was only to fill the vacuums that existed in the community.

Turin's Institute was a magnet for Brenda. He spoke of God in the deepest way. Brenda shared what she had learned with Arthur, but the language of the Kabbalah was foreign to him. If he had been more conversant with the vocabulary, would he have recognized the danger?

He drew the confidential file before him, determined to be done with it quickly.

Ultimately three women had filed the complaint. Brenda had been the first. She came to Arthur in tears, at the edge of a breakdown, to express her rage and confess her guilt and confusion. She had come only after the police had turned her away, finding not enough substance in her charge to warrant action. She had been furious, perhaps more with the police than with Turin. Turin, at least, had paid her attention.

Arthur lifted her deposition from the file.

She reported her name, address, age, and marital status.

"When did you first meet Rabbi Turin?" the questioner asked.

"In November of 1991."

"What was the occasion?"

"I had seen his ad in the Jewish newspaper for classes in Jewish spirituality. I attended a lecture he was giving at the JCC."

"What did he speak about?"

"He spoke about the power of the Kabbalah, that it was an age-old discipline that brought one into the immediate presence of God."

Turin had rented space in an office building and offered seminars, $150 for the six-week course. More advanced courses were more expensive.

Brenda learned about the realms of experience and the expression of the soul through the various worlds. She learned she was an extension of God itself, the connection immediate and eternal. She had been put into this lifetime to refine and perfect her soul, and whatever trials and tribulations she endured were for a purpose, even if that purpose was beyond her ability to grasp.

In the more advanced courses she learned of the need to surrender to the divine, how to meditate on nothing, closing her eyes and drawing her focus to a spot at the back of her head, so as to offer no resistance to the flux of the *ruach elokeem*, the Spirit of God.

A year into the training Turin advised her she was ready to be initiated into one-on-one study, to learn the secrets of the Kabbalah that could not be taught in a classroom setting. There was risk, he advised her, but she was willing.

She learned of the powers of *gevurah* and *hesed*, constancy and compassion. She understood Gevurah as a male principle, that which was finite and extended into the world. Hesed she considered to be the female, the infinite, willing receiver. She learned the secrets of the words *eesh* and *eeshah*, *eesh* being "man" and written with the letter *ycd*, *eeshah* being "female," written with the letter *hey*. The *yod*, a point of light, was to be deposited into the open receptacle of the *hey*. She learned that the recondite four-lettered name of God was itself divided into male and female components, that the name of God was complete only when the male united with the female. She was taught humans were created in the very image of God, the original human androgynous, male and female. It was not a rib that was separated from the first earthling, but a side. The feminine side was dissected away from the masculine, each but half the image of God. The full image of God was formed only in spiritual and holy union.

In the eighth session Turin told her she was being blocked in her advancement by certain repressive tendencies. Her surrender was not complete. Dance, he said, might help in the process of surrender, sacred dance to sacred music. He had her stand and sway, her eyes closed, to concentrate on nothing except the wind that emanated from God, to feel the energy flowing up her legs into her abdomen, across her shoulders and down into her breasts. Risk and exposure were the keys, he told her. She followed his instructions and removed her blouse. Greater risk, he said. She exposed her breasts and felt a flush of heat through her face and chest, a holy heat, he told her, an offering of *tiferet*, the Hebrew word for beauty, for glory. The eighth session was complete. He reminded her the personal lessons were secret. There were to be two more in the series. The next night she was to wear a long skirt, and she would learn the secret of *rahameem*, the secret of divine compassion.

"Why did you return for the next session?" the questioner asked.

"I was confused," Brenda said. "He was a holy teacher, my rebbe. I had learned so many truths from him. He had shared with me the secrets of the deepest Kabbalah."

"Did you enjoy dancing before him, exposing yourself like that?"

"I don't know. It was a profound experience. I don't know. I was confused."

"Were you a consenting adult in a sexual encounter?"

"I wasn't consenting. I hadn't been asked to consent. I was doing what I was told. How could I not do what I was told? He was a holy teacher. He was uniting the male and the female. He was lifting sparks. He was restoring the world."

The next night she had returned as bidden and danced again, her eyes closed. Her teacher instructed her to lift her skirt and unify the lower limbs by massaging the source of mercy. She touched herself, massaged herself, felt the warmth flow through her, a holy warmth.

"Keep your eyes closed." His words were spoken softly but jarring nonetheless, unnecessary, for her eyes were closed. She opened them and saw him reclining in his chair, his penis exposed, erect, untouched, his pelvis thrusting at some imaginary target.

"Close your eyes!" he ordered. "It is not for you yet to see the source of judgment!" She did not close her eyes. His semen shot into the air seemingly of its own accord. She at once marveled he had come to orgasm without any physical contact and at the same time was repulsed by the ugliness, the unseemliness of it all. She reached for her clothes. In spite of his commands she left the room and managed to start her car before the first sobs burst from her.

The next day she had gone to the police with her complaint. After a week of degradation, repeating her story from one office to the next, sensing at last she was not so much making a charge as providing an entertainment, she came to Arthur, the rabbi, in his study, to share what had happened. "You have to do something," she said. "You have to stop him. He must be doing this with others, too. He has to be stopped."

She made the calls and found four others who had suffered similar abuse, two of whom were willing to give depositions. They had completed the ninth session, which culminated in holy fellatio, the tenth in which they had straddled the holy teacher to unify the male and female aspects of the divine. It was good Brenda had stopped when she did, Arthur thought again, as he had every time he had reviewed the material.

The matter came before the ethics committee of the Board of Rabbis which hoped to manage the matter discretely. Rabbi Rafael Turin was summoned to appear before a *bayt din*, a rabbinic court. Arthur had a copy of the summons in his file.

Brenda and the two others testified against him. Turin did not deny the charges but rallied several of his students, male and female, to his defense. "He is a holy master," they said, "and ordinary standards do not apply to him. Whatever his actions, their only purpose was the service of God, and though they may appear to be base on the surface, at their depth they were necessary for the ultimate redemption of the world."

Word that the rabbinic court received and considered such testimony infuriated Brenda even more than Turin's violation. "Turin never fucked me," she told Arthur, "but I feel like these bastards have!"

Arthur counseled patience and assured her the court would come to an appropriate judgment. That judgment was also in his file. Ultimately it was not that Turin had taken advantage of women that did him in, but that one of the women, while divorced from her husband by a secular court, had never been issued a *geht*, a religious divorce. Therefore, in the eyes of the rabbinic court, she was still technically married. Turin was found guilty of adultery, and a judgment of *herem*, excision from the community, was passed against him:

Rafael Turin has no part in the God of Israel. It is forbidden for him to be counted among the quorum for prayer, to be called upon to recite a blessing over the Torah, to hold any office or membership in any Jewish organization or synagogue. It is forbidden for any Jew to stand in his immediate presence. It is forbidden even to have conversation with him or to engage in business with him in any way.

This was the edict pronounced by the rabbinic court to the Board of Rabbis. Turin was advised it would be published at large should he remain in Miami. His defiance lasted but two weeks. He announced to the community he was returning to a teaching position in Jerusalem. Before a farewell party could be arranged, he was gone.

Arthur returned the file to the cabinet, embarrassed by the flush that overcame him. "I'm only a man," he reminded himself. "Flesh and blood. I'm only a man."

"I am all right," Brenda protested when Arthur, Charlotte, and others among her friends encouraged her to seek help for her depression. Hospitalization might have been warranted, were it not for Daniel. She could not be separated from him for any extensive period.

After a year of medication and intensive therapy Brenda came to visit the rabbi again.

"It wasn't all bad, what he was teaching," she said. It had taken the year to separate the bad from the good.

"No, I'm sure it wasn't," Arthur agreed, "but he misused it."

"What do I do now?" she asked.

"What do you mean?"

"My needs are the same. I have the same questions, the same concerns. Helping the homeless doesn't answer the questions. With Rafi, it seemed I was learning how to ask, even get answers. I can't do that anymore. How can I ever trust such a teacher again?"

Rafi. Arthur was alarmed by her use of the intimate name. She was vulnerable. He had to find a safe situation for her. Without that impetus he might never have remembered Moshe's letter.

That letter was at the top of the stack on his desk. "Hi Artie," it began. That should have been reason enough to discard it unread. If only he had done that.

10

Hi Artie,

I regret I have been out of touch all this time, but I suspect you may know Rivie died a year ago. I have been considering ever since what to do. My work here in the Bay Area is done.

I have developed a program for family education, something to supplement and perhaps even someday replace what is happening in conventional religious schools. What I would like to do is borrow a dozen families for a year, to meet one morning a month. Adults and children will learn together.

Would you bring me in as a consultant? As a consultant, not a rabbi. I suspect the word *rabbi* will get in the way. And would you assign someone to record the sessions, on tape or in a journal? A book might come out of this, a guide others can follow.

I am writing this letter to you and all our old friends from the Upper West Side, those who are likely to remember me and Rivie. Salary is not important. The situation is. If this interests you, please be in touch, and we'll develop a strategy for integrating the program into your synagogue.

Moshe had signed the letter in Hebrew and in a postscript left instructions for reaching him at a post office box in New Mexico.

"I have been thinking of bringing in a consultant to do a special program on family education," Arthur told Brenda. "He's a remarkable person." He was on the verge of adding they had been classmates at the seminary but remembered Moshe's caution he not be identified as a rabbi. "I met Charlotte at his place on the Upper West Side. He and his wife introduced us. Rivkah. She died last year of cancer. Moshe is a specialist in family education, something he developed in California. He wants to come and introduce it here in Miami and asks that we provide someone to record the sessions."

Arthur found himself selling the program to Brenda. He had kept the letter, entertaining the notion only because it dovetailed with another he had received, but until Brenda had come to him looking for something to do, he had not really expected to extend an invitation to Moshe. The other letter was from the Jewish Federation, offering a grant of $40,000 to any synagogue willing to develop a family education program. He'd had every intention of requesting the grant but had meant to staff the program with in-house talent and supervise it himself. He did not need Moshe, yet here he was, proposing Moshe to Brenda. "His name is Moshe Katan. He's brilliant. Creative and innovative. Whatever he does will be a challenge."

Contemplating the materials piled on his desk, Arthur reached for a coffee cup that had been missing for months. Why had he made that offer? He'd had no obligation to Moshe, didn't even care for the man.

Yes, Moshe and Rivkah had introduced him to Charlotte. The Katan apartment on the Upper West Side provided cross-fertilization between the seminary and the Columbia school of social work, resulting in a good many rabbis married to MSWs.

Yes, Moshe was brilliant. He had won nearly all of the academic prizes. Talmud, Bible and Outstanding Student had gone to Moshe. History had been Arthur's. Arthur had no complaint. Moshe deserved his awards.

It was not jealousy that made him ill at ease. It was Moshe's attitude, his disrespect for the rabbinate, for the sanctity of the institution. The synagogue was the center of Jewish life, but even at the seminary, Moshe had denied it. "The paradigm has shifted," Moshe said, quoting a rebbe with whom he had learned in Jerusalem. "The day of the synagogue as we know it is done, the day of the rabbi as well. We are fossils, trained in techniques of no avail, masters of a discipline that no longer has a purpose. Our words will be as powerful, our diction as good, our message as clear as those who have preceded us. Their synagogues were full, but ours will be empty." Arthur remembered the essence of Moshe's words. They rang now like a curse come true.

Arthur's career had followed the conventional course, an assistantship in Cleveland with the prestigious Howard Lowenstein, then this emerging monolith in suburban Miami, eight hundred families that had become eighteen hundred. Moshe too had begun in the conventional fashion, assistant to a distinguished rabbi in California, then, nothing. Moshe disappeared, gone from the rabbinic landscape, while Arthur gained in prominence, first a member, then the chair of national committees. His name became known, his congregants proud of it. Still when he preached, his polished words fell into an empty sanctuary.

Arthur had heard Moshe preach only once, to fulfill his requirement for ordination. Arthur remembered Moshe's sermon, if not word for word, step for step. Moshe had said student rabbis served in one-step congregations, two at the most. In casual tones he spoke of driving to his pulpit in New Jersey where only one step separated him from his congregation. When he was ordained, he said, perhaps he might move to a three-step congregation, even a four. His tone of voice deepened, his posture straightened. He projected his message to the students and faculty with words more carefully chosen. After years of service, he might be called to a six-step pulpit, with yet another four ascending to the holy ark, from whence he might stand in robes ten steps high and pronounce his most eloquent phrases. In a clipped accent he said the words might drop from his mouth like pearls to roll down the steps among the feet of . . .

He had left the sentence unfinished. Those familiar with the New Testament completed it without difficulty, the allusion unsettling. Swine was not a kosher metaphor.

Why in heavens's name, Arthur now asked himself, had he extended an invitation to Moshe Katan to come to his congregation to teach?

Because of Brenda.

No, because of Charlotte. His wife the saint. The saint of lost causes. Ever patient and forgiving.

He himself was such a cause, he felt, down deep, but not so deep as to be unaware. Charlotte would not give up on Brenda, therefore Arthur couldn't. Should Arthur give up on Brenda, Charlotte might give up on him. She wouldn't, of course. Arthur knew that even as he thought it. That was his weakness, giving up, not Charlotte's. She was a rock, he but a river flowing with the path of least resistance.

"Bless her," he said, though it sounded to him more a curse as he reached with determination for the documents at the top of the stack. Because of Charlotte, Brenda. Because of Brenda, Moshe.

"Now let's see what the bastard did."

The first document was his initial letter to Moshe.

> Dear Moshe,
>
> So good to hear from you. I am sorry I was not in touch with you after your loss. News of Rivkah's passing came to me late. I apologize for not offering my sympathies sooner.
>
> Concerning your request to facilitate a family education program at Temple Emet, we would be delighted to have such a program, and I am pleased to extend an invitation to you to conduct it.
>
> We already have a person eager to assist you and record the sessions, as you requested. I think you will find her an able assistant.

I look forward to hearing from you soon so we can discuss the format of the program and, of course, determine an appropriate honorarium for your services.

Charlotte sends her best.

In friendship,

cc: Brenda Karman

The only mistake, he thought on rereading the letter, was to include Brenda's name. Bar that and the nature of the program might well have been different, more under his control. This whole matter might have been avoided.

Arthur had expected an opportunity to shape the program. He had been waiting for Moshe to call.

"Good to hear from you, Moshe," he would have begun. "I'm so happy you'll be joining our faculty. I'm sure we'll have no difficulty finding twelve families to work with you. As soon as I put out the word we have such a dynamic teacher coming to town, the roster will be full.

"Now, as for the honorarium. If we paid you, let's say, five hundred dollars a weekend, plus airfare back and forth to, where is it? New Mexico? That's where you are now, New Mexico? That's maybe another five hundred. Figure a thousand dollars a session. Let's make it twelve hundred to include your expenses while you're in Miami. We could arrange home hospitality. You'd be welcome to stay with me and Charlotte, of course, but you'd probably want your own space. Maybe the Marriott. We have an arrangement there. Ten programs at twelve hundred dollars each.

"Now for the program. The Garfinkel Youth Center has one big room where the children could have their class and a lounge in the back we could set up for the parents. Are you going to be working with the children or the parents? Do we need to hire another person to work with the group you're not with? If so, we have to know so we can budget for it.

"I must tell you I had been thinking of starting a program like this myself. I know the value of having the parents present to appreciate and reinforce what the children learn. Occasionally we have opportunities in our religious school for parents to participate with their children. Your idea of establishing this on an ongoing basis is excellent. I am happy you will be available to help us with it."

That's the way the phone conversation should have gone, but there had

14

never been such a conversation, or any conversation, until the program was already established.

Instead of calling him, Moshe had called Brenda. Arthur had given him the name. All Moshe had to do was ask Miami information for "Karman, Brenda," and Arthur was out of the loop. Never before and never again would a program generate in his congregation over which he had no control.

That, too, had been Howard Lowenstein's advice. All activities in the congregation were to emanate from the senior rabbi. "Not my fault," Arthur whispered, but he heard an admonition echo from a Cleveland cemetery. "Whatever happens in your congregation is your fault. Always. Don't forget that."

The first he had heard from Moshe was through Brenda. She strutted into his study with camera-ready copy for the brochure. His astonishment must have been apparent. "I don't like the title," he began. "Nobody will understand what 'Family Bayt Midrash' means." He had opened not with words of support or praise, as was his custom, but with criticism.

Brenda was too effusive to be taken aback. "It means 'family house of learning.'"

"I know what it means," Arthur said. "It's just that the congregation won't know what it means. It won't have any appeal."

"Mr. Katan says—"

Mr. Katan. Not Rabbi Katan. The "Mister" irked Arthur, but not as much as "Moshe" might have. At least Mr. Katan was keeping some professional distance.

"Mr. Katan says we should treat our people like intelligent adults. They will learn as they go along. I didn't know what *bayt midrash* meant, but I know now. It didn't take me long to catch on. It won't take our members long to catch on either."

Arthur scanned the text of the brochure. "He has it taking place in homes, not here in the youth center."

"We have it in homes," Brenda agreed. "Mr. Katan says the challenge isn't to make the synagogue Jewish but the homes Jewish. If we do Jewish programming in the homes, the families will remember that. They will learn the home is also a place where we do things Jewish."

Arthur was thankful for the *also*. At least the synagogue wasn't left out of the picture entirely. He continued his way through the brochure. "The adults and children study together. I imagined they would have separate classes and come together at the end."

"Mr. Katan says it's important the families work together as families. He's developed a system that works on several levels at once. When the children have had enough, they can go off and play. Most of the adults continue to study. Mr. Katan says the kids learn, the adults learn, but most important, the kids learn that the adults learn. That's the essence of it. Mostly all the kids ever see is kids learning and adults playing tennis. Here the kids see adults learning and enjoying it. They have role models, adults learning Torah."

"We have adult education in the synagogue," Arthur responded.

"He asked me what the budget was for that."

"Two thousand dollars," Arthur said without hesitation. He knew every line of the budget.

"Then he asked what the entire operational budget was. I didn't know the answer to either question."

"Two-point-two million."

"He said it would be something like that. A thousand to one, funds spent for children. Even when some adults are learning, the children never get to see it. Besides, it's not their parents doing the learning."

"How will you find your families?" Arthur asked.

"I have four already. The Kantors, the Garfinkels, the Lopezes, and the Schwartzes. I could have twelve if I wanted. You'd be surprised how many are looking for an alternative to religious school. But I thought I would leave the rest of the positions open and see who would come forward of their own accord. I have an article in the next temple bulletin, and we'll send this out next month. That should take care of it."

Arthur tapped a pencil on his desk pad as he thought about that conversation with Brenda. The tapping made little noise. Ten months before, as Brenda had been speaking, he had also been tapping. It had taken some little time to absorb the shock of Brenda's words. It was a fait accompli. He couldn't do bupkis about it, a violation of everything he had learned in his apprenticeship. Beyond that, the four families were among the most generous donors to the temple. In large measure he was depending on them to lead the way in the funding of his new buildings.

"Dollars," he had said in an attempt to regain control. "We haven't yet decided if we can afford this. The cost of airfare alone will be prodigious, and I don't know what he will require by way of salary. We'll have to get all of this approved by the Executive Committee."

"We talked about cost," Brenda continued in the same matter-of-fact

16

tone. "Mr. Katan doesn't want a salary. He says his funding comes from another source. There won't be any airfare. He will be staying here in Miami."

Signed and sealed. A done deal. Arthur could not dispose of Moshe without alienating Brenda and the other families already dedicated to the project.

Charlotte had invited Moshe and Brenda to dinner. "He's single," she'd explained to Arthur. "He did as much for us."

"Rivie did that," Arthur countered. "That was all Rivie. One hundred percent."

Rivie had died of ovarian cancer. Charlotte's mother and grandmother had also died of ovarian cancer. As balanced, as solid, as wonderful as Charlotte was, even she had fears and limits. No argument came from her as to whom had invited whom. "Even if Brenda wasn't going to assist Moshe," Charlotte continued without acknowledging Arthur's contention, "I would have invited her. She's looking for someone spiritual."

"Whatever that means," Arthur said.

Moshe was late for that dinner. Arthur opened a bottle of Chivas Regal some congregant had given him at a Hanukkah party only God knew how many years before, poured some for Brenda, Charlotte, and, for himself, more than he could finish. The cheese dip was nearly done when the doorbell rang.

God, Arthur thought, Moshe still looked like a student. Twenty-five years had salt-and-peppered his beard and grayed him at the temples, but the curly brown hair was still too long and the jeans—he still wore jeans—too baggy.

Charlotte was effusive in her greeting. After a hug and kiss she said, "You've lost so much weight."

"A long time ago," Moshe said.

Arthur hadn't noticed that. What he saw mostly was Moshe's vacant smile, there and not there at the same time, as if he was looking at something amusing in the background. Arthur remembered that smile, how Moshe used to make him want to turn around to see what he was missing. But it was Moshe who had become missing, Arthur reminded himself, missing in action, missing from the Rabbinic Union for the last two decades, missing from the committees that set policy and direction for Liberal Judaism. Even as a student, Moshe had seemed missing even when present, though for all his seeming inattention in class, Moshe was the cistern who held everything. He spoke rarely, answered questions only when no one else could. His answers were always correct.

Dinner conversation was limited. Charlotte did not want to speak about Rivkah. Arthur could not talk of the rabbinate without somehow implicating Moshe as a colleague. Moshe had not been inclined to include Arthur in the planning and could not be expected to discuss the program. That left Brenda to carry the evening. She did so by telling stories from the Kabbalah she had learned from Turin, speaking of him as if the abuse had never occurred, every mention of Turin's name contributing to Arthur's indigestion. Moshe listened to the stories, nodding his head, enjoying his meal.

To Charlotte's question Moshe said he had rented a small house in Coconut Grove, in the old section where the neighborhoods were mixed, poor African American homes yielding year by year to gentrification. Charlotte said, as she had on other occasions, she would like to move from Pinecrest to the Grove. She claimed the Grove had character. Arthur was content in the comfort and security of Pinecrest.

Dinner done, Charlotte and Arthur accompanied their guests to the street, Brenda to her Mercedes, Moshe to a gleaming silver Porsche. "This is yours?" Arthur asked, feeling stupid in the question.

"I'm not sure whether she is mine or I am hers," Moshe said.

Seventy thousand dollars, Arthur thought as he watched Moshe drive away.

"Did you see that car?" Arthur asked his wife.

"What car?"

"Moshe's Porsche. Seventy thousand dollars minimum for a car like that, and it's German. Rabbis don't drive Porsches."

"Brenda drives a Mercedes."

"Brenda's not a rabbi."

"Moshe's not either. Didn't you tell me he didn't want to be a rabbi anymore? I guess he can drive a Porsche now."

In his study Arthur pondered the Porsche and fiddled with the first videotape. The Porsche was a paradox. Arthur would like to own one. With his salary he could afford it, especially now that Tamar was on her own. No more college expenses, not another penny for Oberlin. She should have gone to Kenyon. Even with a smaller Jewish student population, it would have been better, less damage done. One incentive to anger opened the door to all the others. Better to think of the Porsche. That was enough. He would like to have a Porsche, but should he buy one, he might be out of a job and have no salary.

"Rabbis don't drive Porsches," he said aloud, slamming the door shut on his anger.

Arthur recalled his discomfort following that dinner. It did not fade as the Porsche diminished in the distance, rather it moved into his stomach, a presentment immune to Tums and Maalox. His father-in-law, Aaron Deutsch, of blessed memory, had taught him not to ignore such conditions. They would only get worse. Better to confront them at the outset, over martinis.

The Captain's Table, a haven of cool, nautical-themed darkness buried in the flank of a strip mall on South Dixie Highway, was his venue of choice for such encounters. If Arthur had a difference with a member of the board, it was at the Captain's Table such differences would be aired. But not in the first meeting, never in the first meeting. Sometimes not even in the second. In the third meeting differences might be brought safely to the table.

Arthur invited Moshe to lunch at the Captain's Table the first day of September, the Thursday before Labor Day weekend, a wasted Labor Day because Rosh Hashanah followed immediately after, so there was no vacation, no getting away. Pressed as he was, this was something for Arthur to do before the Holy Days, to settle his stomach.

Maybe Moshe played tennis, Arthur thought, as he cruised through the parking lot in search of an open space. He was looking also for the silver Porsche. He didn't want to be first to this luncheon. He wanted Moshe there, waiting for him. He found a parking space but no Porsche.

Maybe Moshe played tennis, Arthur thought again as he opened the door and crossed the threshold, a familiar transition from light to shade, from the blast of Miami summer heat into the envelope of Miami air-conditioning.

The oak bench in the vestibule was empty. No Moshe. Arthur checked the bar, scanned the tables for a man sitting alone. No Moshe. The bench was his to sit on and wait. Several times the door opened. Light and heat, but no Moshe.

Five minutes Arthur waited, an eternity, until Moshe entered blinded from the Miami sun, not able to see Arthur directly in front of him.

"I'm right here," Arthur said.

"Hi, Artie," Moshe said and smiled. "I'm sorry if I'm late. Couldn't find a parking space."

Their table was by one of the aquaria that supplemented the nautical paraphernalia that hung on the wall and from the ceiling. Bright blue and yellow fish circulated among the artificial coral.

"A gin martini, straight up, two olives," Arthur said to the waitress. "What will you have, Moshe?"

"I've never had a martini," Moshe admitted.

"Two martinis," Arthur said. "If you don't like it, we'll get you something else, and I'll have the pleasure of two."

They had the fish to look at.

"Do you play tennis?" Arthur asked.

"I scuba dive," Moshe said. "Do you dive? You have some of the best diving in the world only forty-five minutes away."

"No. We have friends with a boat, though. We go out on the bay, fish a little, have lunch."

"Off Key Largo. Pennekamp Park, an underwater park. No spear fishing. So many fish. Coral gardens, twenty, thirty feet deep. How often do you play tennis?"

"Twice a week."

"That's good. I've been diving only once since I've been here. Maybe I can dive every week. Rivkah and I used to go on diving vacations. Here, actually, down in the keys. And the Bahamas. Do you get over to the Bahamas?"

"No. I was sorry to hear about Rivkah." The martinis arrived, full to the brim. "I don't know how they do that," Arthur continued. "They don't spill a drop from the bar to the table, and I can't get it from the table to my mouth without slurping it all over my hand."

The olives, pierced through by a plastic sword, were served on the side. Moshe examined his with care. "Do we say the blessing over the olives or the drink?"

Arthur had never said a blessing over a martini.

"For the olives," Moshe said, reciting *boray pree ha-etz*. "It was like a scuba dive, those last months with Rivkah. I hadn't thought about it like that before." He looked up from his drink. "Are you happy here, in what you do?"

The question startled Arthur. If anything, that was for the second meeting, surely not the first.

"What does that mean, like a scuba dive?"

"Dying. A scuba dive is like a little lifetime. You go down with a full tank of air, thrash about the reef looking for fish. Then in mid-dive you settle down. The fish come out to look at you. When you have only a few hundred pounds of air left, you slow down, stop moving to conserve air and prolong the dive. You settle on a few square inches of coral. During those last minutes you see more wonders in that small world than you did in the entire dive. Then you drift off to the ladder, a pair of angel fish with you, and climb up to the higher world. The captain greets you and asks how the dive was.

"That's a scuba dive. That's what it was like with Rivkah. Her world closed in and in, down to a few square inches. The angel fish were with her, and she climbed to a higher world."

Arthur sipped at his martini. "You were with her?"

"I was with her. I died, too, Artie. I died with her. She went on. I came back. I don't know why."

"What do you mean, you died?"

Moshe shrugged. "Died. Dead. I stopped breathing. My heart stopped beating. But I didn't stay there. I came back. Are you happy in what you're doing?"

"Why do you keep asking that? I don't seem happy to you?"

"I don't know. I find most people aren't happy in what they're doing, especially rabbis. I don't know many happy rabbis, do you?"

Arthur sipped from his drink and eyed Moshe's. "Do you like your martini?"

"It's good. I'm happy to have it. Something new. Have you ever had a margarita? I think I'll try that next. Not today. Next time. This is a good thing, lunch together. Next time a margarita. That's the one with salt around the rim? Rivkah and I weren't much for drinking. Wine. She liked red wine. We used to go up to Sonoma, a place there, up in the hills. It used to be off the beaten path, but then all the paths got beaten. Poor paths. Beaten all to hell, tourists trampling all over them. Like us. Tourists like us. We were guilty, too. We just found those paths and beat the hell out of them. I don't think you can find an unbeaten path in all of northern California, now."

Golf, Arthur thought. Maybe Moshe played golf. But he didn't ask. He finished his martini and looked around for the waitress. "All of the fish is good," he said to Moshe. "The trout Françaises, especially, if the captain himself is cooking. If it's someone else in the kitchen, don't order the trout Françaises."

"Whatever you're having, Artie. I'll have the same."

The captain was cooking. Arthur ordered trout Françaises with capers. Blue cheese dressing for the salad, no sprouts. "You never know about sprouts," he told Moshe. "Bacteria."

"Are you happy in what you're doing?" Moshe asked. "I heard there was a rabbinic conference last year, I forget whether it was Traditional or Liberal or something else. Rabbis only, not open to the press. Someone asked how many of the rabbis would be members of their congregations if they weren't working there. Not one raised his hand. Or her hand. Not one."

"I wasn't at that conference," Arthur said. "Where are you going to be for the high holidays? Do you have a pulpit?"

"A pulpit? No, I haven't had a pulpit in a long time."

"I forgot. You stopped being a rabbi."

"I stopped. I stopped being a rabbi before being a rabbi stopped me."

The salad arrived.

"I asked for no sprouts," Arthur said.

The waitress made to take the salad back. "Not to worry," Moshe said. He reached over and picked the mound of sprouts off Arthur's salad and added them to his own. "This much risk I can take."

"Where will you be for the holidays?" Arthur asked him. "Do you need a ticket? Call the office, and I'll make sure one is waiting."

Moshe laughed. "Thank you, but I'll be in California."

"Where do you go to services?"

"With the Havurah. There are about three hundred of us."

"I thought a havurah was a small group."

"This is a large group made up of a lot of small groups. The only time all of us get together is for the Holy Days."

"Do you lead the services?"

"I used to. I don't anymore."

"Since Rivkah died?"

"Since long before. I might lead one of the services now and then." He seemed about to add something, stopped, began again. "I didn't go to services at all last year. I was out in the desert. I lost track of time, somehow. When I realized what time it was, the Holy Days had already passed."

"It was hard for you, Rivkah's death."

"It was hard. Her dying, her death. My dying, my death."

Arthur didn't know how to continue. He had counseled any number of people in mourning, those who had lost parents, spouses, even children. Moshe seemed to have lost something more. Himself. Was that possible, to be in mourning for the loss of oneself? "Are you happy in what you're doing?" he asked Moshe, turning the question back on him.

"This is very good, to be here," he said instantly. "It's very good to be here," he repeated. "With the martini." He held up the glass. "With the fish." He nodded toward the aquarium. "With you. I remember you. How many years? Twenty-five? I remember your paper on the Pharisees. What do you think would have happened if the Temple hadn't been destroyed by the Romans? Would we still be offering animal sacrifice? You never addressed that question. No one ever addressed it."

Arthur was saved by the trout Françaises, a generous portion, with capers and scalloped potatoes on the side. They ate for a while in silence. Moshe ate slowly, putting his fork down between bites.

"You like it," Arthur said.

"I wonder if it would be as good without the martini."

"The captain is a good cook, but I'm sure the martini helps. Would you like another?"

Moshe hadn't heard him. He was lost in his fish, chewing slowly, his eyes almost closed. The man was damaged, Arthur realized. "Moshe, what's happening with you? Are you okay?"

"Time isn't quite right with me, Artie. Time and space aren't quite what they used to be. I have to be careful now, to stay attached. But I understand things better. The fish is good. The potatoes are good. I don't care much for the capers. Next time, no capers. I've learned how to do one thing at a time. Fish. Potatoes. Capers. No, I haven't quite learned. I'm still learning. Do you know the story of how the Baal Shem Tov fasted?"

Arthur shook his head more to dispel his astonishment at the disjointed responses than to acknowledge he did not know how the Baal Shem Tov fasted.

"There was a student," Moshe said, "a young man who wanted to be very holy, so he told his teacher he was going to fast from Shabbat to Shabbat. The teacher said it was forbidden, to fast like that. The student said the Baal Shem Tov used to do it. 'Ah,' said the teacher. 'You want to fast like the holy master fasted. That's okay, then. You can fast that way.' So immediately the student knew he was in trouble. He had no choice but to ask his teacher how the holy Baal Shem Tov used to fast. The teacher said, 'Saturday night, after havdalah, the Baal Shem Tov would bring to his table enough food to sustain him a week, so he wouldn't have to be disturbed in his studies. Sometimes, at the end of the week, he would be astonished to find the food was still there, untouched. To fast like that is all right."

"That's a nice story," Arthur said.

"I wonder about Yom Kippur," Moshe said. "Last year, when I was alone in the desert, I don't know if I fasted on Yom Kippur or not. I like to think I did. I like to think Yom Kippur was during one of those weeks."

CHAPTER 2

SUNDAY, 1:20 A.M.

Had it not been for the sloping ceiling, the coarse walls, and the odd windows, Arthur would have considered his study the epitome of comfort. His private bathroom was complete with a shower even though he had never used it, had never so much as turned it on to determine if the plumbing worked. His tea service was sterling, the china, Spode. The mahogany bookcases held not only his rabbinic volumes but also a television and a VCR. These he did use, mostly to review tapes of his own television appearances. Arthur was a regular guest on religious dialogue programs. The archbishop was a personal friend.

The wall opposite the bookcase held pictures, diplomas, plaques, framed newspaper articles. Some of the pictures were mere poses, but of some he was truly proud. The one with Jimmy Carter, that was a pose, but the one with the Reverend Garrison, that was a reason to be proud—the march in Overtown, a protest, black and Jewish leaders together. That march had made a difference. The articles were of such events, each one a significant moment in the history of Miami, turning points in the development of the black, the Cuban, the Haitian neighborhoods. Arthur had never hesitated to put his body on the line. He was the first of the rabbis called. Others followed. The causes of the disadvantaged communities burned within him. The pictures were important reminders to all who visited his study. They spoke of where he had stood, where he would stand, and they encouraged others to stand with him.

Such courage, Arthur thought as he was about to delve into Moshe's program. Such courage, but he hadn't been able to take a stand with Moshe, to ask him about the program and his intentions. Moshe was somehow frightening, even terrifying. All of Arthur's courage was consumed in that first lunch. He had intended to draw the line, bring Moshe and his program under control, but he hadn't been able to make so much as a hyphen in Moshe's strange chain of logic. Like Charlotte with Rivkah, Arthur thought, so it was with himself and Moshe. The family history of ovarian cancer was enough to deter Charlotte from reflections of Rivkah. That was understandable. But what was there in Moshe that so disturbed Arthur?

He sat in the wing chair and pressed the remote to cue the tape to the first session, "Genesis at the Garfinkels, Sunday, September 18." He had known Brenda had taped the sessions, but he had never before asked to see them. With a chill he realized he might have incurred some liability, not having viewed the tapes to provide proper supervision for a temple activity. With some apprehension he turned the volume up.

The Garfinkels had a large home at the end of a cul-de-sac in Gables-by-the-Sea. They had built on a double lot to afford themselves the luxury of a tennis court and a large back yard. It did not surprise him that Brenda and Moshe had chosen such a home to initiate the series. The living room was large enough to accommodate two dozen families, let alone a dozen.

The tape showed not the home but the cul-de-sac. Brenda had set her camera up high, perhaps on top of a car or van. Cars lined the perimeter of the circle. Neither Moshe's Porsche nor Brenda's Mercedes was in sight. He heard Brenda speak as from a distance, "Sound check, Moshe."

"Checking, one two three four." Moshe's voice was clear. He was wired for sound. Brenda had sophisticated equipment. Whatever platform the camera stood upon jiggled as Brenda descended from it. He expected to see her enter the frame and was not disappointed. Brenda was wearing shorts, her blond ponytail an exclamation point above a derriere and legs that needed no such punctuation to attract attention. She set out bait, he thought, then complained when someone nibbled at it.

A stucco wall and a wrought-iron gate protected the house. There was a sign on the wall by the entrance. The video image was not clear enough to allow Arthur to read it, but he remembered its message. It bore the picture of a Doberman and the caption, *I can reach this gate in 2 seconds. Can you?* Adults and children walked from the yard onto the asphalt. At least the program had begun inside, Arthur thought, realizing it bothered him Moshe was using the street rather than the house.

"Come to the center!" Moshe said. "Right here, to the center!" Moshe wore jeans, a black T-shirt emblazoned with a gold Jewish star, cowboy boots, a cowboy hat. "To the center!" He began to sing a Hasidic tune Arthur had not heard before. Those courageous enough to be the first to the center sang along with him. They must have learned the tune inside the house. The words were, *Ya ba bim bam,* over and over again. The song pulled in the stragglers.

"Closer still," Moshe encouraged them. "Closer. Squeeze in close, as close to this spot as you can get." Moshe pointed toward his feet. "Imagine this spot is the most powerful magnet the world has ever known and you are bits of iron and all you want is to be close to that magnet. Push in. Allow yourselves to be pulled in, as close to this spot as you can possibly manage."

The milling focused inward toward Moshe. "Imagine all of us are standing on this single point. All of us *are* a single point. We all merge into one if we get close enough. If we're far enough away from each other, we're just a bunch of individuals. If we come closer, we're a group. Closer still, we're a crowd. Maybe a mob. But if we get so close, we become one. The Hebrew word for such a oneness is *yihud.* It means a unity, a singularity, a oneness. Who has the string?" Moshe asked, the question seeming to Arthur incongruous. A hand popped up with a ball of twine. "Pass it out and around the perimeter so we're all inside a circle of string," Moshe instructed.

Children giggled at the pressure. Adults laughed. "Pull the string tighter," Moshe instructed. The laughter increased. "This is a yihud," Moshe said. "A singularity. When God began to create the universe, there was nothing but God. God's desire was so great God allowed the universe to be created within itself. At first it was no more than the tiniest dot. It was a yihud. A singularity. As soon as it was made, it began to expand. God said, 'Let there be light,' and it expanded at the speed of light. We won't move so fast. Before we begin to move, I'd like to hear the niggun once again." Moshe began, *Ya ba bim bam.* The song swelled up around him to a substantial volume.

When the energy drained from the song, Moshe said, "I'm going to count to three. When I say three, everybody take a tiny step back with your right foot. Everyone knows which foot is your right? Just a tiny step back, when I say three. Ready? One, two . . . three."

The compression pulsed outward. "We'll do another step back, this time with the left foot. Ready? One, two . . . three." Another pulse.

"We're no longer a yihud," Moshe said. "Before we were one, a unity, a singularity. You couldn't measure across us. Now you can measure. We'll take another step back, with the right foot. One, two . . . three. Let the

27

string out so it stays around us. As we expand, let the string out. Now slowly, a step back. Don't wait for me to count. Another step. Another. Another."

Arthur watched the circle expand, the string maintaining the circumference. "Notice what's happening," Moshe said. "We're getting farther and farther from each other." The circle became large, not quite out to the perimeter of the cul-de-sac but large enough so the adults and older children were not touching each other. Some of the younger children stood close to parents.

Moshe said, "Notice how you feel as we move farther away from each other. Was it nicer when we were closer? Did you like being closer, or do you like being farther away? Let's try this. Maybe this will help. Let's sing the niggun again." He began with the *Ya ba bim bam*. Others joined in with him, but the singing did not reach the same volume.

"Was it easier to sing when we were closer together, or now that we're farther away?" There were murmured responses.

"Take another step back," he instructed. "Another. Notice the momentum has us going outward. How would we ever get back to the middle?"

"What's on the other side of the string?" one of the parents asked.

"The cars!" one of the children answered.

"I wish it were that simple," Moshe laughed. "Some say what's on the other side of the string is God. The universe expands like a bubble into the body of God, as much as one can say such a thing. It's as if God is blowing the bubble from the center of the circle, and the bubble expands inside God itself. Outside we have God, and inside the breath of God. The breath of God is called soul. We'll learn more about this later. Let me show you how to get back to the center."

Moshe reached into his pocket and took out the biggest piece of chalk Arthur had ever seen. Quickly he walked around the perimeter of the circle and made six marks. "We need some volunteers to make some lines. Use the string. Hold it here," he said, pointing to a mark by his feet, "and there." He pointed two marks away. "Hurry! We need a way to get back!" Adults held the string. One of the older children ran the chalk along it and drew a tolerably straight line.

"Now from here to here," Moshe pointed. The string moved, was held, another line was drawn. "Now here." A triangle took shape on the asphalt of the cul-de-sac.

In as short a time a second triangle was drawn on top of the first, creating a star of David. The children had seen it coming and announced it.

"Into the triangles!" Moshe commanded. "Quickly! Into the triangles." Seven, maybe eight people scurried into each of the triangles. Moshe stood in the center of the star.

"Now we learn how to get back," he said. "Now we learn how to get back," he repeated. "Tradition teaches God created the world in six days. Do you remember what God created on the first day?"

"Light," came the response.

"Light," Moshe agreed. "God created day and night, separating the light from the darkness." He pointed toward one of the triangles, perhaps the one from which the answer had come. "You are the first day," Moshe said.

Turning around, he asked, "What did God create on the second day?" When there was no correct answer, he said, "God separated the waters above from the waters below. God created the oceans and the seas." He pointed down. "Then God created the waters above, the clouds." He pointed up. To the next triangle he said, "You are the second day, the waters above, the waters below, and the sky between.

"What did God create on the third day? The dry land." He did not wait for answers. The energy was beginning to dissipate. "The dry land and the trees and plants. You are the third day. And what on the fourth day?"

"Sun, moon, and stars," came the response.

"Yes," Moshe agreed. "This triangle is the sun, the moon, and the stars. Notice you are directly across from the triangle where God created the light.

"And on the fifth day? The birds and the fishes. This triangle is the fifth day. You are the birds and the fishes. Notice you are right across from the waters above, the clouds where the birds fly, and the waters below, the oceans where the fish swim.

"And now for the sixth day."

"Man," a male voice proclaimed.

"Men and women," said a female voice.

"Men, women, and animals," Moshe said, "to inhabit the land that was created right across there, on the third day. This triangle is the men, the women, and the animals.

"Now what I would like you to do is to choose a song for your day. This triangle come up with song for light, for night and day. This one for the sky and the seas. You for the land and the trees. You for the sun, moon, and stars. Here, the birds and the fish. And you, men, women, and animals. Talk together. Find a song. You have just a minute or two to decide."

Moshe waited for a moment, circled to see that each triangle was engaged, then left the circle, stepped off camera. He was wired, so his voice could still be heard clearly even though he could not be seen.

"Hi. I don't remember your name, but I remember where you were sitting inside, leaning against the wall by the piano."

The response was not clear.

"What's your name?"

"Andy."

"Andy?"

"Andy Perlman."

"I noticed you had a knife. Could I see it?"

"You going to take it from me?"

"No. I'd like to see it, if that's okay." There was a silence. "This looks like a good knife. We don't need a knife this morning. In our next session we'll need a knife. Will you bring it then?"

"Okay."

"But we don't need it today. If people see the knife today, they won't know what it's for, and they may be disturbed by it. So put it away for today. Don't take it out again, all right? Next session you can take it out, because we'll have to use it. Okay?"

"Okay."

Arthur stopped the tape to ponder what he had just heard. He did not know the Perlmans. He went to his desk, spun his chair around to the computer, and drew up the database. Perlman, Morty and Marsha. One child, Andy. Age twelve. He had been scheduled for a bar mitzvah in December but had withdrawn from the program.

If Andy had shown a knife during religious school, he would have been sent to the principal's office. His parents would have been called in for a consultation. He might have been suspended or even expelled. At the very least the warnings would have been grave. Arthur had not seen Moshe confront the knife-wielding Andy, but he had heard it. Moshe had encouraged the child to bring the knife to the next session. That was hardly temple policy, but Moshe was not on temple grounds and obviously had no interest in temple policy.

Arthur rewound the tape and listened again to Moshe's words. The video clung steadily to the Magen David in the cul-de-sac and the groups in each triangle laughing through the process of choosing songs.

The video progressed. Moshe returned to the center of the circle. "How are we doing?" he shouted. "Are you ready? Do you have your song? Only a few more seconds and we begin!"

Moshe walked from point to point with words of encouragement, then back to the center. "We'll begin!" he said and held up his hand. Adults around the perimeter held up their hands and soon there was quiet.

"Day one, please sing your song," Moshe requested.

"Night and day, you are the one," two grandparents began.

"No!" some protested. *"Day-o, is a daaay-o—evening come and I wanna go home!"*

That was the song, and it generated some laughter.

Moshe moved to the second point. With enthusiasm they sang, *"Mayim mayim mayim mayim, hey mayim bi'sasson,"* the Hebrew Water Song.

The third point sang, *"This land is your land, this land is my land."*

The fourth, *"You are my sunshine, my only sunshine."*

The fifth, *"Let me tell you 'bout the birds and the bees."*

The sixth, *"If I could talk to the animals."*

Moshe asked them to sing all together. They began with a confusion that became cacophony. "Louder!" Moshe encouraged them, and they responded. "Now, begin to walk slowly toward the center." As they gravitated toward him, he began to sing, *"Shabbat Shalom, Shabbat Shalom, Shabbat Shabbat Shabbat, Shabbat Shalom."* Those closest joined him, and soon all were together in the center singing *Shabbat Shalom,* a Sabbath of peace.

"Back out to your triangles!" Moshe shouted. Arthur reached instinctively for the remote to lower the volume. "Back out into the days of the week!"

The crowd disbursed into the triangles, and each again resumed its weekday song.

"To the center again!" Moshe instructed.

They rejoined in the center, singing *Shabbat Shalom,* then once again returned to the points of the star.

Moshe signaled for silence. "So the way back is built into the system," he said. "Six days we do our work and sing our songs out at the perimeter, each of us going our own way, then on the seventh day, we stop working, and come back into the center. One more time!" He motioned them inward. The families joined together in the center singing *Shabbat Shalom.*

Moshe held up his arms for silence. He was in no hurry. Others held up their arms, mimicking Moshe, inviting those nearby to be silent.

"It's written in the Torah we are to observe the seventh day as a Sabbath, as Shabbat, to keep it holy, to keep it separate from the other days of

31

the week. I think now you know why. It also says if you don't do that, you die. Die? Don't you think that's a little extreme? But then have you ever heard the expression 'Get a life?' Can you imagine someone who works every day and never takes a break, never has a Shabbat? You call that living, working like that? To such a person you would say, 'Get a life.' And why would you say 'Get a life,' unless the person didn't have a life? And if the person didn't have a life, I guess that's the definition of dead.

"This may be the most important thing we learn this year. The whole purpose is to get a life. That's what Judaism teaches, to get the best life we can possibly get, and it begins with Shabbat.

"Okay, that's enough out here in the street. Those children and adults who want to play, there are some games waiting for you in the yard. Those who would like to learn some more are welcome to meet with me in the dining room."

Happy voices accompanied the scene of movement away from the cul-de-sac, some families choosing the driveway, others the front entrance into the yard. Brenda walked toward the camera, Moshe just behind her. "Be careful, Daniel," Brenda said. "Give me room." Arthur realized for the first time Daniel had been present. The cul-de-sac jiggled with the motion of the camera, and the screen went blank.

Arthur rewound the tape and pondered what he might have done had he viewed that video back in October when Brenda had offered him the opportunity.

"Eventually," he had told her, being diplomatic. "I'll look at it eventually," his words prophetic, even though he had no intention of ever viewing the tape. They hadn't consulted him when they established the program. Why should he bother to critique it? Such was his reasoning at the time. He chided himself for his petulance.

Would he have intervened in the matter of Andy Perlman? Moshe had addressed the matter of the knife and seemed to have it under control. That would have sufficed.

The families had been happy. The program was successful. Arthur was troubled somewhat that the Genesis story had been taught as if it were real, that God had been portrayed as the creator of the world in six days who had a need for rest on the seventh. Perhaps in his introduction Moshe had talked of the other Mesopotamian creation myths and placed the biblical story of creation into its proper perspective. There was a stack of audio tapes on his desk. Perhaps one of them held a recording of the introduction.

Arthur consulted his watch. One forty-five. He couldn't stop. Monday morning at nine Brenda would demand to know what course of action he would take. Would he have enough time to view, to hear and to read everything on his desk? He had not anticipated there would be so much, but Friday afternoon she had stormed back into his study with the box of materials and made a show of removing the journal and the tapes, piling them high on his desk. "Go through it now!"

"Brenda," he protested, "it's Shabbat in a few hours. And tomorrow night I have a wedding."

"Then Sunday," she said in a tone that admitted no further negotiation. "You look at them on Sunday. Monday morning, nine o'clock, I want to know what action you're going to take. If you don't do anything, Monday morning I go to the police myself."

Friday afternoon Arthur had sorted the materials. The journal was a bound volume covered with a floral fabric. It was stuffed with papers, some loose, some pasted in. He had resolved to examine nothing until after the Sabbath but had opened to the first page nonetheless.

The date of the first entry was the evening of the dinner at his home. The opening sentence had filled him with dread.

What is the difference between Rafi and Moshe?

"God help me," Arthur had said aloud and continued reading.

Rafi was there. Moshe is not.
Rafi spoke incessantly. Moshe speaks hardly at all.
Rafi paid attention to me. Moshe knows I'm here.
Rafi took advantage of me. I don't think Moshe could.

Arthur had wondered what she meant by that. She was not attracted to Moshe? She was too strong to be controlled by Moshe? She had such an attraction for Moshe she might take advantage of him rather than the other way around? He had read no further, putting the matter aside until Sunday.

Arthur read the first entry again, then the second, dated a week later and labeled *Greenstreets in the Grove*. He imagined them sitting at a table outside on Commodore, among the beautiful people. The entry was no more than a list of materials needed for the first session.

String
Street chalk
Shabbat guides
Notebooks
Bibles
Call the host family to ask what to bring
    Bagels
    Juice
    Donuts
    Cream cheese
        No lox or whitefish. Keep it simple, affordable.
        Only bagels and cream cheese.
    Host family makes the coffee?
Paper goods
Street space. Garfinkels?
Names and addresses
What to wear

Arthur closed the book. "Rafi took advantage of me. I don't think Moshe could," echoed through him. He reached for the top audiotape and knocked the pile over. Fatigue washed through him. He pushed it away. "It's going to be a long night."

The tape began with shuffling sounds, people coming to a table, some effusive mumbling. Arthur turned the volume high and left his study for the office to start a pot of real coffee, caffeine be damned.

"The purpose of the first creation story . . ." Moshe began and paused. Arthur heard the sound of chairs dragged along a tile floor. "Among the purposes of the first creation story is to teach Shabbat. The Sabbath is among the greatest gifts we have given to the world. There are some gifts we have kept for ourselves, but others we have shared with the world. Their intrinsic value is so great it is recognized at once and the world absorbs them, and then of course forgets where they came from. Torah is such a gift. And the Sabbath. Especially the Sabbath. We celebrate it on Saturday, the Christians on Sunday, the Muslims on Friday. It's still the Sabbath. Our gift to the world.

"Sometimes when someone says they are not religious, I ask if they observe a weekend. If they say yes, I tell them they're religious.

"The seventh day. The seven-day week is the only period of the calendar not determined astronomically. Did you know that? A year, what's a year? What happens in a year?"

A child's voice responded, "The earth goes around the sun."

"And a month?"

The same voice said, "The moon goes around the earth."

"Something like that," Moshe said. "The moon and earth go around each other. They complete one cycle. The Jewish month is a lunar month. Now, what's a day? A day is the time it takes the earth to turn once on its axis. And then a week? What's a week?"

"Seven days," an adult male contributed.

"Why seven? What's the significance of seven? There is no significance to seven other than God created the world in six days and rested on the seventh. That's why I say that if you observe a weekend, to some degree you are religious.

"Outside on the street you experienced the lesson of Shabbat in a deeper way. Six days a week we go out into the world, each of us doing our own thing, and on the seventh day we come back to the center, together, all of us. That coming to center is very important. Imagine what it would be like if we never came to center, if we just continued out and out and out, farther and farther from each other, until the string around us broke."

Moshe paused. Arthur gave him credit. The image was good.

"When we come to center," Moshe continued, "there are things we traditionally do."

"Light candles," the child's voice said.

"Yes, we light candles. There are lots of things we do. I remember once when . . ." He stopped. "What do you think the most important thing is that we do on Shabbat evening?"

"The candles," the same voice said again.

"I remember when my wife and I were engaged and we met with one of my teachers, a traditional Jew. He asked us what wedding presents we expected to receive. China, silver, crystal. He said the most important thing we could do for our marriage was to use those presents every Friday night. He didn't say anything about candles or wine or bread. He said, 'Just use the china. Everything else will fall into place after that.'"

"That's silly," the child said.

35

"Robert, be quiet," an adult voice admonished. "Let Mr. Katan finish what he's saying." Arthur recognized the voice, Michelle Kantor.

"Brenda, do you have the Shabbat guides?" Moshe asked. "Before you leave, be sure to take one of these. They're from my havurah in California. There's lots of good stuff in them, but the most important thing for you to consider is . . ."

"Lighting candles," Robert interrupted once again.

"Robert!"

"Mrs. Schwartz said it was lighting the candles."

". . . the section on blessing children," Moshe continued, ignoring the interruption. "For newlyweds, it's using the china. For us, it's blessing the children. The sooner you start, the better. Every month we're going to be scheduling a Shabbat dinner at one of our homes. We don't expect everyone to come to every dinner, but now and then. We can learn by doing."

"Do you have children, Moshe?" Arthur did not recognize the woman's voice.

"No," Moshe said. "We had no children. I was looking forward so much to blessing them, but we had no children. Once when I visited my teacher on a Friday evening in Jerusalem—he and his wife were in their sixties—a son, maybe forty years old, had come to visit. I remember it so clearly. Before the kiddush, before the blessing over the wine at the dinner table, the son came to the father for a blessing. The father placed his hands on his son's head and said the words of blessing. I was blown away. I had never seen anything like that before. I realized every Friday night when this son was in his father's presence, he would come to his father for a blessing. He had been blessed as a infant. He had been blessed as a child. He had been blessed when he was a rebellious teenager. I could imagine father and son arguing all Friday during the day, but Friday night, the son would come to his father for a blessing. The blessing was real. The argument was hormones. They both knew that. I could imagine the father in his nineties, the son seventy, coming to his father for a blessing. I can't tell you what that did to me, that one moment in Jerusalem. I couldn't wait to have a child, just to bless him or her. But we had no children.

"It's not too late for any of you. If you wait till they're fifteen, it may be too late. But the oldest child we have here is twelve. Even at twelve it's not too late. We'll do a Shabbat dinner, and I'll show you how it's done. It may be awkward at first if you've never done it, but if you do it from the heart, it will pay dividends you can hardly believe."

36

Moshe paused. The tape was silent. No one coughed. No chairs moved on the tile floor.

"Now," Moshe continued, "the second creation story. If the first story comes to teach us about the Sabbath, the second story comes to teach us about sex."

Arthur sat erect.

"Sex," Moshe repeated. "Let me ask you some questions about the story and we'll see how much you remember. What fruit was it that Adam and Eve ate in the garden of Eden?"

"An apple," came the response from several sources.

"A fig," Robert said.

"Why a fig?" Moshe asked.

"Because they made clothes out of fig leaves."

"And it doesn't say they ate an apple?"

"No. Mrs. Schwartz says it was a fig, not an apple."

"Good for Mrs. Schwartz," Moshe said. "Since you know so much about the story, Robert, perhaps you'd be kind enough to let the rest of us answer the next few questions, okay?" He paused. "Robert is right. The Torah never mentions an apple. It doesn't tell us what the fruit was, but it might have been a fig. Now another question that has no real answer, though that doesn't mean there isn't an answer. Each of us has an answer in mind, and there is no right or wrong here, just what you have in mind. How old was Adam when he was created?"

"Twenty," came an answer. Other voices added, "Thirty." "Eighteen." "Twenty-six."

"A young man," Moshe agreed. "Now how old was Eve when she was created? In your imagination, now, in the story. What do you imagine?"

"Sixteen." "Eighteen." "Twenty."

"A young woman. Now another question. When Adam was created, what was he wearing?"

"Nothing." "Naked."

"Nothing at all? Right. Nothing at all. Now if you had to choose a movie star to play the role of Adam, who would you choose?"

"Brad Pitt." "Christian Slater." "Mel Gibson."

"Well, let's choose one. Brad Pitt, okay? And his costume? No costume. Stark naked. Now who would we choose to play Eve?"

"Cindy Crawford." "Julia Roberts." "Bo Derek."

"We'll stay with Cindy, okay? Okay. And what is she wearing? Right.

37

Nothing. Nothing at all. So we have a naked Brad Pitt and a naked Cindy Crawford playing Adam and Eve. Now, a serious question. Before they ate that fruit, the fig or the apple or whatever it might have been, did they have sex? Did they fool around? What do you think? Think it over carefully, because the way you answer it can be a matter of life or death."

Arthur listened intently. Robert was present, twelve years old. Were there other children? Was he the only one? Was Daniel there? The buzz on the tape indicated discussion in earnest.

"A vote," Moshe interrupted. "You can change your mind later. A straw vote now. How many say they had sex before eating the fruit? How many after? About half and half.

"Let's see what the consequences might be of having no sex before eating the fruit. Eating the fruit is sinful. They see they are naked and they are ashamed. Only after the sin of eating the fruit do they have sex. So sex is sinful and shameful, and the word you would associate with sex would be sinful and shameful, you know, like the *f* word." Moshe paused. "Fooling around." Laughter. "It indicates sin and shame. More than that, anything born out of a sinful act would be born in sin and would have to be cleansed of its original sin. So the need for baptism, to cleanse a child of original sin.

"Now consider the consequences of separating sex from the sin of eating from the fruit of the tree. Sex before sin. Adam and Eve, Brad and Cindy, sinless, shameless sex in the garden. No parents to tell them what to do or what not to do. No law against it. The only law was not to eat the fruit of the tree. So sex is not sinful and it is not shameful. Does anyone know how to say *fuck* in Hebrew?" Laughter. "I'm serious. How many of you went to Hebrew school? Do you know how to curse in Hebrew? How about Spanish?" More laughter.

"You can't say *fuck* in Hebrew," Moshe continued. "The words for sex are not dirty words. You could say *couple*, but *go couple yourself* doesn't have the same impact as *go fuck yourself*. The rabbinic words for sex are *ta-anug*, which means '*pleasure.*' Or *tashmish mitah*, which means '*use of the bed.*' Go pleasure yourself? Go use your bed?

"I was once playing poker with an Israeli friend. Draw poker. Nothing wild. I drew four fours. He had four tens. He was so proud of himself. I wanted to say something sharp and penetrating. Now I know some Hebrew, but for the life of me I couldn't think of how to say *go fuck yourself*. All I could do was to say, *lech vi-hiz-da-*fuck *et atzmechah!*" Laughter. "I had to take the English word and put it into Hebrew context. Now listen closely, Robert. I don't want you going around repeating that. It will get you into a lot of trouble in the wrong places, especially with Mrs. Schwartz."

So Robert was the only child present, Arthur thought. Even so . . .

"So it makes a substantial difference, whether they had sex before or after. Before, sex is not sinful, not shameful. After, just the opposite. It is reflected in the vernacular, in the way we speak."

"But you said life and death," an adult said.

"Yes, even life and death. You have a Catholic hospital here in Miami? Have any of you had children there? I asked a Catholic physician about this once. You know abortion is not permitted at any Catholic hospital. What if in the process of a delivery a doctor had to make a decision to save either the mother or the child, which would you prefer? Sacrifice the mother for the sake of the child, or the child for the sake of the mother?"

"Save the mother," was the unanimous response.

"That's the Jewish answer, but if it should come to that in a Catholic hospital, the decision would be to save the child and sacrifice the mother. The mother has been cleansed of original sin through baptism and merits heaven. The baby has not been baptized. Save the baby, sacrifice the mother. My Catholic doctor friend said it never comes to that anymore. They would do a caesarian long before it ever came to that. But I assure you, Jewish law is quite clear. If the fetus threatens the life of the mother, the fetus is destroyed so the mother might live, just the way a gangrenous limb is removed to save the person.

"It's all a matter of fruit," Moshe concluded. "Whether they had sex before they ate or only after. You might think Adam and Eve is just a story. It's much more than a story. It's much more."

"I've never heard anything like this before," a male voice commented.

"Are you a rabbi, Moshe?" a woman asked.

"How could I be a rabbi?" Moshe answered. "I thought once I might be a rabbi, so I went to school and learned Hebrew and studied in Jerusalem. But it didn't take very well."

"You could be a rabbi." "What do you do, then?" The two voices spoke over each other.

"I teach families now and then."

"No, I mean for a living."

"I'm a trader. I buy and sell."

"What do you buy and sell."

"Soybeans, live cattle, Japanese yen, works of art. Commodities of one kind or another."

"Works of art are commodities?"

Moshe laughed. "You have it backwards. Soybeans are works of art. Live cattle are works of art. The currency systems, the very blood of the world economy, this too is a work of art. I trade in art. It's all art. Every bit of it."

"What about the snake?" a man asked.

"I don't trade in snakes." After the laughter Moshe apologized. "I'm sorry. Let me turn the question back on you. What about the snake? What did the snake look like?"

"It had legs," a woman said. "Afterwards it had to crawl on its belly."

"It could talk," another voice added.

"Some snake," Moshe said. "The Torah says the snake was *arum*. It's a double entendre. It means both cunning and naked. It has sexual connotations. Maybe this was a snake like Rudolph Valentino. Maybe this snake saw Adam and Eve making love and wanted to seduce Eve away from Adam with some sexy fruit."

"Who's Rudolph Valentino?" a young girl's voice asked.

Moshe laughed. "Ask your grandparents."

"So where was Adam?" a guy asked.

"Sleeping," a woman answered. "The man always falls asleep afterward."

More laughter.

At least two children were present, Arthur thought. This was not a conversation for young children.

"After the fruit, sex has consequences. Eve bears children. Adam works the land. They are locked out of the garden of Eden. An angel bars the way back, lest they eat from the tree of life." Moshe paused.

The second young voice asked a question. "Why did God kick them out?"

"So they wouldn't eat from the tree of life."

"Why didn't God just cut down the tree of life? Why did He leave it behind?"

Another pause.

Moshe asked, "I'm sorry, I've forgotten your name."

"Orly. Orly Zedek."

"That's a nice name. A nice question too."

"So what's the answer?"

40

"I asked one of my teachers the same question once."

"What did he tell you?"

"He said to think on it. Think on it, and eventually you figure it out. It isn't the answer that's important. It's the thinking on it.

"A story!" Moshe announced. "I'll tell you a story I learned from one of my teachers. And an assignment. The assignment is to tell the story, not to hear the story, but to tell it. Tell it to your children, and you Robert, Orly, and you too, Daniel, learn the story yourselves, then retell it to your parents. Here's the story."

Moshe paused. When he resumed speaking, his voice had the affect of a storyteller.

"There was once a king who reigned in a land of perfect harmony. Really perfect. Everything went well. There was always rain in its due season. The crops never failed. All the inhabitants worked side by side without quarrel. This harmony flowed from the king, for he knew everything that happened in his kingdom, the nature of each of his subjects. He knew when to speak with strength, when to speak with kindness. He knew the land and the seas and the seasons, the winds, the currents. He knew how to measure and how to weigh.

"He also knew himself, and he recognized within himself a yearning he did not know how to satisfy. Perhaps if I learn how to sing, he thought, I will learn to satisfy this yearning. So he learned how to sing. He studied for years, and finally he sang before his subjects, and all praised his singing. No matter what he sang, all praised his singing. All of his songs were surrounded by uniform praise.

"Perhaps I do sing well, the king thought. Perhaps not. But I will never be able to sing any better, because I never get criticism. My subjects love me too much. His yearning was not satisfied.

"Then he thought he might be able to satisfy that yearning through dance. For many years he studied dance, and finally he danced before his subjects. All praised his dancing. No matter what he danced, all praised his dancing. All of his dances were surrounded by a uniform praise. Perhaps I dance well, the king thought. Perhaps not. I will never know, and I will never be able to dance any better. It does not matter whether I sing or dance. I have a kingdom that utters only praise and never criticism, and so I will never sing or dance again. The king's yearning remained unsatisfied.

"After many years of thought the king decided to become an artisan. He studied glass blowing and shaping. His skill became very great. At last he displayed a glass globe that seemed to fold in upon itself, cheating the laws of dimension. The appearance of the globe took one's breath away. All who saw it praised it, and with the praise, the globe resonated and finally shattered. The subjects of the king were taken aback. 'It's all right,' he reassured them. 'I will make another.' And he did, another more beautiful than the first. Again, all who saw it praised it, and again the globe resonated with the praise and shattered. 'I will make another,' said the king. He did, and this one also suffered the fate of the first two.

"Word spread throughout the kingdom of the wonder of the globes, their beauty and their frailty. To praise them was to destroy them. For months this was the only topic of discussion among the king's subjects. They were perplexed and did not know what to do.

"All this time the king was busy with the shaping of his fourth globe, a fabrication of beauty beyond ordinary words. At last he announced to the kingdom it was ready and all might come to see it, but no one came. No one dared to come. All were afraid to come. So the king's most wonderful creation existed by itself with none to see it except the king himself.

"Into it he expressed his yearning. Day after day, he opened his heart into it, and all of the yearning his heart contained poured into the globe until the globe began to glow and shimmer with a light of its own. The light grew and pulsed and shifted throughout all the bands of the spectrum. The king could relate to it, and he sensed the pulsing globe could somehow relate back to him. With that the king held nothing back and poured all his yearning into the globe, but it was too much for the globe to contain. It shattered.

"The cry that went out from the king's palace was so great and filled with such anguish that everyone in the kingdom shuddered and hid. The king had never known a loss like this. He turned into himself in mourning.

"For a week the king was in mourning. For a week the sharp fragments of the shattered globe lay untouched. No servant dared enter that room. At the end of the week of mourning, the king himself went to remove the pieces. When he bent over, he saw to his astonishment and amazement each shard contained some of the light of his yearning. The globe had shattered into myriad pieces, but each piece, no matter how small, no matter what shape, contained some of that light.

"The king considered what he should do. To sweep up the shards and throw them away was unthinkable. To touch them, to rearrange them, to try somehow to reassemble them was also unthinkable. He feared should he so much as touch one of them, the delicate balance that sustained the light would be destroyed. All that would be left would be pieces of broken glass.

"So the king kept his distance and continued yearning toward the pieces of his creation, the pieces that contained his light, and over time he noticed that, with a will of their own, the pieces slowly moved toward each other and established bonds.

"The king was patient, his yearning constant. As each piece joined another, his joy increased."

The tape remained silent so long Arthur thought perhaps the recording had been finished. He reached forward for the stop button just as Moshe's voice resumed in a different tone. "It's getting late. Let's go out and see what the kids are doing, and remember we have a responsibility to restore this house, pick up the paper, put the chairs back."

"That's all right. You don't have to bother." That was Jessica Garfinkel.

"We do have to bother," Moshe said. "It's not your job to do that. It's our job."

Arthur heard the sound of chairs clacking along the ceramic tiled floor as the recording came to an end.

In spite of himself Arthur was filled with the story. He did not understand it, but he knew it had some kabbalistic significance. It wasn't for children, though. With all the talk of sex, the crude language, that was not a session for young children.

He returned to the journal. Brenda had summarized the entire session. They had begun in the living room. Moshe had sung a niggun as a means for the families to introduce themselves to each other. Brenda liked the tone it set, ordered but still informal. She described the exercise in the street. There was no mention of Andy Perlman and his knife. She outlined the story and summarized its references to the Lurianic concept of creation including more than Moshe had taught. He must have done some teaching not recorded. Brenda used Hebrew terms, and Arthur realized with a start she might have learned them not from Moshe but from Turin, damn him.

Damn them both.

At the end of the summary, this note:

Moshe is not a rabbi. That makes it so much better.

Now what the hell did she mean by that?

43

CHAPTER 3

SUNDAY 2:20 A.M.

Brenda wrote in blue ink with flowery strokes, mostly legible.

> *Moshe drinks his coffee black. I wonder what he thinks of me?*
> *Rivkah died a year ago. Fourteen months. Is that enough?*
> *Just his smile opens me, but he doesn't hold my hand.*

Arthur had no difficulty following the report of their progress through the Grove. They had window-shopped on Commodore and walked back roads to Moshe's place, a small house with a stamped brick driveway, a one-car garage in front, a pool in back that filled most of the fenced-in yard. Brenda wrote more of what was not in the home than what was. The living room needed furniture, and if Moshe liked modern, she knew just where to go. Or traditional. She furnished the room in the journal several times in different styles.

But the Dali was real, she wrote, and underlined it. The Dali was real, not a copy, not a print. An oil on canvas. A real Dali. It was the only painting on the wall and shared space unceremoniously with charts and weather maps. When she asked why the weather maps, Moshe had said, "Orange juice." She wrote the answer as if it were gospel. Why were there weather maps on the wall? Moshe said, "Orange juice," and that was that. No explanation given.

Arthur learned Moshe's bedroom had no bed. A futon was laid out on the floor, a comforter rolled up behind it. So sparse, she thought, and then many more *I woulds*, all the things she would do if she decorated Moshe's home. She would go to Luminaire and buy a platform bed in ebony, a good

44

man's bed, a queen-size bed with a solid rubber mattress because Moshe was accustomed to sleeping on the floor. She would buy a dresser, to bring his things out of the closet. She had been in his closet? She would buy a carpet. She argued in the journal the advantage of one form of carpet over another. Kilims weren't good, Arthur learned, because they would slip on the tile floor, but Moshe liked kilims, and Arthur for a moment found himself taking Moshe's side.

"Damn it!" he said. But Arthur continued reading. He had to read. He had to understand, to find something, to explain it away, to make it go away, like it never happened. He read in hopes of turning back the clock, stopping time, extinguishing the fuse, yet in his stomach he felt it was futile. It would explode. Poof. A quiet explosion that would expand and expand, and maybe even do him in.

She was in Moshe's bedroom. He had not dragged her there. Her curiosity had brought her, her fascination with her new guru, her spiritual leader. She wanted to know all about him, down to the brown towels in the bathroom. Moshe brushed with Viadent, whatever the hell that was. Fluoride Viadent. The bathroom needed redoing. The sink was chipped. She thought a pedestal sink would be better than whatever unspecified style of sink was there.

Noah, she wrote, finally getting down to business. The next session was Noah, and they needed cardboard boxes, big boxes, as many as each family could bring. Refrigerator boxes, book boxes, anything out of heavy cardboard. They were going to build an ark. They needed a big yard. *Shuk*, Brenda wrote and crossed it out. Arthur understood why. The Shuks lived in Gables Estates, and Gables Estates was not a place to build a boat out of cardboard. Each home had a very real boat tied up behind it. *Lopez?* The Lopez family lived only two blocks from Arthur in Pinecrest. They had a big yard. A good choice, Arthur thought.

Each person, or each family, was to bring four things. It was as if they had to leave their homes in a hurry and could carry only four: one to serve as a tool, one to make them feel good, one from which they could learn, and one to tie them close to God. "Whatever that means to you," Brenda wrote.

Moshe had given her examples. Nothing more than could fit in a Porsche. That was his ark after Rivkah died. He had taken four things, one from each world, to put in his ark, to save himself, and he drove for forty days and nights. He took a Swiss Army knife, a picture of Rivkah, Whitman's *Leaves of Grass,* and his tefillin. He ventured into primitive New Mexico, beyond the reach of credit cards, and went to ground.

How romantic, Arthur thought. Brenda was looking for salvation, and he had introduced her to the devil.

Arthur stood and stretched at his desk, found the Noah videotape, dated October 9, inserted it into the VCR, and took refuge in his wing chair.

The Lopez house had a big back yard. The camera had been placed either in or close to a tree. A single leaf, out of focus, appeared in the upper left corner of the frame. The wide angle encompassed most of the yard and one side of the bronzed aluminum and fiberglass screen enclosure that covered the pool.

"Sound check, Moshe," Brenda said.

"One two three four," Moshe responded off camera. Moshe's words were accompanied by a tearing sound Arthur guessed to be a knife ripping through corrugated cardboard. His guess was confirmed when someone threw a sheet of cardboard onto a pile that was forming not far from the tree.

"Be careful," Moshe said. "Make sure no part of you and no part of me is in the line of your cut. That's it."

Again the sound, then more cardboard.

"Are your parents here, Andy?"

"My mother."

"Your father doesn't come? Watch your line, now. Watch your line." The knife ripped through cardboard again. "What about your father? He doesn't come to these sessions?"

"No. Just my mother."

"Which one is she?"

"Over there. With sunglasses."

"What's her name?"

"Marsha."

"And your father's name?"

"Morty."

"Do you have any brothers or sisters?"

"No."

"When is your bar mitzvah?"

"I'm not going to have a bar mitzvah."

"Why not?"

"Don't want to."

"What about your parents?"

"They want me to. My father wants me to. I don't want to."

"Do you go to Hebrew school?"

"I don't learn anything there. It's foolish. I don't like it."

"What do you like, Andy?"

"I like your car. You have a neat car."

"Would you like a ride sometime?

"Yeah. I'd like that."

"Well, maybe we'll find some time to take a ride. Let's get this finished."

Arthur rewound the tape to listen to the dialogue again, thinking perhaps it was important, but he had no deeper insight on the second hearing. The tape progressed to the building of the ark. He would have liked to fast forward, but the audio cut out during fast forwarding. How would he know if Moshe was speaking? He resigned himself to watching and listening to it all.

With some considerable excitement adults traced the outline of the ark on the lawn. Children dragged cardboard sheets to the perimeter to be taped into walls. Bulkheads? Arthur found himself wondering about the correct nautical terms. The bow was made high, and the poop deck, if that's what it was in the stern, was roofed over, so those who desired could have shade.

Moshe said a few words of encouragement. He was in jeans and the cowboy hat. His T-shirt was white with a yellow star of David smiley face. Instead of boots, Moshe wore sandals. Brenda was in shorts. Some of the younger children made attempts to capture Moshe's hat and occasionally succeeded. George Lopez was in charge. "Give Mr. Katan his hat back!" he commanded, somewhat harshly. The ark went up, and spirits were not dampened.

George herded the families on board. Brenda walked from the boat toward the camera, loomed large on the screen and mouthed, "Daniel," gesturing for him to join her. She reached under the camera frame. Daniel emerged in tow behind her toward the ark.

Moshe held his hands up for silence. Others did the same. He had made a similar gesture on the last tape. This time it triggered something in Arthur. With a start he realized it reminded him of the biblical Moses. When the children of Israel were waging war against Amalek, Moses climbed to the top of a nearby hill. As long as he held his hands high, the children of Israel prevailed. Whenever his hands fell from fatigue, Amalek prevailed. Seeing that Moses was no longer able to keep his hands raised, Aaron and Hur provided support, holding Moses's hands aloft so the children of Israel could emerge victorious. Arthur noted when others raised their hands, calling for attention and silence, Moshe lowered his.

"Pretty soon it's going to rain," Moshe said. "It will be a most unusual rain. When Noah told all of his friends it was going to rain, they didn't believe him. Noah built his ark anyway. Then it did rain, suddenly, and the rain continued for forty days and forty nights."

"It can't rain," a child said. "There aren't any clouds."

"Maybe there weren't any clouds in Noah's time, but it rained anyway." Moshe looked at his watch. "Just in case, you've all brought what you need should we have to start civilization all over again? Every family has brought something so we can make our way in the new world? Things to make you feel good? Something about the great ideas you want to save? Something to bring you close to God?" He looked up at the sky again. "We don't have much time. Get together in small groups and share with each other what it is you've brought. It's going to start raining soon. We don't want anything precious to get wet."

Arthur could not see anything of the sky, but judging from the shadows cast by the trees, the sun was not obscured by clouds. The families bent to their task, sharing with each other the items they had brought. Moshe sat with each group in turn, offering words of encouragement.

When he joined with Brenda's group, she turned to him and asked, "How much time do we have?"

"Enough," he responded. "What did you bring, Daniel?" Daniel seemed to be concentrating on the piece of cardboard closest to him. "Daniel, if you could bring only one thing with you from your home, what would you bring?" No response. Did Moshe really expect one? He stood and spoke to the entire group on board. "Another minute please, then we'll share together. Please finish up." To Daniel he said, "Listen when the others tell us what they brought. See if you agree. See if it makes sense to you. Ask yourself if they brought the right thing." He turned to the group. "Let's share!" Moshe said so loudly Arthur winced. "What did you all bring to assist you in making your way in the next world? What did you bring that you might use to make things?" Andy's hand was the first up. "What did you bring, Andy?"

"A knife."

"Will you show it to us?" Andy opened his knife proudly. "And what would you use it for?"

"I already used it to make this boat. A lot of things will need cutting."

"Indeed. Who else brought a tool for the World of Action? That's what we're talking about here. There are four worlds of experience, and the one in which we work with things is called the World of Action. Who else brought something?"

Hands were raised with urgency. Arthur watched a child demonstrate how to focus the rays of the sun with a magnifying glass and start the cardboard smoldering. Another family had brought a compass, so they might find their way in the new world.

"Now for the World of Formation," Moshe said. "What did we bring to help us with our feelings? We might need something to make us feel better when we get out of the ark and find everything we used to know is gone."

Photo albums were the article of choice. And one violin.

"Why the violin, Orly?" Moshe asked.

"Because it makes me feel good when I play."

"Would you play something to make us feel good?"

Orly tuned her violin with facility and played something Arthur did not recognize, but she played it well.

"How long have you been playing the violin?" Moshe asked.

"Since I was five."

"You play nicely."

"Thank you."

"I think you were right. The violin makes us all feel good. Would the photo albums make us all feel good, or just the families that own them?" Moshe didn't wait for an answer. "Is there anything else that might make us all feel good?"

"Art," an adult said.

"Poetry," said another.

"Now we're moving between worlds. Music, art, and poetry can make us feel good, but they can also convey profound ideas. We might ask what world they belong to, feelings or ideas. Feelings are in the World of Formation, and ideas in the World of Creation. What did we bring for the World of Creation, the world of ideas?"

"A book," a child said. He held it aloft. "*The Way Things Work*, so we'll know how to put things back together again."

"How many people brought books?" Moshe asked. Many hands were raised, some containing volumes. Shakespeare, a dictionary, a one-volume encyclopedia, a notebook computer. Arthur wondered what a person would do with a notebook computer in the brave new world. As he wondered, the sharing from the World of Creation was completed.

"And now what did you bring that might draw us close to God?"

They had brought Bibles, as Arthur had guessed, and prayer books. No one had brought tefillin, even though some of the men might have been trained in a traditional synagogue before bar mitzvah in the use of the boxes and straps that bound the arm and the head into a devotional attitude before prayer. Tefillin were not used in Temple Emet. Arthur did not use tefillin, had never used tefillin, didn't own a pair of tefillin but was not surprised when Moshe produced his own tefillin. "God help me," Arthur said aloud. "Is he going to put them on?"

"These were a gift to me from my grandfather before my bar mitzvah. He had been given his by his grandfather, and his grandfather had received his from his grandfather, almost back to the beginning of time. My teacher showed me how to put them on once, and I never did it again for many years, but when I went to Israel to study, I took them with me.

"Do any of you have a drawer at home where you keep precious things you never use? That's where I found these, in my parents' home. We had a drawer in the dining room where we kept things too precious to throw out, but things we never used. I found them, and I took them to Israel with me on spec. You know what that means? On speculation. I had no idea what I would do with them, but I figured if there was any value to them at all, I would find out in Israel. I suspected if they had been passed down through the generations for so many years, maybe there was some worth to them. But I had no idea what that might be. Maybe there would be someone in Israel to teach me. So I took them, and there was. There was a fellow from South Africa who knew how to use them. Even more, he knew how to teach me to use them in a way I could understand." He paused and looked up. "I would take them out now and show you how to put them on, but I think pretty soon it might begin to rain." That was greeted by laughter.

Moshe kissed the bag that contained the tefillin, then looked about as if for a place to put it. "Did anybody bring an umbrella?" he asked. More laughter.

"I'll tell you a story. There once was a village where they hadn't had any rain in the longest time. The farmers were upset because the crops were dying. So what did they do? They sent for a rebbe, a rabbi who could pronounce miraculous blessings, and paid him a substantial sum of money to come to their village and pronounce a prayer for rain. So the rebbe came, and the people of the village gathered for their morning service, waiting for the rebbe to say his prayer. When the time for the prayer came, the rebbe stayed in his seat. The president of the congregation came forward and asked the rebbe why he didn't say the prayer. The rebbe said, 'Why bother. It won't work.'

"'What do you mean it won't work?' the president asked. 'We've paid you a lot of money to come and say a prayer for rain.'

"'Do you really think it's my words that cause the rain to fall? It's your faith. Without your faith, how do you expect my prayer to work?'

"'We have faith,' the president insisted. 'Why would we pay you so much money if we didn't have faith?'

"The rebbe looked out over the congregation and said, 'You don't have faith. If you had faith my prayer would bring rain, you would have brought umbrellas.'"

When the laughter stopped, Moshe asked again, "So who brought umbrellas?" There were no umbrellas. "You brought knives and magnifying glasses and tool boxes. You brought your most precious photo albums and books. All of these you brought to Noah's ark, knowing what happened to Noah's ark, and no one brought an umbrella?"

"Moshe," an adult asked, "did you bring an umbrella?"

"No, but I brought these." Moshe opened a knapsack and withdrew a box of plastic garbage bags. "Pass these around," he said. "Anything you don't want to get wet, put them in these, and hurry. We don't have much time." He extracted handfuls of black plastic bags and threw them fore and aft. "Hurry," he urged again. "We don't have much time. Anything you don't want to get wet, into the bags." The parents played along and urged the children to protect their possessions.

"Is everything protected? Good. Now, what do you think a prayer for rain might be? Does anyone know a prayer for rain?" No one responded. "There was once a Jew named Honi Ha-ma-agal, Honi the Circle Maker. When people needed rain, they would call on Honi, and Honi would draw a circle on the ground and stand in it. He would talk to God and say, 'Listen, please. These are your people. They are a good people. They need rain. You have a special relationship with these people. Why don't you give them some rain? I'll tell you what. I'm going to stand in this circle and keep kvetching like this until you give us some rain, so I suggest you do it soon.'

51

That's what Honi Ha-ma-agal used to say. Can we get someone here to try it?"

Hands went up. "Okay, Robert. Give it a shot. Use your toe to draw a circle, stand in it, and say your prayer."

Robert was too far away for Arthur to hear the prayer clearly.

"Don't sit down," Moshe said. "You have to stand in the circle until it begins to rain. That's all part of the prayer. You can't say you're going to do it, then not do it. Honi's credit was such that God wouldn't delay, the rain would come almost at once. Let's see how good your prayer was."

Arthur heard a gurgling sound. Before he could analyze and comprehend it, the yard was full of streams of water. The sprinkler system had erupted. George Lopez had traced the outline of the ark to fall between the sprinkler heads. Within a few seconds no part of the ark remained dry. Screams of delight and consternation erupted from the speakers. "Enough!" Moshe shouted over the screams. "George! Enough!" The rain ceased. Everyone was standing, laughing, not quite soaked, but wet. Like a Disney ride, Arthur thought.

Arthur could not see Brenda in the camera frame but heard her voice speaking from a distance. ". . . in the patio with Margolit Zedek. Adults and children who want to learn with Mr. Katan will meet in the family room." After a protest from those who had not heard, she repeated, "Those who want to paint a special rainbow project meet in the patio with Margolit. We have plenty of watercolors. Those who want to learn more about the Noah story will meet in the family room with Mr. Katan."

The ark had suffered some from the sprinklers. Families exited through the walls as well as through the door. For some time Arthur watched the empty ark until he realized no one was going to come to turn off the video camera. There was no audio. Moshe must have removed or disconnected his microphone. They had left Arthur to watch the ruins of an empty ark steaming in the sun while they went off to play or study. How inconsiderate. They had left him in his study alone and not turned off the camera, Arthur thought, knowing full well how absurd his thought was.

Arthur shook himself out of his reverie and looked to the desk to count the tapes remaining. How many more would he have to sit through? Too many. And the audiotapes. And the journal. The wing chair was so comfortable he thought he might sleep for a moment, but he knew better. The moment would stretch into hours, and he did not have hours for sleep.

At his desk he found an audiotape labeled *Noah*, inserted it into the machine, and opened Brenda's journal. The section was labeled "The Baal Shem Tov on Prayer." As if on cue, Moshe's voice began, "The Baal Shem Tov was the first of the Hasidic rabbis. What he did was revolutionary. He brought the Kabbalah, Jewish spiritual discipline, to the masses. There had always been study of the Kabbalah, but it had been reserved for the elite. Without an infusion of spirituality, the tradition had become dry and brittle. The Baal Shem Tov broke ranks with the rabbis and chose to share the deepest secrets with whoever might listen, and there were a lot of people who listened."

"When did he live?"

"In the eighteenth century, in eastern Europe. We have all sorts of legends about his early life. He was a teacher. He used to teach children."

"A religious-school teacher?" It was a girl's voice.

"There wasn't any difference between school and religious school," Moshe answered. "There was just learning. It might not even have been in a school. Not all learning takes place in a school. Would you pass me that book please? This is a book of the Baal Shem Tov's commentary to the Torah. What's especially interesting is the Baal Shem Tov never wrote a commentary to the Torah. He never wrote anything. His students used to write down what he said, or later, they would teach in his name. They would say, 'This is what my teacher, the holy Baal Shem Tov, used to say.' So we have a record of his teachings, and they have been gathered and written down in a book. Unfortunately the book is only in Hebrew.

"This is his commentary to the story of Noah's ark. He writes about this one verse, Genesis 6:16. 'You are to make a *tzohar* for the ark and finish it to a cubit from the top and put an opening in the ark in its side. Make it with bottom, second, and third levels.'"

"What's a *tzohar?*" an adult asked.

"The Baal Shem Tov asked the same question. Sometimes we come across a word in the Torah and we don't know what it means. That's the problem with translations. The translator chooses a word in English, and you understand the word, so you think the translator knows what the Hebrew means, but the translator doesn't really know. He's guessing. Or he's choosing between words. That's why when you study in English, it's good to have several different translations. If everyone has the same translation, everyone has the same understanding. But if you have different translations, that's an indication the Hebrew word is difficult to understand. Then you know there's a problem with the Hebrew.

"We're not certain what *tzohar* means. *Tzohar* might be an opening for daylight, or a window, or a skylight, or a source of light, or a spark of brilliance. It's not a common word.

"We'll see in a moment what the Baal Shem Tov does with it, but first let's step back and look at the ark as a whole. When we learn the Noah's ark story as children, we think of a boat. We just built ourselves a boat outside. But the Baal Shem Tov steps back even more. He sees the ark as the instrument of salvation. The people were in a bad way. They had been misbehaving. They were in danger of being destroyed completely. They needed to be saved."

"What were they doing that was so bad?" A boy's voice. Robert?

"Does anybody know?" Moshe asked. "Does anybody know what they were doing that was so bad?"

"The earth had become corrupt," a woman said.

"Why?" Moshe pressed. "What had made it corrupt?"

"They were doing bad all the time."

"But what bad were they doing?" When there was no response, Moshe continued, "They were having sex with angels."

Sex again, Arthur thought. Moshe had taught the Adam and Eve story as a sexual encounter, and now again with Noah.

"They were having sex with angels," Moshe repeated. "The borderline between heaven and earth was becoming confused. Creation and creator were merging back into one. God was about to wipe out the whole thing and start over again but gave it one last chance with Noah and his family. The ark is what saved them from destruction. So the Baal Shem Tov steps back and thinks, 'What is the instrument of salvation?' What do you think his answer might be? What is the instrument of salvation?"

Moshe continued into the silence, "We're not comfortable with that word. *Salvation* is a good Jewish word, but most of us aren't comfortable with it. Do you know what a twelve-step program is? Like Alcoholics Anonymous? Gamblers Anonymous? Anyone in such a program knows what salvation is. There are all sorts of addictive disorders. There's a sexual addiction, and we might say that's what Noah's generation suffered from. They needed their twelve-step program."

"What does this have to do with salvation?"

"Salvation is the action of an agency outside of yourself to get you out of a difficulty you can't get out of yourself. You're drowning in a pool and the lifeguard jumps in and saves you. He's your savior. He's the agency outside of yourself who came in and got you out of your difficulty. The alcoholic can't cure himself. He needs the agency outside of himself to help him. He refers to that agency as a Higher Power. God is what saves him. God becomes his partner."

"The Baal Shem Tov was an alcoholic?"

They thought that was funny. "I don't know," Moshe continued. "I do know what the Baal Shem Tov thought about salvation. He steps back and asks, 'What is the instrument of salvation?' and then he looks to the Torah for an answer. God says to Noah to build a tayvah. *Tayvah* is the word we translate so often as the ark. But what is an ark? Has anyone ever seen an ark?"

"It's a boat," a girl answered. "A big boat."

"Have you ever seen one?"

"We have one on our coffee table."

"I mean a real one. Has anyone seen a real ark? If you wanted to buy an ark, a real one, where would you go? You might buy a boat, or a yacht, or a ship, or a barge, but where would you go to buy an ark? What else does the word ark mean?"

"The *aron ha-kodesh*," a man answered.

"The holy ark," Moshe agreed, "in the synagogue, where the Torah scrolls are kept. That's an ark. So the word *ark* even in English has different meanings, and the primary meaning isn't a boat at all. It's a place, a box where the Torah scrolls are kept. The original tayvah was where the Ten Commandments were kept. Did anyone see *Indiana Jones*? That was a tayvah."

"Are you telling us the Baal Shem Tov says Noah built himself an ark for the Torah scrolls? The Torah hadn't even been given yet." Arthur recognized the voice of Leonard Shuk. Leonard was a regular at the temple's Adult Institute for Jewish Study. Twice each year Arthur taught courses for adults.

"No," Moshe said. "The Baal Shem Tov looks into a third meaning of tayvah. Tayvah can mean a word, or sometimes even a letter. The Baal Shem Tov says words are the means of salvation. On one level God teaches Noah to make a big boat to save his family and all of the animals. On a deeper level, God teaches Noah how to pray. The words of prayer are the instruments of salvation. God says, 'You are to make a tzohar for the ark and finish it to a cubit from the top and put an opening in the ark in its side. Make it with bottom, second, and third levels.'

55

"This is what the Baal Shem Tov has to say. He says God told Noah to make a tzohar in the tayvah. *Tzohar* is a source of illumination. That way the tayvah . . . Here *tayvah* means 'word.' That way the word one says in study and prayer will be illuminated. It's not just enough to pronounce a word. You have to fill it with light. The Baal Shem Tov goes on and says every word has levels within levels. It has aspects of the physical world. It reflects on matters of the soul. And it reveals something of the divine. When you illuminate the tayvah, the word of prayer, the letters and the meanings all bind together, and this draws the attention of God. So what you do when you pray is to include your soul in each and every aspect of the word, and then all of the words are united in ecstasy. Your prayer becomes ecstatic."

The silence continued for some time. Moshe spoke into it, "Here's some more from the Baal Shem Tov. I'll translate without any comment. See what you make of it. 'In prayer it is necessary to put all of your strength into the verbalization. That way you go from letter to letter until you forget you have a body. You ponder how the letters are joined, one to the next. This is a great delight. Now, if there is delight that comes from physicality, how much the more so that which comes from the spirit. This is the World of Formation. After this you enter the letters into your consciousness. Then you are no longer aware of what you are saying. This is the World of Creation. Then you arrive at the state of nothingness, in which every attribute of the physical disappears. This is the World of Emanation.' What do you make of that?"

Arthur wondered why Leonard didn't speak up. Leonard knew how to answer. Leonard had studied with him the relevant portions of the Babylonian poem *Atrahasis* and the myth of Gilgamesh. Surely Leonard knew Noah was the Jewish equivalent of the flood story common to all the peoples of Mesopotamia. The greatness of the Jewish story was the imposition of law and the involvement of God in human history. But Leonard was silent. All were silent until Moshe resumed his discourse.

"The Baal Shem Tov was very serious about prayer. For him, prayer was the instrument of salvation. There are many wonderful stories of how the Baal Shem Tov prayed. Once he was in a town and went from synagogue to synagogue on a Shabbat morning looking for a place to pray. He would open the door, look in and leave, then go on to the next. At one synagogue when he closed the door to leave, the shamas followed after him and asked why he hadn't entered. 'I couldn't come in,' the Baal Shem Tov answered. 'The place was too full of prayer. There wasn't any room for me.' Do you understand the story? Tell it to each other, and see if it makes sense. Work on it a little."

The tape dissolved into a murmur of discussion. Arthur fretted, not knowing when Moshe might return to his discourse. He reduced the murmur to a slight distraction and followed the text Brenda had pasted into her journal, a teaching of the Baal Shem Tov.

Sometimes it is necessary to worship the Blessed One with soul alone, that is to say, in the consciousness, with the body standing in its place, so you shouldn't have to use it overmuch. And sometimes a person can say the prayer in love and awe and with a great ecstasy without any movement, and it may appear to someone else he is saying his prayer without any adhesion to the Blessed One. But this is a technique a person might use to establish adhesion to the Blessed One. Then one can worship God with the soul alone in a great and expansive love. This is the very best worship and leads quickly to a greater adhesion to the Blessed One, more so than the prayer that becomes apparent outside through the limbs, and such prayer is not attached to any outer shell since all of it is internal.

". . . outside through the limbs . . ." Arthur was lost in an image of Brenda, outside through the limbs, swaying, dancing in place, in ecstasy, so much lost he was startled to hear Moshe speaking. ". . . so the prayer was falling from their lips and piling up on the floor, prayer after prayer, none of it taking wing. Soon the entire building was so full of prayer the Baal Shem Tov could not enter into the space. There was no room for him. For the Baal Shem Tov, prayer was not lip service. It was the real thing. It connected him to his creator . . ."

Arthur jabbed the tape recorder into silence and slammed the journal shut. If it were not for the damage it would do to his temple, Arthur would have liked nothing better than to sic the dogs of authority on the hypocrite's heels. How perverse. The only way to save himself was to save Moshe!

Why was he so angry?

Brenda was the problem, more than Moshe. If he could solve Brenda, then Moshe would fall into place, and his feelings would return to normal, whatever normal was.

57

Semi-numb, Arthur thought. That was his normal feeling.

Brenda first, then Moshe. But that had been his resolve from the beginning, to work with Brenda, but Brenda kept her distance.

Reports began to drift in, from the Kantors and Garfinkels, from George Lopez, good reports about Moshe's program, what Mr. Katan was doing, how much the children loved it, loved him. The better the program, Arthur feared, the greater would be the damage. The stronger the impact, the greater the crater when Moshe would depart for some other project.

The fault was mostly his. He had encountered Brenda from time to time, inquired after her program, but professed no serious interest. He was satisfied with a polite response. A cancer patient inquiring after his inoperable lesion, asking but not listening, in denial. No, he wasn't being fair to himself. He had no notion the lesion might be malignant. Rather it was a self-limiting inclusion that would disappear when the year was done. There had been no need for him to do anything more than be polite.

As for Moshe, he had been reluctant to face him head on. That first lunch at the Captain's Table had shaken Arthur. After that the card labeled "Another Lunch with Moshe" kept rising to the top of his organizer only to drop again and again to the bottom of his list of things to do. The high holidays passed, then Sukkot, and Simhat Torah. There was nothing left in the calendar to obscure "Another Lunch with Moshe." The call was made, the date set.

Arthur arrived ten minutes late and crossed the threshold expecting to find Moshe waiting for him on the oak bench. The bench was empty. Moshe was waiting at the bar, a martini in front of him.

"Hi Artie," he said. "I hope you don't mind." He raised what was left of his drink. "I started early."

"What about the margarita?" Arthur asked.

Moshe slapped the bar. "That's what it was. I couldn't remember. A margarita. Next time." He carried his martini to the table, the same table, by the aquarium with the same fish, yellow and blue circling the artificial coral.

"How have you been?" Arthur began.

"From time to time," Moshe answered. "The captain is not in the kitchen. We'll have to do something other than trout."

"Tuna," Arthur said. "Rare. It has to be rare. With caramelized onions and mashed potatoes."

"But no sprouts on the salad. What should I know about Brenda?"

Sprouts and Brenda. This was not going to be an easy lunch. "What do you mean?" The waitress brought Arthur his martini.

"Spiritual retreats. Everyone came with a need, some with a need to know, some just needy. Something missing. Brenda has that kind of need."

Arthur had one olive left on his plastic sword. He held it high in the air like a specimen. Plastic crabs and shells rested in the furrows of the fishnet suspended from the ceiling. "Brenda," he said. "A widow with a child like that, you would expect she would have some needs."

"Those needs, yes, and something from before."

A ship's hatch, wooden planks with metal braces, hung between two columns behind Moshe. Painted on it was a drunken sailor holding a mug of grog. Arthur considered his response with care, speaking more to the painting than to Moshe. "I didn't know her from before. She was married to a friend, a wonderful man, his second marriage, someone to keep him young. He was my mentor in many ways. Charlotte and I maintain the friendship." Arthur thought he had answered well.

Moshe sipped from his drink. "Do you think I might borrow a sefer Torah?" he asked.

Arthur wasn't sure he had heard correctly. "A Torah scroll?"

"A Torah scroll."

"From the temple?"

"From the temple."

Torah scrolls were never removed from the temple. "Why?"

"I don't have one."

Arthur didn't have one either. Not many individuals had Torah scrolls. They were written by hand on parchment, sacred text, holy objects. "Why would you need one?"

"To study."

"But no one studies from a Torah scroll," Arthur said. A Torah scroll was for ritual use only.

"You're right. You're right." Moshe seemed sad, even forlorn. "Once it was a pathway to God. It isn't any longer."

The waitress served the tuna. "Is it rare?" Arthur asked her.

"It's rare," she said.

He motioned her to stay while he cut into it.

"Animal sacrifice," Moshe said.

"What?"

"If the Temple in Jerusalem hadn't been destroyed by the Romans, do you think we'd still be offering animal sacrifice?"

"Of course not," Arthur said. "How could you imagine such a thing?"

"I couldn't imagine it, but I wonder how it would have come to an end. Morning and afternoon the priests offered up the animals on the altar, collecting and sprinkling the blood this way and that. It's what God wanted, just what He told us to do. He says it right there in the Torah scroll, the one we don't study from. Perhaps the Romans did us a favor. If they hadn't destroyed the Temple, how else would we have stopped?"

"The people would have stopped it."

Moshe chewed his tuna deliberately. "Like steak," he said. "It's like I'm eating steak again."

"You don't eat meat, Moshe?"

"Not often. Sometimes I miss it. I haven't had a steak in a long time. You don't talk about that in your paper on the Pharisees."

"Talk about what?"

"About what would have happened if the Temple had not been destroyed."

"You read my paper?"

"You won the history prize. I wanted to see why. They had your paper on reserve in the library."

"That was twenty-five years ago."

Moshe drained the remnants of his martini. "I have a confession to make," he said. "That was my second. I forgot what time we said. I got here early."

Arthur was somewhat more comfortable. Two martinis might explain Moshe's inability to hold a steady course in conversation.

"So, if the Temple in Jerusalem hadn't been destroyed, what would have stopped animal sacrifice?"

"The people would have stopped it," Arthur said again.

"I think you're right. The people would have stopped it. They would have stopped bringing animals. They would have stopped going to the Temple. The Pharisees would have replaced the priests. Rabbis instead of priests, a new age for Judaism. I think you're right. You know, someday our children will consider us barbarians because we eat our tuna rare."

Arthur checked his fork halfway to his mouth. "Why so? What difference, rare or well done?"

Moshe laughed. "No difference. That we eat tuna at all. A hundred years from now, two, maybe five hundred years, our children won't be eating meat, maybe not even fish. The very notion you and I are sitting here eating our tuna rare, that will be considered an abomination." Moshe held his fingers to his lips, looked left and right in mock conspiracy. "But not for five hundred years, Arthur. Not to worry. The temples, though. The temples and the rabbis. Now that's something else again. I don't think they will last five hundred years. Martinis will last. Five hundred years from now you and I can have lunch here together. We'll still have our martinis, but the captain will be in the kitchen cooking broccoli. Broccoli, rare."

No meat, Arthur thought, and no rabbis in five hundred years. Moshe had broccoli in mind to replace the meat. What did he have in mind to replace the rabbis? Asparagus?

Arthur's distaste was such he did not enjoy his tuna, or the onions, or the mashed potato. He ordered his second martini, determined to get to business. "How's the family program going?"

"Fine," Moshe said. "I'm learning as I go."

"What are you learning?"

"What comes next."

Arthur suspected Moshe's "next" meant not what the next program would be but what would come next after the rabbis. He didn't want to pursue that. "What have you been teaching?" That was safer.

"Creation. Noah. The tower of Babel. No, I haven't taught Babel yet. They're all the same. I get them mixed up. The process of creation. Why it is God brought this universe into being. The purpose. That's what I'm teaching, what I've been teaching so far."

Arthur was at a loss. He didn't know how to continue.

Moshe seemed content to sit in silence, watching the blue and yellow fish. Without looking at Arthur he said, "I'm sorry if this is confusing. I don't mean it to be. I don't see things the way I used to. Time is confused for me. It's getting better. I was lost for a while. You know, the deeper you go, the less time you can stay. You risk damage. I was with Rivie when she went, watched her go. I know you don't understand that."

Arthur didn't understand that, but Moshe was crying, and tears he understood. Arthur knew when to say nothing. Moshe cried in quiet sobs, so quiet no one else in the darkened restaurant was likely to have noticed.

"I can't fix myself," Moshe resumed when he was able. "I can see what to do for others. Big picture, small picture, it doesn't matter. If I don't know what to do right away, I wait. Then I see what to do. But I can't fix myself."

He looked at his empty glass, as if contemplating a third martini.

"My friends keep me in the world. They brought me back. They hold me here. But they can't fix me."

Arthur had no words to insert. He searched for some, but Moshe's discourse was far beyond his experience.

"They died young," Moshe said.

Arthur didn't know who he was talking about.

"The early masters, so many of them died young. They didn't have anyone who could intercede for them. They didn't teach us how to do that at the seminary, did they, Artie?" Moshe thought that was funny. "To sweeten the difficult things at the root. More than that, make changes, real changes. Sometimes you can only sweeten things, and that's a lot, to change perspective. Ro-ah ha-gizayrah. But sometimes you can even change the gizayrah itself."

Arthur understood the Hebrew. It was from the liturgy of the high holidays. *Gizayrah* was the decree. The *ro-ah* of the gizayrah was the evil of the decree, the adverse aspect of what had been determined from above. To change the ro-ah of the gizayrah was to see the positive in one's situation, not just the negative. Tradition taught a person could do that through repentance, prayer, and charity. But to change the gizayrah itself, the very decree? To go back to the divine source and make a change at the root from which judgment came? Of that Arthur knew nothing. If there were such texts, they did not teach them at the seminary.

Moshe had been waiting for him to understand before continuing. Arthur shook his head to let him know he was lost, but Moshe continued anyway.

"So I had those who could intercede for me and keep me in this world. But they can't fix me. I'm not anchored like you are, Artie. I see you sitting in your chair as if you're attached to the world, but I see where you're not fixed also. I see how to fix you, but not how to fix me." He reached across the table to hold Arthur's hand. "But you help. You really do. Thank you, Artie. You're a friend."

Arthur did not feel like a friend. He had not been helping, did not need fixing, and he wished Moshe would stop calling him Artie.

CHAPTER 4

SUNDAY, 3:25 A.M.

I asked Moshe what Rivkah was like.

We walked a long time before he answered.

"Like when?" he asked. "Like when I met her? When we first got married? When we were in California? When she got ill the first time? The period after? When she got ill the second time? When she was dying?"

As I read back over that, it sounds angry, but he wasn't angry. He was thinking back through his life with her, like in a few moments he had relived everything.

I asked him how he remembered her, what came to mind first.

"Israel," he said. "When I first saw her. She was . . . present. There was an aura about her."

I asked him if he saw auras.

He shook his head. "No, not an aura. It wasn't something I could see, but it was something she radiated. A presence. A connection with everything about her. That's the way she was. Whatever, wherever, she was present to the situation. Most of the time."

I picked up on "most of the time" and asked him when she wasn't so present.

His answer came without the slightest hesitation. "When she was angry. When you're angry, presence departs."

When you're angry, presence departs.

I don't know why he bothers with me. I am so angry, most of the time.

The next video was "Babel: November 6. Kantor." Arthur knew the home, about twenty blocks from his own in Pinecrest, but those twenty blocks were in the right direction. Property value seemed to double every quarter mile. Mario Kantor manufactured fabric somewhere in South America and sold it to design houses throughout the world. Their house was more marble than concrete, their yacht berthed more often in Nassau than Miami.

This was Robert's home. Robert was scheduled for bar mitzvah the following October. Nearly a hundred bar and bat mitzvahs were celebrated each year in the congregation, so many that two families were scheduled for each Saturday morning service. Even so, Arthur knew only too well when Robert's was. The scheduling had been a major issue. The president of the synagogue and a half dozen members of the board of trustees had called to suggest Robert Kantor be scheduled by himself, center stage, no other family. Mario didn't even have to make the request himself.

Brenda had selected the Kantors for the program on the Tower of Babel. Babel on eggshells, Arthur thought. A touchy family. He was surprised, as he started the tape, to find himself wishing Moshe well.

The camera focused on a large pine tree. Arthur was startled. Almost all of the large Dade County pines had been destroyed by hurricane Andrew. If they hadn't been toppled outright, the stress was such that they died shortly after. No pines remained on Arthur's property, but then the Kantors lived twenty blocks north, and that, apparently, made a difference.

The camera pulled back to expose an open area of the yard. Two acres, Arthur thought, in an area where the average was one. He was pleased to see some mounds, an indication of trees felled and stumps removed, then chastised himself for his perverse satisfaction. The Kantors had taken damage, too.

Hurricane Andrew had been terrifying, a bullet shot out of Africa on a straight line for Dade County, nothing to move it from its path. Day after day, it held true to its track. It had come ashore through Homestead twenty miles to the south, leaving rubble in its wake. Even in Pinecrest it had blown so hard it caused chimneys to whistle like soda bottles. Arthur, Charlotte, and Tamar had huddled in the guest bathroom, the room with the least exposure to flying glass, fearful the roof would be torn from above them, too terrified to dash across the living room for the garage and the safety of the Volvo inside. They spoke of it above the roar, the Volvo would protect them if they could get to it, but they remained huddled in the bathroom until daybreak.

In spite of his protests, Tamar had braved the diminishing winds in the predawn light to scout the damage. Their home was intact, she reported, except for the pool enclosure. Instead of a screened-in pool they had a pooled-in screen. Minor damage. But so many trees were down.

For days chain saws whined on the surface and helicopters beat through the heavens, deafening noises above and below. Weeks went by without power. They had no county water supply, only a well, and no pump to draw from it. Instead they drew buckets of water from the pool to flush the toilets until the insurance company provided a generator, power enough to turn some fans, provide some light, and run the pump. Such a blessing.

The streets became canyons of dead foliage, walls piled eight feet high. Uprooted ficus, pine, and avocado trees. Even hard oak branches had snapped. But not the gumbo limbos or the palms. Those trees had weathered hurricanes for eons, from the time Florida emerged from the coral reef to form dry land.

Friday night, after the hurricane, Arthur opened the synagogue for services in the dark. Two dozen people in shock gathered in candlelight and said prayers, most for the first time in their lives.

The Kantors still had a pine tree, a big one. Healthy.

Arthur watched the yard. Nothing was happening. He fast forwarded in short spurts, fearful he might miss Moshe saying something off camera. Still nothing. Then a parade of boxes, children carrying boxes, some almost too large for them to carry. Static, and then Moshe. ". . . rules. Don't forget. No talking at all. One tower, no ladders, can't lean against anything, stay away from the tree, in the middle of the yard. All sixteen boxes, one on top of the other. The world record is fourteen. It can be done."

The parade of boxes proceeded in silence. Some were big enough to hold a child. Several had a Pampers logo, but these weren't the cartons one brought home from Publix. These were boxes the Pampers company sent to Publix, each containing a half dozen cartons.

They began eagerly, piling one on top of the next. Stupid, Arthur thought, not to arrange them according to size.

"They should arrange them according to size," a voice said within the range of Moshe's mike.

"Let them figure it out themselves," Moshe said.

A tower of four boxes rose at once. Then the children threw the boxes. Five, six. Robert lifted a young child to his shoulders. Seven. A breeze, and down they all came. No talking, but laughter from children and adults.

Again, the same mistake.

"The big ones at the bottom," the adult voice said, "the small ones at the top."

"They should lean them against the tree." A woman's voice.

"No leaning," Moshe said. "No support. Straight up."

Orly took charge, her delicate hands directing. Wordless, the boxes were laid out according to size and assembled. Still no more than six high, and the seventh toppled the tower.

One of the fathers, a man Arthur did not know, entered the frame and lifted a child to his shoulders. Six boxes rose, then seven. Then eight. The ninth brought everything down.

"From the bottom," Orly said aloud.

Another father entered the frame. Arthur didn't understand what Orly meant, but another father did. The two men lifted the boxes from the bottom, and the children slid boxes in from underneath. The tower grew, but the larger boxes were now on top. Eight, nine, ten, and the tower tumbled.

Two more men entered the frame. Half the children had withdrawn. The adults were taking over. Sixteen boxes, from the smallest to the largest. The smallest went up first. Four, five, six. Then the medium-sized boxes underneath. Then the larger ones. Ten, eleven, twelve. Awesome. Thirteen.

Four adults shifted underneath, leaned to counter for imbalance and the effects of the wind. Fourteen.

A gust of wind was too much to counterbalance. In awe and delight the children screamed, the adults echoing their cry, as the tower fell.

"Can't do it, not all sixteen," said an anonymous voice.

"We can do it," said another.

Only the taller children remained. Men and women had taken over. Thirteen, fourteen, fifteen. The tower fell.

The men were determined. "One more time." Mario gave directions. With precision, one box under the next, precisely aligned. Fourteen, fifteen, sixteen.

Applause.

"How long do we have to hold it?"

"Ten seconds," Moshe said.

". . . three, four, five, six, seven, eight, nine, ten."

The tower tumbled to shouts of joy, achievement, triumph, satisfaction.

"A new world record."

"Call the Guinness people. Sixteen."

The adults walked off frame. A few children kicked at the boxes, threw them at each other. Two took one of the smaller boys and shut him into a box until he began to cry. Soon only the boxes remained.

Arthur watched the videotape, a yard full of empty boxes. "What the hell am I doing?" he said aloud. "It's four in the morning and I'm watching a bunch of empty boxes."

He was about to eject the tape when Moshe came into view, walking directly toward him.

"You were watching that?" he asked.

"Who are you talking to?" Arthur asked the television.

"You were watching all the time, weren't you?"

Arthur began to tremble. Was Moshe talking to him? Did Moshe know somehow he would be watching?

"What did you think of that? Had you figured it out? When did you realize the way to do it was to put boxes in from the bottom?"

"Who are you talking to?" Arthur asked the television again. "Stop it! Stop talking to me!"

"Did you know it right from the beginning?"

Moshe was looking through the television screen directly at Arthur, had pinned him to his wing chair. "This is ridiculous," Arthur said, but he didn't move. Moshe looked at him, through him, for a minute, maybe more, saying not a word, then turned aside, leaving behind the empty boxes.

Arthur was astonished to find his shirt soaked through. He watched for another five minutes, ten. Moshe did not come back. Nothing. Nada. Bupkis. Emptiness.

"What the hell," Arthur said, struggling to his feet. "What the hell." He ejected the tape, returned it to its box. "I'm just too tired, that's all it is."

On the desk, the journal contained a sketch of the tower and a text Brenda had pasted on the adjoining page.

The Tower of Babel: Genesis 11
1. The whole earth had one language and common words.
2. When they traveled from the east they found a valley in the land of Shinar and they settled there (*sham*).

67

3. Each person said to his neighbor, "Come, let us make bricks and fire them in fire." So they had for themselves bricks as stone and material they had for mortar.
4. They said, "Come, let's build for us a city and a great thing with its head in the heavens (*shem-a-yim*) and make for ourselves a name (*shem*) lest we be scattered over the face of the earth.
5. *Ha-shem* descended to the city and the great thing which the children of Adam had built.
6. *Ha-shem* said, "So, one people with one language to all, and this is what they have imagined to do! Now nothing that they plan to do will be unattainable for them.
7. "Come, we'll go down and confuse there (*sham*) their language, so one person will not understand the language of the next."
8. *Ha-shem* scattered them from there (*sham*) over the face of all the earth, and they ceased from building the city.
9. Therefore its name (*shem-ah*) is called Babble, because there (*sham*) *Ha-shem* babbled the language of all the earth, and from there (*sham*) *Ha-shem* scattered them over the face of all the earth.

Arthur started the audiotape, heard the sound of chairs moving. He could not remember the inside of the Kantor house, only rooms within rooms within rooms. A living room, a family room, a media room.

"So many creation stories," Moshe said. "First God created the world in six days and then . . . ?"

"Shabbat." Several voices.

"And then Adam."

"Adam and Eve." A young girl.

"At first just Adam," Moshe said. "But that Adam wasn't quite a man yet. He was an earthling, made out of the earth. How many commandments are in the Torah?"

Arthur wondered where that question came from, trying to follow Moshe's direction.

"Six hundred and thirteen." Probably Robert Kantor. Mrs. Schwartz would have told him that.

"Six hundred and thirteen," Moshe repeated. "According to tradition, that's how many Moses received at Sinai. How many did Adam receive?"

Silence.

"Adam had one commandment," Moshe continued, "to name all the animals. He named them all, found each had a mate, and then went back to God and said, 'I did what you asked me to do. All of them are named, and all have a mate except me. I'm all by myself here. That's not fair. Take me back.' Adam didn't want to be alone. He didn't want to be separate from God. But God didn't take him back. What did God do?"

"He put Adam to sleep, took out a rib and made Eve." Robert again.

"Maybe. Or you can read it like this. God put the earthling to sleep, then divided one side from another. The Hebrew word for *rib* is also the word for *side*. One side became male, with the name Adam, the other side, female, with the name Eve."

"So male and female were created together." Orly's voice, or perhaps another girl's.

"Yes."

Arthur stopped the tape, a chill going through him. Where had he heard that, the original earthling being both male and female? He looked back through the materials he had already examined. Nothing. But he had just read it, just heard it.

"Shit," he said aloud.

He went to his personal file, unlocked it, withdrew Brenda's deposition and scanned through it, standing, not willing to bring it back to his desk. There it was, what Turin had taught her. The feminine side was dissected away from the masculine, and each was but half the image of God. The full image of God was formed only in spiritual and holy union. And following that, Turin had attempted in the most perverse way to affect such a union.

"Holy shit."

Arthur returned to his desk and restarted the tape.

"What does this have to do with the Tower of Babel?" An adult.

"Adam set a precedent. The original earthling didn't want to be separated from God. Later Eve tried to eat her way back. Then the generation of Noah—"

"Sex with the angels." An adult.

Sex again, Arthur thought. There it was, in every lesson. Any judge and jury would be listening for it. No doubt the Turin deposition would come out as well. That would make the matter only worse.

"Yes, and now with the Tower of Babel. How did they try to get back?"

"They built a tower." Several voices.

"What do you know about that tower?"

"They wanted to build a tower to reach heaven. They were going to climb their way back." Robert.

"What happened to the tower."

"God scrambled their languages so they couldn't understand each other. They got angry and started throwing bricks, and the whole tower came down."

"Everybody agree?" Moshe asked. "Well, let's go build our tower and see what happens. Maybe we'll get it high as heaven."

They hadn't built the tower yet, Arthur realized. He should have listened to the audio before watching the video.

"These are the rules. First of all, no talking. See if you can do it without any words at all. Secondly, kids only. Adults, stay out of it. We'll have enough fun watching. Third, one box on top of the next, sixteen boxes, one on top of each other. You can't lean it on anything. Find an open place in the yard. Okay? Let's go."

The sound of chairs moving was interrupted by Brenda's voice. "Let me get you wired up."

The order wasn't important, Arthur thought. Audio, video, it didn't matter. He could examine the material in any order he pleased. He was in charge, not the stacks of media on his desk. The thought brought him some comfort.

What had alarmed him? The androgynous male-female union thing—everyone knew that midrash, not just Turin and Moshe. Arthur himself knew it, had used it in his own teaching of Genesis. It didn't prove anything.

He watched the audio reel turn in silence, revolving within the player. Maybe he should have listened to it first, before the video. A judge and jury would have the order straight. He resolved to be more careful, but at four in the morning thinking straight was a bit beyond his capabilities. He reached to eject the tape.

"What's your name?" the tape player said just as he pressed *Stop*.

"Shit!" Arthur shouted as he jerked his hand back. "My name is Arthur! That's what my name is, damn you!" He ejected the tape and stared at it. There were two sessions on it, that's all it was. One session before they built the tower, some empty space between, and then a session after they built the tower. He put the tape back in.

70

"What's your name?" the tape repeated. "That's the important question. It all has to do with names and the importance of language. We tried to build the tower without words, but we couldn't do it. Look at the text. The whole earth had one clear language. No confusion. They traveled from the east. Where have we heard the word *east* before?"

"East of Eden." An adult.

"Right. The generations after Adam and Eve traveled east. They came to a level place and wanted not so much to make a physical tower but rather a name for themselves, a divine name. So, again, what's your name?" He didn't wait for an answer. "Your name and you are not the same. But God and God's name are. If they could create a divine name, they could get themselves back to heaven. The Hebrew word for name is *shem*, and the Hebrew for heaven is *shem-a-yim*, the place of the divine name. So that's what they were doing. They had this clear language, and they were using it to get back to shem-a-yim. God didn't want them back so fast, so God confused their language. He deprived them of the name and scattered them over the face of the earth.

"So this is, really, on a deeper level, a story about names, not a tower. You can use names to build things up, and you can use names to tear things down. We can call you a name and destroy you, or we can make your name great so the world knows and honors it.

"Names are serious business. That's what this is about. What I'd like you to do is divide into small groups, adults and children. Don't go with your parents, find some other adults to learn with. Read through the text. See how often the word *shem* or *sham* appears. See that it's talking about names. Then talk about your own names, what you like to be called, what you don't like to be called. When have you been hurt by a name? When have you hurt others? Throwing a name at a person can be like throwing a brick. Go and learn. I'm going to get some breakfast.

"Where's Daniel?"

"Still outside, looking through the camera."

"Daniel and I will get breakfast. You go and learn."

Silence.

Arthur hesitated to touch the tape player. He didn't want it talking back at him.

Daniel was behind the camera. Moshe had been speaking to Daniel, had been looking not into the camera but behind it. Moshe had been speaking to Daniel, not to him. Not to Arthur. *That* was his name, Arthur. Not

Artie. His parents had called him Artie. His brother had called him Artie, demeaning him in front of his friends.

Arthur, not Artie. I am Arthur, not RT. That's what the kids called him. RT-Doo-Dee. That was the name they'd throw at their rabbi, like a brick, ever since *Star Wars* and that damned robot.

R2-D2.

RT-Doo-Dee.

RT.

Artie.

I am an Arthur, he thought, as he lay down on the couch. For only a few minutes. He needed a nap.

"Artie," Jonah said.

"You're dead," Arthur said back.

"Artie, where you at, you little fuck?"

"You're dead. Don't you talk to me like that."

"I talk to you as I damn well please. I put your nose in the mud. You remember that?"

"I remember that. You keep reminding me. Why do you do that?"

"I don't do that. You do that. It's your dream, Artie, not mine."

"I'm not dreaming," Arthur said aloud, sitting straight up, "no time for dreams," the image of his brother still with him. Jonah, the last time he had seen him. Thin. Wasted.

Arthur stood, stretched, went to the desk.

The journal was open. He turned the page. A sketch of Moshe. Brenda was good, certain enough of her line to draw in pen. Black ink against blue-lined paper. Moshe in three-quarter profile. Handsome. Was he really that good-looking? He turned the page and was astonished by what he read.

Thanksgiving in California

They had the most wonderful house in the hills, Moshe and Rivkah, before she died. Moshe won't live there anymore. Sidney and Stephanie do.

As if Daniel is married to the deck. He won't leave it, and Stephanie won't leave him. Daniel, I think, is in love with the trees, eucalyptus, like the melaleuca back home, bark coming off in his hands. Stephanie is so quiet, so patient, with Daniel for hours, watching Daniel watch the trees, as if meditating.

Sidney is Jewish. Funny, he doesn't look Jewish. His family is from Hong Kong. He's a Chinese version of Moshe. I never know quite what he's looking at, as if he sees through things.

Sidney cooks. Turkey, tzimes, rice, stir-fried vegetables. To please Daniel, dinner on the deck.

Walking through the hills, a path down to the lake. Moshe hand in hand with Daniel, like father and son, so natural.

Shabbat. Stephanie, the candles. Sidney, the kiddush. Moshe showed me how to bless Daniel.
He says the Hebrew, but the English works.
How does he know the English works?
  May God make you like Efraim and Menasseh.
  May God bless you and keep you.
  May God's light shine upon you and be gracious to you.
  May God watch out for you and grant you shalom.
Efraim and Menasseh, the sons of Joseph. Two tribes out of Joseph. A special blessing.
  A kiss.
  A kiss works. I know that. How do I know a kiss works?

What's the difference between a kiss and a blessing?

Saturday morning with the Havurah minyan. What wonderful people. How happy they were to see Moshe. What a welcome for us. Any friend of Moshe's, I guess.
English works, but so much was in Hebrew. Moshe prayed in English, I think to make me comfortable.

Daniel likes to fly. I think he flies sometimes without a plane. In his mind. I imagine him soaring. I imagine him in the clouds, above the clouds. Soaring.

The page was puckered. Dried tears, Arthur suspected. In Brenda's mind, Daniel was always soaring, in the highest of places.

A few years before, Brenda had come to Arthur with reports of a miracle, autistic children communicating through a computer keyboard with the gentlest of guidance for their fingers. Daniel's autism wasn't of the sort described. It wasn't of any sort described. No one knew quite what to make of it, this beautiful child who seemed perpetually lost. Still Brenda had rushed to try.

She sat Daniel before the computer. His attention was not on the keyboard or the monitor, perhaps out the window or on the pattern of the wallpaper. She didn't know where he was. No one knew. But his fingers hit the keys.

"Where are you?" she asked, and the fingers typed out, "Clouds."

She gasped. "Where are you?" She asked again, and again came, "Clouds."

No mistake.

The answers to her questions were immediate. "Are you okay?" "I am okay. Don't worry about me."

She had rushed to tell Arthur. It was a miracle for her friend and rabbi to witness. He had heard of this, not only with Daniel, but with others. He knew of the skeptics. "I hope it is so," he told Brenda, though he had his doubts.

Arthur asked questions. Brenda guided her son's fingers. Daniel responded through the keyboard, making mistakes in spelling, but the answers made sense.

"Let me try," Arthur said. He sat before the monitor, looked out the window, and tried to type answers to Brenda's questions. He couldn't do it, and he knew how to type. "You guide my fingers," he suggested. Then his answers made sense.

It was obvious to him. The questions and the answers were both Brenda's. Daniel had nothing to do with it, but Arthur didn't say so. The evidence was there, whenever she was ready to see it.

For months her longing overwhelmed her ability to see the truth, but bit by bit, reality seeped in. She stopped bringing Daniel to the computer. He remained lost, looking out the window, into space, at the pattern in the carpet. Lost, neither happy nor unhappy. Content.

CHAPTER 5

SUNDAY, 4:15 A.M.

The tape was labeled "Dec. 4, Hanukkah in the Park."

The park was Dante Fascell in South Miami, in honor of the veteran congressman. Was it named for him before he died or after? Arthur couldn't remember. The building committee wanted to name one of the new buildings on the synagogue campus after their rabbi. The Arthur Greenberg Study Center or the Arthur Greenberg Library. He had declined the offer, but the committee had insisted. It would make fund-raising easier, they said. That was the only reason he hadn't dismissed the proposal outright. But the whole matter might be moot, he knew, if he could not find a way out. His heart fell as he looked at the stack of materials remaining. How long did he have? One more day and a few hours. But he had to have it resolved before then. He didn't have enough energy for one more day and a few more hours.

The videotape was silent. To the left, a pavilion, picnic tables covered with cloth, adults eating breakfast. Older children played Frisbee on the field. Were they part of the program? Neither Moshe nor Brenda was in sight.

How long did he have to watch this?

The scene shifted upward, tree limbs, sky through the trees. Someone must have bumped into the camera. When it came back down, the scene swung right, toward the tennis courts. Children were busy under trees, collecting things. Litter. Cans, paper.

Two men stood in the distance, by the soda machine. Moshe, in shorts and a white T-shirt, a baseball hat. A man in jeans, with a stomach. The man was agitated, couldn't stay still, shifted back and forth, side to side, approaching Moshe, as if threatening. Moshe held his ground. The man spoke, gestured, pointed. Moshe moved not at all.

Arthur stopped the frame but still could not recognize the man.

The tape running again, the man became still more agitated, as if about to throw a punch. Moshe did not move, held his ground. The man retreated, approached, retreated again, withdrew to the right and off the screen.

Arthur rewound the tape and reviewed the drama in the distance. The man with the stomach was angry. And Moshe? If anything could be determined with the images so far away, Moshe's countenance was sad.

Now what the hell was that about?

Moshe remained alone by the soda machine for a minute, maybe more, still not moving. At last he turned toward the trees, said something. The children looked up and moved off camera toward the pavilion.

Arthur was left alone with the soda machine.

". . . one two three four." Moshe's voice. He was wired for sound. "Okay, over here. Bring everything you've found. We'll make a Hanukkah menorah. Right here."

The camera shifted to a swarm of children. On the ground they laid out a Hanukkah menorah, or at least a semblance of one, with the litter they had collected. Silver Diet Coke cans, bright in the sunlight, became the candles.

Something to enter in the menorah contest, Arthur thought. The menorah contest was a temple tradition Arthur had inherited from his predecessor. If Arthur had his druthers, there would be no menorah contest. To him the very notion was silly. Popular nonetheless, it continued.

The original intent was for children to create the menorahs. Awards were given for each of the religious school grades. Soon it became apparent the menorahs were most often the product of parents, the child doing no more than providing the means of delivery. So the contest was made into a family affair, and any family might participate. The difficulty was that many families still thought the contest to be for the children and encouraged their children to participate without parental assistance. These juvenile menorahs were then judged in the same category as the adult entries. The children were almost always disappointed, their parents angry.

There had been fewer entries than usual that year. The grand prize had gone to an eight-branched candelabra pieced together from broken glass, a memorial of Kristallnacht. The theme of Judah the Maccabee had been superimposed over the tragedy of the Holocaust. The imposition did not appeal to Arthur, but he had not been on the jury. The winning menorah was the epitome of everything wrong with the contest. Surely no child had so much as touched a menorah made of broken glass.

What was the point?

Arthur would have brought an end to the contest but was powerless to do so. Another program over which he had no control, but one, at least, that was benign. Cut fingers and bruised feelings were the extent of the damage.

Moshe was wired for sound, but had said nothing. Arthur could hear the children, some words from the parents, nothing from Moshe. Why so silent? Something to do with the man with the stomach?

"I saw what happened over there." Brenda's voice. "You didn't tell him where they were?"

"No. Of course not," Moshe said.

"I thought he was going to hit you."

"Not me. Not here."

Silence. Children arranging the outline of the menorah on the ground.

Arthur rewound the tape to listen to the dialogue again, especially the tone of Brenda's voice. She was afraid. What was that about?

"Beautiful," Moshe said at last.

Adults came into view, sat with the children around the menorah.

"Who can tell me the Hanukkah story?" Moshe asked. No response. "Someone begin."

No one began.

"Anyone. Someone start."

Arthur recalled the mounds in the Kantors' yard, evidence of fallen trees. Moshe was taking damage, too. Moshe doing frontal teaching. He wasn't any better at it than anyone else. A few more seconds of withering silence, and he too would topple.

"Won't someone begin?" Still no one began. Why not? The children seemed intimidated. No one snuck up behind Moshe to steal his hat. They kept their distance.

"My fault," Moshe said. "That's not fair. You all know the Hanukkah story. Let me begin again.

"There was a Jewish family in Modeen, about, oh, two thousand two hundred years ago. You know where Modeen is? Not too far from Jerusalem. The Greek-Syrians were in control of the land, and they wanted everyone to worship the Greek gods and live in a Greek style. You all know this?

77

"The Mattathius family put out the word, Mattathius and his sons. He had lots of sons. They were zealots. They said, 'All who will fight against the Greek-Syrians, stand with us! Anyone who does Greek things, fear for your lives!'

"Eventually it was Judah the Maccabee, Judah the Hammer, one of the sons, who became the leader of the rebels. He fought and killed the Greek-Syrians, but he also killed Jews who followed Greek customs. Did you know that?

"It was on the twenty-fifth of the winter month of Kislev. Judah won the final battle and rededicated the Temple in Jerusalem. That's why we celebrate Hanukkah."

That was not the way to tell the story, Arthur thought. Not that Moshe was wrong. The idea of elevating Judah the Maccabee to hero status gave the early rabbis lots of problems. Judah became a hero, but just as Moshe said, at the expense of a lot of Jewish lives. So the rabbis created a new story and eliminated the books of the Maccabees from the Jewish Bible, so the story would not be told that way.

"But why do we celebrate for eight days?" Moshe asked.

Because a dedication holiday lasted eight days, Arthur answered silently. When Solomon dedicated the Temple in Jerusalem, that was eight days. Or to compensate for the eight days of the holiday of Sukkot that had been lost because the people were at war. But that also was not the way to tell the story.

"Because of the miracle of the oil," one of the children risked.

"Yes, Judy," Moshe said. "Because of the miracle of the oil. That's the story. When they rededicated the Temple in Jerusalem, they found only one jar of holy oil to light the menorah, but that one jar lasted eight days. So eight days of Hanukkah for the eight days of the miracle."

"Seven days," a boy said.

"Why seven, Robert?"

"There was enough oil to last one day, so that wasn't a miracle. The miracle was for only seven days."

"I see. Very clever."

Moshe paused, turned to look at Arthur through the camera.

He's not looking at me, Arthur reminded himself. He's looking at Daniel. Even so, Arthur felt Moshe was looking at him. More than a glance, a steady gaze, his eyes not quite focused. What was he doing?

"We need a new story," he said at last, turning his attention back to the circle of adults and children. "The old one is flawed. We need a new one. I know how to begin it, pretty much, but I don't know yet how to end it. All I have so far is the beginning. Let's see what we can do together."

Just like that, the tenor of the session changed. The energy jumped to a high level. Arthur saw it, electric around the circle. Something was going to happen. Everyone knew it.

"It begins with either a little girl or a little boy," Moshe said. "I can't see the child clearly." His eyes were closed.

"A little girl," a girl said.

"A boy!"

"A girl!"

The girls had it. "A little girl," Moshe agreed, "It might have been a little boy, but if you want a girl, it's a girl. It was about twenty-two hundred years ago. She lived with her family in . . . where was it she lived?"

"Modeen," came the response.

"That's right. Modeen." He paused. "You know, the adults can participate in this story too. We'll need all the help we can get.

"This family loved to celebrate Jewish holidays. Most of all the little girl liked Shabbat. Why Shabbat?"

"Because it comes fifty-two times a year." That was from one of the adults.

"Thank you, Linda," Moshe said. "Because it comes every week, she liked Shabbat more than all of the other holidays. She got to do it more.

"She and her family had just sat down to the table on Friday night for their Shabbat dinner when a Jewish soldier burst into the house. 'Let's go,' he said. 'Hurry! The enemy is coming! No time! Into the woods!'

"The family had their bags already packed. 'What about our Shabbat?' the little girl asked.

"'No time for that. We have to save our lives,' her father said. And they rushed into the woods.

"They marched through the woods, sometimes fighting, mostly running away. Soon it came time for Passover. The family sat down with other families to begin their Passover seder, but again, a soldier burst into their camp and said they had to run. The enemy was coming. So they missed out on having a Passover seder that year.

"For seven weeks they were on the move. At the end of seven weeks there was another holiday. Do you know which one?"

"Shavuot." An adult voice.

"The festival of the giving of the Torah," Moshe agreed. "And they missed that one too. So the little girl was upset for three reasons. First she had missed . . ."

"Shabbat," came the response.

"And then?"

"Passover."

"And now?"

"Shavuot."

"Right. She had missed her Shabbat, her Passover, and her Shavuot. She wasn't happy about that at all.

"It was a difficult summer. How many of you go to summer camp?" Several children raised their hands. "Well, this was a military camp, not a summer camp. Not much fun. They were marching, fighting, tired all the time. At the end of the summer came another holiday. A holy day."

"Rosh Hashanah."

"Yes, the Jewish new year. And you know what?"

"They missed that one too."

"That's right. So now the little girl had missed Shabbat, and . . ."

"Passover, and Shavuot, and Rosh Hashanah."

"Ten days later came Yom Kippur. She thought, all you have to do on Yom Kippur is to fast. No eating, no drinking, all day. But Judah the Maccabee, the leader of the Jewish army, said no one could fast on that Yom Kippur because they had to be strong in case they had to fight. So now she had missed her Shabbat, and her . . ."

"Passover, and Shavuot, and Rosh Hashanah, and Yom Kippur."

The responses came in unison, in rhythm.

"Just a few days after Yom Kippur comes the festival of . . ."

"Sukkot."

"The little girl thought, all you have to do on Sukkot is camp outside in temporary shelters, and that's what we've been doing all along. They can't take this one away from us. But all that week, they had to march. There was hardly any time to sleep at all. So now, altogether, she had missed her Shabbat and . . ."

"Passover, and Shavuot, and Rosh Hashanah, and Yom Kippur, and Sukkot."

"Eight days later came the eighth day of assembly. Shmini Atzeret. Then they used to rejoice with the Torah scrolls . . ."

"Simhat Torah," a child said.

"Do you think they were able to celebrate?"

"No." Another child. "They had to fight a war."

"Right. So now they had missed Shabbat and . . ."

"Passover, and Shavuot, and Rosh Hashanah, and Yom Kippur, and Sukkot, and Simhat Torah."

"Then came the biggest battle of all. The Maccabees fought for days. They finally won the war and marched into Jerusalem to the Temple steps.

"Now Judah the Maccabee was about seven feet tall and must have weighed three hundred pounds, all muscle. We need a Judah."

George Lopez stood up.

"And a little girl."

Lots of hands.

"Taylor," Moshe said. Taylor was maybe ten years old, cute. Arthur didn't know which family she came from.

George Lopez and Taylor stood side by side.

"Judah the Maccabee stood on the Temple steps and said, 'Tomorrow we will have a holiday.'"

"Tomorrow we will have a holiday!" George said in a big voice.

Moshe continued, "It will be a holiday to celebrate our victory. We will rededicate the Temple. We will call it Hanukkah, a holiday of dedication!"

"Tomorrow we will have a holiday," George repeated. "A holiday of Hanukkah, to rededicate the Temple."

Moshe said, "It will be a day we will remember throughout all of our generations, forever and ever. But before Judah could finish, the little girl spoke up. 'One day isn't enough.'"

Taylor needed some urging. "One day isn't enough," she said, barely loud enough for Arthur to hear.

"No," Moshe continued, "we need a day to replace the Shabbat we missed, and . . ." He opened his arms to encourage the response.

"And Passover, and Shavuot, and Rosh Hashanah, and Yom Kippur, and Sukkot, and Simhat Torah."

"That's right," Moshe said. "We need one day for Hanukkah, but seven more days for each of the holidays we missed.

"Now Judah was a very smart man. All of the people heard what the little girl had to say, even if she didn't speak very loudly, and they liked it. She wasn't the only one who had missed the holidays. But Judah was a practical man. There was much work to do. He couldn't afford to take eight days off. So what did Judah do? He appealed to a higher authority. The priests had found only one jar of oil suitable for use in the menorah in the Temple. He said he would leave the matter in God's hands." Moshe stopped and pointed toward George. "Do you know what Judah said?"

George nodded. "We'll leave it in God's hands," he repeated. "We have only this one jar of oil that the priests have found, holy oil, for the menorah in the Temple." He held up the imaginary jar for all to see. "As long as this one jar of oil lasts, we will have our holiday. It's out of my hands. God will decide."

"A nice story," said one of the adults.

"A good way to negotiate," George said.

Moshe laughed. "That's not the end of the story," he said. "I know the rest now. That was only the beginning." He closed his eyes, as if somehow with his eyes closed he could see the story better. He opened them and continued. "The little girl wasn't happy with what Judah had said. That night, she got a coil of rope and put it on her shoulder." He nodded toward Taylor. She put an imaginary rope on her shoulder. "And she took a jar of ordinary oil." Taylor held up her hand. "And she climbed up a vine to the roof of the Temple." Taylor made climbing motions. "She found a hole in the roof of the Temple, tied the rope to a pole on the roof, lowered herself over the menorah, and poured the jar of oil into it. Then she climbed back up the rope, and down the vine.

"The next day, Judah stood on the steps of the Temple and announced, 'Our holiday is over. Back to work!'"

"Back to work," George said.

"But the little girl pointed to the menorah."

"Look at the menorah. It's still going," Taylor said, without prompting.

"Judah looked at the menorah and was surprised. It was still burning. He must have figured the amount of oil wrong. 'Okay,' he said, 'we'll celebrate for one more day.'"

"One more day," George said.

"For the Shabbat we missed," Taylor added.

"That night, the little girl climbed up the vine again, lowered herself over the menorah, and added another jar of oil. Imagine Judah's surprise when he saw the menorah was still burning.

"The little girl said, 'Yesterday was for the Shabbat we missed. Today is for the . . .'"

"Passover," everyone said.

"She did the same thing the next night, climbing up to the Temple roof, lowering herself through the hole, adding more oil to the menorah, and the next morning the menorah was still burning. That was for . . ."

"Shavuot."

"And the next day for . . ."

"Rosh Hashanah."

"And the next day?"

"Yom Kippur."

"And the next day?"

"Sukkot."

"Seven days," Moshe said. "Judah was fit to be tied. Seven days when he had planned on only one. He knew something fishy was going on. You know what he did? That night, just after sunset, he took his sword and climbed up the vine to the roof of the Temple to see what might happen. Pretty soon the little girl came up. He saw her, the coil of rope, and the jar of oil in her hand. She tied the rope around her waist, and when she was about to lower herself through the hole in the roof, she looked up, and what did she see?"

George Lopez rose up to his full height, and raised his arm with the imaginary sword.

"A huge figure that blocked out the stars, a sword raised high in his hand!

"'No,' said the little girl. 'It's only me.'"

"No," said Taylor, "It's only me!"

"Judah looked at the little girl, at the hole in the roof. He examined the rope tied about her waist. Then he lifted her up." Moshe nodded. George lifted Taylor up. "High in the air." He lifted her higher, above his head. Taylor giggled. "Then, carefully, he lowered her through the hole, swung her over the menorah, and she poured in the last jar of oil. Then he lifted her back up to the roof. And this is what he said to her."

Moshe whispered some words into George's ear. Arthur could hear them through the mike but wanted more to hear them coming from George.

George smiled, turned to look down at Taylor, and said, "Don't you ever tell anybody about what happened here this night, and neither will I."

"And," Moshe said, "nobody has ever talked about it to this very day."

George and Taylor bowed to the applause of the circle.

Arthur pressed pause.

That was wonderful. Had Moshe just made the story up on the spot, or had he learned it somewhere else?

He started the tape again.

Moshe looked at Arthur and asked, "Did you like the story?"

Arthur was startled. It took a moment to remember Moshe was talking to Daniel behind the camera, not to him.

"I asked for a story just for you," Moshe continued. "I thought you might like it. If we had decided it was a boy instead of a girl, would you have played the part? Maybe next time we tell it, you'll play the part, okay?"

Did Moshe really think Daniel understood? And what did he mean, he had *asked* for a story? Asked whom?

It didn't matter. Arthur stopped the tape, stood to stretch. The story was wonderful. Moshe had preserved the festival of lights, made Judah fearsome and likeable at the same time, but what was especially nice, the little girl was now the hero. Or the little boy. The miracle was no longer a violation of the laws of nature. The miracle was the cooperation of Judah and the little girl.

A sudden trembling overcame Arthur. There was something of the Kabbalah in that story. He felt it. He had been pulled into it. He didn't know enough of the Kabbalah to identify all the motifs, but Judah was Gevurah, the aspect of judgment, and the little girl, Hesed, the aspect of compassion, and the mixture of the two was compelling.

Where did Moshe get that story? Where had he gone when he had closed his eyes, searching for it?

Arthur restarted the tape. It was as if a spell had been cast upon the group, adults and children alike. No one moved until Moshe spoke.

"Now for a real miracle," Moshe said softly, a hypnotist speaking to his subjects. "Tonight will be the seventh night of Hanukkah, seven candles. Can you feel how hard the wind is blowing? Do you think we could light seven candles in a real Hanukkah menorah, and keep them lit, with the wind blowing like this? We can, if all of us do it together, and doing it together like that would be a miracle.

"Everybody stand, gather round. Like a football huddle. Closer. Closer. Block the wind."

Arthur could no longer see Moshe, only the adults and children squeezing together. Who was managing the camera? It was moving, trying to find its way to the center of the circle. Down low, between legs. Arthur could see some of Moshe, on his knees, holding the menorah.

"Let's begin." He started singing, *Hanukkah, O Hanukkah, a holiday of joy.* The families joined in. The candles were lit. They remained lit throughout the song. It was powerful, and intimate.

84

Exclamations of delight, and, unexpectedly, the camera was off, only static on the television screen. Arthur waited, waited some more to be sure he had seen it all, that the tape wouldn't spring alive to bite him when he reached to turn it off. Even so, he felt apprehension when he pressed *Stop*, relief when he pressed *Eject*.

Arthur stood, stretched, returned to his desk and the open journal.

Following the Thanksgiving entry were two pages of doodles: crystals, prisms, and pyramids. Brenda was a devotee of all such things. At one point she bought crystals by the dozens, for herself, for her friends, to be worn around the neck or free-standing to place on desks and night tables.

In the middle drawer of his desk Arthur found among those things he didn't want to keep but couldn't throw away the crystal she had given him. When? Three years ago? Four? She had invested so much in it, he couldn't divest himself of it. At least she hadn't given him a pyramid. A pyramid wouldn't have fit into the drawer. The crystal was purple. Quartz? Amethyst? He didn't know. It had power, she said, to attract and concentrate energy.

Then it was magnets. Magnets to wear in shoes, in belts, in bra straps. She had tried to give him a magnet. He was afraid it might corrupt data on his computer disks and credit cards and refused it, politely.

And after that? Angel cards.

Those were the things she gave away. A missionary on behalf of so many New Age causes. It wasn't enough to have them for herself. The benefit was increased by sharing them with others. Perhaps all of the benefit was in the sharing. The sharing focused energy. Of that Arthur had no doubt.

He turned the page.

> *Moshe said it would be okay. I don't know if it is or not.*
> *Moshe said a week or two. It's been a week.*
> *Marsha can't stay still. She paces, as if always looking over her shoulder to see what's coming up behind her.*
> *Andy lit the first candle. He was happy to do it. He tried to get Daniel to, but Daniel was content to watch.*

Her penmanship was large and filled the page. On the side opposite, a portrait of a woman in sunglasses, Marsha, no doubt.

Perlman, Arthur thought, comprehension growing. He turned to the

85

computer to remind himself, the name already on the screen once he brought it back to life. Perlman, Marsha and Morton. Son, Andrew, scheduled for bar mitzvah in December. Bar mitzvah canceled.

The man with the stomach by the Coke machine had been Morton, Andy's father.

> *Moshe said he was more worried for Andy than for Marsha. He was afraid of what Andy might do. Sweet kid.*

> *Moshe came to light the candles with us. Four candles. Andy first, Marsha, Daniel, and me. He had dreidels for each of us, with different letters. Not "A great miracle happened there," but "a great miracle happened here." Miracles are better when they happen here.*

> *Marsha made the latkes. Thin, crisp. Applesauce, no sour cream.*

> *I am a witness to an offer. A trade. A contract. A knife for a bar mitzvah, that was Moshe's deal with Andy. Andy gives up the knife, he gets a bar mitzvah.*

> *Moshe says a bar mitzvah can't be canceled. The celebration, but not the bar mitzvah. If Andy gives up the knife, he gets both the celebration and the bar mitzvah. Moshe guarantees it.*

Not possible, Arthur thought. The vacated date surely would not still be vacant. December dates were in great demand. A quick computer check proved him right. The Perlman date had been taken. In a year, perhaps, something would open, if a family moved away, or if they chose a date during the summer, but no one ever did.

> *Moshe said we don't need a rabbi, only a Torah scroll.*

> *Hanukkah in the park. Make latkes or bring them? Grate the potatoes there or here? More fun there.*

> *Clark and Davidson; applesauce and sour cream.*

The next page was titled *Abraham & Isaac.*

Arthur wasn't ready for the next session. He carried the journal to his wing chair, rewound the video and watched once again the confrontation in the park. Morton Perlman, making threatening gestures, demanding to know where his wife and son were. Moshe holding his ground.

"Good for you," Arthur said.

There were Jewish men who beat their wives, Jewish homes with battered women. Arthur had been briefed by the Shalom Bayit committee, the Federation committee to increase awareness about such matters. Arthur knew of no such homes within his community, no such families in his congregation. But Moshe had found one.

"Good for you," Arthur repeated, and good for Brenda, that she had the courage to take them in until arrangements could be made.

How did Moshe know?

He had befriended Andy, perhaps given him a ride in the Porsche. Andy had told him what the situation was at home. Maybe not. Maybe Marsha had. Sunglasses when the sun wasn't out. Perhaps that was it. Moshe suspected. Moshe knew.

Moshe had taken Andy for a ride in his Porsche. Moshe had guaranteed Andy a bar mitzvah. Moshe gave presents, made promises. What was Moshe looking for in return? Marsha couldn't stay still. She paced, back and forth. Her husband was no longer a threat. Why was she pacing back and forth?

Arthur was tired, not ready for Abraham and Isaac, still contemplating Marsha pacing and Morty threatening and Moshe promising, a rabbi who wasn't a rabbi saying you don't need a rabbi for a bar mitzvah. Maybe not, but a synagogue and a Torah scroll, and the synagogue wasn't available. Maybe in the summer, a bar mitzvah. But how, on a week's notice?

Arthur's hands didn't know where to go next. They reached for the journal, riffled through the pages as through a deck of cards, to the end. He looked down and was surprised to see the writing upside down. He turned the book around. It was notes from a lesson, in Brenda's hand, the heading, *The Merkavah—The Work of the Chariot.* So Moshe had been teaching her the Kabbalah, one on one, just like Turin, picking up where Turin had left off. The front of the journal was for the family lessons, the back, notes for her private lessons.

Private lessons. What was he doing with Brenda during the private lessons?

Only four pages of lesson notes. Not so many. He could manage that. Arthur sank back into the wing chair. Four pages, then, maybe, a nap.

Just a short one.

What is the difference concerning the songs a person sings who desires to descend to the Chariot? To descend safely and to ascend safely?

Everything is in that question. Everything.

More in the question than in the answer.

That's the question they asked when they made the transition from animal sacrifice to prayer. What is the question to ask now that we are making the transition from prayer to . . . to what?

Maybe that's the question.

What is the difference concerning the songs a person sings?

Margolit says the Hebrew is more difficult than that.

Who was Margolit? Was it important to know? Not important enough to lift himself out of the wing chair.

The word for songs in the text is shirot. *The usual Hebrew would be* shirim. *That means these songs are really different. Different from what? From the ordinary songs one sings.*

These are the songs the angels sing twice each and every day before the throne of glory. The early rabbis descended to the place where they could hear those songs, and those songs were included in the prayers.

Why descent?

Margolit doesn't know, but I know.

It makes such good sense. If you meditate upwards you have to come down. How do you get down safely? Do you fall and crash?

This makes so much more sense. You meditate down, into the depths, and then, when you are tired, you float to the surface. Float up toward the light.

But it's dangerous.

They used to make fun of the rabbis who did this. They used to insult them. Margolit says the text has curses for those who insult the mystics, blessings for those who do the discipline.

One of the blessings is insight. They can look into a person and see his merits and sins, like a smelter can tell the trueness of the metal, how much gold, how much silver, how much iron, how much lead. They can look into a person, and see the history—if the person is a murderer, a thief, an adulterer. Incest.

Can Moshe look into me? Does he see my history?

Margolit is learning the discipline. Moshe teaches her.

Why won't he teach me?

Because I'm not married. That's what he learned from his rabbi.

I would have to be forty, have a beard, be married.

Forty I can understand. Old enough.

A beard, he says, is like a graduate degree.

And married?

Margolit isn't married, and he teaches her.

Arthur had no choice. He raised himself from the wing chair, leaned over his desk, didn't want to sit at it, as if that would be some form of surrender. He punched the keyboard and searched for Margolit. Who was Margolit?

Zedek. Margolit Zedek. She lived in the Gables, one of those old, small houses just east of Red Road. Charlotte liked those houses, wanted to move into one when they were first looking. Maroglit Zedek, an Israeli, divorced. One child, Orly.

Orly. The violinist.

Moshe wasn't teaching Brenda. Moshe was teaching Margolit.

Moshe wouldn't teach Brenda because she wasn't married. Margolit wasn't married.

A riddle, and Arthur was too tired to solve it.

A nap, a short nap, in the wing chair.

The house on Green Street, the living room. The plastic on the sofa and chairs, to be removed for the company that never came. The museum. The mausoleum on Green Street.

Mother wore a hat. Proper women did, but not in the house.

She was so embarrassed when, at the market, left outside by the vegetable stalls in the carriage, he pulled the tips off the asparagus. A planted memory that sprouted anew now and then.

She had denied it, defended him. At home, lifting him from the carriage, all the tips.

The tips.

The customers tipped the driver. The driver gave them tips.

His father in his chair on the porch, closed in. Even in the winter, in his chair on the porch, with the space heater on. His father chomping on the cigar he never lit.

Smarter than all, his father knew the worth of a man. How much gold, how much silver, how much iron, how much lead.

He never packed a gun, not his father.

"Make your money sitting down." His father's wisdom. Others drove the cabs, took the bets, made the payoffs.

The neighbors knew. They never came into the living room.

Jonah drove the cabs. Artie rode his bike. To Clifton, Little Falls, anywhere but Paterson. He rode great distances, so everyone would admire him, how far he'd come.

Jonah took the bets from the many phones downtown in the garage. Not him. Not Artie. Not over his mother's dead body, she said. It was enough Jonah followed in his father's footsteps. Arthur was going to college, even in the third grade.

Even then he rode great distances, so everyone would admire him, how far he'd come.

In Clifton, how would they know how far he'd come, that he'd pedaled all the way from Paterson?

Pop was to Jonah as Mom was to . . . ? A question on the SAT.

Jonah never took the SAT. Jonah peddled dope and made Pop turn purple.

"Make your money sitting down. Stay out of the streets. No place for a Jewish boy." Pop's wisdom.

Mom took him to the shul for Sunday school. In the sanctuary, brick walls halfway up to heaven. Safe space, far away from the porch in winter, when he could not ride the bike to Clifton or Little Falls. He could walk through the snow to the shul, sit in the sanctuary and count the bricks halfway to heaven.

Pop never hit him. Jonah, he hit. Jonah's face turned purple.

"Make your money sitting down."

One small hole in Pop's forehead. A trickle of red on Green Street. Artie was the first to find him, on the porch, the big man in his chair, sitting where they shot him.

"Shit," Arthur said suddenly awake, not that he had been sleeping, only dozing. "Shit," he said again, when he saw by the clock it was 7:30. Two hours. He had wasted two hours. There wasn't any time to waste.

CHAPTER 6

SUNDAY, 7:30 A.M.

Walking in the orchard, with Moshe. Daniel takes his hand. They look good together, natural.

Such trees, fruits I never heard of. Paradise. The Garden of Eden couldn't have been any more wonderful.

Pomelo, a giant grapefruit. Carambola, star fruit. Jack fruit, huge, pendulous.

Rows and rows of lichees. Bill and Linda are hoping for a good crop. I don't know if this is their livelihood or their hobby. But it is paradise, and they know it.

Paradise comes from pardes, Moshe said. Hebrew for orchard.

No apples in this orchard, but it wasn't an apple that Eve gave to Adam.

We spent the afternoon walking, eating from the trees.

A clearing. A place for a bonfire, Moshe said. A Lag Bi-omer bonfire. But that won't be until May sometime.

Abraham & Isaac.
Chuck & Cindy's.
Sheets & broomsticks.

That was it, the complete list of instructions for Sunday morning, December 18.

"Sheets and broomsticks." Arthur shook his head, not understanding.

"Chuck and Cindy." No problem there. The Schwartzes. They lived in Coconut Grove, a townhouse down near the bay. Chuck was on the Adult

91

Education Committee, always complaining they weren't doing enough, wanting to bring in this person, that person, when there wasn't enough in the budget for this person, let alone that. Three thousand dollars for a weekend two dozen people might attend.

"Abraham and Isaac," the one section of Torah Arthur knew by heart in Hebrew, having read it every Rosh Hashanah to a packed house. He couldn't get by reading from the Humash with vowels, not on Rosh Hashanah. He read the text from the parchment itself, a line in Hebrew, then looking up toward the congregation, to translate the line into English. Back and forth, Hebrew then English, a powerful story, a powerful reading. They loved it when Abraham lifted the knife to slaughter his son, and Arthur, in his white robe, raised up the *yad*, the dagger-shaped pointer. So dramatic, they loved it, year after year.

The brief instructions were followed by a text, pasted in.

Genesis 22

1. After these things happened God tested (or made a banner out of) Abraham. God said to him, "Abraham!" He answered, "I am here."

2. God said, "Please take your son, your only one, the one you love, namely Isaac, and get yourself to the land of Moriah, and raise him up there as an offering on one of the mountains that I will tell you about."

3. Abraham got up early the next morning. He himself saddled his donkey. He took two young servants with him, and Isaac, his son. He chopped wood for the offering. He got up and went to the place that God had told him about.

4. It was on the third day when Abraham looked up and saw the place in the distance.

5. Abraham said to his young servants, "You stay here with the donkey. The boy and I are going up there to worship, and then we will return to you."

6. Abraham took the wood for the offering and placed it on Isaac, his son. He took in his hand the fire and the knife. The two of them continued together.

7. Isaac said to Abraham his father, "Daddy." He answered, "I am here, my son." He said, "Here is the fire and the wood, but where is the lamb for the offering?"

8. Abraham said, "God will see to the lamb for the offering my son." The two of them continued together.
9. They came to the place God had spoken about to him. He built an altar there. He set down the wood. He tied up Isaac his son and put him on the altar on top of the wood.
10. Abraham put out his hand and took the knife to slaughter his son.
11. An angel of God called out to him from heaven saying, "Abraham. Abraham!" He said, "I am here."
12. He said, "Don't touch the boy! Don't do anything to him! By that I will really know you respect God, for you will have not removed your son, your only son, from me."
13. Abraham looked up and saw a ram to offer instead, caught by its horns in a bush. Abraham went and took the ram. He offered it up instead of his son.

Should he go home and have breakfast? Arthur scanned the familiar text and pondered his question at the same time. The translation wasn't bad. A few words here and there he might have argued with. No, he wouldn't go home. Not yet, anyway. He liked the "Daddy," more intimate than "father." Charlotte liked to sleep late on Sundays. So did he, for that matter. He wouldn't wake her. But how did Moshe intend to teach this story to children? It was a minefield to be traversed with care. He'd finish the Abraham text first. A video, an audio. After that, he'd consider what to do about a shower and breakfast.

The living room in the townhouse was not large enough to accommodate so many people comfortably, but they didn't seem to mind. The camera must have been set low, perhaps on the floor, inclined upward. Arthur saw legs passing by. In the distance, the dining room, some adults eating bagels. Brenda, as usual, in shorts. Children eating doughnuts. Moshe wasn't visible.

"Let's begin." A voice, not Moshe's. "Sheets and broomsticks."

Sheets and broomsticks moved into the living room. Arthur imagined a moment from *Fantasia, The Sorcerer's Apprentice*, broomsticks coming to life. No, the broomsticks were tent poles. Brenda and Chuck fixed the sheets to the broomsticks with rubber bands, sheet to sheet with safety pins. A tent was erected through the living room, one broomstick high. Children and parents sat underneath.

Moshe appeared and sat, back to the camera. He was wearing a T-shirt, a large blue Torah scroll on the back with some words in Hebrew Arthur could not make out. Moshe sang a single note, the vowel "I." Everyone responded, "I," mimicking him.

"I, I, I, I," followed by, "I, I, I, I."

The Italians sang "me," and the Jews sang "I," Arthur thought, smiling at his own joke. Ego, ego everywhere, and not a drop to drink. He looked about for his coffee. No, no more coffee.

Everyone sang. The niggun built in energy, subsided, ended with a whisper. Silence.

So nice the way he did that, bringing them to order. No shouting. No banging. No words. A song without words, and he had everyone's attention.

"What was great about Abraham?" Moshe asked, his back still to the camera.

"He was the first to know there was only one God." A quick answer from one of the children, maybe Robert.

"He was the first? Really? Do you think Adam didn't know there was one God? Noah didn't know? There must have been something else, some other reason why we consider Abraham so great. What did he do that was so wonderful?"

"He smashed the idols." A male adult voice.

"Do you all know that story? How many of you know the story of Abraham and the idols?" About half of those Arthur could see had hands up.

"Tracy, you know the story. Would you tell it?"

A voice off camera, a young girl. "Abraham's father was an idol maker. He had a store where he sold idols."

"What was Abraham's father's name?" Moshe asked.

"Terach." A boy's voice.

"One day," Tracy continued, "Abraham's father—"

"Terach." The same boy.

"Terach, went away on a trip . . ."

"A convention."

"A convention. And he left Abraham in charge of the shop."

"How old was Abraham?" Moshe asked.

"Twelve," Tracy said and paused. When no one rebutted her response, she continued. "Abraham took a hammer and smashed all the idols, except the biggest one. He put the hammer into the hands of the biggest one.

When his father came home, he asked who had done it, who had broken all the idols. Abraham pointed to the big idol with the hammer. His father . . . Terach . . . said idols can't do anything. They're only made out of wood and stone. Abraham said, 'Aha! So why do you worship them?' And that's why Abraham was so great. He broke the idols."

"Beautiful story, Tracy. Thank you. Is that story in the Torah?" No answer. "No, it's midrash, a story about the stories in the Torah. I used to know that story when I was twelve years old myself. I remember once when I was in the navy, I had a Bible with me, and I figured it was a good time to read it. I read all about Abraham, but that story wasn't there, so I figured my Bible was defective. But a lot of stories aren't in the Bible. We create midrash all the time.

"What else did Abraham do that was so great?"

"He was willing to sacrifice his son." An adult.

"But he didn't." A child.

"Yes, he was willing, and he didn't. Which do you think was harder? To be willing to do it, or not to do it?" He held up his hand. "Wait. Before you answer, let's go back four thousand years and see how the story might have happened.

"It's four thousand years ago. We lived in tents, pretty much like this one. The entire family lived in tents, in the Judean desert. Outside the tent we kept sheep and camels. It wasn't an easy life. People had been scattered over the face of the earth.

"First Adam and Eve had been chased out of Eden, and then came the flood in the time of Noah, and the Tower of Babel. With each story we see people getting farther and farther away from God, farther and farther away from each other.

"Abraham begins the process of return. He put up his tent in the desert and began to welcome strangers. He was known far and wide for his hospitality. For twenty generations people had been moving away. He began to bring them back, filled his tent with travelers.

"Whenever he saw strangers approaching, he himself would get up to welcome them. Once, three angels came to see him. He didn't know at first they were angels. He welcomed them as he would anyone else.

"One of the angels told him God was going to destroy the city of Sodom, because the people were wicked there. Abraham argued and argued, doing whatever he could to save the city. In the end, he couldn't save it, but he did the best he could.

95

"Now, remember this. It's four thousand years ago. Things were very different back then. Today we live in houses. Then we lived in tents. Today we have our way of worshiping God. Back then they had their own way, and that way was to sacrifice a child. That's what people did back then. They sacrificed a child. They thought that's what God wanted."

Arthur had reached to stop the tape, to rewind it, to be certain he had heard what he thought he had heard, that Moshe had said the way we worshiped God was to sacrifice children. But before he could find the right button to press on the remote, Moshe himself repeated it. "They sacrificed a child. They thought that's what God wanted."

Moshe paused. No one questioned him. No one challenged him.

"We know that, because Abraham had argued to save the city of Sodom, but when God asked him to sacrifice his own son, Isaac, he didn't argue at all. Why not? Because that's the way things were done four thousand years ago.

"He wouldn't have been the first to do it. The Garfinkels would have done it. The Lopezes, the Schwartzes, the Kantors. Now it was his turn. He would do it too.

"He got up early in the morning, saddled his own donkey, chopped the wood himself, took his son and his servants, and off they went, three days, to Mount Moriah. He told the servants to stay where they were, and he and Isaac went up the mountain, Isaac carrying the wood for his own sacrifice. Do you think Isaac didn't know what was going to happen? He asked where the lamb was for the offering, and his father said, 'God will see to the lamb. For this sacrifice will be my son.' If Isaac didn't know then, surely when his father tied him up he knew. But he didn't run away. Why not? Because that was the way things were done four thousand years ago.

"Abraham put his son on top of the wood on the altar. Then he reached out and lifted up the knife." Moshe lifted up his hand, but there was nothing in it. Arthur preferred the way he did it, with the yad, the Torah pointer. "Suddenly an angel called out of heaven saying, 'Abraham!'

"Abraham says, 'Leave me alone. I'm busy. Don't distract me.'

"The angel says again, even louder, 'Abraham! Don't do anything to the boy!'

"Abraham says, 'But this is what God wants. This is what God told me to do.'

"The angel said, 'That's the way people heard God yesterday, but yesterday was four thousand years ago. Today is only three thousand, nine hundred, and ninety-nine years ago, and in this age people hear God differently. In this age you should know enough not to sacrifice your children, so don't do it.'

"Abraham spoke to the angel and said, 'But all the other families did it. The Garfinkels did it. The Lopezes, the Schwartzes, the Kantors. They all did it. How can I face them and say we don't do this anymore?'

"The angel said, 'Well, that's the real test now, isn't it? Anyone can do what everyone else does. The difficult thing is to start a new path and convince everyone else it's right.'

"So Abraham didn't sacrifice his son. He was willing to do it, but he had the courage not to. He went back home and told everyone times had changed. God had provided him a ram to sacrifice instead. God would much prefer animals to children.

"So what do you think. Did it take more courage for Abraham to be willing to sacrifice his son or to be willing not to?"

"What kind of God would want us to sacrifice animals?" Brenda asked.

"Better than children," George Lopez said.

"From the time of Abraham we sacrificed animals for about two thousand years," Moshe continued, "and after that we figured out animals weren't what God wanted either. So the rabbis found prayers to offer instead of the animals, and we've been offering prayers for the last two thousand years."

"And now the prayers aren't working." An Israeli accent, probably Margolit Zedek.

Moshe nodded his agreement. "Now it seems the prayers aren't working. We've grown from human sacrifice to animals, from animal sacrifice to prayer, and now it may be time to grow from prayer to something else."

"To what?"

"I don't know. That's why I'm teaching this course. I expect you to tell me. The children will tell me. I'm much too old to know, but the children will know."

He paused as if hoping some child might give him the answer. When no one spoke, he went on. "Do we have anything today like the offering of Isaac, the sacrifice of children?" He didn't wait for an answer. "We still sacrifice our children," he said. "We don't kill them, but we sacrifice them. Consider bar mitzvah. All your friends have extravagant bar mitzvah parties. They spend tens of thousands of dollars. So you have to have one too. What do you do? You mortgage your house, you sacrifice your child's education to have a big party to keep up with everyone else.

97

"What if we had an Abraham in the community, a wealthy family, an Abraham to announce we won't do this anymore? What if this Mr. and Mrs. Abraham proclaimed God did not want extravagant bar mitzvahs? What if, even though they could afford it, the Abrahams chose to have a modest celebration and set a new standard? Would any of you have the courage to stand up to the criticism of your family and friends?"

Oh, the caterer would just love to hear this, Arthur thought. The caterer had contributed half the funds for refurbishing the social hall in return for an exclusive contract for the bar and bat mitzvahs, the weddings, all the celebrations that required fine food and drink.

Not just the caterer. Where would the synagogue be without bar mitzvahs? It was the need for a bar or bat mitzvah that brought families into the synagogue. Four years of mandatory Hebrew education, four years for each family to pay off its share of the building fund, four years of fair-share dues. Most of the children were pressured to continue through age sixteen and confirmation. So, from the time the oldest child reached nine until the youngest reached sixteen, Arthur had them, members of his congregation. After that, most families left, but there was always a new crop coming in. Without the institution of bar mitzvah, the synagogue could not stand.

Not that he disagreed with anything Moshe had said. Moshe was correct, but there was nothing to be done about it. There were no Abrahams in the community. The rebels took their families to Israel and celebrated there, spending as much in the process as they would have if they had stayed in Miami. That made it kosher, Arthur thought, and protected them from criticism. No one could accuse them of being cheap.

"I should have been an attorney," he whispered. "It would have been easier."

"A surprise, outside," Brenda said as the tent was coming down. "A petting zoo."

"Consider what it might have been like to sacrifice an animal," Moshe said. "Could you bring yourself to do something like that today? Could you imagine there was a time when we thought that's what God wanted?"

He's taking them backward, Arthur thought. Regression, forcing them to consider animal sacrifice. There was still animal sacrifice in Miami—Santaria, the Cuban cult. Chickens, goats, whatever it was they sacrificed in Hialeah, found dead in the streets. A Miami jury would just love this, talk of animal sacrifice and a petting zoo. And the talk of offering children, that there was a time when God wanted us to sacrifice our children. Prayer didn't work anymore. We had to find something else.

His building was going to come down, he thought, the despair beginning to twist in his stomach. The building wasn't even up yet, and it was going to come down, his rabbinate as well.

"There's a sheep," Cindy Schwartz said. "No camels, but a llama. I don't think they had llamas. But Abraham had sheep."

"And a pig," someone said.

"Is it kosher to have a pig in a Jewish petting zoo?" someone else asked.

The screen went to static. Arthur watched static, forwarded to more static, to more static still. When it seemed unlikely there were any surprises left on the tape, he pressed stop, and ejected it.

He began the audio.

"Okay," Brenda said.

"So where do we go from here?" Moshe asked.

"*Al shlosha divarim*," Margolit said in Hebrew. "The world stands on three things, Torah, worship, and righteous deeds."

"We have the righteous deeds."

"One leg to stand on."

"We're learning Torah. I've learned more Torah in the last few months . . ."

"But what about worship?"

"What does it mean?"

"*Avodah*," Margolit, in Hebrew again.

"Work," someone translated.

"Or worship," Moshe said, "depending on the intention with which it is done. The word for *work* and *worship* is the same in Hebrew. Work done because you think it might be pleasing to God becomes worship."

"So what is pleasing to God?"

"Righteous deeds."

"We're already doing that."

"Ritual. What ritual does God want?"

"Prayer."

"Who prays?"

Silence.

"One percent," Moshe said. "Outside of the sixteenth-century Jewish world, one percent."

"What does that mean, sixteenth century?" "How do you get one percent?"

99

"The Orthodox world is oriented toward the sixteenth century. That's when the *Shulhan Aruch* was written, the code of law that determines Orthodox behavior. But for those who aren't pointed in that direction, one percent. Only twenty percent of Jews in Miami are affiliated with any Jewish organization. Only five percent of them, at most, have any involvement in prayer. Five percent of twenty percent is one percent. That's it."

"A market share of one percent isn't going to make it."

"No."

"So what do we do?"

"Study Torah. That's what a rabbi once told me. When you don't know what to do, study Torah. And go see what the children are doing. If they're not prophets themselves, they're the children of prophets. Study Torah, and they'll figure it out."

"So what do we learn from Torah?"

"Things change. Even in the time of Abraham. Things change."

One percent, Arthur thought, and Moshe was being generous. Arthur listened to the discussion of the Torah text he knew so well. Abraham became a banner for his generation to rally around, a play on the Hebrew word *nisah*. God either put Abraham to a test, or He made him into a banner. That was the commentary. Nothing new. There was never anything new. No new banners to rally around. Nothing new under the sun.

Bar mitzvah had become the engine that powered the synagogue. Children were the fuel, siphoned in through the school, pumped through bar mitzvah, exhausted through confirmation, occasion after occasion to bring in the parents, grandparents, aunts and uncles. "Take your child, your only one, the one you love, namely Isaac." From this we learned how to break bad news, bit by bit. "Sit down please, Mrs. Greenberg. We have bad news for you. Something has happened. Something bad. No it's not Jonah." Bit by bit, the bad news, even though you suspect what's coming. Three days a journey before the walk up the hill. Three days before the funeral of his father, in panic, searching for his brother, for Jonah, until the call came from only God knew where. "You stay there," Jonah said. "I can't come home. They'll find me and kill me too." Only Arthur walked with his father up the hill, Jonah gone, into exile, his mother in shock, in the hospital. "Where is the lamb for the offering?" The bar mitzvah he offered every Saturday. It's what God wanted. It's what the people felt God wanted. The sacrifice was getting old, beginning to stink. There was nothing to do about it but climb the steps from week to week and raise the *yad*, dagger-like in his hand, to slay the offering.

The commentary had come to an end. There had been nothing new, he decided. Even though he had not paid attention to all of it, he was unwilling to rewind it and hear it again.

Arthur checked the time. Not quite 8:30, still too early to trouble Charlotte, but he wanted something to eat, a shower. Sundays she made brunch, scrambled eggs, lox and onions. Rye toast, sometimes a sesame bagel. Too early to call, but he didn't have the energy for another program. He needed food, a shower.

There was a shower, right there in his office. He had never used it. He had a shower, but no towels. Maybe there were towels, but even so, no change of clothes. Were there towels? He had never checked. Did the shower work?

He lifted himself from the chair, made his way to the bathroom. The door to the shower was stuck. He pulled hard, nothing. Hard again. It gave a little. Hard once more and it burst open. A switch turned on both the lights and the fan. The lights were too bright, the fan too noisy.

In the corner, a brown duffle bag, standing upright. "Isaac," Arthur thought. A duffle bag, large enough to contain a child, a small child, perched upright in the corner. Fatigue was speaking, not his reason. It was a duffle bag, not a child, but what? He lifted the bag, felt the weight, the balance, knew what was in it.

But why? Where from?

Arthur made space on the coffee table and withdrew the Torah scroll, a small scroll in a yellow dress. No crown, no breastplate, no yad, just the scroll in a yellow dress, abandoned, in a duffle bag, in his shower. A miscarriage.

Fatigue overwhelmed him. No matter the time, he sat at his desk and called Charlotte. Twice the phone rang, three times, four. "Hello," his voice said, "this is Rabbi Greenberg. I'm sorry I'm not here . . ."

Mercifully, Charlotte answered, silenced the machine. "Hello."

"I need some help."

"You're still at the temple?"

"Can't leave. Would you do me a favor? Bring me a change of clothes, my toilet kit. Some towels. And breakfast. I can't come home, but something for breakfast? Orange juice? Whatever."

"Are you all right?"

"No. No, I'm not. I'm tired, and things are not going well here."

"You can't tell me what it's about?"

"I'm sorry. Not yet. But come have breakfast with me, please. I need you."

After the call he held the receiver to his forehead as if it were an ice pack. He knew where the Torah scroll was from and had a notion of why he found it where it was, only a notion. The scroll itself would tell him, maybe the tape. He didn't need to check the calendar but did so anyway.

When was it they had discovered the swastikas on the walls of the temple?

January 18. A Wednesday. On Tuesday night, January 17, vandals had sprayed red swastikas on the walls of the synagogue. The custodians had discovered it Wednesday morning. The police had come on Wednesday. The press had come on Wednesday.

The scroll would have been removed from the ark before that, and he hadn't even missed it. There had been no evidence of intrusion, no damage inside the synagogue. When the police asked if anything was missing, he hadn't bothered to check the holy ark. Why bother? The vandals hadn't penetrated the building. But the Torah scroll was surely missing, even then.

Arthur carried the scroll to the sanctuary, switched the lights on from the podium. The amphitheater came alive. He pressed the security code to open the lock on the doors of the holy ark. That lock was new, installed the day after the swastikas had been sprayed on the walls, and that was why they couldn't return the scroll, why Moshe couldn't return it. Not Moshe. Brenda. Moshe wouldn't have hidden a Torah scroll in a bathroom. Brenda wouldn't have known any better.

In the holy ark two large scrolls stood upright on the bottom tier. These were the only two he ever used. Above them, three others. There should have been six more, three on each side, out of sight, but on the left there were only two where three should have been, the bottom one missing. He hadn't noticed, all those months.

On the desk he undressed the scroll. It was set at Parshat Yitro, the Ten Commandments in the book of Exodus. Even without checking the order of Torah readings, he knew Yitro would be the reading for the week of January 18.

He dressed the scroll and returned it to its place in the ark. Grand theft, he thought. If nothing else, he could hang Moshe on a charge of grand

102

theft. Ten thousand dollars, maybe twenty, the value of a Torah scroll, and Moshe had stolen it, removed it from its proper place.

Arthur shook his head. His task was not to get Moshe hung but to get him off. Then a perverse thought. Too bad he had not noticed the scroll had been taken, stolen. The police would have blamed it on the vandals, on the anti-Semites. Anti-Semites were a valuable commodity, increasingly scarce. Because of the vandalism, the sanctuary had been full that Friday night, the congregation rallying around the desecration. Had a Torah scroll been stolen, the sanctuary would have been full for a month, everyone decrying its loss. Contributions would have come in abundance, enough for one Torah, two Torahs, many Torahs. Such an opportunity! The stolen Torah scroll would have become an institution, the anniversary of its loss an annual commemoration.

Arthur had a further thought, while standing at the podium before an empty house. Had the Torah scroll been stolen, the zoning would have been approved instantly, no delays. Funding and zoning, in a matter of weeks. No zoning board could have denied him his request. If he had only noticed the Torah scroll was missing. But he hadn't noticed, not in all those months. February, March, April, May. Four months.

Arthur shut down the lights but paused on the pulpit, reluctant to let go of his fantasy. What would he have done with the lost Torah scroll when he eventually found it? When for some reason, that year, the year after, whenever it might be, he opened the shower door and found the duffle bag, inside the duffle bag the little Torah scroll in the yellow dress?

The Torah had more value stolen than found. He could never admit to anyone it had been found. He would have to dispose of the scroll, sacrifice it, quietly, secretly. One dark night, alone, he would carry the Torah in its duffle bag out back and bury it. He would dress in jeans, carry a shovel, find some space between the trees and the fence. No one would ever know.

The Torah had more value to him dead than alive.

"So stupid," he said aloud. Everyone would know, everyone who had been at the bar mitzvah. Brenda would know. Moshe would know.

But would they say anything?

"What am I doing?" Arthur asked himself, shaking his head. "Stay on track!"

As he approached his study, he heard banging on the outside door. Charlotte. She had gotten things together quickly.

103

CHAPTER 7

SUNDAY, 9:00 A.M.

Charlotte had an overnight bag and a picnic basket. Such an *ayshet hayil*, a woman of valor. Arthur held the door for her, kissed her, followed her through the corridor to his study. She was substantial in her jeans. He became conscious of how aware he was of Brenda in her shorts in each of the videotapes. Brenda wore shorts. Charlotte wore jeans, baggy ones, at that.

Charlotte pointed to the overnight bag. "Khakis," she said. "I figured Memorial Day weekend, no one would be coming."

Arthur nodded. No need for dress slacks, a shirt, a tie. "Thank you."

Charlotte spread a cloth on the coffee table, removed plates, forks, knives, napkins, glasses, orange juice, bagels, cream cheese, lox from the picnic basket.

"Thank you," Arthur said again.

She sliced the bagels, looked around. "I haven't seen anything like this since your thesis." She nodded toward the mess on the desk.

Twenty-five years before it had been books, not tapes, on the desk in his apartment, a month before his ordination, a month before Charlotte had finished her MSW, a month before their wedding.

"I remember. I stayed up all weekend, putting it together."

"I remember too," Charlotte said, invitation implicit in her tone.

Twenty-five years ago they had made love in his apartment, Charlotte eagerly, Arthur with reluctance, his roommate asleep, hopefully, in the other room. Stephen Lipsker slept a lot. His nickname was Ef-ess, "Zero," because he slept so much in class and had so little to contribute.

Arthur had been hesitant about sex before marriage, more than hesitant, afraid of it. Charlotte had taken the initiative, especially that early

Sunday morning, the books piled on the desk, Arthur fearful lest the sixth draft of his thesis not be acceptable. She had coaxed him away from his papers, away from the books, to the old sofa, stroked him, tongued him to hardness until he became a participant, all the time fearful lest Stephen come bleary-eyed through the door.

"I remember too," Charlotte said, Arthur knowing just what she was remembering from the tone of her voice. "It's Memorial Day weekend," she added. No interruptions. No one to disturb them. Nothing to be concerned about.

Arthur shook his head. It was not only that he didn't feel like it, it was his study, the very place where he did his counseling, mostly women. Charlotte thought it exciting to have sex in the rabbi's office, had suggested it before. For Arthur, it was a boundary he would not cross. His office was not for sex, not even with his wife.

He'd always wondered about that one time in the apartment. Had Lipsker really been asleep in the next room?

They had stayed in touch throughout the years, commiserating with each other over the problems of the pulpit. Lipsker had a major congregation in Chicago, bigger, more prestigious even than Arthur's. Every year the two couples, Arthur and Charlotte, Stephen and Gloria, shared a suite in the hotel that housed the Rabbinic Union convention. Stephen brought the brandy, Arthur the rum and Coke. While Charlotte and Gloria visited the shops, the men drank together, laughed together, occasionally attended a study session together. Stephen never gave a hint he had been anything other than asleep that Sunday morning in their apartment.

"It's not going well," Arthur said, focusing on his current difficulty.

"You can't tell me what's going on?"

"Not yet. Maybe there's nothing going on. Anyway, nothing I can talk about. But it's a problem, and it doesn't look good."

Arthur drank a glass of orange juice, poured himself another. He heaped a mound of lox on a half bagel smeared thinly with cream cheese. The fat in the cheese was bad for him, the oils in the smoked fish, good. At last he had a reason to be generous with the lox. In Paterson his mother had cut the slices into thin strips to make the precious fish go farther.

"What are all the tapes about?" Charlotte asked.

"Family programs."

"Brenda's programs? It has to do with her again?"

Arthur nodded.

"Who this time? Not Moshe."

"Can't say anything. You should know that." Charlotte had been a social worker. There were some things which, if you knew, you had to report. "I told her I'd make a decision by Monday morning, put her off a few days so I could go through everything first."

"And it's not going well."

"Not well," Arthur confirmed. He didn't want to talk anymore. The next tape on the stack was labeled "MLK T"U B'Shvat, Jan. 16." Arthur checked the calendar. A Monday. Martin Luther King Day. T"U B'Shvat, the new year of the trees, so easy in Miami to celebrate outside in January. A quick check confirmed Parshat Yitro, no surprise, just where the yellow-dressed Torah had been set. He could make a guess concerning what he would find on the tape. He didn't know the details but was certain of the substance. "Stay and watch," he invited his wife.

Static. Waves of sawgrass seen from a car window. More static. An alligator hole, a big one. Arthur recognized it, the beginning of the Anhinga Trail, about five miles into Everglades National Park. Members of the family group, walking the Anhinga Trail. A close-up of a coot, then a heron, then an anhinga on a tree branch with its wings wide, drying.

"That's Michelle Kantor," Charlotte said, referring to the person, not the bird, though Arthur imagined Michelle with her arms spread, anhinga-like, drying in the sun.

He grunted. The tape wasn't what he had expected.

"What am I supposed to be looking for?"

"Nothing special." There were a lot of people on the boardwalk. A Monday morning, Martin Luther King Day, a school holiday, even in Miami.

A park ranger stood on the walk counseling people to keep their distance from a small alligator that had ventured up onto the grass.

"He's faster than you are," he said, "if he wants to be. A good thing he's probably had his breakfast already and has come up to sun, not to eat."

Nervous laughter. Someone spoke in German. A lot of German tourists came through Miami. The vandals surely weren't German. Teenagers, most likely. They didn't even know how to draw swastikas correctly. They drew them backward, a botched desecration.

Arthur stopped the tape. "I'm going to be here all day."

"You remember Linda and Tom invited us out on their boat?" Arthur shook his head. "We're supposed to meet them at eleven. You don't think you could take a few hours off?"

106

"You go," he said. "I wouldn't have a good time, not till I get this straightened out. Leave the basket. There's enough there for lunch, if I need it."

"I can't remember ever seeing you like this. Whatever it is, it must be terrible. I can't believe Moshe is involved."

"I didn't say Moshe was involved."

"I always liked him."

"I didn't say Moshe was involved."

"And Rivkah," Charlotte added. Arthur noted it was difficult for her to say the name.

"You always liked Rivkah," he said. "You knew her. You went to school with her. But what did you know about Moshe?"

"He used to wear short-sleeved brown shirts."

"Khaki," Arthur corrected. "Probably left over from the navy. He had been a navy officer. Did you know that?"

"Does that have something to do with it?"

Arthur shook his head. "I don't know what has to do with anything. Rivkah was the one you liked, not Moshe."

"I don't know what happened to them. They moved away. I never even knew she was ill."

"They moved away. Moshe left the union. Or the union kicked him out. That was a long time ago."

"How come they never came to the conventions?"

"He left the union," Arthur repeated.

"Then what did he do?"

"I don't know. Something outside the rabbinate, I think."

"They were such nice Friday nights we had together."

Charlotte hadn't been listening to him at all. Rivkah's death from ovarian cancer was too unsettling. It was easier for her to consider the Friday nights. They were an institution on the Upper West Side. Eight around the table, a potluck Shabbat dinner, singing songs late into the night.

How many marriages besides theirs came from those evenings? Arthur could think of two in addition to his own. Charlotte would probably know of more. They should form a club, have a meeting at the convention, Marriages Rivkah Arranged, the name of the group. The MRAs. Except Rivkah would not be there. Nor Moshe. Moshe had been expelled from the union. He had done the inexcusable, violated the guidelines of the placement commission. Sex offenders were placed on probation. Guideline violators were expelled. That's the way it was.

Arthur considered what might happen to him, should he allow the boundaries to break down and get himself into Brenda's shorts. A reprimand, some counseling, but not expulsion. The union was compassionate, understanding of such weaknesses. Should he venture beyond the placement rules, no leniency. Harsh judgment, for that violation threatened the very structure of the union itself.

Arthur walked his wife back to her car. She had left it in the driveway by the door, so certain no one else would be coming. "Enjoy the boat," he said. "Don't get seasick."

"Call me later. Let me know how you're doing." Arthur opened the car door for her, but she hesitated before entering. "Why not call Moshe? Speak to him directly." She held up her hand to stop his protest. "I know, I know. You never said it's about Moshe, but if it's about Moshe, why not call him? Talk to him. Hear his side of it, whatever it is."

Arthur watched her drive away and make the turn out of sight. Why hadn't he thought to call Moshe? The call wouldn't come as a surprise. All he had to say was, "Moshe, I need some help. Brenda is angry. Can you tell me anything about it?"

He filled his coffee cup before returning to the wing chair. It wasn't too early. Nine-thirty. Moshe would be up, and even if he wasn't up, he deserved waking.

Arthur dialed the number. Three rings, four, then the answering machine. "Hi. You've reached the home of Moshe Katan. I'm happy for your call and sorry I'm not here to take it. Please leave your number. I'll call back as soon as I can."

Beep. Arthur hung up.

That wasn't adequate. He couldn't leave it there. He pressed redial. The line was busy. He hadn't given the machine time to recycle. He redialed again. The phone rang. He waited the requisite number of rings, listened to the message, the beep, and said, "Moshe, this is Arthur. I need to speak to you. Please. As soon as you can. You can reach me in my study at the temple." He left the number and set the receiver gently into its cradle.

Where was Moshe? Out for breakfast? Out for a walk? Out.

The taped tour of the Anhinga Trail continued. Why did they bother to tape it? Nothing was happening. Sawgrass, birds, and alligators. Hardly any sound at all, and that of no significance.

He left the video running and returned to his desk. The journal was face down on the blotter, still open to the Abraham and Isaac text. Arthur turned the page and discovered a story in Brenda's handwriting.

Abram and Sarai: A Story by Moshe Katan

Sarah's name was originally Sarai, and Abraham's name was originally Abram.

I asked Moshe if there was a story behind that. He said not yet and asked what kind of story I would like.

I asked for a fairy tale, and he said he would have a fairy tale for me that evening, one that had never been told before, if I would come out with him to dinner, and to bring Daniel, too.

We went to the little Italian place on Bird Road, and we sat outside under the awning.

I'm writing this with Moshe's permission. I think it should be published somewhere.

Always with Daniel, Arthur thought. To break down barriers, create an atmosphere of trust, familiarity. Which restaurant on Bird Road? Arthur could think of only one, in the North Grove, not particularly romantic, but the food was good.

Once upon a time there was a young man who came from a family of idol makers. His uncle designed them, another uncle built them, and his father sold them. They were fabricated out of wood and stone. They cost almost nothing to make, but the family sold them at a huge markup because they said they were gods and had great power for healing, for livelihood, for all sorts of other things. In this fashion the family became wealthy, taking advantage of the poor, superstitious people. But the family had no respect in society because of the business they were in. The educated people knew the idols had no power, that it was all a scam to make money.

The young man who was born into this family was named Abram. Abram taught himself to read and write. Abram found teachers. The teachers liked Abram and got him a scholarship to the university.

In his theology class Abram met a beautiful young woman whose name was Sarai. Sarai was from a royal family. Her name meant "my princess." She was as bright as she was beautiful. She and Abram had long discussions and arguments. Sarai knew there was only one God, and that God's name was spelled yod hey vav hey. She taught this to Abram.

When Abram went home and told his father and his uncles what he was learning, they laughed at him. "What do you want to do?" they asked. "Make us shut down our shop? Close our business? What difference does it make if the idols aren't gods as long as people keep buying them?"

The more and more Abram learned, the more and more distressed he became.

Sarai began to invite Abram to her home for dinners. Pretty soon her parents suspected she was falling in love with him. They cautioned her, "You know his family background, don't you? Do you really think this is the right man for you?"

The more time she spent with Abram, the more convinced she became he was the right man. At last she went to her parents and said she was thinking of marrying Abram.

"But you can't do that," they said. "Consider the family he comes from. Just look at his name. Abram! Alef bayt resh mem. What kind of name is that? He is so far away from God, his name doesn't include even one letter of the Divine Name. Better put this young man aside and find someone worthy of you."

Sarai went to her room and cried all night. She prayed to God for guidance and fell asleep. When she woke up, she knew just what to do.

After class that day, she took Abram with her to a name changer. She told the name changer her name was Sarai, spelled sin resh yod. She had in her name a letter of the Divine Name, the letter yod. It had the numerical value of ten, because it was the tenth letter in the Hebrew alphabet. She told the name changer she wanted to exchange her yod for two heys, since the letter hey had the value of five, being the fifth letter of the Hebrew alphabet.

What did Sarai do? She kept one hey for herself and changed her name to Sarah, sin resh hey. She gave one hey to Abram and changed his name to Abraham, alef bayt resh hey mem.

When her parents learned what she had done, they knew her love *for Abraham was great. They approved of the marriage. Sarah and Abraham were married, and they lived happily ever after.*

It's the most beautiful story, and to think Moshe made it up for me. And Daniel liked it too.

Arthur sat numb, the journal like lead in his hands, the inane video of the Anhinga Trail rustling in the background. The story wasn't about Abram and Sarai so much as about himself and Charlotte.

Could Moshe have possibly known the impact the story would have on him? Arthur had never spoken of his family those Friday nights on the Upper West Side. Everything else he discussed across that table, but never his life in Paterson.

After several weeks of earnest and ardent dating, Charlotte had brought her Arthur home, a Park Avenue home, to meet her parents, Aaron and Elizabeth Deutsch. They liked Arthur but made their inquiries and uncovered the story of Barney Greenberg, shot by the mob in Paterson, New Jersey. They cautioned their daughter, only a caution. Charlotte had a head of her own.

"Why didn't you tell me?" she asked Arthur.

"It's not something I'm proud of," Arthur said. "My father was a good man, a smart man. He had a hard life. No opportunities, no breaks, no support. No education. He didn't finish high school, had to make his living early on the streets. He was a good man, in his own way. He knew where he was, why he was there. He did what he did. He didn't want us to follow him."

A half truth, that. True for himself, not so true for Jonah, five years older and made in his father's image. She didn't know about Jonah. The inquiries hadn't gone that far.

It was true, Charlotte told her parents, Arthur came from such a family, but consider how much he had accomplished. He had bootstrapped himself, a teenager alone with a sick mother, through high school. A scholarship to Rutgers, the endorsement of his rabbi, into the seminary, where he excelled, second in his class, second only to Moshe Katan.

Arthur wondered if it was possible Moshe knew. Could he have known Arthur would ever read that story, that Arthur would be sitting at his desk after a sleepless night, watching a relentless video of a walk through the Everglades, reading a story written for Brenda but meant for him?

111

When Charlotte had championed Arthur before her parents, they had little choice but to champion him as well. Arthur attached himself to the family and learned through the footsteps of Aaron how to walk in those circles, at the dining table from Elizabeth how to sit.

Charlotte was proud of her discovery. She had redeemed a diamond from the depths. They were married in Temple Emanuel, the gothic synagogue on Fifth Avenue. She was the fourth of the generations of Deutsches to be married there.

The scene shifted, still in the Everglades, among the trees in one of the hammocks, chairs around a picnic table, the Torah scroll in the yellow dress visible. The tape could be used as evidence, Arthur thought. How had they taken the Torah from the sanctuary? Not difficult when the ark wasn't locked. Any Friday night, or a Saturday morning after services.

Brenda, in white shorts, set a microphone on the table, tapped it, looked up at the camera. "Okay, George?" George Lopez walked in from the left.

The screen went blank, started again, this time with people present. A lot of people—adults, children, some in jeans, some in shorts. Andy Perlman sat in a chair to the left of the table, wearing jeans, and, incongruously, a dress shirt and tie.

Where was Moshe?

George Lopez called the service to order and asked everyone to stand for the morning blessings. The camera wasn't positioned well. All Arthur could see was the backs of those in the last row. A child's voice began chanting rhythmically, "You are blessed . . . Lord our God . . . sovereign of the universe, who has opened my eyes to see, opened my eyes to see. You do the first part," she instructed, "then hear what the blessing is, then repeat it. Let's do it again."

"You are blessed . . . Lord our God . . . sovereign of the universe," everyone chanted.

"Who has opened my eyes to see," the child said.

"Opened my eyes to see," everyone repeated.

"You are blessed . . . Lord our God . . . sovereign of the universe," the next blessing began.

"Who has given me clothes to wear."

"Given me clothes to wear."

"You are blessed . . . Lord our God . . . sovereign of the universe . . ."

"Who lifts me up when I am down."

"Lifts me up when I am down."

"You are blessed . . . Lord our God . . . sovereign of the universe . . ."

"Who protects me while I sleep."

"Protects me while I sleep."

Different voices provided the filling for the blessings that followed. "Who causes the trees to grow." "Who causes the sun to rise." "Who gives me cause to smile."

The rhythm was contagious. The backs on the screen began to sway, people began to clap. Eventually the words stopped altogether, and only the rhythm was chanted. *"Yi lie lie, yi lie lie, yi lie lie, yi lie lie . . ."*

"Let's take a moment, before we sit, to consider our bodies." An adult voice. "We are made mostly of holes and holes and spaces and spaces. If one of them should be shut when it should be open, or open when it should be shut, we could not stand like this. That we stand at all is a miracle.

"And into these holes and spaces you cause our breath to flow. Our soul-breath came from you pure. You created her, formed her, and now you breathe her into us so we can move about and do your will in the world. You are blessed, that You breathe life into us in such miraculous fashion."

Everyone sat down, including the speaker. Arthur had no idea who she was.

No one stood, not even the readers. Leadership of the service moved about the congregation. Some blessings were sung, some read. They must have rehearsed it well. There were no lapses, no awkward moments.

They sang Psalm 148 in English to the tune of "Michael Row Your Boat Ashore." Tedious, Arthur thought, but effective. Everyone knew the melody.

Praise the Lord from the heavens, Halleluyah,
Praise God up in the heights, Halleluyah.
Praise God all of the angels, Halleluyah,
Praise God all of the hosts, Halleluyah.
Praise God sun and the moon, Halleluyah,
Praise God all you stars of light, Halleluyah . . .

George Lopez held up his car keys and encouraged everyone to reach into pockets and follow suit. He jangled his keys. The congregation joined with him, creating a rhythm of gentle percussion, and all sang Psalm 150.

113

Praise God with the sound of horns, Halleluyah,
Praise God with the lyre and harp, Halleluyah.
Praise God with the drum and dance, Halleluyah,
Praise God with the strings and flute, Halleluyah . . .

Margolit Zedek led the blessings before the Sh'ma, then, in Hebrew and English, *Hear O Israel, the Lord is our God, the Lord is one.*

Michelle Kantor led the standing prayer, all facing what Arthur presumed to be east, toward Jerusalem. Again he could see only the backs. The words were mostly muffled and would have been difficult to understand if Arthur had not known them so well.

Andy Perlman came forward and lifted the Torah. Everyone stood and sang as Andy walked around with the scroll. The Torah was undressed, placed on the table. George Lopez took charge of the service. He called up all those who had come in from out of town. Perhaps a dozen people stood and chanted the blessing before the ritual reading of Torah. Margolit Zedek came forward and read in Hebrew. "*Vayishma Yitro . . .*" Correct, Arthur thought. She was reading from the beginning of the portion. The guests chanted the concluding blessing, shook Andy's hand, kissed him, returned to their seats.

"And now," George said, "the parents of the bar mitzvah." Marsha and Morton came forward. Arthur hadn't expected to see Morton at all, but recognized the man who stood by his son as the same pot-bellied figure that had threatened Moshe in the distance in the park. Some serious work must have taken place, quickly, for Morton to be there.

Margolit read a few verses beginning, "*Vi-shem ha-ehad . . .*" The parents chanted the blessings.

"And now, the bar mitzvah himself, Andy Perlman, *Asher ben Mordecai vi-Miriam.* Andy will be reading from Exodus 19, beginning with verse 12."

Morton wrapped a tallit around the shoulders of his son. It was a large prayer-shawl, too big for him. Morton picked up the ends and draped them over his son's shoulders. Andy chanted the opening blessing and read in Hebrew, "*Vi-higbal-tah et ha-am . . .*" He chanted the closing blessing. His parents hugged him, kissed him, and sat down.

Andy read in English, "'Set a boundary for the people all around, and tell them to take care lest they go up on the mountain, or even touch the edge of it. Anyone who touches the mountain will surely die. You won't have to lay a hand on such a person. It will be as if he had been stoned or

114

shot by some agency outside of himself.' The message is that there are some things which, if you do them, become the punishment in themselves. You don't have to do anything to the person. The sin is the punishment. Here, it was like if you crossed the boundary and touched the mountain, you died right away, like it was high voltage and you were electrocuted. The sin becomes the punishment.

"Can you think of other things like that?"

Andy stopped, looked around for help, not certain how to continue.

George stood and said, "Divide into small groups, and see what you can learn. When is it that the sin becomes the punishment?"

Whenever you crossed the boundary to touch what was forbidden, Arthur thought. The answer was in the text itself. Eat foods that were damaging to you, the sin became the punishment. Arthur knew that only too well. Sugar and coffee. Take drugs, the sin became the punishment. Poor Jonah.

The groups did well. Food, drugs, and sex.

Sex again. Always sex.

"What do they have in common?" Andy asked, a rehearsed question. He must have been advised the discussion would come to such a point.

Again, discussion in small groups.

"Appetite," was the answer. "They all have to do with the appetite. Appetite for chocolate, for alcohol, for sex."

"For gambling," someone said.

It was turning into a twelve-step meeting.

"For control," Morty said.

"Workaholic," someone added.

Andy consulted his paper. "Why a mountain? When it says, 'Don't cross the boundary and touch the mountain.' Why a mountain?"

This time, silence. The question was too abstract.

"It's easy to cross the boundary," someone said at last. "You don't know the burden will be mountainous until you have it on your shoulders. Once you cross, it isn't that you are shot. You are crushed."

"Not until someone knows about it," a new voice said. "You can pretend everything is okay until someone knows about it."

"With God's mountain, God knows right away, so it's like you are shot."

"With other things you pretend it's not a burden, but when someone finds out, you are crushed. Then the guilt falls on you like a ton of bricks."

Sometimes, Arthur thought, the bricks fall on everyone in the neighborhood. What would happen when Brenda went public and made the accusation and the matter was found out? No, he wouldn't let it happen like that. He himself would go public. Better that way. Not that it was conclusive yet, but bit by bit a foundation of support was being laid for the charges, and those charges, when ignited, would explode and bring him down, like a ton of bricks, a mountain collapsing on top of him.

"Playing with guns," someone said, still involved in step one of the argument.

"Guns is the same thing as control," Morty said. "Knives and guns. It takes courage to live without them."

Whatever intervention Moshe had made, and Arthur had no doubt it was Moshe, it was remarkable. That the bar mitzvah was taking place, that Morty was there, that Andy had given up his knife, and all in such a short time . . . stunning.

Moshe had done good work.

But where was he?

With something of a shock Arthur realized Moshe had not been at the service, was not at the service.

"So why am I watching the damn thing?" Arthur asked aloud. Still, the tape droned on, but without Moshe's presence, Arthur's attention drifted away.

The rabbi had saved him. Rabbi Perlstein had taken him to the cemetery in the rabbi's own car. They had walked together, up the hill and down. They went to the hospital together after the burial to see his mother. The rabbi was a support, a pillar, a foundation.

They met together twice a week, to study Hebrew, but mostly so they could talk. The talking was important, the Hebrew secondary. Still, he learned the Hebrew well. He mimicked the rabbi's pronunciation, slightly foreign. Not foreign, the rabbi said, just Boston. Decades later people would ask Arthur if he had been raised in Boston.

Arthur's bar mitzvah, like Andy's, had been on a Monday morning, but with the minyan at the synagogue, a proper minyan in the brick-walled chapel. His mother was there, but not his brother. They heard from Jonah rarely, didn't know where he was. "I'm out of town," he would say. That was all, as if he was afraid someone was listening.

Arthur continued to study after his bar mitzvah. He became the rabbi's assistant. He learned the prayers, practiced leading them, first before a mirror, then before the minyan.

116

Good for Moshe, Arthur thought, seeing something of himself in Andy. Then a sudden chasm in his heart, an emptiness where Jonah should have been. Jonah had no Rabbi Perlstein. But then Perlstein couldn't have done it, not for Jonah. Moshe could have. If only there had been a Moshe for Jonah, to bring Jonah back to this side of the boundary. There had been no rabbi to walk with Jonah up and down the hill as there had been for him, as there had been for Andy. No one for Jonah. Jonah had been alone.

"Artie, you little fuck. I put your face in the mud. You remember that?"

"I remember," Arthur said.

Those were the opening lines in all the memories, Jonah laughing and pushing him into the mud. For years it worked well enough to keep concern, guilt, fear, and horror away. Artie had wanted so much to hang out with the big boys, but Jonah had knocked his little brother down and pushed his face into the mud. Disgraced, his face more red with shame than brown with mud, Artie had sulked away.

"I remember," Arthur said. "I remember you."

CHAPTER 8

SUNDAY, 10:05 A.M.

With determination Arthur stood and strode to his desk. He would read the next section of the journal then reward himself with a shower.

They are so quiet sometimes I think they are not here.
Sidney has the old bicycle completely apart. He ponders each piece as if it were a religious artifact.
Stephanie would live in the lake if she could. It's so cold, I don't know how she stands it. She laughs when I tell her that. Daniel goes with her. I'm terrified he'll go into the lake alone. Stephanie assures me he would not, but how does she know? She says the lake is good for Daniel.
Her father doesn't have long.
They are here for the duration.

Moshe, Margolit, and Sidney learn in Hebrew.
That bothers me, but not Stephanie. She doesn't know Hebrew either.
They learn, and we walk. Stephanie, Daniel, and me.

Stephanie says the Tarot cards have their origin in the Kabbalah. She turns them slowly and laughs.
I like her laughter. She's laughing with the cards, not at them.

I told her about the Torah scroll, made her promise not to tell Moshe. He thinks Arthur gave it to me. I showed it to her, in the bedroom.

She doesn't know how to read from it but says Sidney does. I made her promise not to tell Sidney, either. Having it in the house frightens me. I don't know how to get it back. The ark is locked now. I don't know what I will do when Arthur discovers it is missing.

Stephanie wants to take Daniel to see her father. I don't know. I think it would be disturbing for him. Her father sometimes recognizes her, sometimes not. Sometimes he thinks she's his wife. He sees things that aren't there. I would find that disturbing. Stephanie doesn't.

She had Daniel hold his hand. That seemed to settle her father down. Whatever he said, it was in Yiddish. Stephanie understood some of it, but mostly it didn't make sense, even to her. She spoke to him in Yiddish. He called her by some name, not hers, not her mother's.
I can't believe this doesn't disturb her.
Daniel wasn't disturbed.
It disturbs me.

Stephanie says it takes forty years to get born. We don't get born all at once. The body is a vehicle for the soul, but it takes that vehicle a long time to pull the soul down into it. The soul exists before life, and it is pulled into life gradually.
I don't understand that, even now that I've written it down.

I understand it now.
Imagine a train track that goes through a valley, the valley of life. The track comes out of a tunnel on one side of the valley and goes into a tunnel on the other side. The tunnel it comes out of is before life. The tunnel it goes into is afterlife.
It takes ten years for the first car of the train to come out of the tunnel into the valley of life. That ten years is spent learning how to run and jump and use your body.
It takes another ten years for the second car, and that ten years is learning how to make relationships.
Another ten years for the third car, and during those ten years you learn to make your way in the world. You get your degrees, start a family, earn a living.
And then another ten years to wonder what it's all for.

119

Forty years.

Then another forty years with all four cars on the track.

Then the train begins to go into the tunnel of afterlife.

We don't die all at once either.

The first car begins to go into the tunnel on the other side of the valley. We can't run and jump the way we used to.

Then the second car. We don't form new relationships so much as hold on to the old ones.

Then the third car. New developments aren't important to us. Computers, VCRs.

Then only the fourth car remains on the track. The borders of things begin to break down. We see in symbols and archetypes, not the way we used to.

That's where Stephanie's father is. Borders breaking down. Everything confused. Then the last car disappears into the tunnel of afterlife.

One hundred and twenty years. Forty to get born, forty all here, forty to die. That's what Stephanie says.

What's the purpose of the last ten years?

Daniel likes going to see Stephanie's father. She says there is a connection.

Stephanie says the last ten years don't last long. Going from five to six is twenty percent of a lifetime. Going from fifty to fifty-one is two percent. Going from one hundred to one hundred and one is one percent. We live by the percentages, not by the years.

I remember how long it took to go from five to six. It took forever. If my mother was ten minutes late picking me up, that was an eternity. I remember going from ten to eleven, before my mother took me away. That was forever. But the last ten years, so fast. Even now, time is going by so fast.

Sidney rides the bicycle everywhere. He says it is paradise.

Stephanie says that this is paradise, not the afterlife. It's as if God ad-

dresses the soul before life and says, "You deserve a trip to Disney World. Roller coasters and merry-go-rounds. The haunted house. Ecstasy and fear, exhilaration and terror. I give you a ticket for one hundred and twenty years. Go enjoy. Go learn. Go grow. Then come back to me."

I asked Sidney what Stephanie meant. He was cleaning the dishes. He stopped as he was scraping the leftovers into the garbage. He said, "This is paradise. This very moment. It doesn't get any better than this."
I think I understand him. But when I tried it, it was still garbage.

When I asked if we needed a rabbi for the funeral, Stephanie thought that was very funny. Sidney did the service.
We were just Sidney, Stephanie, Margolit, Moshe, me, and Daniel. And the funeral attendant. And the grave diggers. And the planes overhead.
Why do they build cemeteries in airport flight patterns?
Sidney read the Hebrew. Stephanie spoke about her father, his life in Poland, how difficult it must have been to cross Europe and set up a new life in a strange country. He had been damaged by the trip.
She felt lucky to be with him during the last year. It had been a healing for both of them.
There was no healing with my father. I would not approach him and kept him far, far from me. I know he is dead. I don't know where he is buried.

Stephanie shoveled some earth to begin covering the casket. She used the back of the shovel first, then the front. Sidney and Moshe did most of the work. Margolit and I did a little. When we couldn't see the casket anymore and turned to leave, Daniel scooped a handful of earth and dropped it into the grave. I've never seen him do anything like that before.

We returned to Margolit's for the meal after the funeral. She had bagels and lox and eggs. Traditional foods. It's not traditional to hear music after someone died, but Stephanie wanted to hear Orly play the violin. She played some Bach. So beautiful. Sad and beautiful. It

121

*seemed just right to hear that after a funeral. Why wouldn't it be tra-
ditional?*

*I'm going to miss them. Stephanie said she would likely be back in a
few months. She suspected there would be a wedding.*
Whose wedding?

The words about the California people were scattered among a myriad
doodles. It seemed they had been staying with Brenda in January.
Stephanie's father had been ill, had died.

The mystery of the Torah scroll was mostly solved. Brenda had taken it.
Somehow she had returned it to his study, if not to the ark.

Some light had been shed on Brenda's past. What the father had done
to her between the ages of ten and eleven Arthur could only guess. He did
not want to.

Arthur had watched a bar mitzvah without a rabbi. Now a funeral without a rabbi. But they had a rabbi. Brenda didn't know it. The California
people knew. They laughed. But then a rabbi didn't do the funeral, unless
the Chinese man was a rabbi, too.

There were stranger things under the sun, Arthur thought.

Then there was to be a wedding. Would the wedding also be without a
rabbi? Were they going to put him out of business completely?

Whose wedding, Brenda didn't know.

"Wow," Arthur said aloud, his face suddenly flush with the heat of realization. Margolit and Moshe. Please, he thought, let that be it. It made
sense. They both spoke Hebrew. He and Margolit had been learning together, she a single mother, beautiful, with a talented child. Please, let that
be it. Brenda would be crushed when she found out, angry, venomous, ready
to make any accusation.

A first ray of hope surged through him.

A shower. He deserved a reward. He had done some good work.

Charlotte had packed two towels, a bath mat, a washcloth, his toilet kit.
The kit contained soap on a rope, a birthday present from his daughter. He
had never used it. This would be a celebration. What time was it in Los Angeles? Seven-something in the morning. Too early to call Tamar. Later he
would call and thank her again.

How long had it been since he had spoken with her? A week? Two? The calls had become polite. If Cindy answered, no pretensions, no small talk. She didn't like him; he didn't like her. That's the way it was. There were still enough things to talk about with Tamar. Her work, the dog, the weather.

Why did so many kids from Miami move to Los Angeles?

It was all Cindy, her influence, like that of a cult leader. Eventually Tamar would be strong enough, with a head of her own. She would come home. Charlotte had an easier time with it. It wasn't something he could talk through rationally with his wife. Each time she raised the subject, he became emotional, angry, and she had let it go.

Arthur peeled off his shirt, sat to undo his shoes, wiggled his toes and relished the freedom. Why hadn't he done that earlier, gone in socks or bare feet? He laughed. Even with no one to see him, he couldn't do that. He stepped out of his pants. Wrinkled as they were, he hung them up carefully. He carried all the paraphernalia with him to the bathroom. He opened the door to the shower, made sure it was empty. No more duffle bags lurking in the corners. Why had he never taken a shower in his study before?

He stepped back from the shower head, out of harm's way, and turned on the water.

No water.

He turned both hot and cold wide open.

Not a drop.

Such exposure, even with no one to see. He reached for a towel as if he were wet. Wrapped, he stepped out of the shower into a profound sadness.

Even when he brushed his teeth, he didn't look at himself.

His bare feet felt so strange on the rug. He thought he might brush his teeth, then realized with alarm he had done that but seconds before.

"What's happening to me?" he asked aloud.

The towel fell. He stood naked in his study.

"This isn't going well."

He found clean shorts in the overnight bag, socks, khakis, a short-sleeved shirt, tennis shoes. He dressed but, unshowered, didn't feel fresh. He wanted to call Charlotte, but she would be on her way to Linda and Tom's, perhaps out on the boat already.

What time was it in Los Angeles?

He needed a rabbi, someone to walk with him up and down the hill.

He had no rabbi, and he couldn't be a rabbi unto himself.

CHAPTER 9

SUNDAY 10:35 A.M.

Arthur returned to the journal and read again the section about the California people. There was something out of place. The Torah scroll. Brenda had made Stephanie promise to tell no one about the Torah scroll because Moshe did not know she had taken it. But Moshe did know. That's what was wrong.

He and Moshe had had a breakfast together. Arthur could not bear another lunch. Those two experiences had been unsettling. But a breakfast, that he thought he could manage, check in on Moshe's progress in the family program, reign him in if necessary.

It had been a Monday morning in January, at the Bagel Time Deli. While Arthur was saying good morning to the half dozen temple members he recognized, or recognized him, Moshe arrived and clapped him on the back. They found a booth in the rear of the restaurant. Privacy was not possible at the Bagel Time Deli. A rear booth as far as possible from the deli counter was the best Arthur could do.

"Have you ever been to Alabama Jack's?" Moshe began.

Arthur had hoped for a better beginning, something like: How are you? Good to see you. How have you been? It seemed as if Moshe started instead in mid or late conversation, as if all the precursors had been completed. Had Arthur ever been to Alabama Jack's? He could only shake his head that he hadn't.

"It's out on Card Sound Road, just before the bridge, right on the water, in the water. Country music on the weekends. I don't like country music. You don't have to go on a weekend. The gulls hover right at the railing, waiting for a french fry or a piece of bread. Mangroves."

"Mangroves?" Arthur asked. Moshe's one word alone did not seem quite a sentence. Arthur had become aware of a crack underneath him in the red vinyl seat cover. How many years had he been coming to the Bagel Time Deli? Why had they never recovered the seats? He shifted his position, only to discover another crack.

"Mangroves," Moshe repeated. "Those trees with the roots that stick up, the ones that grow just where salt water becomes fresh and fresh water becomes salt. Mangroves."

"I know what mangroves are," Arthur said.

"They are trees that exist between worlds. Alabama Jack's is a restaurant that exists between worlds. Between worlds and between worlds. It's wonderful, a restaurant on land and water, where the mangroves grow, with the birds hovering, and the country music, even if you don't like country music."

The waitress came to take their order. So early in the morning, she was already chewing gum. "Oatmeal with raisins and brown sugar, black coffee, sesame bagel, well toasted," Arthur said.

"I'll have the same," Moshe said, "but an onion bagel, and cream with the coffee."

"Well toasted?" the waitress asked.

Moshe closed his eyes. "Well toasted." He turned to Arthur as the waitress walked away. "You're under a lot of pressure, Artie. What's going on?"

"What do you mean? Why do you think I'm under a lot of pressure?"

"I felt the order, what it was like to order the bagel well toasted."

"Well toasted doesn't mean I'm under a lot of pressure."

"No, it doesn't. You're right. I'm wrong. It's just the way it felt, and I get confused sometimes."

A busboy brought cups of coffee. Arthur reached for his eagerly, raised it too quickly to his lips. Moshe blew over the surface of his coffee to cool it. The two men sipped in silence. Arthur made a mental note to bring bagels home, a bakers' dozen. Sesame for him, pumpernickel for Charlotte.

"What's happening in the family program?" Arthur asked, getting down to business.

"Re-creation."

"Recreation?" Arthur asked, not sure he had heard right.

"No. Re-creation. We are repeating the process of creation, re-creating. The families are beginning to feel the distance, beginning to feel the pain of separation. We're about to begin the process of return. There's no creation without exile. Do you know any good Isaac stories? I don't. He re-dug the wells his father dug, reswore the oaths his father swore, repeated his father's stories. Not very interesting. But it's always Abraham, Isaac, and Ja-cob, the three of them together. Rebecca was interesting. Not Isaac."

Arthur searched his memory for an Isaac story but found none.

"He was a good son," Moshe said. "Is that enough of a story, to be a good son?"

Arthur sipped more coffee. He had been a good son. Why did Moshe bother him so?

"I keep asking for an Isaac story, and nothing comes. How do you write your sermons?"

From the newspaper, Arthur thought, but he did not say. From the movies, the books, whatever he had been seeing, reading. Those became his sermons. He had learned over the years how to do it. He lived the week as research for sermon material, anxious already by Tuesday if nothing came forward to present to the congregation. By Thursday he had written the ser-mon, Friday morning reduced it to an outline. He preached from the out-line, not from a text, creating an illusion of spontaneity. It worked. Those who came liked it.

"Posthumously," Moshe said.

"What?" Arthur asked.

"A joke. A rabbi gave a sermon, an adequate sermon, but one of which he was not proud. In the receiving line after the service . . . Do you have a receiving line? In the receiving line after the service an elderly woman thanked him profusely for his wonderful sermon and asked when it might be published. 'Posthumously,' the rabbi said. 'Well,' said the woman, 'I hope it's soon.'"

Arthur had heard the joke before. Yes, he did have a receiving line. If Moshe had ever come to a Friday evening service, he would have known that. "The line is useful. Those who have personal difficulties use it as a way to make contact. I encourage them to be in touch during the week." He felt a need to justify himself. Why should he have to justify himself to Moshe?

"It's not such a bad thing to live posthumously," Moshe said, just as bowls of steaming oatmeal were placed in front of them, and a saucer full of raisins, another with brown sugar.

Arthur considered to ask what it meant to live posthumously, chose not to go there. "What do you mean when you say you keep asking for a story?"

"Just that. Stories don't come out of nowhere. I put myself in the place

126

where stories happen, express my need, and wait. Sometimes stories come. Sometimes not. But when they do come, no one is more surprised by it than me. It's like I tell it and hear it at the same time. Sometimes I'm astonished. I understand it fully. Sometimes I'm puzzled. I don't understand it all. But I tell it anyway. I've already told it. All I can do after is consider it and wonder why it came. It always comes for a purpose."

Arthur stirred raisins into his oatmeal. They disappeared under the surface. He added more. The new ones disappeared and the old ones came up. "You've always been able to do this, ask for stories?"

"Not always," Moshe said. He had been watching Arthur's oatmeal, not paying any attention to his own. "In recent years, more now since Rivkah died, I find stories everywhere. Sometimes I have to be careful not to trip over them. Sometimes I have to be quiet or they start bubbling out of me."

"You could go off and tell the stories to yourself," Arthur suggested.

"No. A story isn't a story unless someone hears it. The person doesn't have to understand it, but he has to hear it. Otherwise I haven't told a story."

"Like a tree falling in a forest with no one to hear. Does it make a sound?" Arthur was doing his best to participate.

"Depends on the definition of sound and the definition of a story." Moshe paused and cocked his ear, as if listening for the sound. "I didn't say it right. Let me try again. I could tell the story with no one to hear, but the story would have no effect on me. For it to have an effect, it has to bounce off someone else and come back to me. Then it becomes real. A sound becomes a sound when it bounces off an eardrum. Otherwise it's just waves in the air." Moshe waved his hand in the air. "Like that."

The man was unbalanced, Arthur thought. Confused, still in mourning. How long had he been in a coma? How long did it take to recover from such a trauma?

"You just ate a story," Moshe said. "Your oatmeal. There was a wonderful story in it, and you didn't even see it."

Arthur pondered the spoonful of oatmeal halfway to his mouth and returned it to the bowl. "What are you teaching the family education program?" he asked, thinking he had already asked that question, but not quite sure.

"Torah stories," he said sadly. "I'm sorry. I have no choice. They need those before we can go on to Talmud. You know, by age fifteen, Torah is finished in the traditional community. Torah, Prophets, Writings, all finished.

127

After that it's Talmud. The only reason we read Torah on Shabbat is so we don't forget it. But these families, they have to know first what not to forget. Then we can begin to teach Talmud. Next year."

"You're going to continue the program next year?" Arthur asked, not certain he had concealed his concern.

"Not me," Moshe said. "It's like the raisins. You put raisins into the oatmeal, stir it, they go down. Then you add new ones on top of the old. You stir those, the old ones come up. You eat the old ones, add new ones, stir it, they go down. You eat the second ones. You understand?" Moshe looked up from the oatmeal. "What is the purpose of the Old Testament in the Talmud?"

"We're careful not to call it the Old Testament," Arthur said.

"Torah, Prophets, and Writings, then," Moshe said. "But I assure you, whatever we call it, it's the Old Testament. The New Testament for Jews is the Talmud, and the purpose of our Old Testament is to provide proof texts for the new one. If we're going to create a new Judaism, it isn't going to come out of the Torah, Artie. It will come out of the Talmud. The Talmud will be the proof texts for the new Judaism, the Judaism that will come after us, after the rabbis."

"After the rabbis?"

"We came after the priests. You don't think there will be something that will come after us? The priests had their Torah and animal sacrifice. We have our Talmud and prayer. Something will come next. But it won't come out of the Torah. It will come out of the Talmud."

That was as much as Arthur remembered about the breakfast with Moshe. It was the last time they had been together. They talked about oatmeal and raisins, Torah and Talmud, priests and rabbis. The priests were extinct, and in Moshe's mind, the rabbis were following close behind.

Moshe had any number of opportunities to thank him for giving Brenda the Torah scroll, but he had not done so. Moshe knew Brenda had taken the scroll from the ark without permission.

Arthur reached for the phone and pressed redial. He wasn't surprised to hear the message. "Hi. You've reached the home of Moshe Katan. I'm happy for your call and sorry I'm not here to take it. Please leave your number. I'll call back as soon as I can."

Nearly eleven o'clock on Sunday morning. Where was the man? "Moshe," Arthur said, "I really need to speak with you. Please. It's important. Call me in my office." Again he left the number.

His annoyance had value. It kept him on task. He turned his attention to the journal.

> *Daniel has become a chaperone. I think Moshe uses him to maintain a distance between him and me.*
> *I think he was hurt by Rivkah. Then by her death. I don't think he was happy in his marriage. He's afraid he can't be happy with me.*
> *But he comes by often, drops in. As if he's trying to be close.*
> *All I can do is keep the door open.*

> *Jacob & Esau: January 29 at the Holsteins'*
> *Piggy banks, zedakah boxes, penny collections*
> *Buckets*

Arthur didn't know who the Holsteins were, or what piggy banks had to do with Jacob and Esau. He could find out about the Holsteins. All he had to do was punch a few keys and they would come up on the screen.

Cows. They would be cows. Were Holsteins cows, or was it something else that was cows?

A shower would have served well to awaken him. Without the shower he wanted to sleep. He deserved sleep. He had earned his sleep, he couldn't remember how.

Margolit Zedek. That woke him. Moshe and Margolit. Brenda, when she found out.

In the journal, doodles of buckets overflowing with coins. Was there a hole in the bucket?

Instead of sitting, Arthur stood behind the wing chair.

Whoever the Holsteins were, they had a lovely back yard, a flagstone patio, unusual in Miami. The weather must have been chilly. Some of the adults wore sweaters. Not Brenda. She was still very much in shorts and a T-shirt, sitting beside Moshe more sensible in jeans and turtleneck.

"So Jacob had to leave town," Moshe began. "His mother . . . What was his mother's name?"

"Rebecca," came the answer from several sources.

The tape had started in the middle of the story. Arthur pressed stop, rewind, and started again. Static, and then Moshe saying, "So Jacob had to leave town. His mother . . . What was his mother's name?"

The recording was late. The tape was on time.

Had Moshe already told the story of Jacob and Esau or did he assume everyone knew it? There were two stories to tell. Esau coming in hungry from the field and Jacob poaching the birthright with a bowl of lentil stew. Then the deception, Jacob pretending to be Esau, at his mother's urging, to appropriate his father's blessing. It was a common theme in the Torah, the younger brother supplanting the older.

"Rebecca."

"That's right. Rebecca. Rebecca told Jacob he had better leave. Esau was angry. Why was Esau angry?"

"Because Jacob had tricked him."

"So Jacob's the bad guy."

"Jacob's the good guy," a young voice said, most likely Robert.

"If he's a good guy, why does he have to leave town?"

"Because the bad guy is going to get him."

"And the bad guy is . . . ?"

"Esau."

"What makes Esau a bad guy?"

"He cheated Jacob out of his birthright." Another young voice.

"No, it was the other way around." Arthur could see the speaker, Orly Zedek, Moshe's stepdaughter-to-be. "Jacob cheated Esau. Esau came in from the field hungry, and Jacob wouldn't give him anything to eat until Esau gave up the birthright."

"Again, what made Esau the bad guy?"

"Something about the blessing and his father," the suggestion coming from off camera.

Moshe shrugged, looked toward Orly.

"It was Jacob again," she said. "He tricked his father into thinking he was Esau and stole Esau's blessing."

"So who's the bad guy?"

"Jacob deserved the blessing." Arthur recognized George Lopez's voice.

"Why was that?"

"Because the Jewish people were to descend from Jacob."

"Why not Esau? He was also the son of Isaac and Rebecca, the grandson of Abraham and Sarah."

"There must have been something wrong with Esau." Robert's voice.

"Like what?"

"Some moral problem." An adult speaker.

"Like what?"

"Something the Torah doesn't tell us," Orly said.

"Why not?"

"Because it's ashamed to." Andy Perlman, off camera.

"So what might be so shameful?"

Arthur knew what was coming. It didn't apply to him. It was backwards. The story had nothing to do with Artie and Jonah, because Jonah was Esau and Artie stayed home.

"Drugs. Esau did drugs." Correct, Arthur thought. Jonah did drugs. Not Artie, not Jacob.

"Maybe it was drugs," Moshe conceded. "Something shameful."

"A temper." Morty Perlman.

"A temper. Maybe Esau had a short fuse. When he found out his brother had cheated him, he wanted to kill him, so Rebecca told Jacob to leave home. That's where we begin, Jacob leaving home. "

Jonah left home, Arthur thought. Jonah was the Esau and Jonah left home. Artie had been the Jacob, and Artie stayed behind in Paterson. The story was giving him a headache. It was right and not right. Jonah was the man of the streets, and Artie was the kid who stayed home. Jonah was his father's child, Artie his mother's. The story was backward, mercifully backward. It didn't apply, but the hint of a headache remained.

Someone Arthur did not know, perhaps Mr. Holstein, distributed a text, presumably the same text Brenda had pasted into her journal.

Genesis 28

PART ONE

10. Jacob left Beer Sheva heading toward Haran.

11. (*Vayifga*) He encoutered a place (*makom*) and camped there because the sun was setting. He took one of the stones (*eh-ven*) of the place (*makom*). He put it under his head. He lay down in that place (*makom*).

12. He dreamed. There was a ladder standing in the ground, its top reaching heavenward. There were angels of God ascending and descending on it.

13. There was *YOD HEY VAV HEY* standing on it saying . . .

PART TWO

16. Jacob woke up from his sleep. He said, Surely *YHVH* was in this place and as for me, I did not know.

17. He was frightened. He said, How awesome is this place (*makom*). This is nothing other than the house of God, and this is the gate of heaven.

18. Jacob got up early in the morning. He took the stone which had been under his head and made a marker out of it. He poured oil on top of it.

19. He called the name of that place (*makom*) Bayt El. However the name of the town originally had been Luz.

Moshe said, "Let's imagine how Jacob feels as he's leaving home. Esau is angry with him. His father can't be too pleased. His mother is afraid for him. Jacob has probably never been away from home before.

"How many of you have been to summer camp?"

Many of the children raised their hands, many of the adults as well.

"Do you remember how you felt when you went away for the first time? What that first night was like? How old were you?"

A jumble of responses.

"How old was Jacob?"

The consensus was about eighteen.

"Time to study. Break into groups, no more than four. You know how to do it. Parents and children not in the same group. Begin with that first night you were away from home, your first night at summer camp or at college. Whenever it might have been. Then, the text. We're going to learn about Jacob's first night."

Arthur had no one to learn with. He envied the groups on the screen, each immediately energized. The children gravitated quickly to favorite adults. They must have done so many times before.

"Jacob left Beer Sheva heading toward Haran." Heading North, Arthur thought, back toward Syria.

Arthur had never been to summer camp. His first night truly away from home had been in the dormitory at Rutgers, across from Bishop Hall. He had been so eager to go it was weeks before he realized he was terrified.

"He encountered a place." *Makom* was the Hebrew word. Arthur could see where Moshe was going. *Makom* was a Hebrew euphemism for the name of God. Jacob was to have an encounter with God. Arthur had an encounter with a dean in Bishop's Hall.

"He took one of the stones of the place." To build a foundation, Arthur thought, for an institution. That stone, he remembered vaguely, became a cornerstone for something, perhaps for the Temple in Jerusalem. The dean had comforted him, reassured him. The institution would take care of him. All freshmen had such fears. Counselors were available to help.

". . . A ladder standing in the ground, its top reaching heavenward." A symbol, better even than the radiant sun of Rutgers College. Arthur turned from the television to the diploma framed and hung on the wall behind him, *Magna cum laude* under a radiant sun. But the ladder was better, a symbol first for a fund-raising campaign, then for the new institution. He would use it, a ladder reaching heavenward. "Contribute so much, become an angel." The ranks of angels, one above the next, donor categories escalating rung by rung all the way to heaven.

Magna cum laude. Then second in his class at the seminary. With Moshe on the screen, he felt like chopped liver.

"Together," Moshe said. Arthur heard him, but no one else did. "Let's come together." He began to sing a niggun. The buzz of conversations ceased.

"'Jacob left Beer Sheva heading toward Haran.'" Moshe quoted. "Why Haran?"

"That's where you go when you run away from home," an adult voice said. "He had an uncle in Haran. I used to run away from home when I was a kid. I had an uncle who lived about a mile away. That's where I would always run. My father called ahead to tell them to expect me."

"'He encountered.' *Vayifga*. A strange word. Do you recognize it, Orly?" Orly shook her head. "Maybe it means he had an appointment. A strange word for a strange encounter. How could he have an appointment, if he was running away from home?"

"An appointment with himself," Margolit suggested. "He was growing up. He was going to have to face himself, who he really was, and meet who he was to become."

"Beautiful," Moshe said, almost in a whisper.

Yes, thought Arthur. Beautiful.

"'He took one of the stones,'" Moshe continued. "*Eh-ven* in Hebrew. The last two letters, *vet* and *nun*, they might have the meaning 'to build' or 'to understand.'"

"*Ben* means son," Orly said.

"A son is a form of building also," Moshe said. "But if it represents an understanding, he takes a stone that leads to an understanding and places it under his head. Then he dreams. What's unusual about this dream?"

133

"He sees a ladder." A child's voice.

"And what's on the ladder?"

"Angels."

"And what are the angels doing?"

"Going up and down."

"And what's unusual about that?" When no one answered, Moshe asked, "Were they going up and down or down and up?"

"Up and down."

"If they were going up and down, were the angels with him before he went to sleep, or did they come only after he went to sleep?"

"Before."

"So angels aren't just something you see when you are asleep. They are with you even when you are awake."

"But maybe you can see them only when you are asleep."

"Maybe," Moshe said. "What do you think?" He looked directly at Arthur.

I don't believe in angels, Arthur almost said, taken by surprise again but recovering quickly. Moshe was looking into the camera, not at him, looking at Daniel who, it seemed, liked to stand behind the camera. But the camera never moved. Daniel stood behind it but did not touch it. Did he look through it?

"A tradition says we have four angels about us at all times, Mi-cha-el to the right, Gabriel to the left, Uriel in front, and Rafael behind."

"I know Rafael," a young voice said.

"Not the turtle," said another. "He's talking about angels."

"Mi-cha-el is the angel of compassion, Gabriel the angel of strength. Uriel, the angel of light that goes in front of us, and Rafael, the angel of healing. He comes up behind to help when we fall down."

"Can you see them?"

"Jacob probably couldn't, not until he went to sleep. Later in his life he might have been able to see them when he was awake, but here he was just starting out. He went to sleep and saw the angels going up, then coming down."

"What were the names of the angels who came down?"

Moshe laughed. "What a wonderful question! No one has ever asked me that before. The names of the angels who came down were Mi-cha-el, Gabriel, Uriel, and Rafael."

"But those were the same ones who went up."

134

Moshe laughed again. "There isn't just one Mi-cha-el. There are a great many who go by that name. Hundreds. Thousands. Enough for each of us, more than enough." He looked toward Margolit. "One set for each of us when we're children, another set when we're teenagers, another when we become adults. Maybe Jacob had an appointment to meet his new set of angels.

"Then Jacob woke up from his sleep and said, 'Surely God was in this place, and as for me, I did not know.' How come he didn't know?"

"He was still a teenager," George Lopez said. "Teenagers don't know much." The adults laughed.

"There's some wonderful teaching about this line," Moshe continued, paying no attention to the laughter. 'And as for me, I did not know.' Hear it a bit differently. Because of the 'me,' I did not know. Because the 'me' got in the way of my knowing.

"Jacob thought he was such hot stuff, the younger brother getting the birthright, the primary blessing. When he went to sleep he had no idea where he was, no idea angels were all around him, because his ego got in the way."

"You're right," he said to George. "Teenagers don't know much. They're too busy learning who they are. That's important to them, their development. They can't be expected to know much. That's why we forgive them their behavior. When adults act like teenagers, we have them committed to an institution. But when teenagers act like teenagers, that's to be expected.

"Jacob had an appointment with a new set of angels. As a teenager he was never able to see his angels. He was too wrapped up in himself. But the dream woke him up. He became an adult. He said, 'God was in this place, and because I was so busy with me, I did not know.'

"Then he became frightened. Why frightened?"

"He saw how little he was," Orly said. "How awesome the place was, how little he was."

"Then Jacob got up. He wanted to remember what had happened, so he got some oil and put it on a stone. Does that make sense?"

"He wanted to be able to find the stone again," Robert said.

"There might be better ways to mark a stone. Maybe he could have written on it, 'Jacob was here.' Did any of you ever leave your name in a cabin at camp?" Hands went up. "Did you carve your name into the wood? Draw on the walls with a marker? How about pouring oil on a stone?

"Oil was used back then to mark a transition. Kings were anointed with

135

oil. Oil was poured onto their hair to make it shine. Maybe the stone that was anointed was the understanding Jacob had gained. Maybe it was his own hair he anointed, marking the transition from being a teenager to being an adult."

"But I thought that stone became part of the altar in the Temple." The voice was Leonard Shuk's, but Arthur couldn't see him.

"Maybe it could be both at the same time," Moshe said. "There are layers and layers and layers of understanding. It starts with a stone and ends up with a realization.

"Jacob names the place Bayt El. What does Bayt El mean?"

"House of God," Orly said.

"House of God," Moshe repeated. "Is there any place which is not a house of God?" When no one answered, he said, "Every place can be a house of God if you only open your eyes to see it.

"Time to do some work," he announced, his tone of voice sharper, bringing even Arthur to attention. "Those of you who have made it through your teenage years into adulthood, can you remember when that was? One particular event, perhaps? Think it over, and if you like, share it with your group."

The groups began to buzz. Moshe sat and stared at the camera, straight through the camera, into Arthur. Arthur did not turn away. "One particular event," Moshe repeated.

Arthur's sophomore year, his mother in the hospital in Hackensack, her leg amputated below the knee, and Jonah was there. How had Jonah heard? He hadn't been there for the toes, for the foot. But when it was time for the leg, he materialized.

"Hey, Artie," he said.

"Hey, Jonah."

"I gotta go. Can't stay. You take care of her now, you hear? I can't come back for the funeral."

In that moment Arthur knew his mother was going to die. In that moment he ceased being a teenager.

"Going home is harder than running away," Moshe said. "Jacob had been gone a long time. He had married, twice, had lots of kids, lots of sheep, lots of goats. The time had come for him to go home, but Esau was at home. He didn't know if Esau was still angry with him or not. What did he do? He sent messengers to find out. The messengers came back, and this is what they said: 'We went to your brother, Esau, just like you told us.'

"'Good,' Jacob said.

"'And he's coming to meet you.'

"'Good,' Jacob said.

"'And he's bringing four hundred armed men with him.'

"'Not so good,' Jacob said.

"Jacob had to figure out what to do about Esau. The first thing he did was divide everything he had into two separate camps, so if Esau destroyed one of them, the other would be left. Then he worked out a plan, a clever plan. We're going to act it out so we can see what happened."

The screen went to static.

Arthur lowered the volume, checked the materials on his desk and found an audiotape labeled "Jacob and Esau."

". . . part three," Moshe began, the audio starting in mid-sentence. "What would you like to hear God promising you in such a situation? You have just left home. You are afraid. You don't know what's going to happen. You have a dream or a vision and hear something you think is God speaking to you, and the voice says something reassuring. What would you like to hear? Read what God has to say to Jacob, and while you are reading consider what would you like God to say to you."

In the journal Arthur found a "Part Three" to the text, three verses taken out of sequence from Jacob's encounter with the ladder of angels.

PART THREE

13. . . . I am *YHVH,* the God of Abraham your father and the God of Isaac. The land which you are lying on I will give to you and your descendants.

14. Your descendants will be like the dust of the earth and will spread out to the west, to the east, to the north and to the south. All the families of the earth will be blessed through you and your descendants.

15. Now I will be with you and guard you wherever you might go. I will bring you back to this land because I will not abandon you until I have done what I have said to you.

Arthur reviewed the text even as he heard the groups of adults and children doing the same.

Moshe was good. A powerful exercise. Writing what you would like to hear from God wasn't the same as hearing it from God, but it was close. The writing forced one to focus on one's wants, one's needs. Focus alone might satisfy them, even without God's intervention.

Static continued on the television screen, mumbling on the audiotape. Arthur had little choice but to consider what he would like to hear from God, should God be so considerate as to address him.

"It will be all right, Arthur. It will be all right. As it was with Abraham, Isaac, and Jacob, so it will be with you. There is a way out, and I will show it to you." Nice words, if he could only bring himself to believe them. What belief he had did not allow him to put words into God's mouth, comforting as such a thought was. If there was a way out, he would have to find it for himself.

The television came to life. ". . . into groups, one after the other. The leader of each was to approach Esau and say, 'This is a gift from my master Jacob to his older brother Esau, and Jacob himself is coming right behind us.'"

Moshe motioned a young boy to stand in front of the camera. The two of them looked at Arthur. "This is Esau," Moshe said. "He's been angry for years, angry at Jacob, thinking of what he's going to do to him when he gets his hands on him. Messengers have told him Jacob is coming, and Esau can't wait." Moshe gave the boy a bucket. "Stand over there, and remember, you're angry."

The boy walked to the end of the yard.

"First messenger," Moshe said.

A girl came forward with a bucket too big for her.

"This is the first messenger," Moshe announced, "but Esau doesn't know that. He thinks it's Jacob. He just can't wait to get his hands on Jacob, but when the messenger approaches, it isn't Jacob at all. It's a messenger with a gift from Jacob." Moshe pointed the girl in the right direction. "What are you going to say when Esau comes up to you?"

"This is from your brother Jacob," she said, "and he's coming right behind me."

"Good. Okay, go ahead. Don't be afraid. Esau won't do anything to you. He's angry at Jacob, not the messenger."

The girl started slowly toward the figure in the back of the yard.

"Esau sees the messenger," Moshe said, his tone that of a play-by-play sports announcer. "Esau is angry. He thinks it's Jacob. But wait! It's not Jacob! It's a messenger. And what does the messenger have? A gift! A gift from Jacob to Esau!"

The girl poured something from her bucket into Esau's. Coins, Arthur realized, from the piggy banks. Pennies for Esau.

"Next messenger," Moshe said.

Again, the same action, the same commentary.

"This is from Jacob, a gift for you," the messenger said.

"What else are you supposed to say?" Moshe asked.

"And your brother Jacob is coming right behind me." The child looked back to be certain he had spoken correctly.

"Give him your pennies," Moshe said. "Each time Esau received a gift, some of his anger was taken away. As the gifts got heavier and heavier, the anger became less and less."

The boy poured his coins into Esau's bucket.

Another child with a gift, and another, and another. Esau's bucket became so heavy he could barely carry it with both hands.

"Okay, time for Jacob," Moshe said.

Another child came before the camera. "This is Jacob," Moshe announced. "He doesn't know if Esau is still angry. He's done everything he could think of. He's sent Esau gift after gift after gift. Each time Esau rushed forward, thinking the next messenger was Jacob, ready to kill him, but each time he came forward with less and less anger. Now Jacob will see if his plan has worked, if Esau is ready to forgive him, or whether Esau is still angry and will kill him.

"Are you ready?" he asked Jacob.

The child nodded.

Esau was no longer in the back of the yard. He had stepped forward to each of the messengers. When Jacob turned, Esau was only a few steps away.

"I am your brother," Jacob said.

Esau put his bucket on the grass, stepped forward, extended his hands toward his brother's neck, pulled him close and gave him a big hug.

So stupid, Arthur thought, not because of what he was seeing but because he was crying. The program wasn't that good. He was just tired, worn thin, labile.

Exercise, Arthur thought, shaking his head to clear the tears, reluctant to wipe them away with his hands, too much an admission they were really there. He would exercise.

Arthur stood and stretched toward the slanting ceiling, bent at the waist and pushed his fingers toward his toes. There was a time he could touch them. He extended his arms like wings and made small circles, then big circles, then giant arm swings, clockwise, then counterclockwise. Swimming motions. There was a time he could do twenty laps, freestyle, and twenty more, backstroke.

He had never been an athlete, but he had tried. When he was twelve he had pumped iron to build muscle, an attempt to be bigger than Esau. Bigger than Jonah. At thirteen, his father dead and Jonah gone, he pumped no more iron. He had his bike to ride, to run away, then the tennis courts behind Bishop Hall. Tennis had served him well. When the new building campaign was secure, he would take up golf. For his birthday Charlotte had given him a putter and a contraption to putt on the carpet, a hole that spit the ball back to him.

He swung his arms until his breath came quick. "I will be with you," he said aloud, his eyes closed. "As I was with Abraham. As I was with Isaac. As I was with Jacob, so I will be with you. And I will show you a way out of this place. There is a way out, and you will find it."

The words helped, even if he didn't believe them.

CHAPTER 10

SUNDAY, 11:15 A.M.

SOUTH BEACH. OCEAN DRIVE.

Moshe sits and watches the hotels, the old ones, art deco. Daniel watches the waves.

Moshe says the hotels are waves also. They just move more slowly.

The ocean is considered mayim hayim, living water. Every ocean is living water. Every river that goes down to the ocean. Every spring that bubbles up from the earth. Every lake that has water flowing into it, through it. All mayim hayim, living water.

The hotels have life flowing through them also. They were living, then they weren't, and now they live again.

Not all of them. Some are restored and beautiful. Some wait to be restored.

In time, Moshe says, they will all be restored, decay, and be restored again. Like waves in the ocean.

They sit on the same bench, Daniel looking at the waves, Moshe at the hotels. I wish I had a camera. This is beyond my ability to draw. It is so beautiful, it makes my heart ache.

They have the same expression.

RED ROAD. AIRPLANES AND CEMETERIES.

Why would Daniel like cemeteries?

It was Stephanie's idea to park by the runway at the top of Red Road and watch the planes take off and land. He likes that. Twice I've brought him back, and each time we go to the cemetery, just down the street, to visit Stephanie's father.

Daniel sits under the oak tree and looks at the gravestones like they were airplanes.

Hotels and waves. Gravestones and airplanes.

Such a strange way of seeing things.

That was Stephanie's idea too, to bring him to the cemetery. She said he would like that. How did she know?

She said he had a bond with her father.

Her father was lost between worlds, and so is Daniel. Is that the bond?

Her father is no longer in this world. Does the bond continue?

We visit Nathan's grave, too, but Daniel doesn't know it. His bond is more with Stephanie's father than his own.

Where Nathan was is only a numbness for me now.

I'm forgetting what he looked like.

And my father. The pain is I remember what he looked like.

In the journal, the portrait of a woman Arthur did not know. Stephanie? Sketches of a man and a boy on a bench, one facing this way, the other that. No hotels. No waves. No gravestones. No airplanes.

February 12. Joseph.
At the Clarks. Jim and Stacy.
• Kimono
• striped bathrobe
• remind Barry to bring tuxedo jacket
• ask George if he still has his army uniform

The home was modest. Arthur did not know the Clarks. He paused the tape to check the database. They lived in Kendall Lakes, way out, twenty minutes in traffic. Two boys, Chris and Sean. Such names for Jewish children. The parents were Jim and Stacy. A mixed marriage? The computer didn't tell him. Chris was eleven, bar mitzvah set a year from October. The family paid below fair share, were behind in their building pledge. All that would be taken care of prior to the bar mitzvah. Temple policy.

Moshe and Daniel sitting on the bench on Ocean Drive, Daniel facing one way, Moshe the other. Arthur couldn't get the picture out of his mind. He went back to the journal to look at it again. Brenda was right. It was difficult to draw. The proportions were wrong, or the perspective. The figures were not recognizable. The drawing was depressing.

What time was it in Los Angeles? Still too early. Tamar would be asleep. Charlotte was somewhere on Biscayne Bay. She should have a cell phone. Did cell phones work on the bay? No matter, he wouldn't call her. She would want to know how things were going, then Linda and Tom would want to know what was happening. Nothing was happening. Nothing at all.

He reached for the phone, pressed redial. After four rings he expected to hear Moshe's message, but instead, a fifth ring. A sixth. A seventh. Strange. He checked Moshe's number, to be sure he had it right, dialed it again, digit by digit. Four rings, five, six, seven. The answering machine was off. Or full. Or something.

Arthur restarted the tape.

Brunch. Bagels and cream cheese. Coffee, orange juice. Doughnuts. The camera was moving.

"What do you need?"

Arthur didn't recognize the voice.

"Here. Let me get you set up." A woman speaking, not Brenda.

The camera followed Moshe from the family room, through a small dining room, to the living room.

"Okay?" Moshe asked. "Are we ready? Perhaps a niggun to begin."

Sing along with Moshe.

"A problem with Joseph," Moshe began. "He was his father's favorite. Anything Joseph wanted, Joseph got. Not that he wasn't worth it. He was smart. He was good-looking. The only problem was, he knew it. And there's nothing worse than a smart, good-looking boy who knows it. None of you are like that, are you?

"Well, his brothers became jealous. Can you blame them? When Joseph was only seventeen years old, his father sent him out to check up on his older brothers to see how they were doing.

"Then Joseph had these dreams, how his father, mother, and brothers would someday bow down to him. It's one thing to have dreams, another to brag about them.

"Jacob gave Joseph a special coat. A designer coat."

"A coat of many colors," a girl said.

"A special coat," Moshe said as he opened a suitcase Arthur had not seen. How could he not have seen it? Moshe withdrew and displayed four garments. A small, colorful Japanese kimono. Red, blue, yellow, green. An army officer's jacket with medals attached. A black tuxedo coat. Striped red flannel pajamas. Who would have flannel pajamas in Miami?

Arthur consulted the journal. A striped bathrobe was called for, not pajamas. Why did that annoy him?

Moshe laid each garment carefully on the carpet. "They went shopping," he said. "Jacob and Joseph together. Jacob never took any of his other sons shopping, only Joseph. Jacob wanted to buy his favorite son a present. Which one do you think Joseph chose?"

"This one." "This one." Voices overlapped.

"We need a Joseph." Moshe beckoned a tall boy forward. "Chris. Put on the kimono."

He looked handsome in it. The colors set off his blond hair. Chris paraded in his coat of many colors, a fashion model.

Moshe said, "You are the brothers and sisters of Joseph. How do you feel when you see Joseph in his beautiful new coat?"

"Jealous."

"Jealous," Moshe agreed. "Now, I'm going to tell you a secret, something very few people know. The Joseph story is all about clothes. That's all it is. A story about changing clothes. Changing clothes can be very important." He stopped to look about the room. The camera did likewise, progressing from person to person, each attentive, pondering the secret as if it held the deepest wisdom in the world.

Arthur wondered how Moshe did that, command attention so completely. What had Moshe said? A great secret, changing clothes, and they listened to him as if he were speaking profound truth.

Something else. The camera work was different. In all the previous tapings, the camera had remained still. This time the camera was moving about the room. Someone other than Daniel was behind it. Where was Daniel?

Where was Brenda?

"The brothers were fed up with Joseph," Moshe said. "What's more, his father saw it. His father knew how the brothers felt. Jacob had made a mistake by giving Joseph such special treatment. Jacob realized it. The question was what to do about it.

"Joseph had to grow up. His father took a risk. The brothers were up north taking care of the sheep. Jacob told Joseph to go see how his brothers were doing.

"Somehow I don't think Joseph was eager to go. He went, but he would just as soon not find his brothers. The Torah says an eesh found him wandering around. The word *eesh* means person. Whenever a person is mentioned without a name, the rabbis say the eesh is an angel. The purpose of an angel is to give you a message. That's all such an angel is, a messenger. The eesh, the person, the angel, found Joseph wandering around and asked him what he was looking for.

"'My brothers,' Joseph said.

"'They went that way, toward Dotan,' the angel told him.

"So Joseph had no choice but to encounter his brothers. That was something he had to do if he was to grow up. It was risky. Jacob had known that when he sent him. But sometimes risks have to be taken."

Moshe paused, apparently uncertain how to continue. "A difficult question," he said. "Has there ever been an eesh in your life, a stranger who made a connection for you, who pushed you into a situation where your life changed as a result? This is a hard question. It's for the adults to share, if they like."

Silence.

Moshe was right. The question was hard, too hard.

"I'll give you an example," he said. "When I met my wife in Israel, there was an eesh. In this case an eeshah, a woman. She sat down between us in the dining room and kept us from talking with each other. She drove us nuts, chattering away, first to me on the right, then to Rivkah on the left. All we wanted was to talk to each other."

"I thought you said an angel came to make a connection," Michelle Kantor said.

"She did make a connection. She gave us a common experience. By the time she left, we felt such exasperation it broke through whatever reticence we might have had. We began talking on a much deeper level than we would have otherwise.

"She made it easier for us to talk to each other," he explained to the young people.

"Your turn now, if you're willing. You might have to think really hard on this one. It's not easy to see angels. They do their work and get out of the way. You may not be aware of them at all. Try discussing in small groups. It might be easier."

Angels. Arthur sat back into his chair. Moshe was speaking of them as if they were real, not a metaphor or an allegory. The very notion of angels

145

being real made Arthur uncomfortable. Were his teachers angels because they conveyed messages to him? Was Rabbi Perlstein an angel because he had saved him after his father's funeral? Were Moshe and Rivkah angels because they had introduced him to Charlotte? Another might say such a thing as a metaphor, in a poem, maybe, or a eulogy. But they weren't angels. Acting as angels, maybe.

The study groups worked earnestly, Moshe moving from one to the next, the camera following him, zooming in now and then on individuals. This camera work was decidedly different from that of the other sessions. Was the cameraman an angel?

When the group reassembled, George Lopez was the first to speak. "This was an easy one for me. I've known about this angel from the moment it happened. In Vietnam, in combat once, a voice shouted, 'Lopez, over here!' I turned and, for whatever reason, ducked. A bullet took off a tree limb where my head would have been. I never knew who shouted at me, yet I think I knew, even then, it was an angel."

And what about all those who didn't duck? Where were their angels?

"Playing soccer once, at West Point." Bill Capstan was speaking, a balding, paunchy man, anything but the image of a soccer player.

"You went to West Point?" a woman asked, off camera.

"No, Cindy, I didn't go to West Point. I went to Cornell. We were playing at West Point. We had unlimited substitution in those days. The Army team came in waves, expecting to wear us down. Then there was this moment, toward the end of the game. We were down two goals, but everyone on the field just knew the game was ours. We knew it. I think they knew it. It was so . . . I don't know the right word for it. I felt something telling me to go somewhere on the field, out of position. The ball came to me. I didn't do much, just made a one-touch pass. We scored one goal, then a second. We won in overtime. No surprise. No celebrating. We just won. Like an angel was with us. That's the way we talked about it."

And where was the angel for the losing team?

"It's how I decided to be a nurse," Linda Capstan said. The camera shifted to focus on her. "I was in my third year at Swarthmore, not an idea in the world what I wanted to do. All my friends knew what they were going to do. I didn't. I didn't want to be in school anymore. I left my classes, in February I think, went home, a bus, a Greyhound bus. A woman sat beside me and started talking. She was a nurse. All I wanted was for her to shut up. I got off the bus, took a cab home. During the cab ride, something changed in me. My mother opened the door, not all that surprised to see me, even though I hadn't called ahead. 'I'm going to be a nurse,' I told her." Linda's discourse came to an abrupt end, as if she suddenly realized there wasn't any more to add.

The children were listening, every one of them. The camera panned to show their faces.

"So Joseph encountered an eesh, an angel, who directed him toward a meeting with his brothers. Sometimes the experience is on the upside. A bullet misses you, you win the game, or you find a new direction in life. Sometimes the new direction doesn't seem to be on the upside at all. Joseph was in for a rough time. What happened?"

"The brothers stripped the coat off him."

"They wanted to kill him."

"They threw him into a pit."

"They sold him to a caravan that was going to Egypt."

All of the answers, all at once.

"Yes," Moshe said. "They stripped the coat off him." He nodded at the children closest to Chris.

Chris said, "I'll do it myself." He took off the kimono and threw it to the boys across the room.

"Remember," Moshe said, "This is a story about changing clothes. What did the brothers do with the coat?"

"They dipped it in blood."

"Sheep's blood."

"They brought it back to their father and said Joseph was dead."

"Did they really say Joseph was dead?" Moshe asked. He opened a large purple-covered volume to consult a text. "No, they didn't say that. They let the coat speak for itself. They said, 'We found this. Is it your son's coat or not?' They didn't have to say anything. The coat told the story.

"Become the coat," Moshe said. "If you were the coat, how would you feel? What would you say?"

He wanted them to be a coat? Arthur struggled with the concept of becoming an inanimate object. The children had no difficulty.

"Sad."

"Angry."

"Look what has happened to me," Susan Cohen said. Susan was a lawyer, president of the sisterhood. "Look what has happened to me. I used to be so beautiful, and now I am all bloody. I used to shine in the sun, make

147

my master feel so good, and now I'm nothing more than a soiled piece of colored cloth."

"Nice," Moshe said. "What do you think Jacob did with the coat?"

"He buried it."

"He sent it to the dry cleaners."

"He kept it in the closet."

"Did he just throw it away?" Moshe asked.

"No. It was special."

"Why didn't he throw it away?"

"Because it reminded him of his son."

Moshe nodded. "Joseph had to grow up. Jacob had taken a risk. He sent Joseph off to a meeting with his brothers. It was a dangerous trip. When Jacob saw his son's coat, soaked with blood, his heart must have broken. 'I took a risk,' he said, 'and I lost.' Not all risks pay off. That's why they're called risks. Sometimes you lose."

"Jacob didn't lose. Joseph was still alive." A child, off camera.

"But Jacob didn't know that." Another child.

"No," Moshe agreed. "At that time, Jacob didn't know." His aspect brightened. "What happened to Joseph?"

"Joseph was sold as a slave into Egypt."

"He became a servant."

"To Potiphar."

"What kind of a servant?" Moshe asked.

"A butler."

"A secretary."

"Head of a household."

"What would he wear?" Moshe asked.

They dressed Chris in the tuxedo jacket.

"Joseph became the head of Potiphar's household. Just as he had reported everything that happened to his father, Jacob, so he reported everything that happened to Potiphar. Potiphar put him in charge. Things were good for Joseph once again, until . . ."

"Until Mrs. Potiphar upset things," one of the adults said.

"Mrs. Potiphar wanted Joseph to pay more attention to her," Moshe continued, "but this made Joseph increasingly uncomfortable. We need a Mrs. Potiphar." Jennifer Garfinkel was the first to her feet. "She reaches for Joseph, but grabs . . . what?"

"His coat."

"There we go again," Moshe said. "This man keeps losing his clothes."

Jennifer stripped the coat from Chris.

"What does she tell her husband when he comes home?" Moshe asked.

"Joseph tried to attack me. I chased him away, and he left his coat behind."

"Do you think Mr. Potiphar believed his wife?" That was a new question, one Arthur had never heard before. "Do you think Mr. Potiphar thought his wife was telling the truth?"

"No," Susan Cohen said. "No. He knew his wife, what she was like. He knew Joseph, trusted Joseph. But his wife had the coat. She was going public with her accusations. He had to say she was a liar, or he had to get rid of Joseph. He knew Joseph hadn't done anything, but he didn't have any choice. Joseph had to go."

"So he had Joseph killed," Moshe said.

"No!" the kids shouted.

"Well, what happened to him?"

"He got sent to the Federal Correctional Institute at Danbury," Susan Cohen said. "That's where they kept all the government officials who had to go to prison."

"He went to a special prison. What did he wear there?"

"A prison uniform."

The kids dressed Chris in the striped pajamas.

"Another change of clothes," Moshe said. "How do we know it was such a special prison?"

"Because the chief baker and the chief wine steward were there."

"The Minister of Agriculture and the Chief of Staff," Moshe said. "What happened to Joseph in prison?"

"He interpreted dreams."

"He became in charge of the prison."

"He became second-in-command once again," Moshe said. "He had been second-in-command to his father, supervising his brothers. He had been second-in-command to Potiphar, supervising his household. Now he became second-in-command to the warden, supervising the prison. What happened next?"

"Pharaoh hung the baker and took the wine steward out of prison."

"Joseph had interpreted their dreams."

"The wine steward forgot all about Joseph."

"Until . . . ?"

149

"Until Pharaoh had a dream."

"Two dreams."

"And no one could interpret them."

"Then what did the wine steward say?"

"*Et ha-ta-eye anee mazkir ha-yom*," Margolit said.

"'I just now remember my mistake,'" Moshe translated. "The wine steward had promised Joseph he would help him. He had forgotten to do so for two full years. But now, when no one could interpret Pharaoh's dreams, the wine steward told Pharaoh about Joseph. What did Pharaoh do?"

"He ordered his soldiers to bring Joseph to him."

"Could Joseph come before Pharaoh in a prison uniform?"

"No. He changed his clothes."

"Into what?"

The only garment left was the army uniform jacket with rows of campaign ribbons.

"Oops," Moshe said. "Not enough clothes. Jim, do you have anything Joseph might wear to go to the oval office in Egypt?"

Jim Clark hurried off to the left and returned with a blue blazer. The children removed Chris's pajamas and dressed him in the blazer.

"Another change of clothes," Moshe said. "They brought Joseph before Pharaoh. We need a Pharaoh. Jim, stay and be Pharaoh. Do you remember what Pharaoh said to Joseph?"

"I had a dream. No one could interpret it. There were five—"

"Seven," came the correction.

"Seven lean cows that ate seven fat cows. What does it mean?"

"Joseph interpreted the dream. Do you remember what he said, Chris?"

"There will be seven fat years, and then seven lean years," Chris said.

"Pharaoh needed someone to be in charge of gathering the food during the seven good years, of passing it out during the seven lean years. Who did he choose?"

"Joseph."

"What would a man in charge wear?"

The children stripped Chris of the blue blazer and dressed him in the army jacket, much too big for him but impressive with all the medals attached.

"So Joseph is second-in-command once again, this time to Pharaoh. And yet another change of clothes. It looks like he has a coat of many colors once again," Moshe said as he ran his fingers across the medals. The only one Arthur recognized was the Purple Heart.

"So, what do we learn from the story. In small groups. Three things we learn from the story."

The groups formed quickly and began to buzz. Again the camera passed from group to group. Someone was in charge, but not Brenda. Where was Brenda?

Arthur left the buzz of the groups to consult the journal. It took him a while to realize Brenda was in California.

So Moshe used to be a rabbi. I should have guessed that.

It's Saturday night, midnight, after the first session.

They limit the storytelling sessions to twelve people. It's a marathon, really, four sessions, from Saturday after sunset through midnight Sunday. I don't know why they do it that way. No recording permitted. No note-taking. Everything present tense, real time.

Sidney says if we take notes or if we record, we won't be as present to the experience.

Stephanie says it's just Sidney's hangup. He's afraid if a recorder is on he'll tell the stories to the recorder rather than to the students.

We had Shabbat with the Lees, in the house. Such a beautiful house, a California house. I try to imagine Rivkah from her house. I think I would have liked her. I couldn't find any pictures of her.

Saturday morning with the Havurah minyan. So nice they remembered us. Especially nice to Daniel.

Shabbat afternoon, picnic down by the lake. So still. Sidney skipped stones across the surface of the water. Daniel sat, watching, as if waiting for the stones to jump up and skip some more.

A holy convocation, those who gather for the storytelling. For some this is a repeat. They've been through it before. To hear them differently, they say. To learn how to tell the stories. To learn how to tell their own stories.

Stephanie is comfortable in them, more so than Sidney. For Sidney, it's as if the stories are outside of him. He sees them, hears them, remembers them, retells them. The stories come through Stephanie. She says they are her—that even the stories about Moshe and Rivkah

151

are her, that we don't learn about Moshe and Rivkah from the stories; we learn about Stephanie.

I don't pretend to understand that.

Maybe. Maybe I'm afraid to. Afraid to tell stories that expose so much.

It doesn't seem to me Moshe and Rivkah were happy together.

Were Nathan and I? I don't remember.

I understand Moshe better, now. He teaches the way Stephanie tells stories. He is his teaching.

I understand why he doesn't want to be a rabbi. The title would get in the way of him and his teaching.

I don't think I would like him so much as a rabbi.

Daniel spent the evening looking through the window. When we were in the living room, he looked through the window toward the deck. When we were on the deck, he looked through the window toward the living room. Or he was looking at the reflections.

Maybe he was looking into the glass, like the surface of the lake, waiting for the stones to begin skipping again.

". . . a person is what he wears."

"Change the clothes, change the person."

"It may be better to be second-in-charge than be in charge."

How long had the groups been reporting? Arthur wondered. How much had he missed?

"One more change of clothes for Joseph," Moshe said. "Do you know what it is?" The camera panned a series of silent faces. "Joseph died at the age of 110 years . . ."

"Shrouds," someone said.

"Yes," Moshe agreed. "A final change of clothes. Joseph was embalmed and placed in a sarcophagus in Egypt."

"A mummy?" one of the children asked.

"A mummy," Moshe agreed.

"Was he second-in-command once again?" Orly asked.

Moshe paused. "Second-in-command?" he asked.

"To God."

"In heaven," another child said.

"What did he wear?" asked another.

"What does God wear?" still another.

Arthur hated teaching children. They were so unpredictable.

"There is a tradition," Moshe began, "that God wears a garment. It needed cleaning. So what did God do? God created a universe, a world of space and time with things in it—rocks, plants, animals, and us. God took off the garment and put one sleeve into this, another into that. Everything in creation holds a piece of it. So there's a piece of God's garment in me, in you, in everything. When we talk like this, when we ask such questions and struggle with the answers, it's as if we're cleaning God's garment.

"If your shirt was dirty, you wouldn't clean it while you had it on, would you?" he asked Mario Kantor, who was wearing a dress shirt with jeans. Mario shook his head. "You'd take it off. In the old days, before there were any dry cleaners or washing machines, you'd take one sleeve in one hand, and one in the other, put them into a washing tub and rub them together to clean them.

"It's as if that's what's happening here. God put one sleeve in you, one in me, and we rub them together. When we've done the best we can do, God takes the garment back, and puts it on."

"So we become God's garment," Orly said. Moshe waited for her to complete her thought. "And Joseph became God's coat of many colors," she continued.

Moshe held up George Lopez's army uniform jacket, with all the medals. "This coat is second-in-command," he said. "The soldiers salute not the officer, but the coat, and the coat salutes the officer."

Moshe's words made a much greater impression on the families than on Arthur. Sleeves were Moshe's metaphor for souls. God put souls into the world. But into rocks and plants? Rocks and plants had souls? They accepted that without argument? No one was going to object? No one? They simply took Moshe at his word, as if everything he said was gospel. If he, Arthur, had said such a thing, they'd be all over him. But Moshe said it and got away with it. Moshe hadn't even said it with conviction. He'd said it as if the idea was new and he was trying it on for size.

A theology, Arthur thought. Moshe was trying on a theology to see how it fit, if he could make it fit. A theology was like a garment for God. One needn't believe in God. The theology would do.

Moshe was right, Arthur realized. The theology, the belief system, was God's garment. He wanted to share that with someone, to add it to the discussion. But the discussion was inside the television, inside the VCR, on tape and far away.

That was a good idea, a theology as the garment of God. Most religious people related to the theology instead of God Himself. It wasn't God that became holy; it was the theology. There was a sermon in there somewhere. Was it worthy of the Holy Days? It wasn't too early to be thinking about the Holy Days. Something for Yom Kippur morning, perhaps.

But would people tolerate a sermon about God?

Had he ever given a sermon about God?

While Arthur probed for an answer, a sermon title that had to do with God, the tape went to static.

He couldn't remember any sermon he had ever given concerning God.

Lunch break.

Daniel is off somewhere with Stephanie, and I have a corner of the deck to myself. Stephanie's amazing. If I had put out that much energy, I would no more have anything left over for Daniel. But she says she's not working when she's telling the stories. That's one thing she learned from Reb Hayim.

This is what she told me yesterday about Reb Hayim. I don't know if Reb Hayim is real, or if he's a story, but either way, it's not one of the stories from the cycle. Reb Hayim is the name she gives to an itinerant Hasidic teacher. She said it took her a long time to appreciate Reb Hayim and understand what it was he does.

The first time he came to the Havurah he taught niggunim. The niggunim were wonderful. Most of the members of the Havurah had never heard tunes like those.

The next time he came back, they couldn't wait to hear the niggunim. He sang some and everyone sang along. Then he began to tell stories, and most of the members of the Havurah had never heard stories like those. They realized that the purpose of the niggunim was to prepare them to hear stories on that level, at that depth.

The next time he came back, he sang some tunes, old ones and new. They were okay, but the haverim were waiting to hear the stories. Then he began to tell the stories. Some were new. Some they had heard before. Then he stopped telling stories, reached down, picked up a book, and began to teach Torah. They had never heard Torah taught like that before, and they realized that the purpose of the niggunim was to get them to hear stories so they would be ready to learn Torah.

The next time he came, he sang some tunes. Everyone sang along, waiting for the stories. Then he told some stories, but everyone was waiting for the teaching. Then he taught some Torah, at such a deep level. Then he said, "Let's take a break."

That's when he did his real work.

He went from person to person, knew each person's name, and asked, "So, holy brother, how are you? So, holy sister, how are you?"

That was his work.

The tunes were to get us to hear the stories. The stories were to get us to learn Torah. The Torah was to open our souls so he could ask how we were.

So Stephanie told me she learned that from Reb Hayim. She liked his songs, didn't care all that much for his stories or his teaching, but learned from him how to work the intermissions. She learned to coast through the stories and work the time in between.

Me, I'm exhausted just having heard the stories.

Again, I don't know if all of that is for real, what happened to Moshe and Rivkah, but the stories are powerful. What they went through.

And the Kabbalah.

This is so different from what Rafi taught, so out there. Spirituality without the mystery.

Arthur turned the page and found drawings of trees, two pages of eucalyptus trees.

So Brenda had been in California in February, during the Joseph program. She had been taking a course, a story cycle in Rivkah's home, with stories of Moshe and Rivkah. Cultic. The very discipline of the cult. Long hours, little time to ask questions. Bombard them with information until they couldn't distinguish between what was real and what was not. Two teachers, one relieving the other, to keep up the incessant pressure. Bend the minds of the disciples, break them.

Brenda would not be so easy to break. Rafi hadn't been able to do it. She bent only so far. Swayed, Arthur thought, recalling the images in spite of himself. But then, she broke away. And again, this time also, she had broken away, but not, apparently, before significant damage had been done.

The television was still static. Something had happened in the program. The children were off doing something, Arthur guessed. What they were doing he did not know. He did not care to know. Moshe was likely sitting somewhere with the adults, pontificating, spinning his web that allowed no room for questions.

Push on. No time to rewind. No time to unwind. He muted the TV, let the static play, just in case some image should present itself. Who knew what might be on the back end of the tape? Maybe Moshe and Margolit, together. That was his hope.

Cobwebs. He shook his head to clear them, stood, stretched and still standing, started the audiotape at his desk.

". . . write home," Moshe said. Arthur didn't bother to see if he had the tape at the beginning or not. "He was second-in-command of all of Egypt through the seven years of plenty, and now well into the seven years of famine. Did Joseph write home? He certainly could have. Did he tell his father he was still alive? Did he say, 'Don't worry, Dad. I'm okay. My brothers sold me down to Egypt, but I've made good, done well. You'll be proud of me when you see how well I've done'?"

Joseph didn't write home, Arthur thought. Jonah never wrote home, nothing that could ever be traced. They must have found out eventually Jonah was in New Orleans, but so long as he stayed there, that must have been all right with them, whoever they were. Whatever it was Jonah had been doing on the streets, it had resulted in his father's death. Arthur was certain of that. But in those glancing meetings with Jonah in New Jersey, he had never asked, had been afraid to, didn't want to know. Jonah materialized a few minutes at a time, to check in on his mother, not his brother. After his mother died, to Arthur's knowledge, Jonah never came back to New Jersey. No messages, no questions, no contact. For years.

Joseph did not write home.

"If he did," Moshe said, "the brothers didn't know about it."

Arthur never knew when Jonah might show up, but his mother never seemed surprised.

"If Joseph did write home, somehow, to let his father know he was all right, why didn't the brothers know about it?"

Joseph did not write home.

"There was work to do with the brothers. Let's see what happened."

Arthur pressed the pause button, stopped Moshe in his tracks. So easy to do.

Why hadn't he done that earlier?

In the airport, waiting. Fog has things closed down.
Daniel watches the fog, intrigued with it, as if it were alive.
It could be alive. An angel, intended for some purpose.

I think I cried all night.
I cried for Rivkah and Stephanie and Sidney. For Nathan. For
Daniel. For me.
I didn't cry for Moshe, the Moshe in the stories.
The Moshe I know in Miami doesn't seem to need my tears.

Stephanie's stories took so much courage to tell. And Sidney's.
Some, he said, he had never told before, never knew before.
Each cycle is different. Maybe that's why some students take it
more than once.
I don't think I could take it again.

I don't see any connection between Moshe in Miami and the
Moshe in the stories. The Moshe in Miami is so patient, so percep-
tive, so considerate, so kind.
The stories may not be right. Sidney said so. The stories were en-
tities unto themselves, each told for a purpose, a stepping stone, a
path around a given frame, the four worlds and the ten Sefirot.
You can't believe stories, but you can have faith in them.

Arthur closed his hand and snapped the journal shut. There was no escape. What time was it? Just after noon. Nine o'clock in California. Maybe
she would be awake. He reached for the phone and called Tamar. The
emptiness in his stomach deepened with each successive ring. Three. Four.
Surely he would trigger her answering machine. Five.

Cindy picked up. "Goooood morning."

They had a narrow house in Venice, just off the beach, on a pedestrian
street. Two stories and a deck above from which, between taller houses, one
could glimpse the ocean.

"Good morning," Cindy said again.

"Good morning," Arthur said. "This is Tamar's father. Is she available to
come to the phone?"

After a pause long enough for two full breaths, Cindy said, "She's sleeping, Artie. Should I wake her?"

157

Arthur closed his eyes. With his free hand he tried to press his cheek-bone and forehead together to still the pounding in his head. "No, no, don't wake her."

"Should she call when she gets up?"

"No, I'm not at home. I'm in the office."

"Should she call the office?"

"No. It's all right. Maybe I'll call back later."

"Are you okay, Artie? You don't sound well."

"I'm okay. Thank you. I'll call back later."

Arthur laid the phone gently in its cradle, leaned back in his chair. It would be so easy to escape into sleep.

No. There was an urgency. Moshe and Brenda. Moshe and Margolit.

"Joseph recognized his brothers when they came down to Egypt to buy pro-visions," Moshe said, "but the brothers didn't recognize Joseph. How come they didn't recognize him?"

"He was dressed like an Egyptian."

"He had aged, grown up, had a beard."

"They never expected to see him. They thought he was dead."

"He didn't speak Hebrew."

All adult voices.

"There were many reasons why the brothers didn't recognize Joseph," Moshe said. "How is it Joseph was able to recognize his brothers?"

"They looked like his brothers."

"They hadn't aged?" Moshe asked. "Joseph had grown older, but his brothers hadn't?"

"They were already older when they sold Joseph." That was Margolit, in her Hebrew-accented English. "Joseph knew them as men, but they knew him only as a boy."

"Yes," Moshe agreed. "These are all good answers. But let's take it to a deeper level. What if Joseph could recognize them because they hadn't changed at all? They were still the same. The guilt they incurred when they sold their brother into slavery was such they hadn't been able to grow at all. He saw his brothers exactly as he remembered them.

"Joseph had aged. Joseph had grown. His brothers hadn't.

"Imagine this. A new story, to fit between the lines of the old one. Joseph writes home."

Joseph didn't write home, Arthur insisted silently.

158

"He writes to his father," Moshe continued, "and says, 'I'm all right, don't worry about me, but don't tell my brothers. Keep this a secret. Let me know how they are doing. I'm afraid for them.'"

Why would Joseph be afraid for his brothers? Arthur wondered. Joseph was the one at risk, down in Egypt. The brothers were safe at home.

"'They did something terrible,' Joseph told his father. 'Perhaps you and I can devise a plan to help them work through it, to atone for it.'"

Jonah did something terrible, not me, Arthur protested. Jonah was the one to feel guilty, not me.

"'If we put them in the same situation and allow them to choose differently, then they can unload their burden of guilt and continue with their lives.'

"Now Jacob had already suspected the brothers had done something with Joseph. He didn't know quite what, but he wasn't entirely surprised by Joseph's letter. He and Joseph corresponded. They devised a plan.

"If you think of it this way, then it makes sense. Why would Jacob send all the brothers, all except Benjamin, his youngest and his favorite, all of them to Egypt to buy provisions? Wouldn't one or two have been enough? But he sends all of them. They all have to go through the experience.

"Joseph knows they are coming. He recognizes them. He orders that their money be returned in their sacks. They discover it on the way home, and they are terrified. They're afraid they will be accused of stealing the money.

"Even worse, Joseph has said they may not return to Egypt unless they bring Benjamin with them.

"They return home. All the food they brought with them from Egypt is consumed. Jacob tells them to go back to Egypt, and they say they can't, not unless Benjamin goes with them. And so the situation is set up. The brothers will have an opportunity to atone for their sin.

"Joseph recognizes Benjamin. He has his own wine cup placed in Benjamin's sack. As the brothers leave, Joseph's soldiers pursue them, stop them, and find Joseph's cup. They bring all the brothers back. Joseph says, 'You all can go, except the guilty one. This one stays with me. The rest of you go back to your father.'

"So the brothers have the opportunity to do to Benjamin, the favorite, what they did to Joseph. They can go back to their father without Benjamin, leaving him in Egypt. Or they can do something else.

"They do something else. Read this. It's Judah's monologue from Genesis 44."

Arthur heard the sound of shuffling papers. He looked into the journal for the text but found only Brenda's handwriting and a series of doodles, six-winged angels, perhaps from Ezekiel's vision.

No matter. He knew Genesis 44. Judah approached Joseph, not knowing he was Joseph, and said they couldn't do that. They couldn't leave Benjamin behind. One brother had been lost already, and they couldn't do that to their father again.

It was a beautiful monologue. Arthur couldn't remember it word for word, but he wasn't about to get up and read it. Judah offered himself in place of Benjamin. The brothers held their ground.

Moshe's story was clever, Arthur admitted. The rabbis had a simple understanding of repentance. When presented with the same opportunity to sin, make a different decision. Choose not to. The brothers had been presented with the same opportunity. They could have eliminated Benjamin as they had eliminated Joseph, but they chose not to.

It was good, except the writing home. Joseph didn't write home. Jonah didn't write home. There had never been any letters.

Even as Arthur underlined his thought, engraved it with certainty, he knew he was wrong. Jonah hadn't sent letters through the mail; still, his mother had known when he would show up. She was never surprised. Arthur was always surprised.

Whatever messages she had been receiving from Jonah, she had not shared them. Information reached New Jersey in such a way it couldn't be traced back to Jonah in New Orleans. Suddenly it seemed obvious, but Arthur had never known, never admitted it to himself. He had not been taken into their confidence, not by his mother, not by Jonah. He had been out of the loop, like Joseph's brothers.

But what was his guilt? What was his guilt, that he should have been kept in the dark, not trusted?

"Joseph had been holding himself back, behind a strong facade," Moshe said. "After Judah had finished his presentation, after the brothers had nodded their acknowledgment, Joseph could not restrain himself any longer. The brothers had atoned for their sin. Joseph made himself known to them. The word of the reunion spread throughout all of Egypt."

Arthur pressed stop and ejected the tape.

CHAPTER 11

SUNDAY, 12:15 P.M.

Just me and Moshe, walking in the Grove. I wanted time with him alone. He seemed to have expected it. He didn't ask about Daniel at all.

I wanted to know if the stories I had heard in California were true. He said he didn't know. He hadn't heard the stories. He knew Sidney and Stephanie taught the framework of the Kabbalah through their stories, that he and Rivkah were part of those stories because they were part of the experience of Sidney and Stephanie, but he didn't know if the stories reflected reality as he understood it or not.

I asked him what his reality was.

He didn't answer for the longest time. It was like he was trying to answer but couldn't find the right words.

He said he no longer had certainty about his reality. Everything was real, and nothing was real. Time wasn't the same for him anymore.

I asked him if that was because Rivkah had died. He said it was because he had died. In that ultimate descent with Rivkah, he had died. It wasn't just that his heart stopped beating and he had to be resuscitated, but that something had shifted within him. He was no longer attached to the world the way he had been. That had happened before his heart had stopped beating. He had felt it happen, had known what was happening, felt himself tear loose.

But he was walking on the ground, holding my hand. He was right there beside me.

He said he was, and he wasn't. He was with me, but before me and after me at the same time. That space, time, and soul stretch through all the worlds. That his soul had become unattached while still in his body because of that experience. He could feel me right then, walking in the Grove. But he could also feel something of where I had been and something of where I would be.

I asked him if he was a fortune-teller. He thought that was funny, not the telling part, but the fortune part. Everyone had a notion that fortune always meant what they wanted, that if you uncovered a fortune you found a treasure. But he wasn't a fortune-teller. As space, time, and soul stretched away from the present, shapes and events lost their sharp edge and became blurred, uncertain.

He said he could see something about me and my father, or a father figure, but that was because whatever happened then I carried with me into the present. But any good therapist could see it, too. Or a fortune-teller.

One's experience is one's fortune, and it isn't always a treasure.

I was afraid he could read my mind, and more certain of it when he told me not to worry, he couldn't read my mind.

I tried to block out everything my father had done to me, but suddenly every other man I had been with was in my thoughts, too. I'm sure I was blushing, but he didn't look at me. If he could see them, he was kind enough not to mention them.

He was also in my thoughts, that I wanted him, like no one else in the world I wanted him. If he felt that, he did not respond. He did not speak to it. I could feel nothing different in the way he held my hand.

I asked him if he had been with a woman since Rivkah had died. A stupid question.

He didn't let go of my hand, but he didn't answer either. He waited and waited, until I became aware of what I had really asked, the invitation I had given him.

It was I who broke the silence and said we should see how Daniel was doing.

He took me home.

A portrait of Moshe. Sensitive. Pensive.
Good, Arthur thought. Damn good. She had talent.

March 5—the Davidsons'
Young Moses

Arthur could see from the camera placement Brenda was back and in charge. The camera was set up high, covering a large living room, modern furniture, sliding glass doors open onto a terrace with a swimming pool that seemed to fall off into Biscayne Bay.

Five million dollars for a house like that. Who were the Davidsons? Arthur consulted the database. Frank and Louise. Two young children, Lindy and Larry. Such a house, and they weren't even members of the President's Circle. What kind of name was Lindy? But there it was again, in the school registration. Lindy. Her first year in the religious school. Larry wasn't enrolled at all.

A niggun again, the usual one, sung along with Moshe, grabbing attention, building in energy. Arthur was tired of it. How often could he repeat it?

Not fair, he thought. For Moshe and the families, they heard it every few weeks, but he was hearing it in his study on tape seemingly every hour, on the hour.

"So, what did you learn?"

Learn about what?

"Pharaoh had ordered all the boy babies to be thrown into the Nile."

"What else?"

"Moses's mother was able to hide him for only three months."

"What else?"

"She put him into an ark when she couldn't hide him anymore. His sister hid in the reeds to see what would happen to him."

"What happened?"

"Pharaoh's daughter came down, saw him floating there, and took him to be her son."

"What did the sister do?"

"Went and got the mother to be a nursemaid."

"She got paid to be a nursemaid," another young voice added.

"To take care of her own baby."

Moshe waited for additional responses. "You've all read the text? It's not very long. You know it well? You understood it? Good. Let me ask some questions now."

As if he hadn't been asking questions all along.

"What tribe did the baby's father come from?"

"Levi," an adult answered.

"The baby's mother?"

"Levi."

"They got married, yes? And they had a baby? Was the baby a boy or a girl?"

"A boy."

"What did they name the boy?"

"Moses."

"Everyone agrees?" He waited. What was he waiting for? "Everyone agrees they named him Moses?" Arthur shook his head, knowing what was coming. "You haven't read the text. Go read it again, please. Really read it. Every word of it. Question everything. One minute, that's all you get."

Cute. He was teaching them how to read. He checked the journal for a text and found one folded between the pages.

Exodus 1

22. Pharaoh commanded all of his people saying: "Every boy who is born (among the Hebrews), throw him into the Nile, but let all the girls live."

Exodus 2

1. A man from the tribe of Levi went and took a woman from the tribe of Levi.

2. The woman became pregnant, gave birth to a son. She saw he was healthy. She hid him for three months.

3. She couldn't hide him any longer, so she took an ark of papyrus, waterproofed it, put the boy in it, and placed it in the reeds by the bank of the river.

4. His sister stood off at a distance to learn what might happen to him.

5. The daughter of Pharaoh came down to the Nile to wash while her maidservants walked alongside the river. She saw the ark among the reeds. She reached out for it and grabbed it.

6. When she opened it, she saw the boy. The baby began to cry. She took pity on it and said, "This must be one of the Hebrew boys."

7. His sister said to Pharaoh's daughter, "Shall I go and get a nursemaid for you from the Hebrew women, to nurse the child for you?"

8. Pharaoh's daughter told her, "Go." The young girl went and summoned the boy's mother.

9. Pharaoh's daughter said to her, "Take this child, nurse it, and I will pay you a salary." The woman took the child and nursed it.

10. The child grew. She brought him to Pharaoh's daughter, because he was like a child to her. She called his name, "Moses . . . "

"Again," Moshe said. "A man from the house of Levi went and took a woman from the house of Levi. They got married. Right?"

"They had sex." A girl speaking, Orly.

Margolit said something in Hebrew too quickly for Arthur to understand. He sighed. If this was about sex, he had better rewind and listen again. Even the second time Arthur couldn't understand what Margolit was saying. Something sharp in Hebrew, but the words were beyond him. His modern Hebrew wasn't adequate.

"It's okay," Moshe said to Margolit. "When Torah says 'A man took a woman,' she's right. It means they had sex." To Orly he said, "Here it also means they were married."

"Having sex means you're married?"

Arthur shook his head, despair rising in him. This did not sit well, would not sit well if heard by a judge and jury.

"Not every having sex means you're married, but here it was well enough known what the relationship was between them so it would be all right to translate it, 'A man from the house of Levi married a woman from the house of Levi.' Okay?"

Arthur pressed pause. What was Orly questioning? Moshe and her mother? Were they having sex? Did she know it? Was she wondering if they were married, getting married? Should he rewind and listen to the dialogue again? Probably, Arthur thought, but he did not. Whatever it was, it was.

"They had a baby. A boy or a girl?"

"A boy."

"And what did they name him?

"Moses," some said.

"We don't know," said others.

"Why don't we know?"

"We don't know what his parents named him because it was Pharaoh's daughter who named him."

"So what the baby's parents named him, we don't know."

"No."

Moshe let the word stand. He looked from face to face, to see if anyone had another word to insert. When none was spoken, he continued, "So you're telling me that Moses, the one who comes and leads the Hebrews out of slavery, has an Egyptian name. The daughter of Pharaoh speaks Egyptian, not Hebrew. She names the baby Moses, as in Tut-Moses or Ram-Moses. We don't know what the baby's parents named him. For some reason it's not important for us to know."

No one challenged him, not even Arthur. Moses's name was a mystery.

"Let's see what else you've learned from your reading," Moshe continued. "A man from the house of Levi marries a woman from the house of Levi, and they have a baby boy, right? They hide him for three months. Why do they hide him?"

Robert answered, "Because Pharaoh would throw him into the river."

"When they can't hide him anymore, they put him into a little basket, an ark, a tayvah, and float it in the Nile. Then his sister sits back in the reeds to see what will happen to him. All right so far?"

Cautious nods of agreement.

"Good. Was this an older sister or a younger sister?"

"Older."

"Where does she come from?"

Silence.

"Where does she come from?" he repeated. "A man and a woman get married, have a baby boy, then, suddenly, the baby boy has an older sister. She just appears, out of thin air. Where does she come from?"

Even Arthur, in his thoughts, was silent. There was a midrash, a rabbinic interpretation about that, but he had read it so long ago it had faded from his memory. Only a tickle of the memory remained, and he wasn't able to reach in and scratch it.

Where had the sister come from?

"A stepsister," Robert said.

That wasn't it. Arthur knew it was something else.

"A stepsister," Moshe repeated. "There are two ways to have a stepsister. Either Moses's father had been married before and had a child from his first marriage, or his mother had been married before and had a child from her first marriage. But there's another possibility."

That's it, Arthur thought, remembering the answer. The whole midrash came back to him. He had learned it once. Why had he never taught it?

"There isn't any other possibility," Robert said.

"There is," said Orly. "What if my mother and father got married again and had a baby boy. I'd be the baby's older sister."

"Yes," Moshe said. "And that's the one the rabbis chose to teach. Does anyone know Moses's father's name?"

"Amram."

"And his mother's name?"

"Yoheved."

"A story. A midrash. When Pharaoh ordered all the newborn male babies to be thrown into the Nile, Amram divorced his wife. He was afraid he might have to kill his own child if she gave birth to a boy. Amram was a leader among the people. When the Hebrews heard he had divorced his wife, all of them divorced their wives." Again Moshe had everyone's attention. Amazing the way he did that. "What was the name of Moses's sister?"

"Miriam," several voices said.

"The story is that Miriam scolded her father. She told him he was worse than Pharaoh because Pharaoh had ruled only against the boys, but her father had ruled against both the boys and the girls. Still, Amram protested. He couldn't bear the thought of having to kill a newborn son.

"Then Miriam said he had no faith in God. God said that Abraham's seed would be like the sand of the sea, like the stars of heaven. Still Amram wasn't moved.

"Then she said he had more faith in Pharaoh than in God. God said the Hebrews would have a myriad children—a lot of children—and Pharaoh said they wouldn't. 'Who do you believe,' Miriam asked her father, 'Pharaoh or God?' And with that Amram remarried his wife Yoheved, and you know the rest of the story from there.

"Or do you?

"Sometimes it's not enough to read what is written. You have to read what isn't written as well. You have to learn to ask questions. I have a question. Are you ready for it?" Nods indicated readiness. "We know Pharaoh ordered the male babies to be thrown into the Nile. When did he rescind the order?" Blank faces. "When did he take the order back?" Still no understanding.

What was he getting at? Arthur wondered.

"This is a question that doesn't have an answer, yet," Moshe continued. "We know Pharaoh must have canceled the order, because when Moses came back to Egypt to tell the Pharaoh to let his people go, if the Egyptians were still killing the baby boys, Moses would have had to say something about that first. But he doesn't say anything. Therefore, it had to have stopped at some time. When? Why?"

"Do you know the answer, Moshe?" That sounded like Josephine Shuk asking.

"No," Moshe admitted. "I don't know the answer. All I know is the question."

Arthur had no answer either, but he had his own question. Not so much how Jonah stayed in touch with his mother. That could have been done by second-party mailings or any number of other ways. But why hadn't his mother told him? Why had she kept it to herself?

She had been ashamed to tell him.

Why ashamed?

Because Jonah had been sending her money, money from his drug business. Arthur flushed as the answer rose in him.

She was ashamed, too ashamed to share that with Arthur. That was where the money came from. He had a scholarship to Rutgers, but not spending money. Not money for clothes or activities or . . .

His mother gave him money, always had money to give him. Cash. Where had the cash come from? He had never asked the question, never wanted to ask the question.

"Something stopped it," Moshe said. "What?"

"God intervened," said an anonymous voice.

"Too easy," Moshe said. "Besides, God doesn't speak to Pharaoh. God speaks to Moses."

"Then a plague happened to stop it," said the same anonymous person.

"The plagues came later," came a response from somewhere else, with a sense of annoyance.

"We're going about this the wrong way." A Hebrew accent. Margolit. "We don't need something miraculous. Moshe's right. That's too easy. We don't learn from something God does that we can't do."

"What do you mean?"

"I mean, if we say God stopped Pharaoh by tying up his tongue magically, or forcing his hand to write a new order, we don't learn anything. We can't do that. What we have to find is something that might have happened then that we could do now. Or we could do it the other way, find something that happens now that might have happened then."

"Nice," Moshe said, his admiration apparent.

"Nice," Arthur repeated, drawing satisfaction from Moshe's admiration.

168

"Do you know what that is, Moshe?" Josephine again.

"No," Moshe said. "The only thing I've seen so far is the question. I woke up with the question, but not the answer."

"The atom bomb on Hiroshima. That stopped World War II." George Lopez's contribution.

"That's a plague," Margolit said. "We're not looking for a plague. We're looking for a reason."

"The student in front of the tanks in Tienanmen Square," Michelle Kantor said.

"Yes, something like that," Margolit agreed. "One person with the courage to stand up to Pharaoh."

"Like who?"

"Like the King of Denmark." Arthur thought that was Mario Kantor's voice.

"Come on, be serious," said Josephine.

"I am serious. The King of Denmark. When the Nazis ordered the Jews to wear yellow stars on their clothes, the King of Denmark wore a yellow star. Then everyone wore a yellow star and the Nazis couldn't tell who was a Jew. One person. He stood up to the Nazis."

"Who was there to stand up to Pharaoh?"

Silence.

"I know," Orly said.

"Who?"

"His daughter. His daughter went down to the Nile to bathe and saw a lot of little bodies floating in the water. Her maidservants told her it was the Hebrew babies, that her father had ordered all the boy babies to be thrown into the Nile. Pharaoh's daughter said it had to stop, it was too terrible. She stopped it."

"How could she stop it. What could she do?"

"She went to her father and told him to stop it."

"Why would he listen to her?"

Silence, the silence of hard work. Arthur himself was drawn into it.

"Oh," Margolit said. One syllable, softly spoken, enough to draw all attention to her. "Oh," she said again, and covered her mouth in astonishment at her realization. "She went to her father and told him her own son, his grandson, the one he loved, the heir to the throne of Egypt, would have to be thrown into the Nile."

"He was a Hebrew baby?" Josephine asked.

"It doesn't matter!" Orly interjected, catching her mother's excitement. "It doesn't matter! Her father was trapped! Either she was telling the truth, or she wasn't. Either way, once she went public, she had him. To save his grandson, he had to cancel his order. It's beautiful. Don't you see it? He either had to drown his own grandson or stop killing the Hebrew babies."

Silence.

Everyone was considering the response, Arthur as well. It was a stunning answer to Moshe's question. Where had that question come from? What had engineered it? How had he seen into the empty spaces of the text to bring it out and give it words?

This was a wondrous teaching.

What a shame, Arthur thought. What a shame he might have to bring it down. The children would never forget that moment. Nor the adults. The tugging and pulling that brought out such a story of courage, one young woman standing up to a tyrant and stopping the flow of injustice with a single sentence. "My son, your grandson, is a Hebrew." Orly had been right. She had seen it instantly. It didn't matter whether his daughter was telling the truth or not. Going public was all she had to do. To save his grandson, Pharaoh had to rescind his order.

No one wanted to disturb that silence. The moment had become precious, a holy moment.

"You know," Moshe said, ever so gently, "there is a tradition. Under every word of Torah is an angel. When you uncover the secret of that word, you release the angel. Maybe that's why we're all so quiet, so we can hear the wings of that angel as it flies back to its source. She flies before the throne of the Holy One to announce that another secret has been discovered and one more word is in place, one more word in the bridge that connects earth and heaven."

One more word, Arthur thought, and he was angry with a new anger. One word from him would bring that bridge crashing to ground.

"That's nice. Really nice," Josephine said.

"But what about the ark in the bulrushes?" Robert asked. "What do we do with that?"

"Tayvah here, and tayvah there," Margolit said.

"Remember the Noah story," Orly explained. "*Tayvah*, the word for ark, is also the word for prayer."

"But if that's the story, then Moses is an Egyptian and not the child of

Amram and Yocheved," Robert said. He wasn't so much objecting as trying to make everything fit. For the story to work for Robert, all the details had to fit into a neat package.

"Pharaoh's daughter could be telling the truth. Her own son could have been stillborn, and she took one of the Hebrew babies to replace him."

Silence.

"And the ark, the prayer, the tayvah, that was the prayer of Miriam, the prayer Miriam said when she was bringing the baby to the Nile. She prayed, 'Please God, help me find some way to save my brother.' Pharaoh's daughter heard the prayer. She was coming down to bathe in the Nile, to purify herself after the loss of her infant son. She heard Miriam's prayer. 'Why do you have to save your brother?' she asked. Miriam pointed to all the dead babies floating in the Nile. 'We have to stop this,' Pharaoh's daughter said. So she took the baby from Miriam and hired the baby's mother to nurse him. Then she went to her father and stopped the killing."

"Is that the right answer?" Josephine asked Moshe.

Moshe said. "The Torah doesn't give Pharaoh's daughter a name, but the midrash does. It calls her Bat-Yah, daughter of God. If what you just told isn't her story, I can't imagine a better one."

Neither could Arthur imagine a better one, and that inflamed his anger still more. All those holy moments the families had celebrated in the course of the year would become profane, desecrated by the unholy action of their teacher. What a waste. Everything Moshe had accomplished would be in vain, never to be mentioned again because it would be associated with a disgraced name.

The excitement these children shared, their enthusiasm as they told the stories, the wonderful stories, to their friends, their classmates, their teachers, silenced, never to be repeated again, because of what Arthur might have to do.

Not just the zoning and funding, but all the learning, brought down. The story of Bat-Yah, Pharaoh's daughter, would never see the light of day.

Holiness profaned, desecrated.

The stakes had become higher. Added to his concern for the zoning, the funding, and his career was a new desire to protect these families. And the learning.

But it wasn't his fault, he reminded himself. The blame, the shame, that was all on Moshe.

Due diligence. Do the diligence, Arthur reminded himself. If there was a way out, it was for him to find it, and he had how many hours? Until nine in the morning. Then it didn't matter anymore. Once it was out, it was out, and the damage would be done. No matter guilt or innocence, the accusation, once spoken, would be damage enough in itself. The stories would never be told again. They would be buried under the headlines, swallowed up by the tabloids.

He looked to the television. Static. Where had the children gone? They had been swallowed up by static, a screen gone blank. White noise, like a waterfall.

> *Nathan died so quickly. There was so much to do. With Daniel and everything, I never thought about it much, what it meant to die.*
> *With Rivkah, it must have been so different.*
> *Moshe saw her going, day by day. Did he really think he could bring her back?*
> *What would happen if I died? Who would take care of Daniel?*
> *Why haven't I thought about this before?*
> *Nathan would have thought about it.*

"Ten," the tape player said.

"More than ten."

"None."

"How many?"

"Once," Moshe said, "and then only in passing. We'll see if they find it."

"Only once?"

"Only once."

Arthur had no idea what they were talking about. He had missed something, still lost in Brenda's words. "What would happen if I died? Who would take care of Daniel?"

"Do you have the energy for more?" Moshe asked.

A murmur of assent, but Arthur had no more energy.

"Torah tells us so little about the young Moses, so little, as if it's inviting us to ask questions, to fill in the blanks. Do you remember why Moses had to leave Egypt, why he had to run away?"

"He killed an Egyptian."

"Why?"

"The Egyptian was beating a Hebrew slave."

"Here's what Torah says," Moshe continued. "'Moses looked this way and that, then seeing no person, he struck the Egyptian.' He killed the Egyptian. You hear the problem?"

Silence.

"Why did he look this way and that?"

"To make sure no one was watching."

"You mean if someone was watching he wouldn't have done anything? He would have let the Egyptian kill the Hebrew?"

Silence.

"No, if Moses was a righteous person, he would have done something whether someone was watching or not. He couldn't have just let the Egyptian kill the Hebrew, could he? So, what does it mean, he looked this way and that and saw there was no person?"

"No person. No eesh. No angel." A woman speaking, but Arthur did not recognize the voice.

"Nice," said Moshe. "So if there was an angel, the angel could have done it."

"No other person. It doesn't have to be an angel." That was Leonard Shuk. Good for Leonard, Arthur thought.

"Also nice," Moshe said. "Why should Moses have the privilege? Maybe someone else would have come forward. But there was no eesh, no angel, no other person, so Moses did it."

"What do you mean, privilege? Since when is it a privilege to kill someone?" Another woman.

"Ah, my mistake. A bad choice of words. A mitzvah, then. A commandment."

"Since when is it a commandment to kill someone?" the same woman asked.

"Take a life to save a life." That was George Lopez, the veteran. "Sometimes it's a commandment to take a life, rather than let a person be murdered."

Silence.

"So," Moshe said, "Moses looked this way and that, saw there was no angel, no other person, and he did what was necessary, reluctantly. Is that okay?"

No one objected.

"Another commentary," Moshe continued. "Moses looks this way and that, as if he's looking into the future of the Egyptian, all the children that Egyptian is to produce, and into the past, all the ancestors from whom that Egyptian has descended, and sees that in all those generations there was no eesh, no person worthy of merit. Only then did he kill the Egyptian."

"If you kill a person it's as if you kill an entire world," Margolit said.

"Yes," Moshe agreed. "You kill not only the person, but all the people who might descend from that person."

"And if you save a person, it's as if you save an entire world," Margolit completed the teaching.

"Yes," Moshe said.

"Something else," Margolit added. "Maybe he didn't look into the future and the past of the Egyptian. Maybe he looked into the future and the past of himself."

"What do you mean?"

"Moses looked into his own past," Margolit said, "when he was living as a prince in the land of Egypt. He looked into his own future. If he killed the Egyptian, he would have to run away. He would no longer be a prince."

"So he didn't want to kill the Egyptian." A young girl's voice.

"No, he didn't want to kill the Egyptian . . ."

"But if he didn't, what kind of man would he be?"

"He wouldn't be an eesh."

"He looked this way and that, saw there was no eesh . . ."

"Unless he stepped forward to protect the Hebrew slave . . ."

"And did so knowing he would have to run away . . ."

"And be a shepherd instead of a prince."

One voice on top of the next, then silence.

"*Bi-makom she-ayn anashim, hishtadel li-hi-ot eesh*," Margolit said, quoting a familiar phrase from the Mishnah. "'In a place where there is no person, try to be one.'"

"Very nice," Moshe said. "Moses looked this way and that, and saw if he didn't do something, he wasn't much of a man. So he stepped forward and changed the course of history."

Silence.

"I think we should write it down," someone said. "This and the story of Pharaoh's daughter."

"We don't need to write them down," Moshe said. "If the words have worth, they'll find their own expression. The children will tell their friends.

174

Their friends will tell their parents. The words will make their way around."

The words would be buried. They would be buried, unless Arthur could find some release, some way out, some explanation. The words would be buried, as beautiful as they were, and Arthur would be the grave digger.

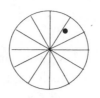

CHAPTER 12

SUNDAY, 1:20 P.M.

The next tape was dated but unlabeled. Wednesday, March 15, 7:30 P.M. Except for the bar mitzvah on Martin Luther King Day in the Everglades, all the other programs had been on Sunday mornings.

Why that Wednesday? And why at night?

He consulted the journal and found folded into it, between the pages of doodles and drawings, a sheet of limericks. One glance and he knew Wednesday, March 15, was the evening of the festival of Purim.

> Hagai put all the girls to a test,
> But Esther pleased him the best.
>   Others thought him a eunuch,
>   But she looked up his tunic
> And pleased him more than the rest.

> It was known all over the town
> Mordecai caused Haman to frown.
>   Before Haman the masses
>   Presented their asses
> But Mordecai would not bow down.

> Those who enter unsummoned aren't wise,
> For surely they're risking their lives.
>   Their only protection
>   Was a royal erection
> Of the king's golden scepter. Will it rise?

Esther considered her plight
And practiced her entrance all night.
    When the king saw her standing
    There was no reprimanding.
His favor rose in her sight!

Complained Haman, "Oh, woe is me!"
And asked his wife for a good prophecy.
    But his shrewish wife Zeresh
    Turned on him with relish
And said, "The screwer will be the screw-ee."

Such poems for family study, Arthur thought. The stories they did not write down, but these lewd limericks, these they wrote down. He considered discarding them, the first thought he had of destroying evidence.

Not that he would do so.

Not that he could do so.

Not that it would be of any benefit to do so.

If Brenda had a copy of the limericks in her journal, how many others had copies? They would be everywhere. Limericks like those spread like the measles. It was a wonder he had not seen them already, that a friend at the country club hadn't slipped them into his locker.

That thought cheered him somewhat. Perhaps they weren't from the family program at all. Perhaps they were from some other source. Brenda had merely inserted them into her journal. The hope was weak, but present as Arthur inserted the tape.

Children in costume. Esthers and Hamans and Mordecais. A Purim party in a home Arthur did not recognize.

Static.

The video restarted, focused on steps leading up to French doors.

"Ladies and gentlemen," an adult male off camera announced, "for your Purim evening pleasure, the Purim players present the story of Queen Esther. Scene one."

The doors opened, revealing a curtain backdrop.

"King Ahashuerus and his two advisors are drinking wine," the narrator said. A child king and child advisors came on stage pretending to drink wine.

"They have been drinking for 180 days. The king has an idea." The child king put his finger to his temple.

"Let's drink some more," the child king proclaimed.

"Then one of the advisors said . . ."

"Let's have Queen Vashti come and dance."

"How would she dance?" the narrator asked.

The three children wriggled their hips seductively to show how Vashti would dance.

Queen Vashti, a young boy in a dress, rouge, and lipstick, was escorted on stage. The others indicated how they wanted Vashti to dance. Vashti became angry, shook her head, and steamed off stage.

"What shall we do now?" the child king asked.

"We'll have a beauty contest to choose a new queen."

A parade of children followed, some dancing, some gesturing, some awkwardly, some with a grace that bordered on the sensual.

Arthur thought perhaps he could dispose of the tape along with the limericks, knowing he would do neither. He would like to dispose of the whole matter, throw it all away, go to sleep.

He opened his eyes to watch a Queen Esther chosen to the applause of the audience.

"End of the first scene," the narrator announced.

The doors closed and reopened.

"This is Mordecai," said the narrator. A handsome boy entered in a Shakespearean costume. "And this," the narrator's voice deepened, "is Haman."

The mention of the name induced a racket of noisemakers, stomping of feet, and pounding of pots and pans.

Two other boys came on stage. "Bigtan," the narrator announced, "and Teresh. They bow low to Haman." They bowed. "But would Mordecai bow?"

Tension on stage as Haman walked in front of Mordecai.

Before Haman the masses presented their asses, Arthur recalled from the limerick, astonished he remembered the words.

Mordecai would not bow. Haman, infuriated, walked off stage. Mordecai sat to one side, Bigtan and Teresh to the other, whispering words.

"What are they talking about?" the narrator asked.

"A plot against the king," someone shouted from the audience.

"Yes, a plot against the king. Mordecai overhears it. Mordecai goes offstage," the narrator waited for Mordecai to stand and walk off stage, "and he informs the king. Soldiers come to take Bigtan and Teresh away." Bigtan and Teresh were taken away. "And the whole story was printed in the morning edition of the *Shushan Herald*.

"End of scene two."

The French doors closed and were reopened to a scene of King Ahashuerus seated on a chair. A butler entered to offer the King some wine.

"Who should come to visit the king?" the narrator asked. "None other than Haman!"

The mention of the name triggered a loud banging and stomping. Purim always gave Arthur a headache. It was his least favorite of the holidays, a sanctuary filled with unruly children. The cantor read the megillah, beginning in Hebrew, continuing in English. Arthur's role was to keep the noise-making within proper bounds. He, too, wore a costume, but no matter what costume it was, he always felt like the Haman. It was his task to impose silence.

"Haman . . ." More noise.

". . . whispered into the ear of the king, 'There is a certain people who do not give the king proper honor. Would you please give me permission to kill all of them, take their money, and add it to your treasury?'

"The king thought about this long and hard, had another drink, and said, 'That sounds like a good idea.'

"No one in the entire kingdom was happier than Haman."

Lots more noise.

Yes, Arthur thought, if he had to mention the name of Haman at all, let it at least be at the end of a sentence. Then the interruption would come with the appropriate punctuation.

"End of scene three," the narrator announced when the noise subsided.

The play would take forever. Surely Arthur had seen enough of it, yet knew he had no real choice. Judge and jury were likely to view it in its entirety. There was some legal expression that pertained, though for the life of him, he couldn't remember it. Some kind of evidence.

"Scene four." Mordecai and Esther.

"You will have to go before the king," Mordecai said. "Don't imagine you will be saved because you are the queen. All the Jews in the land are to be killed."

Mordecai knew his lines, and so did Esther.

"But I can't just walk into the king's chambers unless he calls for me. If I come in unannounced, if he doesn't raise the royal scepter, I will be killed on the spot."

The only protection was a royal erection, Arthur remembered.

"You have no choice."

"Then pray for me. Everyone pray for me." Queen Esther turned to the audience and the camera. "Will you pray for me?"

Like Tinkerbell. What was it they were supposed to do to save Tinkerbell?

"Yes," the audience responded.

"End of scene four," said the narrator. "Scene five. The royal throne room."

King Ahashuerus sat in his chair, his throne. Haman stood by his side. Queen Esther entered, stage right. The king took notice of her and raised his scepter, a stick covered with gold foil.

His favor rose in her sight. Damn the limericks, Arthur thought.

"What can I do for you, Queen Esther? Even if it's half my kingdom, I will give it to you."

"All I ask," Queen Esther said, "Is that you come to my place tomorrow night for dinner. And please bring Haman with you."

Such noise upon the mention of Haman, Arthur turned the volume down. The king said something Arthur did not hear.

"End of scene five. Scene six, the king's bedroom."

"I can't sleep," the king said. "Someone bring the paper."

A servant entered with a *Miami Herald.*

"Who is this Mordecai?" the king asked. "He saved my life. Has anyone done anything for him?"

"No, your highness," said the servant.

"Who is in the court?"

"Haman."

A pounding of noise.

"Send him in."

Haman entered, mercifully without his name being mentioned.

"What would you do for a man the king wants to honor?" the king asked.

The narrator paused, apparently reluctant to say the name yet again. "Haman—" More pounding. "—thought the king wanted to honor him, so he said . . ."

"I would dress such a man in the king's clothes and ride him about on the king's horse and have someone announce, 'This is the man the king wants to honor.'"

"Then do that," the king said, "to Mordecai."

180

Haman appeared appropriately shocked.

"End of scene six," said the narrator.

Scene seven took place among the audience, Mordecai riding an adult or an older child in a horse costume about the room, led by Haman. The children loved it.

"Scene eight," the narrator said. "Queen Esther's chambers."

Queen Esther on her bed, the king and Haman sitting on chairs.

"What can I do for you?" the king asked. "Even if it's half my kingdom, I will give it to you."

"Only one thing," Queen Esther said.

"Anything. Anything at all."

"All I ask for is my life, and the life of my people, for there is someone who would kill me."

"Kill you? Who would do such a thing."

She raised her finger and pointed. "Haman," she said.

Such noise. Such pounding. Arthur closed his eyes. When he opened them, the king had gone, and Haman was on Queen Esther's bed, pleading for mercy.

The king returned and said, "What? In bed with my queen? You would do this, too? Away with him!"

Guards came and took Haman away, struggling and kicking.

"End of our play," said the narrator. "And the end of Haman."

Pounding. Stomping. Applause. Whistles.

The doors opened and the actors took their bows. Robert had been Mordecai. Andy had been Haman. Arthur didn't recognize the boy who played the king. And Esther, when she took off her wig, was Chris Clark. He got the most applause of all. A boy had played Esther, and Arthur hadn't so much as suspected it.

The screwer will be the screw-ee, he thought. *The screwer will be the screw-ee.*

Such a headache, he almost didn't hear the phone ringing. He reached for it, thankful Moshe was at last returning his call.

"Dad?"

"Hi, Tamar."

"Cindy said you called earlier. Is everything okay?"

The question took some time to penetrate. Arthur was speaking to his daughter, not Moshe. He was sweating, felt he might have fever. What time was it? Two in the afternoon, still morning in California.

"I'm okay," he said, no conviction in his voice.

"What are you doing in your study on a Sunday?"

"I have a problem here," he admitted.

"What kind of a problem?"

"Something I have to deal with myself."

"It must be serious."

"It might be."

Silence.

There were always those silences when he spoke with Tamar. How long did it take a phone message to bounce from Miami to a satellite and descend to Los Angeles? Why did so many Miami kids move to Los Angeles? So many questions, he forgot Tamar was on the phone until she spoke.

"I can't help you with it?"

"I don't think so. It's an ethics thing."

"Brenda again?"

How did she know about Brenda, let alone Brenda again?

"I'm sorry, honey. I'm not free to talk about it."

"She's a bitch. Don't let her get to you."

"I really can't talk about it."

Another silence.

It was his turn to break it. "How was your week? I tried reaching you on Shabbat, but you were out."

"We were with friends. Not far from here. Up in the hills. Pacific Palisades."

She was waiting for something.

"Shabbos friends?" he asked.

"Shabbos friends," she said. "It was very nice. A friend of Cindy's. A doctor, her husband, and their two children."

"It sounds nice."

What made her think this had to do with Brenda? Had her mother told her anything? When could she have told her?

And why was Brenda a bitch? Brenda had been like an aunt to Tamar when she was little. Why would Tamar say such a thing? Why did it give him hope?

"Do you remember the Purims we used to have?" Arthur asked.

"When I was a kid, you mean?"

"Yes."

"I remember. I remember dressing up like Charlie Chaplin. You burnt a cork and made me a moustache."

"That was Halloween."

"Are you sure?"

"Purim you would have been Vashti or Queen Esther."

"Vashti, maybe. Not Queen Esther."

"You don't like the Purim story?"

"I like Halloween better."

"Aren't you a little old for Halloween?"

Again, the silence.

Arthur said. "I'd better get back to work."

"We'll see you in July?"

"In July."

"You won't stay here? We really do have enough room."

"No. We don't want to impose. That hotel in the Marina. It's close by."

Still more silence.

"Call me if you want to talk, Dad."

"Okay. Thank you. I love you."

"I love you, too."

CHAPTER 13

SUNDAY, 2:00 P.M.

Arthur opened the journal and found an entry dated March 17, in green
ink.

> Moshe wore a bright green tie, a gift from Father O'Leary.
> Moshe promised he would wear it the entire day.
> Moshe and Father O'Leary have lunch every Tuesday. They talk
> about the difference between prayer and worship.
> Moshe says prayer is asking from God what we want, and wor-
> ship is offering to God what God wants.
> How are we supposed to know what God wants?
> Is wearing a green tie on St. Patrick's Day worship? Is wearing a
> green tie to a Shabbat dinner on St. Patrick's Day double worship?
> This wasn't technically a family Shabbat, just a Shabbat gather-
> ing at our house. No taping is permitted during the family Shabbats.
> That's the rule. But since this wasn't a family Shabbat, maybe I'm
> not really in violation.
> I didn't tell Moshe I taped his story, haven't told him.
> I wouldn't erase it anyway.
> Fran and Hal Rosen came and their son Jesse. Gina and Sol
> Davidoff and Elliott. Moshe, Daniel, and me. Nine altogether, but
> Moshe asked that we set the table for ten. Just in case.
> He and Rivkah always used to have an extra place, just in case.
> I like that.
> Candle lighting. Kiddush over the wine. Sol Davidoff sang it. He
> knows it by heart.

184

*Daniel seems to expect his blessing now. I still can't do it in He-
brew.*

*It was such a nice Shabbat dinner, relaxed. We sang songs. Even
Fran and Hal joined in.*

*I don't know why everyone can't have a Shabbat like that. We
didn't want to leave the table. Fran said it was easy when you knew
how. Moshe said it wasn't difficult to learn how. Fran said Hal
wasn't much interested in learning. Hal didn't say anything.*

I think they've been having that conversation for a long time.

*I talked about the Family Bayt Midrash, how we had learned to
do Shabbat dinners together. Moshe seemed kind of lost, not partici-
pating. He kept looking at the empty chair.*

I thought he was remembering Rivkah, but it was something else.

"I just realized a story," he said.

*That was his word. He realized a story. He didn't remember a
story. He didn't make up a story. He just realized it.*

*I excused myself, told him not to begin until I got back. He
thought I was going to the bathroom. I went to get the tape recorder.*

When I have time, I'll write the story down.

Moshe didn't give his story a title. I call it "The Empty Chair."

Arthur turned the page. Doodles. No story.

On his desk, an audiotape. He didn't have to listen to all of it, he told
himself.

Moshe was humming a niggun, one he had used before in the Family Bayt
Midrash. He wasn't singing. He was humming. Singing would have invited
other voices to join in. The humming, Arthur recognized, was a way of
turning inside.

"A family," Moshe began.

"No, a rabbi's family. A rabbi, his wife, and his daughter. She was maybe
ten, eleven years old. Becky. That would be nice. Her name was Becky. Her
father was a rabbi, her mother, Sheila.

"They had such beautiful Friday evenings, Shabbat dinners, a lovely
table, wonderful guests. Becky's friend, Mindy, the girl from across the
street, was sometimes among the guests. Mindy loved to be in Becky's home
for Shabbat dinner.

"One afternoon Mindy's mother knocked on the door of the rabbi's house. She didn't really know the rabbi or his wife. It took some courage for her to do this, to cross the street and knock on the door.

"The rabbi's wife answered the door. 'Yes?' she asked.

"'I'm Natalie Ginsberg, Mindy's mother, from across the street. Could I talk to you for a moment? Would it be all right?'

"'Of course it would be all right.'

"They sat in the kitchen. They had tea and talked of neighborhood things until Mrs. Ginsberg was ready to speak about what it was she had come to speak about.

"'It's about Shabbos,' she said. 'My daughter, my Mindy, has Shabbos so often with you. She comes home talking about it, so happy. I would like to have a Shabbos like that.'

"'So why not? Is there something you need to learn? I can teach you.'

"'It's not what I need to learn. Not that I don't need to learn. It's my husband.'

"'So he can learn, too.'

"Mrs. Ginsberg sighed. 'My husband doesn't want anything to do with Shabbos. Friday nights, he comes home late from work. He grabs a beer, a cigar, strips down to his undershirt, sits out on the back porch, and watches TV.'

"'What work does he do?'

"'He drives a cab.'

Damn him, Arthur thought. Damn him to hell. What was he doing? Who was this story for? What did Moshe know? How could Moshe know? Where the hell was this story coming from?

"'So if you made a nice Shabbos dinner, he might come home a little earlier.'

"'It doesn't matter what I make. Friday night, always the same thing. He won't listen to me. He won't listen to anyone. He doesn't want anything to do with Shabbos.'

"This was too much of a problem for the rabbi's wife. When her husband came home, she shared it with him. She told him about Mrs. Ginsberg and her husband, what the husband was like.

"'Let me think about it,' he said.

"The next day he told his wife he wanted to see Mrs. Ginsberg. Sheila went across the street to let her know the rabbi wanted to see her.

"'Can you help me with my husband?' she asked him. 'Can you help me make Shabbos in my house?'

186

"'No,' the rabbi said. 'I'm sorry. I can't do that. That's not really why I asked you to come over. It's because of something else. Your husband, what's his name?'

"'Bernie,' Mrs. Ginsberg said.

Barney, Arthur thought, not surprised by the similarity. Something was going on. Barney Greenberg, Bernie Ginsberg. A cab driver. Cigars. The back porch. Moshe knew something.

"'His full name?' the rabbi asked.

"'Bernard. Bernard Haskel Ginsberg.'

"'That's what I thought,' the rabbi said. 'And where was his family from in the old country?'

"'Poland.'

"'Yes, that's right. And do you know just where in Poland?'

"'Near Warsaw.'

"'Exactly right. Exactly right. Bernard Haskel Ginsberg. From Poland, somewhere near Warsaw.'

"'Not him, his father, of blessed memory. Hayim Ginsberg. He was the one who came over. That was a long time ago.'

"'Yes, of course. That's what I heard. Such a coincidence."

Moshe waited until someone asked. One of the young guests broke the silence.

"What was the coincidence?"

"You'll hear in just a moment," Moshe said. "Sometimes you have to have patience. Stories don't come all at once, you know.

"That night," his tone again that of the storyteller, "Mrs. Ginsberg was so excited, she could barely wait for her husband to come home.

"'Guess what?' she asked him.

"'I'm not in a mood for guessing,' he said as he reached into the fridge for a beer.

"'We're having a guest for dinner this Friday night.'

"'A guest for dinner? Since when do we have guests for dinner?'

"'She's a relative, someone from the old country who was related to our family.'

"'What do they want from us? Money?'

"'Just one person, and she doesn't need anything from us. She's royalty. A countess.'

"'A countess. You're telling me you're related to a countess?'

"'Not me. You. Your grandfather's cousin in Warsaw, a Ginsberg, married into royalty. She's been searching for her family. She's coming here to Miami to see you, to see us. She wants to meet us.'

"'You've got to be kidding.'

"'I'm not kidding. The rabbi himself told me so.'"

Moshe knew from Rivkah, and Rivkah knew from Charlotte. That's what it was, Arthur realized. Moshe knew the story, Barney Greenberg who had been shot on the back porch by the mob. Charlotte had talked about it with the girls. Moshe was creating a story of a man in an undershirt who needed to know about Shabbos, so he drew up distant memories of a Barney Greenberg who had something to do with cabs. That hint of a memory became Bernie Ginsberg.

But Moshe could not have known Arthur would ever be listening to the story. Moshe did not even know the story was being taped.

"'My family?' Bernie Ginsberg asked. 'Really? A countess is related to me?'

"Mindy was so excited, to be having such a guest. She told Becky, and Becky told her parents. Her father listened and nodded.

"That Friday night, Bernie Ginsberg came home early from work. He showered. His wife . . . What was his wife's name?"

"Natalie," a young voice said.

"Natalie. Natalie had made a beautiful meal. Mindy had set the table, a tablecloth, flowers, the best dinnerware, and an extra place for their guest.

"Natalie set out candles. Bernie opened a bottle of wine. They were ready.

"They waited.

"The time came for their guest to arrive, but she didn't come.

"They waited some more.

"There was a knock on the door. Natalie rushed to it, Mindy right behind her. They opened the door and saw . . . Becky.

"'My father told me to come to tell you he heard from the countess. She was delayed in New York at the last moment and wasn't able to reach you. She apologizes and says she'll come next week. She hopes she hasn't put you out.'

"You can imagine how disappointed the family was. They sat down to dinner with no one in the empty chair. But their disappointment dissolved in the chicken soup, with matzoh balls. And the chicken, and green beans and sweet potatoes. It was a wonderful meal, with candles and wine.

"Natalie and Mindy cleaned up after dinner. Bernie stripped down to his undershirt, grabbed a beer and a cigar, and went out to sit on the porch.

"But they all looked forward to the next week.

"The week passed slowly. Friday, Mindy set the table again. Natalie cooked, brisket and tzimmis. The candles on the table were lit, the wine uncorked. The time came for their guest to arrive.

"They waited.

"They waited some more.

"There was a knock on the door. Again, they went eagerly to answer it, and again, it was Becky.

"'My father sent me,' Becky said. 'He heard from the countess. She was in Palm Beach, on her way to Miami, and something happened. She had to stay there for the night. She's so sorry she's done this to you twice, but she's here in Florida. She promises she will come next week.'

"Again the family was disappointed, but astonishingly, not as disappointed as they were the previous week. They sat down to dinner and enjoyed the brisket and the tzimmis and the wine.

"Bernie stayed at the table for desert and had coffee before leaving for the porch with his cigar.

"A week passed. Mindy knew how to set the table. It came easily. Natalie prepared the meal. Fish. Baked fish like her grandmother used to make. They lit the candles on the table. Bernie opened the wine.

"The time came for the countess to arrive.

"They waited.

"They waited some more.

"There was a knock on the door, and they weren't surprised to see Becky.

"'My father said the countess is in town. She's on her way, but she doesn't want to keep you. She asks, please, if you would not wait dinner for her. Go ahead and eat, and she will join you for dessert.'

"They did as the countess had asked, conscious of the empty chair, but still very much enjoying the fish. They finished their dinner, cleared the plates, and waited.

"And waited some more.

"There was a knock on the door. They went, eager and apprehensive at the same time. They opened the door and found . . . Becky. And the rabbi. And the rabbi's wife. The rabbi's wife was carrying a cake, a big Bundt cake with yellow frosting.

"'We thought it was the countess,' Mindy said, disappointed.

"'Oh,' the rabbi said, 'the countess has been here all along. She's been here all this time. You just haven't seen her.'

189

"'What do you mean?' Mindy asked.

"'The countess always comes. Whenever you set an extra place on Shabbos and expect her, she always comes, whether you can see her or not.'

"That's how the rabbi taught Bernie Ginsberg to celebrate Shabbos," Moshe said.

That's all it was, Arthur thought. Something subliminal. Moshe was in Miami. Arthur was in Miami. Moshe knew something, not much of Arthur's family, only what Charlotte might have shared with the girls. Nothing more than that. The way he had made the little girl a Becky, a memory from the stories of his wife's childhood, so he had made Mindy's father a Bernie, a subliminal impression of Barney Greenberg.

It couldn't be anything more than that. It was a story to be told once, realized, as Moshe himself had said.

There was no way Moshe could know the effect the story would have on Arthur, in his study, sleepless for more hours than he could count, struggling to stay awake, to keep from crying.

The journal continued, in blue ink.

> *I must have listened to that story ten times.*
>
> *I asked Moshe about it, where it came from. All he could do was shrug.*
>
> *I asked him if he would tell it again. He said, if it came up again.*
>
> *The story was for Hal. I have no doubt about that.*
>
> *I asked Moshe if that was why he told the story, because he was trying to find a way to teach Hal about Shabbat. Moshe said he didn't know why he told stories. He told them because they came to the surface.*
>
> *I should share this story with Arthur. It would be great to use at a family service.*
>
> *But I'd need Moshe's permission first. And for that, I'd have to tell him I recorded it.*
>
> *So, we'll see. Maybe the story will come to the surface again. Maybe not.*

CHAPTER 14

SUNDAY, 2:40 P.M.

Arthur checked the time. Not yet noon in California. He reached for the phone and dialed Tamar, praying he would reach his daughter, not Cindy, not a machine. His prayer was answered.

"I need to know something," he said to her, "if you're willing to share it with me. You said Brenda was a bitch. Why did you say that?"

"Because she is."

"That's not helping me."

It was Tamar's turn to make the silence. Arthur waited. "Because of what she says," Tamar said. "And the way she says it."

"What does she say?"

"Not such nice stuff about Cindy and me."

Arthur considered that. Saying not such nice stuff about a lesbian couple wasn't nice, befitting, or proper, but it also wasn't unusual. There had been a time when jokes about queers, butches, and dykes were part of his own repertoire.

"And others," Tamar added.

"Women couples?"

"Any couple that's working right. You haven't noticed?"

"Noticed what?"

"She always has something nasty to say, some barb to insert."

This wasn't helpful. *Lashon ha-ra*, slander, evil speech, was a serious transgression, but a common one. It was hard to unsheathe the tongue without doing damage to someone. The rabbis considered it the most dangerous of weapons. "I hear what you're saying," he said to his daughter, "but everyone says bad things now and then."

"She does it differently."

"How so?"

"It's like I said. She has bad things to say about what's working right. She maligns couples that are doing well together. Like you and Mom."

Arthur felt a chill. "What does she say about us?"

"Nothing. She just hints that underneath that rosy front you show to the world there's got to be something going on. Little barbs. She can't let well enough alone. About me and Cindy she's been downright nasty, so much so it gets back to us. She can't stand it when something's going right."

Arthur was too tired, and this was too much. He had noticed that about Brenda, but dismissed it as a fundamental cynicism, a residue of mourning for her own marriage. But there was another dissonance with which he was struggling. Brenda was maligning Tamar's relationship with Cindy because it was going right. How could that relationship be going right?

Tamar spoke into her father's confusion. "Cindy and I are okay together, Dad. For right now, it's the right thing." Were his thoughts so transparent? "I've been learning how to talk about it. We go to group together. The best I've heard is that there's a difference between sex and gender. Sex is male or female. Gender is the identification as male or female, and that's different for every person. Even in the same person, different at different times."

Venice, California. The place to learn how to talk about such things. Was that why so many Miami kids went West? "I have to think about this." That was all he could bring himself to say.

"Thank you," Tamar said.

"For what?"

"For thinking about this."

"I love you," Arthur said, knowing as the words were uttered he hadn't said them like that in a long time.

"I love you, too."

He hung up the phone, but, for the first time in many months, without breaking the connection.

Arthur was hungry.

On the coffee table he set out a paper plate, fork, and knife. There was a bagel left, some warm cream cheese. Had there been time enough for it to go bad? He wouldn't trust the remnants of the lox.

He drew a cup of water from the cooler in his secretary's office. He paused at the coffeemaker. Not yet. Later, maybe.

His secretary kept cheese crackers in the bottom drawer of her desk. He borrowed them.

That would be enough. He sat to his banquet and resolved not to think of the case before him, only his repast.

Charlotte would be getting home soon. What was the weather like? Had it been choppy on the bay? What was the difference between sex and gender?

Women talked. That was their nature. They talked about intimate things, whatever was on their minds. Witness Charlotte. She had shared the story of Arthur's family with the girls on the Upper West Side. She had shared it with Rivkah, and Rivkah with her husband, and so Arthur's history had worked its way into Moshe's story. That was all right. It didn't matter. He wasn't that Arthur anymore. He had Charlotte to thank for that, and Rabbi Perlstein.

When Rabbi Perlstein had died . . . how long ago? Four years? Five? Arthur and Charlotte had flown to Paterson for the funeral. He had walked with Rabbi Perlstein for the last time up the hill. After the grave was closed, he and Charlotte visited the graves of his parents. There were no pebbles on top of the granite marker. No one had visited.

"You never talk about them," Charlotte said.

"I guess the memories aren't good."

"You never talk about your brother."

"I don't know much about him. What I do know, I don't want to talk about."

"What do you think ever happened to their baby?"

That was a memory he did not care to pursue. They left a pebble before they started down the hill.

That was the last time he had visited his parents' graves. The pebble was surely no longer there, but the memory was, even the one he didn't care to pursue.

Arthur looked at his hands. His fingers were orange. He had been eating the cheese crackers from the box.

In the bathroom he washed his hands.

One washed hands after returning from a cemetery.

> *March 19th—A Walk through Sinai*
> *10:30 sharp.*
> *Gather at The Falls, in the parking lot west of Macy's.*

193

Bring: Hats, walking shoes, water. No credit cards. No identification of any kind.

All drivers licenses, wallets, keys, will be collected at the beginning of the exercise.

Bring exactly $4 per person. No more. That, too, will be collected at the beginning of the exercise.

Wear jewelry. Gold, diamonds, bracelets, necklaces, earrings.

The Falls had languished until Bloomingdale's built to the east and Macy's to the west. Then the center flourished, a Mecca to well-heeled shoppers from Pinecrest, Kendall, even Coral Gables.

Pasted inside the journal, a text printed on pink paper.

PASSAGE THROUGH SINAI

1. READ THIS ALOUD: Welcome to this side of the Red Sea. You are about to begin a forty-year journey through the Sinai desert. When you left Egypt, you brought only the clothes you were wearing. You had no weapons, no credit cards, no money, no keys, no driver's licenses, no identification. But you did have jewelry. Whatever wealth you had, you wore.

2. Here are the rules for the march through the Sinai desert. If you look to the south, you can see the Red Sea. It's full of crocodiles. If not crocodiles, certainly alligators, and that's for real. Don't go near it. Your task will be to head east, between the mountain range (which looks remarkably like the back of a shopping mall) and the sea. Before you begin, choose a leader—a Moses. Moses in turn will choose an Aaron. When Moses wants to tell the people something, he speaks to Aaron, and Aaron speaks or selects someone to speak to the people.

3. First, remember the story of how you came through the Red Sea.

4. Then elect your Moses and choose an Aaron.

5. NO DRINKING UNTIL YOU RECEIVE INSTRUCTIONS TO DO SO.

6. Instructions come from God. God leaves messages on papers that look like this. Find the messages, bring them to Moses and Aaron, and they will instruct you what to do.

7. Good luck.

BEWARE OF AMALEK!

Moshe had so many things going on at once, on so many levels.
We gathered at the Falls, as instructed.

Word had gotten out about the Sinai march, much as it had for
the Purim hunt. We were no longer the Family Bayt Midrash. We
were a tribe.

Thursday night, the Purim hunters had gathered at the other end
of the mall, as the sun was setting, on the top of Bloomingdale's
garage. Maybe forty of us. The instructions were to wear hats and
bring Bibles.

Moshe had left a packet of information. Hunters were to work in
pairs. Each pair had a map of the mall, a page of code linked to verses
from the Book of Esther, and a starting limerick. We had to find the
verse on the code sheet that best matched the limerick, go to the place
indicated in the mall, and find there a person in a hat to ask for the
next limerick. From store to store, hat to hat, limerick to limerick.
Ten in all. We finished up at Seasons for a late dinner.

It was wonderful fun, I think more so for the newcomers who had
never experienced learning like that.

They heard from us about the Sunday march through Sinai. So
we were a tribe that gathered at the west end of Macy's.

Had there been children at that Purim scavenger hunt? Arthur wondered. Such prurient material. He turned some pages back and read again
the five limericks. *Before Haman the masses presented their asses.* Only five
limericks out of ten. He shook the journal. No more came out.

He felt cheated.

Jews don't hunt. That was Arthur's thought as he sunk into his wing chair
and started the video. But if Jews did hunt, they would do so at a fashion
mall.

There was not much shade, even at 10:30 in the morning. The families,
a great many of them, hugged the building. The camera was shoulder high
and focused on Michelle Kantor, who held a big stick and read from a paper.

"At the Red Sea the people complained to Moses and said, 'Weren't
there enough graves in Egypt? You had to bring us out here to die in the
desert?' Things looked bad for the Hebrews. The Egyptian army was coming
down on them from one side, the Red Sea was on the other. Moses asked
God what he should do. God said to Moses, 'Why are you crying out to me?

195

Tell the people to go forward, and as for you, raise your staff and stretch out your hand over the sea.' So Moses raised his staff." Michelle raised her staff and stretched her hand out toward the families. "Nothing happened. Moses went back to God and asked, 'Nu?' God said, 'Why didn't you do what I told you to do?' Moses went back, raised the staff again. Still nothing happened. 'Do what I told you to do,' God said again."

She folded the paper and put it in her pocket. "A question for those who are new to the Family Bayt Midrash. What had Moses forgotten to do?"

Arthur remembered a midrash about that. He wondered if they taught it in the religious school. He suspected not.

Michelle waited, retrieved the paper from her pocket, made a show of unfolding it. "God said to Moses, 'Why are you crying out to me? Tell the people to go forward, and as for you, raise your staff and stretch out your hand over the sea.'"

"Tell the people to go forward," several of the newcomers said.

"Yes. Moses had forgotten to tell the people to go forward. So he stood on a rock, looked out toward the Red Sea, and told the people to go forward.

"The people said he had to be kidding. They didn't know how to swim.

"'Still,' Moses told them, 'that's what God said to do.'

"One man, Nachshon, had enough faith to do what God asked. He took a step forward into the sea. The water ran away from his foot. He took another step. The water ran away faster. He ran into the sea, and the water piled up in walls, it was in such a hurry to move away. When the people saw this, they all rushed into the sea.

"Moses went back to God and asked, 'So what's the stick for, then?'

"'Oh, that,' God said. 'That's to impress the Egyptians.'"

Walk softly and carry a big stick, Arthur thought.

Mario Kantor stepped forward. "Now that we're on the other side of the Red Sea we have to choose a Moses and prepare for a march through the Sinai. Whoever carries the staff will be Moses, but after a while, hand the staff over to somebody else. We'll let Moses choose his or her own Aaron. Okay? Who's first?"

Several of the children pushed Robert up front. He took the staff and selected the older Shuk girl to be his Aaron.

"These are the rules," Mario said. He held up a burlap sack. "All money, wallets, car keys, identification . . . everything but your jewelry, in this sack. Pass it around please.

196

"No one goes near the canal. There are alligators in it. Stay near the building. We will be looking for messages from God to help us on our way. Messages from God are written on pink paper like this. Be on the lookout for them. We can't miss any of them. This will be a dangerous journey."

The journey began.

The children rushed to the front. One Arthur did not recognize shouted he had found a message from God. He brought it to Robert who passed it to the Shuk girl. She read, "Beware of Amalek."

"Louder!"

"Beware of Amalek!" she shouted. "There is a tribe of robbers who live in the desert. They rob only the weak, unprotected people, people who have no weapons but lots of jewelry. If they think you have no protection, they will come down upon you like a plague. Learn how to march as if you were the strongest people in the world, in formation like an army. Maybe Amalek will be afraid of you. Maybe not."

Several of the adults attempted to organize the children into ranks. The children would have none of it. This was too much fun. They ran in search of the next message from God.

"Be careful," Mario Kantor shouted. He must have been standing close to the camera, his voice was so loud. "The journey is dangerous."

The journey was dangerous, Arthur thought. He found himself walking through the quarter, down Bourbon Street, trying to look as if he belonged there, not like a mark. The streets were full of marks. He was one among many. If Amalek descended from the alleys, they would pounce on the stragglers. He tried not to look like a straggler.

He wore his shirt sleeve over his gold watch, kept his gaze straight ahead. He didn't look at the lurid photos on the right, ignored the hustlers trying to suck him in to the left. He walked down Bourbon Street, beyond the clubs and noise, deep into the French Quarter.

Arthur blinked, opened his eyes, and watched the children searching the nooks and crannies of the back side of the shopping mall. What were they looking for? A message from God.

Jonah had called. "Hey, Artie." No one else but Jonah began a conversation, "Hey, Artie."

"Hey, Jonah."

"I need to see you."

"Another message from God!" a child announced.

"This one is labeled 'The Rock of Moses,'" the girl said.

197

"It's time for someone else to be Moses and Aaron," a child protested.

Without complaint, Robert passed his staff to another boy, and the Shuk girl handed the note to a man standing behind her.

"The Rock of Moses," the man read. "Are you thirsty? Somehow you will have to get through the desert for forty years. Where will you find water?

"The people complained to Moses. They said, 'Better we had stayed in Egypt rather than come here into the desert to die of thirst.'

"Moses said, 'You people have so little faith. Didn't God open up the sea and save us? Surely God will help us find water.'

"Pretty soon Moses was thirsty. He went to God and asked, 'So where do we get water? The people are driving me nuts.'

"God said, 'Speak to the rock by the side of the mountain, and water will come forth.'

"Moses went to the people and said, 'You want water? I'll give you water!' He hit the rock by the side of the mountain. Water came out.

"They continued walking. When the people became thirsty again, Moses hit another rock, but nothing happened.

"'Where's the water?' Moses asked God.

"'I told you to speak to the rock, not to hit it,' God said. 'Why is it you people never do what I say?'

"'But what are we to do for water?'

"'Keep walking. You'll figure it out eventually."

The children continued walking. The back side of the mall was dotted with stairways and railings, Dumpsters and fire hydrants. The children looked everywhere, under everything, searching for another message from God.

Arthur kept walking, down Bourbon Street, beyond the lights, into the darkness. He had become both a mark and a straggler. Jonah had called and wanted to see him in New Orleans. An address, directions, a phone number.

Could Jonah have come to Miami? It was out of the question.

"I've got one!"

Arthur's eyes snapped open.

A child with a pink paper ran toward the camera.

"We have to choose a Miriam," she said. There was an envelope attached to the paper. "It's supposed to be opened only by Miriam."

"Who wants to be Miriam?" Mario asked.

A tall, thin girl with long dark hair answered the door. "You're Artie," she said.

A tall, thin girl with long dark hair stepped forward to be Miriam. She

198

opened the envelope and announced it was a letter from God. There was something else in the envelope. A piece of black plastic that she unfolded, a circle, a bit smaller than a manhole cover.

"What's in the letter?"

She read it. "Dear Miriam. So nice of you to come and visit. I know the people are thirsty, so I'm giving you a special present. I don't want to give it to your brother, Moses. He can be such a pain sometimes. All you need to get water in the desert is a special well. What is a well? A well is a hole in the ground. If you have faith you will find water. When you dig the hole you will find water. If you have no faith, when you dig the hole, you will find only a hole. So in this envelope you will find a black hole. Put it on the ground. If the people have faith, they will be able to reach into the hole and find water. Have a good walk. Love, God."

"There's a PS," she said. "God says anytime we want to drink, you have to ask me to put the hole onto the ground. It's Miriam's well. No drinking without the well."

She laid out the black plastic on the asphalt of the service road. Kids opened their water bottles and drank. The adults also.

"A text for adults only," Mario said. He removed the paper clip from a sheath of papers. "While the kids look for the next message, a text for us to study."

Arthur sighed. Better study than sleep. Perhaps the text was in the journal.

THE WELL AND THE PIT

People congregate around a well and shun a pit like a plague.
Treaties and marriages are made at wells. People die in pits. Pits cause damage.
Hebrew for well is *be-air*. Hebrew for pit is *boor*.
באר well. *BAYT ALEF RESH*
בור = pit. *BAYT VAV RESH*
A well contains water. A well contains an *Alef. Alef* has the value of ONE. At a well one ponders the ONE and comes to an understanding. Understandings lead to treaties and marriages.
A pit is empty. *Boor* can be written empty, without the letter *vav.* No understandings. Only damage and death.
Watch out for the black hole. When you approach it, consider well what is in it.

Nice. Arthur wondered where Moshe had learned that.

"Larry found something," an older child shouted as the mob of children streamed toward the camera.

Larry, maybe nine years old, approached with a bag and a pink paper.

"Manna," the person playing Aaron said. The camera focused on her. She read, "The people became hungry, very hungry. They complained to Moses. Moses said, 'Look, God's not too happy with me since I hit the rock. Whatever God will do, God will do. Don't bother me anymore. Leave me alone.'

"The next day, when the people woke up, there was something on the ground, something unusual. 'What is it?' they asked.

"'Manna,' said Moses, meaning he had no idea, but the people took him at his word and called it manna.

"They ate it, and it satisfied their hunger. It tasted like whatever they wanted it to taste like.

"Moses said, 'Each day pick up only what you will need for the day. On Friday, you can pick up enough for two days, so you will have enough for Shabbat.'

"People who had no faith picked up as much as they could carry, but what was left over for the next day rotted and became worms and gunk that smelled very bad.

"Only on Shabbat could they eat leftovers."

The woman who was playing Aaron scattered wrapped candy across the service road. The children pounced on it.

"Only what you can eat now," she said. "Don't put any in your pockets."

Sesame honey candy, Arthur thought, not that he could see what kind of candy it was. That was what he would have liked it to be, what he wanted at the moment. Sesame honey candy, like his mother brought back from the market in Paterson. That and Indian nuts. He hadn't seen Indian nuts, in the shell, for decades. Pine nuts, they were called now. Pignolia. They tasted better when they were Indian nuts.

He had expected a dump, but the apartment had some charm. The walls were painted New Orleans colors. No confusing that with Paterson, New Jersey.

"Where's Jonah?" he asked the tall, thin girl, her hair so long, so black.

Jonah was in his bed, dying. "Hey, Artie," he said.

"How you doing, Jonah?"

Jonah laughed. The laughter caused him pain.

"Would you like something to eat?" the tall, thin girl asked.

"Would you like something to eat?" the flight attendant asked. He hadn't eaten anything in New Orleans, nor did he eat anything on the flight home.

The bagel and the cheese crackers were not enough. Surely Charlotte would be home. The children were standing in line by a garden hose, waiting to wash their hands. Why were they washing their hands?

Arthur rewound the tape until he saw a flash of pink. "Preparing for Sinai," a man read. "Pretty soon you will reach Mount Sinai. You will climb the mountain to receive the Ten Commandments. Before climbing the mountain, you must be clean. You must wash your hands. The rule for hand washing is this. You cannot wash your own hands. Someone else must pour water into your hands so you can clean them. The blessing for washing hands is—"

Arthur stopped the tape. He knew the blessing for washing hands.

There was something he had missed, something that had flashed by as the tape was running backward. He started it again, endured the blessing, and found what had made the impression. Moshe and Daniel, in line, holding hands. Moshe had Daniel put his hands out and poured water over them. Then he handed the hose to Daniel. Daniel washed Moshe's hands. The camera caught the two of them, singled them out.

Where was Brenda? Brenda must have been doing the camerawork. That was why he hadn't seen her.

Moshe and Daniel. Arthur was certain if he rewound the tape and watched it again, awake, with care, he would find Moshe often with Daniel, hand in hand.

He went to his desk to call Charlotte.

A busy signal. She was talking to someone. If they had call waiting . . . But Charlotte wouldn't have call waiting. Rude, she said, to put one person on hold to speak to another. The person you were speaking to deserved your full attention. The other person would call back.

He would call back.

The tape had been running. The families were climbing Sinai, the Bloomingdale's parking garage, empty on a Sunday morning. The camera followed behind Moshe and Daniel. Surely it was Brenda who carried it.

Jonah lived on the second floor, not an unattractive place. Unusual. The colors. The balcony outside his bedroom, facing the street. A railing of ironwork. Arthur imagined Mardi Gras, women standing on the balcony, raising their tops to shake their tits at the men below. The thought caused him pain, a headache behind his eyes.

Jonah was in pain. A gaunt Jonah. A weak Jonah. Barely able to sit up in bed. No matter if those who had been looking for him knew his address. After all those years, no matter anyway.

"This is Grace." Jonah made the introduction. A toddler stood beside the tall, thin girl, who held his hand. "And this is Jeremy." Jeremy seemed unafraid, unperturbed, unaware. "Our son."

The top floor of Bloomingdale's garage was bright in the noon light. Mario Kantor stood at the center of the families. "Welcome to a new world," he said. "After Sinai, the world was different for the Hebrews. They had a purpose. A purpose, but little else. Ten Commandments and four dollars." He looked at his watch. "In a few minutes Bloomingdale's will open. You have those minutes to memorize the Ten Commandments. When each family knows all ten, go to either Marty Cohen or Bruce Holstein. If you know the Ten Commandments and have them in the right order, they will give each person four dollars. Nothing else.

"Then you enter the promised land. Bloomingdale's." The families laughed. "Heaven and hell at the same time. Bloomingdale's, but only four dollars. No credit cards. No checks. Walk down through Bloomingdale's, through the Falls. See where you can have lunch for four dollars per person. Have lunch. Then find us in front of Macy's, at the other end of the mall." He looked at his watch. "We'll meet there in forty-five minutes."

Jonah had a family.

Mario distributed pink papers. A message from God, no doubt. The Ten Commandments. Families huddled to study. Family by family, they rose to pass through the pearly gates. It was noon, Bloomingdale's was open for Sunday business.

A nice program, Arthur thought. They would have trouble finding lunch in the Falls for four dollars, but that was part of the program. Moshe was an artist. Everything had significance, everything evocative. Such creativity. What price had he paid to gain such creativity? What imbalance had it caused? What damage would come from it?

The phone rang and rang. At last Charlotte picked up.

"I was speaking with Tamar," she explained. "She was worried about you."

"I'm worried about me, too," Arthur said. "How was your day? Smooth sailing?"

"A bit choppy, but fun. Norma and Harry were there. They missed you. We all missed you."

"What did you tell them?"

"You were busy with rabbi stuff."

Rabbi stuff, Arthur thought. That's what he had been doing.

"Are you done with it yet?"

"Not yet."

"Why not come home? I'll fix you something. Take a nap."

Arthur measured the pile left on his desk. How many hours did it represent? Three? Four? "I don't want to leave until I finish it. I don't want to leave and have to come back."

Charlotte was quiet a moment. "This seems worse than anything you've ever been through."

"Yes."

"Worse than the Sneider thing." Sneider was the man who had tried some years back to get Arthur fired and brought the contract to a congregational vote.

"Yes."

"How much more do you have to do?"

"Three, four hours. But I'll stay all night if I have to. It has to be done by nine o'clock tomorrow morning."

"What can I do for you?"

"I really don't want to leave until I've finished it. Would you bring me something to eat? What time is it? Maybe in an hour? I'll take a nap until then. Ring me to let me know you're coming." He was about to hang up. "One more thing! Before you come here, would you drive out to Moshe's house, see if he's there? He's not answering the phone. He's probably not there. It's a long shot. But I really need to speak with him."

Arthur settled on the couch. An hour, a blessed hour. He closed his eyes to sleep, then snapped them open lest he dream. Why should he be afraid to dream? Jonah was in his dreams. He wasn't afraid of Jonah.

The child was in his dreams.

He could keep the child out of his dreams, by force of will. Again he closed his eyes, felt the ache behind them, concentrated on that until the phone rang.

He could stop the ringing in his dreams, but not the ringing on his desk.

203

"Has it been an hour?" he asked.

"More than an hour," Charlotte said. "I ordered Chinese. See you in a few minutes."

He must have been sleeping, because he had that taste in his mouth. In the bathroom he brushed his teeth and saw himself in the mirror. Haggard, he thought, a word he couldn't remember using, surely one he had never applied to himself. That's what haggard looked like, that thing in the mirror. It surprised him. This was worse than the Sneider thing. Then it was ten hours on the phone, his committee, calling congregants, answering questions, getting out the vote. That was him against Sneider. This was him against . . .

Who was he against? Moshe? He wasn't against Moshe. His task was to save Moshe, though he doubted he could do it. He hadn't always doubted it. Only a few hours before, he had hope, but the hope seemed gone. Why?

Because Moshe hadn't been holding Margolit's hand. He should have been holding Margolit's hand.

But Margolit hadn't been in the video, nor her daughter. No Orly. He hadn't seen either of them. They must have been away that day. That explained it. Margolit wasn't there. He couldn't hold her hand. So he held Daniel's instead.

The thought gave him comfort, raised his hopes. He looked into the mirror, hoping to see himself less haggard. Perhaps he was. He couldn't tell.

There would be a wedding. It was on his desk somewhere. Stephanie was coming back for the wedding. Moshe and Margolit, and Brenda furious. What would she not do in her anger? A woman scorned. She would see great crimes in misdemeanors, interpret coincidence perversely. A few questions, sympathetic questions, a point made here or there would be enough to open her eyes and dispel the charges.

He was working so hard to give himself hope, he was astonished by the pounding on the door.

CHAPTER 15

SUNDAY, 5:15 P.M.

"Sorry," he said to Charlotte.

"I thought you'd fallen back to sleep."

"It was like I hardly slept at all."

The food smelled good through the bag.

"Where shall we eat?" she asked.

"What did you bring?"

"Egg rolls. Honey garlic chicken. Orange Szechuan beef."

"We'd better eat in my study," Arthur said. The temple kitchen was kosher, even if most of the congregants weren't. He and Charlotte kept a kosher house but ate non-kosher food outside.

Chinese food was a favorite of Arthur's. It was considerate of Charlotte to bring it. It was not her favorite.

"I went by Moshe's house," she said. "The Porsche was in the driveway, but he wasn't home." She paused. "Or if he was home, he didn't come to the door."

Arthur ate slowly. Chinese food he usually gulped down, a habit acquired at Rutgers. The guys at the dormitory went out once a week to eat Chinese. Shared food, chopsticks only. One learned to use chopsticks with facility. In his study, Arthur put his chopsticks down after every mouthful, chewed his food deliberately. He expected he would have indigestion anyway.

He didn't want to talk about Moshe. He asked Charlotte about her day. They had sailed over to Elliott Key, anchored for lunch. She had gone swimming and had difficulty climbing back into the boat. The water had been warm. There was no more for her to say. She left the direction of the conversation to him.

"What if I weren't a rabbi?" Arthur began. "What if I gave this up?" He looked around his study and shrugged his shoulders, as if throwing off the hands that had ordained him. "What would I do? I'm fifty-two."

"Is it that bad?" Charlotte asked.

"No. Not this. This doesn't have anything to do with me directly. But all of it," he looked around again, "it's wearing me down. I don't look forward to it anymore. I can't wait to be away. Each year, it sets in earlier. June, May, April. I want the year to be over, to go away.

"I'm fifty-two. Thirteen years to retirement, and I'm beginning to count them. This thing," he waved his hand to the stack of materials on his desk, "is just an annoyance. A major annoyance. It may make things difficult for a while. More difficult.

"I've been thinking about Jonah," he added.

"And the baby?"

"Not a baby anymore."

"What have you been thinking?"

"Nothing. Just about him. I don't know what one thing has to do with the other." He paused to look directly at her. She held his gaze, a wife, a social worker. "It's been a difficult day," he said and turned away.

"No way out?"

"Maybe." He walked to his desk and read the label of the videotape at the top of the pile. "Maybe here. Do you want to see?"

The tape was labeled, "Saturday night, April 1." Saturday night was not the time for a family program. This had to be something else.

A back yard. A hupah. The wedding canopy was constructed of four poles and a large tallit. The camera was fixed, up high, maybe in a tree, or on top of a ladder. Moshe was there, wearing a jacket, no tie. He did not look like a groom, but Arthur would not give up hope so quickly. From what he knew of Moshe, he might indeed dress that way for his own wedding.

Some of the people Arthur recognized.

"The Garfinkels," Charlotte said. "The Kantors. That's Shoshana Lopez."

And Brenda Karman. Brenda was there, not upset. There talking with some people Arthur did not know. Not animated, not angry.

A woman Arthur did not recognize beckoned people to come together. Some chairs were in a semicircle about the hupah. Some sat. Most stood behind the chairs.

"My name is Stephanie Lee," the woman said. "Margolit and Dana have asked me to preside over this ceremony. Let's take a moment or two before we bring them forward, so we can consider what is happening, what changes, what becomes different. They have been together for a half dozen years. God willing, they will be together for decades to come. So what changes?

"They have been living in a committed relationship. They will continue to live in a committed relationship. What changes now is the responsibility of the couple to the community, the community to the couple. We acknowledge their relationship is precious to us, and we are to provide for them a fertile ground in which to nourish that relationship and allow it to grow."

Stephanie nodded to Orly, who stepped forward with her violin, tucked it under her chin, and began what might have been a Bach partita, plaintive, complex, profound. Family stood around the hupah, parents of the couple most likely. Margolit and Dana walked together down the center aisle, both in simple white dresses. When they came under the hupah, they turned about to face the community. Arthur recognized them both, Margolit surely, but also Dana. Her face had appeared often in the videos. He simply had never associated the two of them.

Stephanie recited *bruchot ha-ba-ot* to welcome the couple under the hupah. Her words were mostly lost in Arthur's amazement. Only when Margolit placed a ring on Dana's finger and said in Hebrew, *"Ha-ray at mi-kudeshet lee . . ."* and then in English, "By means of this ring you are made holy to me according to the laws of Moses and Israel," did he really pay attention to the words. He felt a flush, then a flash of anger. How could this be according to the laws of Moses and Israel? Dana in turn placed a ring on Margolit's finger and repeated the same formula in Hebrew and English.

"They are made holy to each other," Stephanie said. "Holy means separate, reserved to each other for all intimacies, physical, emotional, intellectual, spiritual . . ."

Arthur looked to Charlotte to see if she shared his feelings. She was crying, making no motion to wipe the tears from her cheeks.

". . . a receiving blanket for a newborn marriage," Stephanie was saying. *"Sheva brachot,* seven blessings that have been passed down through the generations with which to wrap and comfort a new marriage."

An older couple, most likely Dana's parents, walked from the right side of the hupah and stood in front of the couple. They consulted a paper and read, "You are blessed, O Lord, our God, ruler of the universe, for you have created everything to reflect your glory, and we are all blessed to see this glory so wonderfully reflected in this holy relationship."

The community responded, "Amen." The parents kissed the couple.

Other members of the community came forward to offer blessings.

"You are blessed, O Lord, our God, ruler of the universe, who has created humankind. What a blessing we can find in one another strength to compensate for our weaknesses, so we can become together both human and kind."

"You are blessed, O Lord, our God, ruler of the universe, who has created us in the divine image, the very image of God. From Your own essence you have created for us such everlasting wonder. You are blessed, O Lord, creator of humankind."

"May your children, and all that you produce between you, rejoice in your fulfillment and share in your completion. You are blessed, O Lord, who causes us to delight in our children."

"May these two lovers constantly rejoice in each other, and find in each other the delight of Paradise. You are blessed, O Lord, who creates intimate relationships that provide a source of delight, one for the other."

"You are blessed, O Lord, our God, ruler of the universe, creator of joy and happiness, rejoicing and celebration, pleasure and delight, love and good feelings, shalom and friendship. May the joy that you experience here at this moment radiate outward to fill the whole community and the whole world, so that there should be rejoicing even in the streets of Jerusalem, because we are rejoicing in you here. You are blessed, O Lord, who makes unions that become a source of happiness."

The blessings were both right and wrong at the same time. The words were wrong, the feelings were right.

A Chinese man, no doubt Sidney Lee, stepped forward, raised a cup of wine, and began chanting the blessings in Hebrew. Again the words were wrong, the feelings right.

Someone Arthur did not know took a small tallit, wrapped it around the two women to bring them together, and pronounced the priestly blessings. "May the Lord bless you together and keep you together. May the Lord cause his light to shine upon you and be gracious to you. May the Lord watch out for you, and enable the two of you together to find shalom, fulfillment, peace. Amen."

Orly came forward with another girl, a girl about twenty, Dana's daughter, Arthur guessed. They each put glasses wrapped in napkins on the ground. Both women, arms around each other, stomped on the glasses. The community shouted, "*Mazal tov!*"

The women kissed, embraced. Family and friends swarmed to them. The hupah fell over, dropped behind them.

There was nothing else to see.

"Is that it?" Charlotte asked, her tone defiant. "Is that it? Is that what's causing you so much pain and anguish?"

"What do you mean?"

"A lesbian wedding."

"No, that's not it. That's not what I expected at all."

"Who has been giving you trouble over this? Is it a contract thing, they want you out because there was a lesbian wedding?"

"No, nothing like that. I didn't even know about the wedding. Nobody has so much as mentioned it to me."

Charlotte considered that. "Then that's what's wrong."

There was this difference between them. Charlotte from the first was more accepting of Tamar's relationship with Cindy. Should her daughter wish it, Charlotte would surely accept and cherish the sanctification of that relationship. Arthur, on the other hand, had only just begun to wrestle with the nature of the relationship. He still hoped for Tamar's release from the influence that controlled her. Hadn't he just learned from Tamar herself that matters of gender were not permanent? Her inclination might yet shift to something more . . . appropriate. He sensed the bias within himself, but there was a basis for his bias. It rested on traditional ground.

Margolit and Dana were mature women, had lived through their various cycles, had found each other, and if, from that relationship, derived lasting fulfillment, *kol ha-kavod*—all honor to them. But Tamar had no such experience on which to base decisions. It was unfair of Charlotte to reprimand him, even indirectly, for his opinion, his approach.

Had Margolit and Dana approached him, he would have worked with them toward a commitment ceremony of some kind to recognize the value of their relationship to the community, but not what he had witnessed, the travesty of a wedding. The blessings had been emasculated. Every mention of grooms and brides, Adam and Eve, male and female, had been deleted. The relationship between male and female was unique and could not be replaced by any other form of relationship, no matter how profoundly felt. A man and a man, a woman and a woman . . . what next? A person with a pet? With a car?

One part of him was thinking the old thoughts, another observing, knowing the thoughts to be old but not knowing how to replace them. He retreated into sound reasoning. Sense was on his side, common sense, but it made no sense to raise his side of the argument. Surely not when Charlotte was looking at him like that.

Charlotte left the remnants of the Chinese food to his disposal. The kiss they exchanged as he opened the car door for her was correct but not comforting.

Arthur returned to his study, alone, bereft of hope. There was no longer any reason he could perceive for Brenda to manufacture charges against Moshe, to misconstrue anything she had experienced or witnessed. This thing was going to end badly. Still, he had little choice but to see it through to its end.

The tape had run into static. There was nothing more to see. He pressed eject, half expecting, as he touched the button, something to explode.

Pictures and doodles in the journal. Portraits. Stephanie, Sidney, Margolit, Dana, surrounded by charms, signs, prisms, and pyramids. Brenda could go into business, Arthur thought, creating amulets, snippets of portraits and pieces from the pages to be enclosed in lockets or dissolved in water and swallowed.

He turned the page and found her notes concerning the wedding.

> I asked Moshe if Jewish law would countenance what Margolit and Dana were about to do.
>
> He told me to ask a rabbi.
>
> I hadn't put my question in the proper form, so I tried again. If I would ask a rabbi about a lesbian wedding, what would a rabbi say?
>
> He said, First ask about a lesbian relationship. About a lesbian relationship, the rabbis would say it was lewd behavior.
>
> But not forbidden, I asked. He shrugged.
>
> What about male homosexuality?
>
> There he only smiled.
>
> That's forbidden in the Torah, I said. A man who lies with a man as he would with a woman, that's forbidden. So it is forbidden.

210

The Torah doesn't waste words, he said. All it would have needed to say was, "A man who lies with a man." But there were extra words. "As he would with a woman." He said we might understand that to mean a man who would lie with a woman should not lie with a man, but a man who would lie with a man, the Torah doesn't prohibit that.

I asked him if the rabbis understood the Torah that way.

He said no, the rabbis considered male homosexuality forbidden. But he wasn't a rabbi.

Then I asked about the lesbian wedding.

He said gay or lesbian, it didn't matter. Weddings were easy. Divorces were difficult. It doesn't take much to get married. To get divorced, that's another matter. To create wedding ceremonies without procedures for divorce was irresponsible. Gay or straight doesn't matter. Gay couples acquire property, responsibilities, even children. What happens when they divorce? What procedures are there for parenting, alimony, child care, property distribution?

More than that, how would one know when to do a second marriage if there was no system of divorce to conclude a first marriage?

He said just because he isn't a rabbi doesn't mean there isn't wisdom in rabbinic Judaism. The Mishnah speaks of marriage and divorce in the same sentence. So if we speak of gay and lesbian weddings, we need to speak of gay and lesbian divorces in the same sentence.

So I asked him if it was okay, what the Family Bayt Midrash was doing for Margolit and Dana. He said there was a way of handling it. Sidney was working on it.

Friday morning before the wedding, at sunrise, Margolit and Dana came by to immerse themselves in the lake. Stephanie, Sidney, and Moshe came also.

Mikvah, ritual immersion, a cleansing of the soul, so they could begin their marriage from the purest place.

Mayim hayim, Moshe called it. Living water.

In bathing suits, they walked into the lake until they were deep enough to be modest. They removed their suits and took turns immersing, saying the blessing al tevilah, concerning immersion.

Life in life, Moshe said. The place where boundaries overflow.

Pretty.

Daniel liked it.

If Moshe did not consider himself a rabbi, what was he? For the first time Arthur allowed that question to rise in him. He realized it had always been there, an implied threat he did not want to recognize.

Moshe was conversant with Scripture, with Talmud—both biblical and rabbinic wisdom. He was using the Talmud for proof texts the way the Talmud used the Bible.

Moshe was dangerous. He had the knowledge to undermine rabbinic authority. A bar mitzvah, a funeral, a wedding, a lesbian wedding at that, all without rabbinic supervision. If the community took upon itself the creation and conduct of ceremonies, what would become of the rabbi?

Would there be a new institution, with a new literature? As the Talmud added a new layer of understanding to the Bible, would there be a new literature, a new layer of understanding beyond the Talmud? If so, who would write it? If it were written, how would it affect him?

He turned the page of the journal and read the text pasted into it.

Tina-im: Preconditions for a Same-Sex Marriage

Margolit, the daughter of Joseph and Shulamit, and Dana, the daughter of Gabriel and Sophia, agree before witnesses here in the city of Miami, in the State of Florida, that should the union they are about to enter come to the point of separation, either one of them can summon the other before a mediator certified in the courts of the State of Florida, for mediation concerning the division of the assets, privileges, and responsibilities of the union including:

• parenting
• equitable distribution of property
• alimony
• child care
• and everything else that may be construed as pertaining to that union

and, if the mediation is not successful, either one of them can summon the other before an arbitrator certified in the courts of the State of Florida, for binding arbitration concerning all of the above, with the understanding that the decision of the arbitrator will be made in accordance with the laws of the State of Florida to provide similar protection to the partners of this union as would be provided to the partners of a heterosexual union, as best as is possible.

This agreement is made in accordance with the laws of the State of Florida concerning binding arbitration, and in the sight of God, within the Jewish community, according to the laws of Moses and the people of Israel.

_____ Witness
_____ Witness

Who had written that? Arthur wondered. Moshe or Sidney Lee? Which was worse?

How did they presume to attribute such a document to "the laws of Moses and the people of Israel?"

As he pondered the permutations and combinations, the implications and considerations of the ceremonies, the immersion and the marriage, the document and the questions of authority, his hand reached out on its own for the chopsticks. They snagged a piece of honey garlic chicken. He didn't know what he had done until he discovered something cold, sticky, and distasteful in his mouth, something he could not swallow. He looked this way and that to spit it out.

CHAPTER 16

SUNDAY, 7:00 P.M.

Arthur felt a calm he hadn't experienced since the crisis had begun. There was no time pressure. He had all night, if necessary, but he wouldn't need that. There were only four programs left.

This was going to end badly. Of that, he was certain. All he could do was prepare himself, become as informed as possible, so he could answer every question, respond to every charge.

What had happened? How had it been allowed to happen? Why wasn't the program adequately supervised?

Was it technically a temple program if the funds came from outside the temple? If the program didn't take place on temple grounds?

What was the extent of the temple's liability? Of his liability?

Could he be held responsible for what went on in people's homes? In the park? In the Everglades?

This was going to be nasty. Ugly.

> *Remember Daylight Savings Time!*
> *Dante Fascell Park.*
> *Bring the Torah scroll.*

Bring the Torah scroll?

They found ever new ways to annoy him. Where would they get the Torah scroll? Did they steal it again? Come into his bathroom, his shower, to take it? Or did they have it all along and return it only recently? If so, why would it have been set to Andy Perlman's Torah portion?

The video showed the families under and around the larger of the two pavilions in the park. There were many more families than usual.

Adults were studying with children in groups of four or five. They were busy with a text. Arthur found a copy in the journal.

Exodus 24

12. God said to Moses: "Come to me, up the mountain, and be fully present there, and I will give to you the tablets of stone, the Torah and the commandment which I have written for their instruction."
13. Moses and his attendant, Joshua, rose up. Moses climbed up the mountain of God.
14. He said to the elders: "You wait here as you are until we return to you. Aaron and Hur will be with you. Whoever has legal questions can approach them."
15. Moses climbed the mountain. The cloud covered the mountain.
16. The glory of God dwelled upon Mount Sinai. The cloud covered it for six days. He called out to Moses on the seventh day from within the cloud.
17. The appearance of the glory of God was like a consuming fire on the summit of the mountain in the sight of the children of Israel.
18. Moses came within the cloud and ascended the mountain. Moses was on the mountain forty days and forty nights.

Exodus 31

18. He gave Moses, when he finished speaking with him on Mount Sinai, two stone tablets of testimony, inscribed by the finger of God.

Exodus 32

1. The people saw that Moses was taking a long time before coming down from the mountain. The people gathered around Aaron. They said to him: "Get up and make us a god that will go before us, because this Moses, the man who raised us up out of the land of Egypt, we don't know what's happened to him."

2. Aaron said to them: "Remove the gold rings that are in the ears of your wives, your sons and daughters and bring them to me."

3. All the people removed the gold rings that were in their ears and brought them to Aaron.

4. He took possession of them and formed them with a mold, making them into a golden calf. They said: "This is your god, Israel, that raised you up out of the land of Egypt."

7. God said to Moses: "Get down there, because the people you raised up from the land of Egypt have become corrupt.

8. "They have been quick to turn off the path I commanded them. They have made themselves a molten calf. They are worshiping it, sacrificing to it, saying: 'This is your God, Israel, that raised you up from the land of Egypt.'"

15. Moses turned and went down the mountain with the two tablets of testimony in his hand, tablets written on both sides, all the way through from one side to the other.

16. The tablets were the work of God, and the writing, the writing of God, was inscribed on the tablets.

17. Joshua heard the noise the people were making. He said to Moses: "It's the sound of war coming from the camp."

18. He responded: "That's not the sound of victory, and it's not the sound of defeat. What I hear is the sound of singing."

19. When he approached the camp and saw the calf and the dancing, Moses showed his anger. He threw down the tablets from his hands and smashed them at the foot of the mountain.

"Stay in your groups, please," Moshe said by way of bringing the focus back to center. Misdirection, Arthur thought. Moshe always seemed to be limiting his role, dividing into small groups, letting others take the lead in study, in ceremonies, but Moshe was always at the center, even when he didn't seem to be. He would hum a niggun, tell a story, even order people to stay in groups. By giving orders, he kept himself at the center.

"Some questions," Moshe announced. "Don't shout out answers. Talk quietly to each other. Do your best.

"How old was Moses when he went up the mountain?"

Arthur had read the text. It didn't mention Moses's age, but Moses was one hundred and twenty when he died. The children of Israel were in the desert forty years. That made Moses a little over eighty when he climbed Sinai.

"Okay," Moshe said. "Raise your hand when I come to your answer. Moses was thirty years old when he climbed Sinai." No hands. "Forty," two hands, hesitantly raised, quickly lowered. "Fifty. Sixty." A few hands. "Seventy." A few more. "Eighty." A lot of hands. "Ninety." A few. "A hundred. A hundred and ten. A hundred and twenty."

"He died at a hundred and twenty," someone said.

"Yes. He died at a hundred and twenty," Moshe agreed. "The eighties have it. Most of you said he was eighty when he climbed Sinai. So that must be right.

"Another question. In what you read, how many people climbed the mountain?"

"Just Moses."

"And Joshua."

"Two," came the answer. "Two."

"Was Joshua younger than Moses or older?"

"Younger." The response was unanimous.

What was he getting at?

"How old do you think Joshua was? A show of hands. Was Joshua seventy?" No hands. "Sixty?" A few hands. "Fifty?" A few more. "Forty?" A lot of hands.

"So, Moses was eighty, and Joshua was about forty. The two men climbed the mountain. How many got to the top?"

"One."

"Who?"

"Moses."

Moshe paced between the groups, a lawyer before a jury. "So, let me see if I understand this. We have an eighty-year-old man, a forty-year-old man. They both climb the mountain. Only one gets to the top, the older man. How come?

"For this, take some time. Think it through, and come up with what the Torah doesn't tell us."

Only Moses got to the top, Arthur thought, because he was the only one invited. Joshua remained at a distance. That was not difficult.

The camera panned from group to group. Someone other than Brenda was in charge of it. Arthur became certain when it focused on a group that included both Brenda and Daniel. And Stephanie and Sidney. They were still in town. When had this program taken place?

There was no date, just, "Remember Daylight Savings Time."

Arthur stretched, walked to his desk to consult his calendar. Sunday, April 2. The day after the wedding. Of course Sidney and Stephanie were still in town.

In one group everyone had a hand raised, adults and children alike. "Call on me! Call on me!" their hands were begging, waving for attention.

"What is it?" Moshe asked.

A teenager Arthur did not recognize, had not seen before, stood and said, "We have it."

"What is it?"

"The two of them climbed the mountain together. They came to a place where one had to lift up the other to continue. Moses couldn't lift Joshua, but Joshua could lift Moses. So he lifted Moses like this." The boy made a motion as if he were pressing a weight above his shoulders, above his head. "Moses could go on, but Joshua could not. Only Moses got to the top."

"Nice," Moshe said. "So Moses went to the top, and Joshua went back down the mountain."

"No," came an objection from a different quarter. "Joshua stayed there."

"How do you know?"

"Because when Moses and Joshua came back down the mountain, Joshua heard a noise in the camp and didn't know what it was."

"So Joshua stayed on the mountain." Moshe looked about for dissent. "Everybody agrees? How long did Joshua stay on the mountain?"

"Forty days and forty nights."

That was easy, Arthur thought. Almost everything was forty. Forty days and forty nights it rained in the time of Noah. Forty days the spies were in the land. Forty years the children of Israel wandered in the desert.

"So," Moses continued, "Joshua waits one day. He waits two. Three, four. A week. At some point he has to make a decision. Maybe Moses has died on top of the mountain. Maybe not. Maybe he would be back in a few minutes. Maybe never. If Joshua leaves his position, Moses won't be able to get down the mountain. Joshua has to make a decision. He has to say to himself, 'I'll wait one more day. Two more days. Or I'll wait forever, and if I die here, I die here.'

"What would it be like, to be a Joshua, waiting on the mountain? Take a moment, please. Don't talk about it. Just think about it. Imagine you are Joshua. You are on the mountain. You don't know if Moses is going to return or not. You make a decision not to leave your place. You will stay there forever, die there if necessary. Take a few minutes and become Joshua."

Moses told Joshua he would be gone for forty days, Arthur thought. Joshua knew how long Moses would be gone. But there was a difficulty. If Joshua knew Moses would be gone forty days, he didn't have to stay there. He could have gone back to the camp and returned at the appointed time. But perhaps he was afraid Moses might return early, so he stayed nearby.

The camera moved slowly from person to person. Most had their eyes closed. Meditating, Arthur realized. Moshe had suggested a meditation, and they were doing it, becoming Joshua, making a decision. It was as if he had hypnotic control over them.

"So," Moshe said, and he paused, leaving time for them to adjust to his voice. "Joshua waits for forty days. Moses comes down the mountain. What is he carrying?"

"The Ten Commandments."

"What are they written on?"

"Stone."

"How many pieces of stone?"

"Two."

"How big are the pieces of stone?"

People held their hands up accordingly.

"How much do two pieces of stone that size weigh?"

"A lot."

"How old is Moses?"

"Eighty."

"Another question for you to consider. How does an eighty-year-old man carry two heavy pieces of stone down a mountain?"

"Carefully," someone said. Laughter.

Moshe waited for the laughter to cease. "Talk about it. Let's see what we can come up with."

Again the groups became animated. Who cared? Arthur was tired. It was a story. There could be any number of answers.

"They were helium letters!" someone shouted. More laughter. "No, really. It says the letters went all the way through the stone. Written with

219

the finger of God. The stone was heavy, the letters were light. It was easy for Moses to carry them."

"Have you ever done any heavy reading?" Leonard Shuk asked. "But when you get into the book, it becomes light. You don't want to put it down."

"Nice," Moshe said. "Helium letters. Letters so interesting Moses couldn't put it down. The letters made the stones light, so Moses could carry them. And the writing was the writing of God.

"Now that gives us another problem." Moshe walked to a picnic table and lifted up the Torah scroll, the same little Torah scroll in the yellow dress, the one Arthur would have buried had he only known it was missing. They had taken it twice. Or was it once, and returned later than he'd thought? But why was it set to the Perlman boy's bar mitzvah portion? The bar mitzvah had been back in January.

Moshe asked, "Is it okay if I take this Torah scroll and throw it on the ground?" He made a motion as if to do it.

"No," came the shouted response.

"But it was all right for Moses to throw down the Ten Commandments? Written by the finger of God? How could Moses do such a thing?"

"He was angry."

"Even so. Consider it please. See if we can come up with a good answer."

He was angry, Arthur concurred with the anonymous speaker. When you were angry, you did stupid things. What did the Mishnah say? When you were angry, your wisdom departed.

"We have it," a woman said, someone else Arthur did not recognize. Moshe turned to the speaker. "The letters wouldn't stay on the stone when they got close to the golden calf. They flew away."

There was a midrash like that. Arthur had forgotten it. Why had he forgotten it?

"When the letters flew away," the woman continued, "the stones became heavy, fell from Moses's hands, and broke. When they hit the ground, all of the writing was gone."

"Nice," Moshe said, then whispered in Hebrew. "*Eem ayn nivee-im hem, bi-nay nivee-im hem.*" He didn't translate it. He had said it only in a whisper, for his own ears. But the microphone had picked it up. Arthur had heard it. "If they are not prophets themselves, they are the children of prophets."

It was a quotation from somewhere in the rabbinic literature. The rabbis asked what they should do if they didn't know any longer what the law was. The response was to go out and see what the people were doing. That became the law, because if they weren't prophets themselves, they were the children of prophets.

"Consider what you have done," Moshe said, "what you have created, such wonderful stories. Moses and Joshua go up the mountain together, an older man and a younger man. The younger man lifts the older man up onto his shoulders, raises him high so he can continue up the mountain, then waits and waits, resolves to wait forever, if necessary. Moses receives the Ten Commandments, written on two tablets of stone. Heavy reading made light. Old as he is, he can carry the tablets down the mountainside. As he approaches the golden calf, the letters fly away, back to their source. They aren't intended for such a people. The stones become heavy. They fall from Moses's hands and shatter. That's a wonderful story you've created. A wonderful story. I don't think we'll forget it."

The groups of adults and children were quiet, pondering their creation.

"In a moment we'll go out on the field and open the Torah scroll," Moshe said. "All one hundred feet of it. Maybe more." He nodded toward Stephanie. She stood and walked from group to group handing out what appeared to Arthur to be plastic sandwich bags.

"Moses went back up to Sinai again, not only to receive the Ten Commandments one more time but also to receive the entire Torah. Imagine Moses on top of Sinai. God gives him the Torah. It's a hundred feet long. Actually, a hundred feet around. There's no beginning, no end. Imagine the original Torah scroll was one continuous sheet of parchment, no breaks, a cylinder one hundred feet in circumference. That's about thirty feet across.

"God says to Moses, 'Here is my Torah. I give it to you.'

"Moses says, 'Thanks, but how am I supposed to carry it?'

"God says, 'Oh. Well, here.' God hands Moses a special knife. 'Go cut it somewhere. It will roll up into a scroll, and you'll be able to carry it.'

"Moses takes the knife and begins to walk around inside the Torah scroll, looking for a good place to cut. Should he cut in the middle of the Ten Commandments? Should he cut where Isaac was about to be sacrificed, make a cut right where Abraham wouldn't? He walked around and around and couldn't find a place to cut, so he said to God, 'I can't do it. Your Torah is perfect just the way it is. You do it.'

221

"God said to Moses, 'I can't operate on my own creation. You have to do it.'

"With that God told Moses to close his eyes and spin around, walk out to the edge with the knife, and wherever the knife would touch the Torah, there it would be cut. So that's what Moses did.

"We're going out on the field now. Those of you who have sandwich bags, wear them like gloves. That way you won't damage the parchment with oil from your fingers. Sidney and I will unroll the entire scroll, into a circle. Then the children will have a chance to take a tour."

The camera followed behind the Torah. They removed the dress, the belt, walked out into the field. Adults lined up, about five feet apart. The scroll was unrolled in both directions at once, and soon it became a circle, a cylinder. Arthur could not see Moshe, but he could hear him. "You are Noah," he said. "When someone asks you, tell them the story of the flood. . . . You are Abraham. . . . You are Jacob, where he wrestled with the angel. . . . You are Joseph, when he interpreted Pharaoh's dream. . . . You are the end of the book Genesis and the beginning of Exodus. . . . You are the first of the plagues. . . . You are the passage through the Red Sea. You see these columns? That's the song they sang after they came through the sea. . . . You are the Ten Commandments. . . . You are the golden calf. . . . You are—"

Mute, Arthur thought, and made it so with the push of a button. His head was pounding. He couldn't listen anymore. The children came inside the circle, walking around the Torah, asking questions of the people who were holding it.

The program was wonderful. Arthur didn't want to watch it. There was no reason to. Yes, there was. He forwarded to the end, when they began to roll it up, then backtracked a bit.

". . . where Moses cut," Moshe said. "You all see it? If the Torah were really a circle like this, there would be no beginning and no end. So it would read, *Li-ay-nay kol yisra-el beraysheet bara adonai et ha-sha-mayeem vi-et ha-aretz,* 'In the sight of all of Israel God began to create the heaven and the earth.' It's already cut for us. We don't have to make that decision. But we do have one decision to make. How to roll it back up. It's not like a book that can open to any page. We have to decide what section we want to leave open. What shall we choose?"

Arthur turned the VCR off. He knew what they had chosen. The Ten

Commandments. It was just by chance Andy Perlman's bar mitzvah portion had been the Ten Commandments.

They were playing tricks on him, leading him to false conclusions. Had he been right about anything? Wrong about when the Torah had been returned, wrong about Moshe and Margolit, wrong, wrong, wrong.

But one thing would be right. Moshe would come down.

CHAPTER 17

SUNDAY, 8:00 P.M.

It took Arthur a moment to recognize the text in the journal. It was from the Passover Haggadah, the service read during the seder meal in every Jewish home on the eve of the Passover holiday. It wasn't so much the text but the formatting that was strange. The words in parentheses were a commentary to the translation of a difficult passage of the traditional Hebrew.

It once happened that Rabbi Eliezer, Rabbi Joshua, Rabbi Elazar the son of Azariah, Rabbi Akiva, and Rabbi Tarfon (all of them among the great mystics of the second century) were reclining (at their seder table) in B'nai Brak (a religious community in Israel) and were telling how to get out of Mitzrayim (the word for Egypt, but also the word for a very tight place) throughout the night until their students came and said to them, Rabotaynu (our Masters), the time has come for the morning Sh'ma (to say the morning prayers).

Rabbi Elazar the son of Azariah said: "Here I was like one seventy years old (he was really only eighteen, but since he was the head of the rabbinic court, he was considered like one seventy years old) and I wasn't worthy (because he wasn't really old enough) of being instructed in the matter of the meaning of getting out of Mitzrayim 'in the nights' until Ben Zoma taught me this about it: 'So that you might remember the days of your exodus from the land of Egypt all THE DAYS of your life. (The expression) THE DAYS refer to the daytimes. (If the text had said only *the days,* it would have meant only the daytimes, but it says *all*

224

the days.) ALL THE DAYS (is mentioned so we should consider twenty-four hour days and) include the nighttimes as well.'"

(This answer didn't satisfy Rabbi Elazar the son of Azariah. He suspected the older rabbis were still keeping something from him.) Then (when they saw he wasn't satisfied) the sages said further "The days of YOUR LIFE refer to your lifetime in this world. (Concentrate on the words *your life* instead of the word *days*). Expending the meaning to ALL the days of your life bring one to the days of the Messiah (not only the days of your life in this world but the days of your life in the next world)."

(So the purpose of their nightlong meditation was to bring the Messiah, the source of salvation. In the following code they reveal the essence of their meditation.)

י–Blessed is ha-Makom (God).

ה–Blessed is He.

ו–Blessed is He who gave Torah to His people Israel.

ה–Blessed is He.

According to four banim (a word that can have several meanings: children; constructions; understandings) one speaks of Torah.

One is Hacham (wise).

One is Rasha (wicked).

One is Tam (innocent).

One is beyond the place of asking.

Arthur read through the text twice, understood all the words, but not the sense of it. Fatigue was surely getting the best of him.

He inserted the next videotape into the VCR. The families were confined in a small space, a porch with screen doors, not the flimsy sort found behind sliding glass but screen within a solid wood frame. There was not room enough for everyone to sit. Moshe stood in the far corner.

Everyone held a blue booklet, the Maxwell House Haggadah. For generations Maxwell House coffee had distributed the booklet free of charge through groceries.

"The authentic version," Moshe said, holding his up high and waving it.

Authentic to you, Arthur thought. He had written his own Haggadah, which he used in the temple seder the first night of Passover, in his home on the second night. His was a Haggadah much easier to use than Moshe's "authentic" one. He had excerpted sections from the book of Exodus, Moses's confrontation with Pharaoh, the splitting of the Red Sea, and included songs that had become part of the American Jewish Passover liturgy, "Go Down Moses" and other folk melodies. He had been using his Haggadah for twenty or more years and hadn't looked into the Maxwell House version in all that time.

"So, you remember when I asked you to search for the name of Moses? How many times did you find it?"

"Once."

"Only once," Moshe agreed, "and then only in passing. In a midrash about the plagues, added late. So if Moses isn't the major player in the Passover story, who is? Who do we open the door for?"

"Elijah."

"Elijah the prophet. And who is Elijah the prophet?"

"The forerunner of the Messiah," Leonard Shuk said.

"So Elijah is the major player. Passover is more about bringing Elijah than telling the story of Moses. And the purpose is, the hope is, that we bring the Messiah."

"What's the Messiah?" a child asked.

Moshe paused. The anointed one, the savior king to come from the line of David, Arthur thought, trying to put the words into Moshe's mouth so he could get on with it, get through the tapes, all the programs, and be done with it. But Moshe said nothing for a long time.

"I learned this from my teacher," he began at last. "When the Jewish people were in a tough place, a really tight place they couldn't get out of by themselves, they used to hope for a Messiah, someone God would send to save them, to rescue them. Reb Hayim, my teacher, taught it like this. He said we've grown into a new way of looking at things. The Messiah doesn't come in the form of a single person. He comes bit by bit, piece by piece. For example, the Messiah for polio has already come." The adults nodded. "Polio," Moshe explained to the children, "used to be a terrible disease. It killed and crippled lots of people when I was a little boy. But polio is gone now. The Messiah for polio has already come.

"Reb Hayim said the Messiah for women is in the process of coming. It hasn't fully come yet, but it's on the way.

"I've been thinking about this. If the Messiah comes in pieces, then Elijah comes in pieces, too. If the Messiah for polio has come, who was its Elijah?"

"Jonas Salk," the adults said.

"And if the Messiah for women is coming, who is its Elijah?"

"Gloria Steinem, Susan B. Anthony," were among the answers Arthur heard, spoken on top of each other.

"Now the question is, what are you the Elijah for? This makes it easier, in a way. We don't have to bring the Messiah all at once. We can bring the Messiah in pieces. If each of us can be the Elijah for a piece of the Messiah . . ." He stopped, changed the tone of his voice, spoke more slowly. "Look into yourselves. Consider what you might be the Elijah for, what piece of the Messiah you might bring in your own lifetime."

The silence on the porch became profound. He had them meditating. Adults and children.

Arthur became agitated in the silence. He reached for the remote to fast forward just as Moshe resumed.

"That's a difficult thing to find, what it is we're the Elijah for."

He was quiet again.

"Hametz," he said in his teaching voice. "Right now, in some of our homes, we're cleaning out hametz. Give me some examples of hametz."

"Bread," was the immediate response. "Beans, corn, rice," followed shortly after.

"What do they have in common?" Moshe asked.

"They puff up," the children said. "Leaven," the adults added.

"They puff up," Moshe repeated. "To get ready for Passover, we remove from our houses all the food that puffs up. Why do we do that?"

"Because we didn't have time to let the bread rise when we left Egypt," Robert said.

"We had to travel light," someone else added.

"What's the Hebrew for Egypt?" Moshe asked.

"Mitzrayim," Orly said.

"What's the root of *mitzrayim*?" Moshe continued.

Was he teaching them Hebrew grammar? Arthur wondered.

"*Maytzar*," Orly said. "A narrow place."

"So Mitzrayim was a very narrow place. A tight place. If we want to get out of a tight place, we can't take too much with us. We have to travel light.

"What if we were to look at it on a deeper level, in the world of feelings? What puffs us up in the world of feelings?"

"Pride, self-importance," came the answers.

227

"So, if we want to get out of a tight place, we can't be puffed up with pride or self-importance.

"The opening to get out of a tight place is very narrow, both in space and in time. It may be open only for a moment."

"Berlin," Michelle Kantor said. She was off camera, but Arthur recognized her voice. "My father had brothers in Berlin. They could have gotten out, but they were bankers. My father used to say they wanted to take the bank with them. They wouldn't leave without it. So they stayed. They died. My father left. He left the bank behind."

"You have to give up a lot to get out of a tight place," someone else added, as if speaking from personal experience, but he did not add to it.

"Who wants to get out of a tight place?" All the children raised their hands, suspecting the question was intended for them.

"A tight place may be very narrow," Moshe said. "It may be difficult to get out."

No hands came down.

"Lindy." Moshe pointed to a young girl.

Moshe opened the screen door just about a foot. "Not yet," he said, when she looked like she might go. "First, when you get outside, there are twenty-four pieces of hametz in brown paper bags hidden around the yard. Your job will be to find them. But before you try to get out, we have to dress you up Egyptian style."

Brenda stepped forward with a large T-shirt, then pillows to stuff inside it. Lindy became large, then huge.

"Go!" Moses said.

Lindy ran forward and bounced off the opening in the screen door. Again and again. Laughter. Fun.

"Too much hametz," Moshe said. "Help her."

The children reached under her shirt for the pillows. Without them she was able to squeeze through the opening.

"The T-shirt," Moshe said.

Lindy stripped off the T-shirt, passed it back for the next child who wanted to leave Egypt.

Child after child was stuffed, bounced off the screen door, unstuffed and pushed through the opening into the yard to search for the bags of hametz. Child after child after child.

How old was Jonah's child? Arthur asked himself. Was he old enough to enjoy this game? How many years had passed since that walk down Bourbon Street in the French Quarter to find his brother dying and the tall, thin, long-haired girl with the toddler? The child would be Lindy's age, a boy Lindy's age.

"This is my son," Jonah said. "He's okay. He's not sick."

HIV, Arthur realized. His brother was dying of AIDS. His wife? The boy's mother? Were they married? She had HIV also. She was going to die. Drugs. Needles. Jonah's line of work. A deadly business.

Child after child, stuffed, unstuffed, ran through the narrow opening into the yard. How old was that boy? Arthur measured each child who ran through. That old? That big? That happy?

Grace was the mother's name, Jeremy, by an act of grace, a toddler who was not sick. But damaged. Damaged. Born with heroin and cocaine running through his system.

"You will take care of my son," Jonah said.

Arthur didn't know, couldn't promise. He would have to discuss it with Charlotte.

"You will take care of my son," Jonah said again.

The last of the children ran through the opening. Arthur had watched them all.

A moment ago he had been rushed, but there was no hurry. He had all the time in the world. The outcome was known, but the process was important. Due diligence.

"A text for us," Moshe said. Brenda distributed the text Arthur had already read. "We'll do it together. It's difficult.

"These rabbis who were reclining in B'nai Brak, what night was that?"

"Passover. The seder night."

"And who were they, do you know?" He waited for an answer. "Everyone knows the Bible stories," he said, as if to himself, "but nobody knows the rabbi stories." Aloud he said, "These were the great rabbis, the mystics, those who risked their lives to learn from God where to go, where to lead the people. They had to get out of a mitzrayim, a tight place. Not Egypt. You don't have to be in Egypt to be in a tight place. We've already heard that Berlin can be a tight place. Their tight place was caused by the Romans. The Romans had prohibited study, the ordination of rabbis. Times were difficult, tight, very tight. They were meditating all night, so lost in their meditation their students came and found them in the morning, deep in the worlds. The students brought them back, each out of his trance, to say the morning prayers.

"What was the purpose of their meditation? Rabbi Elazar the son of

Azariah wanted to know. Ben Zoma gave him a simple answer he wasn't satisfied with. The sages decided ultimately he was worthy of knowing the truth, so they told him, 'We are developing a discipline to bring the Messiah, to invoke God's help in getting us out of our tight place.'

"Wouldn't it be nice to know what that discipline was?" Moshe asked, looking about the room, from face to face, then up at Arthur, directly into the camera.

"They tell us," he said. "For those who can understand, they tell us what they were doing and how they did it. But they do it in code. It's not for everyone to know. It's written on several levels.

"First, they spell out the name of God. Four times the word *blessed* is used, one for each of the letters of God's name. Blessed is God, *yod*. Blessed is He. Don't read He, but *hey*, the Hebrew letter *hey*. Blessed is He who gave Torah to His people, that's over against the letter *vav*. Then the *hey* again. *yod hey vav hey*. The four-lettered name of God.

"The way to invoke the presence of God is through the letters of the Divine Name.

"Then they go on and tell us how to do that. They say one speaks of Torah to four different kinds of children, the wise, the wicked, the innocent, and the one who doesn't know how to ask. This is a part of the seder we all know. But the word for children, *banim*, has different meanings. *Bayt nun* is at the root of the word for understanding, or building, or construction. According to four different understandings, four different constructions, Torah is learned. In the world where things happen, in the world of feelings, in the world of principles, and, finally, in the world of the spirit, in the presence of God.

"The first child is Hacham, the wise child, who likes to show off how much he knows and asks questions that admit only a detail as an answer.

"The second child is Rasha, the kid who acts out, the typical teenager. We tolerate him because we know he can grow into something wonderful.

"The third child is the Tam, the innocent one, who asks profound questions. He asks, *Ma zoht?* 'What is this?' A question that opens up to a discussion of the principles that sustain the universe.

"The fourth child asks a question so profound it can't even be expressed in words. The answer to that question is the secret of the purpose of the universe.

"What I'm teaching isn't new. Everyone really knows it, on a deep level, even if we haven't expressed it. We can put it to a test, if you like. But first, find a study partner and review the text."

They did that, and Arthur read it through once more. He hadn't studied that text in twenty years, at least not the beginning of it. The four children, that was incorporated into every Passover seder. In his Haggadah, they sang it to the tune of "My Darling Clementine."

"How many have you found?" George Lopez shouted into the yard.

"Twenty-two," someone shouted.

"Bring them back in. You can find the other two later."

He opened the screen door wide, the children returned, sweaty from their adventure in the yard.

"The four children," Moshe said. "You all remember the story? The wise, the wicked, the innocent, and the one who doesn't know how to ask. We want to read the section of the Haggadah that deals with the four children, but we need you to select the children for us. Go back into yard, have a meeting, decide who will be which, come back and tell us."

The children left, taking the mandate seriously.

"So we'll see what they do," Moshe said, then added in Hebrew, "*Eem ayn nivee-im hem, bi-nay nivee-im hem.*"

"If they are not the prophets, they are the children of prophets," Margolit translated.

Moshe seemed startled someone had heard him and understood.

It did not take the children long. They came back into the porch, almost solemnly.

"Who will be the wise child?" Moshe asked. Robert stepped forward.

"Who have you selected to be the wicked child?" Andy stepped forward.

"And the innocent child?" Hands pushed Orly forward.

"And the one who doesn't know how to ask?" All the children looked toward a distant corner. The camera shifted to focus on Daniel, sitting hunched between two walls.

"Yes," Moshe said softly. "They understand."

"Two more pieces of hametz are hidden somewhere in the yard," George Lopez said. "A prize to the children who find them."

They were off in a moment, except Daniel, who sat where he was, the camera still on him.

"You will take care of my son," Jonah said.

Passover.

I am writing in my room, Moshe still asleep. Daybreak, and I haven't slept at all.

231

Nine for the seder. Margolit, Dana, Orly. Morty, Marsha, Andy. Daniel, Moshe, me.

Moshe wanted the Kantors also. I think he wanted Robert there, to have all four children from the program, but the Kantors have their own seder. They have a big family.

Rather than a fourth child we had an empty chair. Just in case, Moshe said.

Moshe changed the order around, beginning with the ritual foods. Parsley, matzah, horseradish, egg in salt water, gefilte fish. Smart. No one got hungry.

"This is the bread of affliction," Moshe said. "Also the bread of paradise."

He told a story, an old story.

There was a worthy rabbi who was given the privilege of visiting both heaven and hell in his lifetime. An angel took him first to hell. There he saw a beautiful orchard, trees laden with ripe fruit. The people could pick the fruit, but their elbows were locked, so the fruit was always held at arm's distance. Then the angel took him to heaven. There he saw a similar orchard, with similar fruit, people also with locked elbows.

What was the difference between heaven and hell?

In heaven, the people fed each other.

So, when we ate the matzah, we fed each other. I fed Moshe, and Moshe fed me.

We poured wine for each other. I poured for Moshe, and Moshe for me.

Throughout the seder, feeding each other. At the end of the seder, chocolate-coated matzah. Then the afikomen, the hidden piece, which Andy found.

The guests left. Daniel had gone to bed long before. Just Moshe and me. The chocolate-coated matzah and the wine. More than the mandatory four cups.

Sexy. Very sexy. At least I thought it was, feeding each other pieces of chocolate. He took it from my mouth, followed me upstairs.

I undressed him. He didn't resist. I undressed me and took him to bed.

I thought he wanted it. He seemed lost, in a reverie, but when I kissed him, he woke up and pulled away.

232

He said no. That's all he said. "No."

Son of a bitch. What a bastard. He said no and fell asleep. In my bed. And I've been up all night.

"Son of a bitch!" Arthur said aloud, echoing the journal, angry at Moshe, then thought it served the bitch right, his focus turning toward Brenda. That's what Tamar had called her, a bitch. But Moshe had transgressed, let the barriers down, crossed a boundary. Naked in Brenda's bed. He should not have let that happen.

It served the bitch right.

Arthur was angry, but the target of his anger not certain.

Moshe had spent the night. He had not seduced Brenda. Brenda had attempted to seduce him.

So what was new in that? It was Brenda's nature, something he and Charlotte had discussed. Charlotte had suspected some trauma. Arthur hadn't been surprised to find hints of it in the journal.

Brenda, a single woman. Moshe, a single man. Why should he be surprised, shocked, upset, angry?

But he was. He felt the anger growing within him, at Moshe. Brenda was not just a single woman. She was Moshe's student. Moshe, rabbi or not, had violated a boundary, even if he hadn't consummated the act. Arthur felt profaned just reading about it. It was akin to the Turin folder he kept behind lock and key so as not to contaminate his study.

It was the reverse of the Turin folder, the student taking advantage of the teacher.

No, the teacher had a responsibility to keep the boundary in place.

With confusion and disgust he put the journal down and began to pace. What did this do to his case? Which case? Was he trying to get Moshe hung, or Moshe off?

Arthur wanted nothing more than to walk away, leave the journal and the tapes behind, let the chips fall where they may, and to hell with it! He turned toward the door, back again, toward the door, back. Such agitation. He had to sit down. His heart was pounding, his head aching.

He thought for a moment it might be his heart, recalled the symptoms of a heart attack, not that he'd ever had one. There was no chest pain, no pain in his left arm. What else was he supposed to look for? He couldn't remember, but just his attempt to remember brought his breathing under control. The panic subsided.

He didn't know what to do.

The journal was trayf, unkosher, taboo.

He had no choice. He picked it up.

> *I damaged him. And I thought I was the one offended.*
>
> *He says it is okay, but I can see that I damaged him. Daniel sees it, too. Daniel is afraid to go near him.*
>
> *I wanted this to be different. No. The wanting was different. Is different. Different from any other wanting.*
>
> *I think every other wanting has been a wanting to get even. This has been a wanting to . . .*
>
> *I don't know how to complete the sentence.*
>
> *I trust him.*
>
> *I don't think I've ever thought that about anyone. I trust him. I hurt him. I hurt me in the process. And I hurt Daniel.*
>
> *This hasn't been a good day.*

Arthur sat confused. He knew what to do. He picked up the phone and called Charlotte.

There were rules he had set for himself in his rabbinate, boundaries he swore never to violate. Matters he heard in confidence were just that, in confidence, not to be shared with anyone, not with his therapist, not with his wife. He was about to stretch such a boundary, if not violate it.

"I need to know something," he began. "A victim of incest, a girl, a young girl, what effect is that likely to have upon her as a woman?"

"Violent? Rape?" Charlotte asked.

"Most likely not. I'm guessing here. I don't know. Fondling, perhaps. Unwelcome advances."

"Not always unwelcome," Charlotte said. "There's a great deal of confusion in such acts. Even unwelcome attention is still attention."

"What might happen as such a girl matures?"

"Most anything," Charlotte answered, "but often movement to one extreme or the other, avoidance of sexual activity, or promiscuity. You're asking about Brenda?"

Arthur was silent, but his silence was an acknowledgment.

"Promiscuity," Charlotte said. "A way to get even."

It was almost as if Charlotte had read the journal. "Does she ever get even?"

"Not even, but she can get better, through therapy."

Arthur paused. "Do you know if Brenda has ever had any therapy?"

"Nothing significant," Charlotte said.

"What if she learns to trust someone, a man, and the man turns her down."

"She'll be confused. Vulnerable. Volatile. Betrayed. Angry. Vengeful." When Arthur was quiet she asked, "It sounds like you're caught in a difficult place."

"I understand it better, but I don't see any easy way out of it," Arthur said, not wanting to stretch the boundary any further.

"I'm here," Charlotte said. "Let me know what I can do to help."

"I love you."

"I love you, too."

CHAPTER 18

SUNDAY, 9:25 P.M.

He needs to be here. He finds it difficult to talk, but he needs to be here. The sentences come out of him disjointed, fragmented.

I feel whole again. He seems in pieces. I wish I could reverse it, go back to the way it was. I know how to handle it. He doesn't.

He has the guest room whenever he wants it. He stays some nights. I think he wants to make peace more with Daniel than with me.

He doesn't touch me.

He plays chess with Daniel. He plays, Daniel watches. Moshe plays both black and white, the board on a lazy susan, on the coffee table. He talks about his strategy, first from one side, then the other. White he plays from the aspect of hesed, with compassion, surrounding, encompassing. Black he plays from the aspect of gevurah, sharp attacks, penetrating. He talks as if Daniel understands, asks him which side has the advantage. He doesn't finish the games. No side wins. No side is defeated.

If he stays, he helps in the kitchen. We pass dishes from hand to hand.

I guess that's a form of intimacy.

April 30.
At Morty & Marsha's.
Posterboard, cut into sixteen pieces.
Scissors, crayons, Scotch tape.

Arthur was too agitated to continue. He looked at the desk. The pile had shifted, those tapes already viewed to the right, those yet to be viewed to the left.

Deuteronomy, he thought. It was coming to an end. As the Torah scroll was rolled from Genesis to Deuteronomy through the course of the year, the weight of the parchment shifted from the left hand to the right. So the tapes shifted, from left to right. At the end of the year, all the weight of the Torah scroll was on the right hand, then it was rolled back to the beginning to start another year.

But not the tapes.

The tapes he would view but once, then on to the district attorney.

He would go for a walk. No hurry. He had the entire night ahead of him, only a few more hours to serve. Like a prisoner. A short-timer, going for a walk in the prison yard.

A full moon hung large in the eastern sky, illuminating the clouds piled high in the west over the Everglades. California had its mountains, but Miami had its clouds, an argument he had begun with Tamar in his last visit. Not an argument, a discussion. No, it had been an argument. It was always an argument with Tamar. Perhaps that would change.

He walked the perimeter of the synagogue grounds, on the grass between the concrete and the fence where he had imagined burying the Torah scroll. How did they get the scroll back into the synagogue, into his study, into his shower? The silhouette of the campus would change. A second story on the school. A new library and chapel. A gymnasium. A swimming pool for the summer camp. His would be the only synagogue in the region with a swimming pool.

The new sanctuary was to be built on the playing field, the old sanctuary to become the new playing field. But the new sanctuary would be larger, the new playing field smaller, and that was the problem with zoning. Land usage, the percentage of land that had to remain open, unbuilt. Two percent in violation, the zoning board said. For lack of those two percent his plans were in jeopardy.

For lack of two good men Sodom was destroyed.

But this wasn't God against Abraham. This was the zoning board against Arthur. Arthur could bargain better than Abraham, but then the zoning board was more powerful than God. God would have granted the permit without argument, a larger sanctuary to proclaim His glory. The zoning board had a perverse understanding. God was served better with unbuilt land.

Two tapes and some testimony, all that was left. Then a phone call. "I have something to report," he rehearsed, and stopped. No need for that yet. No need.

With clarity of mind, certainty of purpose, he returned to his study to complete the work at hand.

An old-fashioned screened-in patio, something from the sixties. They had probably bought the property more for the location in Pinecrest than for the house. A long table. No, several tables pieced together. Children and adults sprinkled around them, finishing breakfast. Doughnuts for the kids, bagels for the grown-ups.

"Who remembers?" Moshe began, off camera. "In the right order. Talk it over with your neighbor while you're eating. All ten, please. In order."

The phone rang. The phone rang again. Why didn't anyone pick it up?

It was his office phone.

"Hello," he said, still watching the families in conversation, eating breakfast. "Hello?"

"Arthur?" It was Charlotte.

"Yes."

"I called a little while ago. I was worried about you. There wasn't any answer. I thought you might be on your way home."

"I was out for a walk. What time is it?"

"About ten. How's it going?"

"I don't know how it's going, but I'm doing better. This isn't going to be pretty, but I'll be all right. I think I see things a little more clearly. The walk was good for me."

"When do you think you might be home?"

"I don't know. Two hours. Maybe three. You must be tired after being out on the boat. Don't wait up for me. I'll be all right here. If I'm tired, I'll take a nap."

"Are you hungry? Do you want me to bring you something?"

He looked at his watch. Why should he look at his watch? Ten o'clock, but she had told him that. Didn't they just have lunch? There was still food on the coffee table. Sweet and sour. He sniffed at it, turned his nose away.

"Fatigue," he said, then realized he hadn't answered her question. "No, I'm not hungry, just tired. That's all it is. Not to worry. This is all going to

238

come out all right. I can sleep all day tomorrow. I don't think I could eat anything."

"Would you like me to come over?"

"No." He felt a surge of guilt. Why guilt? He wasn't the one who had been naked in bed with Brenda. Was he jealous? "No, you don't have to do that. I'm almost at an end, almost done. It will come out all right. Tomorrow morning, it will all be over." What was he saying? "No, that's not right. There will be difficulty, but we can get through it. The temple will get through it. It shouldn't be a concern for you. It's becoming less of a concern for me." Did that express it properly? "There's a program on. A videotape. I have to watch it. Really, if I need you, I'll call."

"I love you," she said.

"Thank you. I love you, too."

He hung up the phone gently, as if the small pieces of his inner ear were in the receiver instead of his head.

"Number one," Moshe said.

"I am the Lord your God."

"Who brought you out of the land of Egypt, out of the house of bondage," someone added.

"Number two," Moshe said.

"You shall have no other gods before me."

"No idols," someone explained.

"Number three."

"Don't take the name of God in vain."

"Number four."

"The Sabbath day, to keep it holy."

"Number five."

"Honor your parents."

"Your father and mother," the second voice added.

"Number six."

"Don't murder."

"Number seven."

"Don't commit adultery."

"No, don't steal." Several voices.

"Which is it?" Moshe asked. "Number seven, steal or adultery?"

"Steal." "Adultery." The voices came on top of each other.

"A vote," Moshe said. "How many say adultery? How many say steal? The adulteries have it. Adultery is number seven."

"But which is it, really?" someone asked.

"If you say it's number seven, then it's number seven," Moshe said. "Have faith in yourselves. Individuals may get it wrong, but the community will get it right. Number seven, adultery. What's number eight?"

"Steal."

"Don't steal," said the second voice. Arthur found that second voice annoying. Was that Robert?

"Number nine?"

"False witness."

"Don't bear false witness." Damn him, Arthur thought. Why couldn't he keep his mouth shut?

"Number ten."

"Don't covet."

"What's covet?" a child asked.

"To desire wrongfully," Robert said.

"Where'd you get that?"

"The dictionary."

Well, at least he did his homework.

"The Ten Commandments," Moshe said. "In order. Nicely done. How many tablets?"

"Two."

"Ten commandments, two tablets. That's as much as we know. How many commandments on each tablet, that we don't know."

Five and five, Arthur thought. Right there, through the door, in the sanctuary, on the wall above the ark. Two tablets, five commandments on each.

"The Torah doesn't tell us. It could be one and nine, two and eight, three and seven, four and six—"

"Five and five," Robert said.

"—or five and five. Or not. That's for you to decide. Two tablets. You know the commandments. Small groups, please. How many on each, and why."

There was nothing to learn from this, Arthur thought, but he couldn't turn it off. He had come this far, he would finish it, see, hear, read everything, so when they came to him to ask questions, he would know how to answer. The police would be easy, the press would be difficult. They would be all over the temple. Should he call the president before he called the police? No, afterward. Immediately afterward.

"Charles, I have some bad news for you. It might involve the temple, so I'm calling to give you a heads-up. It didn't happen at the temple, but it involves people from the temple, and some not from the temple, a program that wasn't part of the temple, but was done with, done for, done to our members."

Those members would be questioned also. The Garfinkels, Lopezes, Schwartzes and Kantors. They needed a heads-up. They shouldn't learn of it from the newspaper or television. Every family would be questioned. And the children. What effect would this have upon the children? Why hadn't he considered that before?

He had a sudden awareness of what that questioning would be like, downtown, each family, one at a time. "Tell us what he did, what you did, what you wanted to do, what you didn't want to do. How many times? When did it start? What is your sexual history? Have you ever . . . ? The children, have they ever . . . ? Did he force you to do it? How did he force you? Why did you? Will you submit to an examination? Is there physical evidence? We have to take samples, to probe, to scrape . . ."

Arthur barely made it to the bathroom. He hadn't vomited in years, was fearful for a moment he had forgotten how to do it. Two heaves, three, and he thought he was done, but there was a fourth that was dry, as if his stomach was trying to expel itself, turn itself inside out.

He was on his knees before the toilet bowl. He had made a mess.

He flushed the toilet and waited for the tank to fill before continuing. What was he going to do? He couldn't let that happen, the probing, the scraping, but there was no way out of this. He used toilet paper to clean the floor, the lip of the bowl, and flushed again. He couldn't subject the families to that. He had to find a way out. Moshe was speaking in the other room. How many commandments were there on each of the tablets, as if it were an open question. The rabbis ordained five and five. It was five and five. Five and five. Balance. Balance was what he needed, enough to stand, enough to see his way through.

He had soiled his shirt.

He stripped it off and left it to soak in the sink. Bare from the waist up, he returned to the study, heard the discussion in progress but paid it little attention as he donned his limp tuxedo shirt, covered his nakedness, tucked the tails into his khakis, rolled up the sleeves.

Down to business, he thought. He sat and rewound the tape to pick up the beginning of the discussion.

"One and nine? Why, Jessica?"

"Because the first is God speaking about himself. It's just a statement, not a commandment. The rest are things for us to do."

Arthur didn't like the way he smelled. It wasn't the vomit. It was his shirt, musty from the wedding. How long ago was that wedding?

"How about two and eight? Michael."

"The first two God speaks in the first person. 'I am the Lord your God,' and 'You shall have no other gods before me.'"

"What about 'You shall not take my name in vain?'"

"Three and seven, then."

His study was a mess. It wasn't just a matter of cleaning himself up but the study as well. He couldn't leave it like this, for the staff to come and see. He'd have to clean out his wastebasket. And the shirt in the sink, he hadn't even wrung it out.

"Anyone else for three and seven? How about four and six?"

Lots of hands were raised.

"Why four and six? Jennifer."

"The first four have to do with us and God. The last six have to do with us and other people."

"Nicely said. Is that it? How about five and five?" A few hands were raised. "Why five and five, Robert?"

He might manage a few hours of sleep before nine o'clock. He'd go home. But he'd have to get back to the study sometime during Memorial Day to clean it.

"Because that's the way it's always been done."

Should he bring the tapes home? No, he would leave them there. Was there something to consider about a chain of evidence? It wasn't as if he was removing something from the scene of a crime. They didn't have to remain in his possession. He could pack them up, leave them in the closet, and deliver them later to the district attorney. Or the police would come to his study to pick them up, so another reason to make sure his study was in order.

"What happens if the way it's always been done doesn't work anymore? Should we continue doing it that way? Hardly anyone comes to the synagogue because we do things the way they've always been done, so we should continue doing it like that? What would happen if we announced that from now on there would be four commandments on the first tablet and six on the second? Then people would have to think about it, at least for a moment. Maybe someone would say, 'If that can be new, then other things can be new, too,' and find new ways of doing things.

"Can you imagine the headlines? Extra! Family group discovers there are four commandments on the first tablet, six on the second!"

Arthur could imagine the headlines but didn't want to imagine the headlines. There had been an incident similar at a church in Perrine. It had been in the headlines for days.

"If there's one thing we've learned this year, it's that we can't do things the way they've always been done. We can't take anything for granted. We have to read every word, challenge every concept. Out of the box. Stretch the envelope."

Violate the boundaries, Arthur thought.

"So it may be five and five, but not because that's the way it's always been done.

"Let's look and see. The last five commandments, what are they? Don't . . . ?"

"Murder. Commit adultery. Steal—"

"That's enough," Moshe interrupted. "Murder, adultery, stealing. They all have to do with civil rights. A person's chief right is to life, so don't murder. Then to family, so don't commit adultery. Lastly, to property, so don't steal. Then, not only may you not do those things directly, you may not do them indirectly, either.

"If I wanted to, I could take a person's life by bearing false witness. How could I do that, just by lying?"

"By giving false testimony," Leonard Shuk said. "By testifying that you saw someone kill someone and having that person condemned to capital punishment."

I will have to testify, Arthur thought. What would it be like, to be on the stand in such a case? Once, in a divorce, he had to testify, but then only for ten minutes. This would be more than ten minutes.

"How could I destroy a person's family by lying? That's easy. By saying I saw such and such a person with such and such a person and creating jealousy in a household."

How many families would be destroyed?

"And what about a person's property? I don't have to steal it. All I have to do is lie about damages, insurance fraud, whiplash, whatever.

"So I may not take a person's life, a person's family, or a person's property either directly or indirectly.

243

"Not only that, I shouldn't even desire wrongfully. I shouldn't covet such things. I shouldn't let my desire build to such a degree I might consider such actions seriously."

God help him, Arthur thought, imagining the tape playing to a jury, Moshe talking about coveting. They would crucify him. The jury would seek just retribution, if not outright vengeance, for the preacher whose desire had led to such behavior.

"So the last five commandments have to do with civil rights, person to person."

All the while, even as Arthur was imagining Moshe's future and fall, he was still with some small part of him hearing the teaching, the last five commandments as a code of civil rights. He could use that in a sermon. The Ten Commandments were discussed three times a year, in Exodus, in Deuteronomy, and on the holiday of Shavuot. It was good to have yet another way to speak of them.

"The first commandment," Moshe said. "'I am the Lord your God who brought you out of Egypt.' Jessica tells us that isn't a commandment at all. Is it a commandment or not?"

Another of those silences that Moshe induced, attentive, working silences. Arthur was jealous of those silences.

"Listen to this and tell me the difference. I am the Lord, *the* God who brought you out of the land of Egypt. I am the Lord, *your* God who brought you out of the land of Egypt. What's the difference."

"The *your*."

"Yes. The first commandment says there is to be a relationship between us and God. This is to be *your* God, not *the* God. The next three all have to do with that relationship. You are to have no idols, no other gods to get in the way of that relationship. You are not to misuse the name of God. You are to have a special day on which to sanctify that relationship.

"Then you are to honor your parents, your father and mother. What do we do with that one? Should we put it on the first tablet or the second? Whatever you decide, that's what we're going to do."

Brenda walked in front of the camera. Arthur could see only her back, not whether she was wearing shorts or not. She distributed posterboard cutouts of the two tablets.

"We're going to make our own Ten Commandments," Moshe said, "two tablets, however we decide. The question is what to do with the fifth commandment, honoring parents."

244

Honoring parents, that was the difficult one, Arthur knew. Difficult for him, difficult for everybody. It was for the children to determine how to honor parents, not for the parents to declare how the children were to do it. Arthur honored his parents by recalling the best of them, that they had done the best they could do, given their situation. He and Jonah had the same parents, but at different times. Something had changed in their mother in the five years between them, something to make her more independent, set her on a different course, strong enough to pull Arthur after her. He was grateful for that, grateful his father had permitted it, by his silence even encouraged it. It was the best his father could do.

Was he doing the best he could do? Had he succumbed to the path of least resistance? In the last hours his concern had become more damage control than damage prevention. Surely he could do better than that.

Moshe and Brenda had slept together. Despicable, but not a crime. When was that? He checked the journal. April 30. Perhaps in the last few weeks Moshe had succumbed to someone else. How would Brenda discover that? How angry would she be?

Would she be as angry as he had been a moment ago? Would she report falsely, bear false witness? Could he, in the hours remaining, find something, anything, that would serve as the root cause of her anger, so that she might falsify such charges and incur such personal damage just to bring the man down?

Please, he begged, let me find something.

Who was he addressing? God, he realized. He was praying. He knew the words but had never prayed them before. "May the one who has blessed our fathers, Abraham, Isaac, and Jacob, and our mothers, Sarah, Rebecca, Rachel, and Leah, also bless me, and allow me to find a way out of this difficulty, not for my sake, but for the sake of the others, for the sake of the families that will be tortured, the temple that will be damaged, the community that will be injured. God help me, please. Amen."

He felt better, a bit abashed, but better. If it was there, he would find it. If not, it would not be for the lack of his trying. He had this program to finish, one more, and what was left in the journal. And the rest of the night, if necessary, to go over all of them again, until he found something. If not, he would make the call. He would make it himself, with a certainty that nothing could have been done to prevent it.

". . . relationship," the tape was saying. "That's what it's about. So it belongs on the side of relationship."

"But relationship between people, not between people and God."

"A model of the relationship between people and God."

"*Aveenu malkaynu,*" a voice spoke off camera. Not Margolit. The accent was American. "Our father, our king. We relate to God as father. It belongs on the first tablet."

"How many for the first tablet?" Moshe asked. "How many for the second? It looks like it's going on the first tablet. Five and five."

"I heard a teaching once. Do you have the energy for it? It was a teaching about this commandment, that of all the commandments in the Torah, this one is the most difficult to fulfill, because it's different for every child.

"Not only that, each child goes through different stages. At first the child thinks he or she is the center of the world, the only purpose of the parent to please him, to please her. When that doesn't happen, the child becomes rebellious, moves away from the parent, wonders why the parent has failed him, failed her. Eventually, sometimes, the child recognizes the parent isn't perfect, has his or her own needs and deficiencies, has been doing the best he or she can do, and the child accepts the parent for what the parent is. Then a real relationship is possible.

"That's what it's like with God. First we think God's only purpose is to meet our needs. We pray for something, our prayer isn't answered, our needs aren't met, so we rebel, we move away. Eventually, sometimes, we recognize the Creator must have a need from its creation. We begin to work in partnership with the Creator to fill that need.

"Just as our parents wait for us to grow up, God waits for us to grow up.

"So we'll put it on the first tablet. That's the way you've voted, and just as well. Otherwise Robert would have to go around to all the churches and synagogues to edit the text."

Brenda stepped forward again. She was wearing shorts. "Five and five, if that's the way you want to do it. We have crayons. Decorate your tablets. Then we're going to cut them into ten pieces, like a jigsaw puzzle. Like the first tablets that were broken. We'll put the puzzles back together with tape."

Marsha Perlman stood and said, "For those who don't want to make puzzles, we have something interesting on the TV in the family room."

The camera moved from child to child, each busy with the posterboard tablets. Then static.

Nothing, thought Arthur. Nothing he could use.

The static was replaced with a scene of the family room. Even in the distance Arthur recognized the movie playing on the television, *The Ten Commandments*, in color, Charlton Heston on the summit of Sinai, fireballs from God streaming out of heaven to explode against the mountain. Four commandments were engraved on the first tablet, six on the second.

"Cecil B. de Mille doesn't know bupkis about honoring parents," someone said.

"What about honoring children?" A young voice. "How come there isn't any commandment about honoring children?"

"How about honoring brothers and sisters?"

"How about grandparents?"

"Why not grandchildren?"

"Grandparents always honor grandchildren. They carry their pictures everywhere. Does any grandchild carry a picture of a grandparent?"

"Who do you have pictures of?" Arthur didn't know who was asking. "Open up. Take out your wallets. Look in your purses. Let's see whose pictures you carry."

"Anyone have a picture of their grandparents? How about their parents? Children?" Several hands were raised. "Grandchildren?" Two hands, a couple that didn't look old enough to be grandparents. "Brothers or sisters?" Two more hands. "Nieces or nephews?" The same hands.

There was no commandment to honor a brother, Arthur reminded himself. No commandment, no obligation.

Moshe stays most nights. After Daniel goes to sleep, we sit in the kitchen and talk. Mostly I talk.

I feel I have to do something to bring him back together.

I keep telling myself it wasn't my fault. Then I get angry at him, that he won't take any of the blame.

But there isn't any blame. Why do I keep thinking there is?

I told him about my father. For a long time, I talked about my father. I wanted to know how a father could do that.

He said he could feel my father that Passover night, the presence of my father touching me. Was that why he turned away?

My father. Can I ever get rid of him? He's dead and buried, I don't know where, but he keeps touching me.

CHAPTER 19

SUNDAY, 11:05 P.M.

What will Moshe do when the year is done?

I haven't asked him. I'm afraid to ask.

Daniel is comfortable again around him. I tell myself I'm worried for Daniel, how Daniel will be if Moshe disappears.

How will I be if Moshe disappears, if he gets into his Porsche and rides off into the sunset?

Daniel drives men away, but for Moshe, Daniel seems to be an attraction, an endless puzzle for him to solve.

Moshe has no plans.

He says he looks for openings, opportunities to make a difference. He doesn't know what they look like until they appear.

The family program was such an opportunity, a tiny opening, to experiment, to create a system of learning that might take seed and grow. He says there are gaping holes in Liberal Judaism. He doesn't know how to fill them. All he can do is plant a seed.

Once he begins something, he has no idea what else might open in front of him. Not doors; lesions. Lesions in the deeper worlds. That's how he describes them. Lesions in the worlds of formation and creation.

He sees them, perceives shifts, how to make room for healing. He doesn't know how it happens. He surrenders to it. Like the programs and the stories. They don't always work the way he expected, or work at all. But then he doesn't have much choice.

He says he doesn't have free will the way he used to. That's why

248

he appears broken to me. It's not that he's broken, he just isn't free the way he used to be. He describes it as a profound sense of partnership and purpose. But during the process, he sometimes struggles against it, because he can see it will be painful for others. That's when he seems to be broken.

What others?

Sometimes I ask such stupid questions.

Morty, Marsha, Andy, but that work was done.

Arthur. When he said Arthur's name, he closed his eyes and disappeared for a moment. When he came back, he said , "6491, 7491, 8491." He thought one of those would be the code to Arthur's study.

He didn't know the code to the ark. He had no insight into that, only into Arthur.

And then there was Daniel and me.

That's when I stopped asking. I didn't want to know any more.

He had told me for a lesion to begin healing, there had to be some debriding. I didn't know the word. He spelled it for me.

To debride: to clean out dead tissue to make room for new growth.

He held my hand, the first time he had really touched me since Passover, but it was an apology, not an expression of love.

Debriding is painful, he said. You have to cut down to healthy tissue.

He told me a joke to cheer me up.

What's the most comprehensive, organized, effective, and efficient adult activity at any suburban synagogue?

I said adult education.

He said carpool.

Arthur felt himself flush with anger. Perhaps fever too, but surely anger. The insolence of the man! All the awards his congregation had won, the recognition received for his programs of adult learning, dismissed with a single word. Carpool!

What did Moshe know about the way he thought, even if he did manage to guess the code to his study? It wasn't so difficult, the year of his birth, backward.

If it were not for the families, for the pain they would suffer, he wouldn't bother to continue. But the innocent shouldn't suffer. The victims shouldn't suffer. If there were only a way to leave them out of it and bring the man down.

> *May 14 isn't Lag Bi-omer, but it is a Saturday night, and that's when we'll celebrate it. Nobody will drive down to Homestead on a Wednesday night, not with school the next day.*
> *Send directions to the orchard. Bring stuff to barbeque.*

Only once in his life had Arthur been to a Lag Bi-omer bonfire. It was the year his father had died, an unusually cool night in the spring. Rabbi Perlstein had taken him along to spend just the evening, not the night, at a youth group retreat at a camp in New York. It was the thirty-third night after Passover, during the period called the Counting of the Omer, a ritual counting ordained in Scripture, seven times seven days from Passover, the exodus from Egypt. Seven times seven days the children of Israel traveled, to the festival of Shavuot, the celebration of the giving of the Torah at Sinai. Seven weeks of semi-mourning, and Arthur was surely mourning after his father's death, perhaps still in shock.

Tradition had it that on the thirty-third day of the counting of the seven times seven days, students of Rabbi Simeon bar Yohai, the great teacher of the second century, trekked through the woods with bows and arrows, pretending to be on a hunt when they were really going to study with their exiled teacher. That thirty-third day became a celebration in the period of mourning, a time for bonfires.

The youth group was for the older teens. Arthur was out of place, except by the side of his rabbi. There was a bonfire, and a storytelling, but what Arthur remembered most was the ride with the rabbi, from Paterson to the camp and back again.

The video began with the barbeque in a shed, a packing shed, Arthur judged from the long tables and stacks of cardboard boxes. The Capstans were farmers. That seemed strange, Jewish farmers, members of his congregation. Several grills were going. The camera was shoulder mounted, moving about from group to group.

Happy people. Happy children.

A tractor drove up, a hay wagon behind it. Adults and children jumped on board, the camera also, and Arthur found himself on a hayride. A fast hayride. Too fast. The children bounced and screamed. The camera bounced and swayed with the turns. Arthur bounced and swayed, felt himself becoming ill again. This he could fast-forward, but that in some ways was worse, a roller coaster instead of a hayride.

What was it he used to do, when he had gone with Jonah on a dare, on the roller coaster? Thousands had been on that ride, thousands more would be on it. All had survived, would survive. He, too, would survive, if he only concentrated on being but one in the thousands of thousands. A meditation to get him through a roller coaster ride.

Jonah laughed at him, pried his fingers off the bar, encouraged him to raise his hands above his head. Arthur triumphed in the end. He did not vomit, though he wanted to puke his guts into the wind and let the mess fly back into Jonah's lap.

The ride was over. The camera returned to steady ground and followed a trail of families through a dark, then darker path to a glimmer of light, of fire, kindling in the middle of a tower of branches, dead fruit trees, no doubt, gathered and stored for this one purpose.

Arthur watched the fire grow, imagined he could feel its heat, wondered again if he had a fever. The camera walked about the fire, capturing images of the gathering, a great many families. Twenty, thirty, forty. How far had the cancer grown? If even one cell was infected, all the others would be examined, questioned, subjected to a battery of tests. Every family that had attended any program. How many on that list?

Mario Kantor stood, large against the fire, several children with him. He began a chant. "When we see three stars it will come to an end, a-ha, a-ha. When we see three stars it will come to an end, a-ha, a-ha." On and on it went, deep into Arthur's headache. The chant was an introduction to the havdalah service to bring an end to Shabbat. The children lit a braided candle, said blessings over wine and fragrant spices. Between each blessing, the chant, "When we see three stars it will come to an end, a-ha, a-ha," again and again.

Moshe stood between the camera and the fire, dark against the light. He walked about the circle, the camera walking with him. He was singing as he walked, another of his damned niggunim, drawing everybody in, closer and closer, louder and louder.

"I have a story I don't know completely," he said. "Will you help me with it?" He must have received nods of agreement, for he continued, "Good. It begins with a wise man, a very wise man, renowned for his wisdom. Now something made him angry, and that's my problem. I don't know what it was that made him angry. The rest of it I can see, but not that.

251

Whatever it was, it was an anger beyond any anger I have ever known, a terrifying anger. If you were in the presence of such an anger, you might have been consumed like this." He threw into the fire a handful of something that burst and crackled.

"But the wise man was not angry at anything in particular. There was nothing to be consumed by his rage. That's what was so strange. If there was something he could reach out and touch, something that was causing his anger, he could push it away, express his rage. But there wasn't anything. All he could do was push himself away. And that's what happened. He pushed himself away, and he was no longer a wise man. He found he was quite an ordinary man, in ordinary clothes, thinking ordinary things. But he remembered that he used to be wise. The memory was all that remained of his wisdom."

Moshe stopped walking and began to hum the niggun again. The families hummed along with him.

"That memory tugged and pulled at him," Moshe said, "at this man who used to be wise. He became angry because he had lost his wisdom, angry because he was reduced to the ordinary. He didn't know how such a thing had happened because he wasn't wise enough to know. So he had no place to put his anger, except to push himself away from it, and he pushed himself out of the ordinary, so he was no longer an ordinary person. He was reduced to a very low state. He became a person among the lowest of the low, an outcast, a beggar, a leper, revolting to see, untouchable.

"He was surprised to find himself in such a state. He had a memory that he used to be ordinary, quite ordinary. And now he was reduced to the untouchable."

Moshe stopped his story and resumed his niggun, the same niggun.

"This poor man was so isolated, so alone in his situation. No one would speak with him. No one would look at him. All he had was a memory that he used to be ordinary, like the people who passed by him. He had no idea how he had been reduced in such a fashion, and he became angry, with a terrible anger. But, since he had no idea what caused his anger, all he could do was push himself away from it, and he found he was no longer human. He had become an animal of some kind, that skulked around the outskirts of the city, fearful lest he be seen by any human or another beast. But even in this state, he knew he had once, not long before, been of a higher state, a person, a speaking, reasoning being."

Again the niggun, slower, sadder.

"This memory, that once he was a higher being, plagued the beast, tormented him. He howled at it and sent a feeling of dread into the heart of every person in the city who heard it, for never before had there been such a howling. The beast had no notion of how it had been confined, restricted to walking on all fours. There had been a time when it had been upright. It howled at the unfairness but didn't know where that unfairness was. All it could do was push itself away, and it pushed itself farther and farther, until it became a vine climbing up a tree.

"The vine felt the coarseness of the bark underneath it, sensed a distance from its roots, and had a vague notion it had not been confined like this always, that once it had been free to roam among the trees, not limited to any one of them. It had this vague notion, and the notion began to smolder and irritate, like poison ivy."

Moshe no longer began the niggun. When he paused, the families themselves raised the chorus, with a sadness and slowness appropriate to the narrative.

"The vine expressed its resentment by coiling and lashing out, but there was no object against which its resentment could be expressed, so the vine pushed and pushed and pushed itself away until it became a rock on top of a hill. The rock sat there, still, ever so still, unmoving, but had within it a resonance that once, whenever once might have been, it had motive power, it could grow, change. But now the rock was unchangeable, unmoveable. It sat there, and deep within it was a discord, a disharmony, a sense of being out of place."

The niggun, ever so slow.

"The dissonance grew in this rock, ever so slowly, the sense that it once was able to move, to grow, and now it could not. It could not become comfortable with its position, felt an imposition, and with that, rolled down the hill, picking up speed, more speed, tumbling down the hill until it struck a boulder and shattered into pebbles.

"The pebbles were astonished to find they were no longer a whole. They had become scattered, inches, feet, yards from each other. There was a sense that once they had been part of a whole. As a sum of its parts they were less than their whole and felt a loss. Such a loss, such a sadness."

Only a few voices picked up the niggun.

"The pebbles were scattered, individual elements of resentment, resentful they had become less than they used to be. They wore themselves thin in their resentment, until they became light, like the dust, to be scooped up

253

by the wind and scattered throughout the atmosphere. They had so little mass, they were pushed about not only by the slightest breeze, but even by the rays of the sun. They had virtually no weight, no influence. But there was the faintest awareness that once they had some influence, though slight. Once there was some gravity to them, but now there was none."

If anyone sang the niggun, Arthur could not hear it.

"The particles of dust resented their loss of gravity, that they had no weight. In their resentment, whatever influence they had was stripped away. They became mere elements, sub-elements, atoms, sub-atoms, the vaguest material of the universe, the closest thing to nothing one might be, and still be there. They found themselves so remote, they had no memory of what they used to be and were, finally, at last, beyond resentment."

Surely no one was singing, Arthur thought.

"Only then," Moshe said, "only then were they able to be moved by an agency outside of themselves, those sub-elements into elements, and the elements congregated together into dust. The dust felt itself and was thankful for its substance. The dust combined with dust to form pebbles, which fell to earth. The pebbles were thankful for the direction of gravity. They fused to become a rock, and the rock was thankful for its substance. The rock burned and churned and evolved into a vine, and the vine was thankful for its growth. The vine evolved and became a beast, and the beast was thankful for its movement. The beast evolved and became a person, a lowly person, but the person was thankful for its reason. The lowly person evolved and became quite ordinary, but the ordinary person was thankful to converse with others. The ordinary person evolved and became a wise man, the wisest of the wise, and the wise man was thankful for his wisdom.

"Only one thing the wise man did not know, could not learn. He never learned why he had been so angry to begin with."

Silence, and then the niggun erupted, such an eruption. It built in energy. Adults, children, rose to hold hands and dance to their own music around the fire. The camera followed, then turned back to find Moshe dancing with Daniel. Moshe and Daniel danced apart from the circle, Moshe swinging Daniel around and around and around.

CHAPTER 20

SUNDAY, 11:55 P.M.

Only an audiotape was left, the one he had recorded on Friday, Brenda's accusation.

Midnight. Surely Charlotte would be asleep. Tamar? Nine o'clock in
California, but he had no reason to bother Tamar. No, it wouldn't be a
bother. They had some talking to do. That was something to be happy for.
But he didn't make the call. It would be a distraction from the business at
hand.

He looked again at the audiotape, again away. A few minutes of sleep,
he thought. The couch was inviting. There was no hurry, he had all night.
He wouldn't go home, anyway. He wouldn't risk waking Charlotte and her
questions. Better he should spend the night in his study, on the couch.

He laid back, placed the pillow beneath his head. A stone would be better, Jacob's stone, something to provide understanding, but all he had was
the pillow. Perhaps he could settle his mind and the churning in his stomach. He turned on his side, lifted his knees, curled up like a baby, a puppy.
A vine, he thought, remembering Moshe's story. It would be so nice to
regress, to dissipate, float away like so much dust.

He imagined a pond, ever so still. Fish. Moshe had forgotten fish. Beast
to vine was too great a jump. Better first a fish. Arthur slipped under the water and saw Jonah there, just under the surface, wasted, dead, floating up
toward him.

Later he could sleep.

Arthur uncurled, straightened, walked to his desk, slipped the audiotape
into the recorder, and pressed start. He uncapped his pen, found a fresh legal pad, and prepared himself to listen. It was his own voice he heard.

"Friday, May 26. I'm with Brenda Karman and want to record what she has to say. Is that okay with you, Brenda?"

"Yes."

"I want you to tell me again what you just told me, so we have a record of it. That's okay?"

"Yes."

"When did this happen?"

"This morning."

"Can you tell me what happened?"

"Before breakfast. I went shopping. There were some things I needed, so I went to the Winn-Dixie in South Miami. I left Daniel at home with Moshe."

"Moshe was at your home early on Friday morning?"

"Yes. He had spent the night. He has his own room. He comes over often, sometimes stays the night."

"So Moshe was taking care of Daniel."

"Yes."

"Does that happen often?"

"That's what I said. He comes over often."

"Was there anything special about Thursday night?"

"No."

"Moshe and Daniel didn't do anything special?"

"Moshe talked to Daniel. He does that a lot. They sit, Moshe talks. Sometimes he reads out loud. Recently he's been playing chess. He talks to Daniel, explaining the moves."

"Daniel doesn't talk back?"

"You know Daniel doesn't talk."

"It's for the tape."

"Daniel sits. Moshe talks. Daniel looks off into the corner, wherever. Moshe talks. Daniel sits. Sometimes Moshe just sits as well. Meditates."

"You don't have to answer this if you don't want to, but someone is going to ask. What's your relationship with Moshe?"

"He's a friend. He was a friend."

"Not lovers."

"Not lovers. Just a friend."

"So, you were at Winn-Dixie."

"I did my shopping. It didn't take long. There wasn't much traffic, hardly anyone in the store."

"You came home. What did you find?"

"I came home. I expected to find them in the kitchen, but they weren't in the kitchen."

"Where did you find them?"

"Outside. I saw them from the living room. They were outside on the dock."

"What did you see?"

"Moshe and Daniel."

"What was Moshe wearing?"

"Jeans. Sandals. A T-shirt."

"And Daniel? Where was Daniel?"

"Standing in front of Moshe. Naked. Daniel was naked."

"What did Moshe do?"

"Moshe reached out and pulled Daniel close to him. He hugged him and kissed him."

"Where did he kiss him?"

"On the forehead."

"What did Daniel do?"

"Daniel put his arms around Moshe and hugged him back."

"And Moshe?"

"Moshe kissed him again."

"On the forehead?"

"Yes. No. More on the top of the head."

"What did you do?"

"I almost screamed. But I didn't. I didn't want to make matters worse. I went out the side door and walked down to the lake. They didn't see me. Even when I said Daniel's name, they didn't see me. When Moshe finally realized I was there, he kept hugging Daniel. He didn't let him go. When he saw how angry I was, his expression changed, and he stepped back. I stepped between him and Daniel and pushed him away. I didn't want to scream. It was everything I could do not to scream. I pushed him and pushed him and pushed him. . . ."

"Take your time. There's no hurry."

"Finally he turned and walked away, into the house."

"Did he say anything?"

"He said it would be okay. That's all he said. It would be okay."

"What about Daniel?"

"Daniel had sat down on the dock, had his knees up to his chest and was

257

hugging them. It took a long time for me to get him to stand and come with me back into the house."

"And Moshe?"

"Moshe was gone."

"He had left?"

"He was gone."

"You had pushed him away?"

"I had hit him, too. I had hit him. I pushed him, and I hit him."

"Did you say anything to him?"

"I said, 'How could you? How could you?' I pushed him, and I hit him."

"So he left."

"I would have killed him."

"Did anything like this happen before?"

"I don't know."

"What do you mean?"

"I never saw it before. But I realized he was always with Daniel, around Daniel, alone with Daniel. I became very afraid."

"What do you want me to do?"

"I don't know. I thought I would go straight to the police, but I thought I would come talk to you first. What should I do?"

"Have you taken Daniel to see his doctor?"

"No."

"Maybe do that first. Then we'll talk some more, go over it again."

"I won't let you get away with it this time."

"What do you mean?"

"Last time, with Turin. You never helped me with the police. If he's done this with Daniel, he may have done it with others. He has to be stopped. Right now. I'm not going to wait for the rabbis to have their meetings."

"We'll do something, Brenda. I promise. But let's look at everything first. Bring me everything you have that might possibly shed some light on this. Then I'll go to the police myself. You won't have to. I'll do it. Just give me a little time."

Arthur checked the clock. He had a little time, but didn't know what to do with it. He didn't know what the hell Moshe had been doing with a naked autistic kid.

Brenda had brought Daniel with her to his study. All the time Brenda was leveling her accusations, recording the tape, Daniel had sat, dressed, in a chair, oblivious, looking at the closet door.

Why would Moshe have undressed him and taken him naked down to the lake? Where had he undressed him? Where did Brenda find Daniel's clothes? Why hadn't he asked her that? What other questions hadn't he asked?

Arthur looked down to his legal pad. He hadn't written anything but the numeral one. One hell of an attorney.

Was there any way he could not report this, convince her not to report it? A cute, naked kid. A rabbi. A man who used to be a rabbi. Whose wife had died. Who had become unbalanced. A teacher of flaky stories and a singer of flaky songs. Who spent a lot of time with children. Who engineered time with children, alone, one on one. Who seduced them with his Porsche.

How many times had Moshe been alone with Daniel? Brenda would be asking herself the same question. How many images had he seen, Moshe and Daniel, hand in hand, dancing around and around? What impression would that make on a judge and jury?

All the sexual innuendos in the teaching, not even innuendo—blatant sexuality. Everything sexual from Adam and Eve to . . . to a lesbian wedding. God help him, he had witnessed a lesbian wedding. A man who would lie with a man, according to Moshe, the Torah itself permitted that. So a man who would lie with a boy, not such a great jump for a judge and a jury.

If the charge was made, Moshe was guilty. In the mind of the community, he would be guilty, even if he was acquitted, and he might well be. Brenda had reason to be angry with Moshe. She had offered herself to him. He had rejected her. A woman scorned. It would come out, had to. It was in the journal, and the journal was evidence.

But they might consider Moshe a man who would not lie with the mother because he had his sights set on the son.

Perhaps it was abuse.

If so, then there would be others. A pedophile wouldn't be content with one victim. There would be Andy and, what was the name of that boy who had dressed up like Queen Esther? Chris. Arthur shook his head at the thought. He had the boys dressing up like girls.

The leadership of the temple, the Garfinkels, the Lopezes, the Schwartzes, and the Kantors, all to be questioned, interrogated, subjected to physical exams. "We have to check, to probe, to insert our fingers and take pictures, to see if your son's rectum has been violated."

The girls, too? Would they do the same to the girls?

Everyone in the family program, the original families, and the twenty or thirty additional families that had joined with them along the way. There would be no way to keep this thing small. It would grow. The press, national headlines, network news. A rabbi accused of abusing an autistic child. The storm would be too great to weather.

Moshe was not a pedophile. He was not an abuser of children.

That was Arthur's new certainty. That was the certainty he carried with him to the couch. But his certainty would not be enough. Even if he had but a suspicion Moshe might be a sex offender, he had no choice but to report it. That was the law. Once reported, the matter was out of his hands, into the public domain. If he did not report it, Brenda would. Better he should do it.

Why was he certain? As he lowered his head to the pillow, the certainty began to fade. What was he doing with Daniel on the dock? Why was Daniel naked? There was a reason. He just couldn't bring it to the surface. Even if he could, even if he could justify Moshe's behavior in his own mind, he could never convince Brenda. This was her father all over again, but worse, her father abusing her son. She saw it there all before her, out the window, down by the lake, on the dock, her father approaching not her, but her defenseless son. Any venom still latent in her would be in her mouth. She would press the charge, spit it out like poison.

No, he would make the call, deliver the journal and the tapes, call it a suspicion, not a certainty.

Lying on the couch he considered the arguments again and again. Moshe was innocent, but he didn't know why, and it didn't make a difference, because there would have to be an investigation anyway. The investigation would become public, and, once public, guilt would be attached to Moshe forever, and to himself by association, and to the temple.

There was nothing to do.

He slid beneath the surface of the pond. Jonah was waiting for him.

"Hey, Artie."

"Hey, Jonah."

Jonah was in his bed, the bilious shade of his skin almost a match for the paint on the walls. "What you up to?" he asked. "You in a fix?"

"I'm doing all right," Arthur said.

"Bullshit."

260

"I've got a problem, Jonah."

"What can I do to help?"

"I don't need your help."

"You've always needed my help."

"I can handle this by myself."

"Then why did you come to me?"

"I didn't come to you."

"It's your dream, asshole."

Arthur almost woke up. He turned his back on the dream, rolled over on the couch, debated whether or not to get up and go to the bathroom. No urgency. He drifted back into the dream.

"I don't see a way out," he admitted.

"So you want to know what I would do? When you have a problem, you dispose of it."

"I don't know how to dispose of it."

"No kid, no mother, no problem."

"I don't do things like that. You never did things like that."

"How do you know what I did and didn't do?"

"I don't know."

"You don't know much, do you."

Arthur withdrew from Jonah to escape to the bathroom. He stood before the toilet, leaned forward, hand against the mirror, forehead pressed against his hand, and waited, like Yom Kippur afternoon, toward the end of the fast, when his body had begun to shut down. Every Yom Kippur afternoon he felt he had to urinate, but there was no urine, just the feeling, and this was like that. His hand began to ache where his forehead was pressed against it. He had fallen asleep, standing over the toilet. He couldn't urinate.

The image in the mirror, did Jonah look as bad as that?

"You will take care of my son," Jonah had said.

Word came that Jonah had died, a few weeks after the visit. Jonah had died, his body cremated. Arthur didn't know what happened to the ashes, or the wife, or the son. She had called, her voice less than sober, to tell him about his brother. She was going with the boy back to Lafayette, where she had family. She had never called again.

Her name was Grace. She had family in Lafayette. That was all he knew. He had never heard from her again. How long ago was that? How many years?

261

Charlotte wanted him to go, would have gone with him, to find her and the boy. It had been his choice not to go. He did not want to go, did not want to chase down that woman, that boy, a damaged boy. He remembered the look in those eyes, a cocaine baby, a heroin baby, emptiness behind those eyes. That was too much to ask of him, to take care of that child.

"I took care of you," Jonah said. Had Jonah spoken those words, or was it only in the dream?

Jonah had taken care of him, in a manner of speaking. No one messed with Artie, not with Jonah on the streets. Artie was safe in Paterson, even after Jonah left. Jonah's name was such as to leave an impression behind. Even from a distance Jonah had taken care of their mother, sent money, cash money. That money had taken care of Arthur at Rutgers after their father had died.

Drug money. Dirty money. A drugged life. A dirty life.

Jonah had no solution for his problem. There was no way out. Not even Jonah could find one.

Arthur washed his face with cold water. It wasn't enough. "I want a shower," he said to his reflection in the mirror. "I want a shower!"

He pulled the shower door open to examine the sheet metal panel under the faucets near the floor. Flat head screws. He was going to have a shower.

He knew where to get what he needed, down the corridor, into the auditorium, up the stairs to the stage, through the curtains, the closet near the exit sign. His master key opened it. A tool chest, heavier than he thought. Back through the curtains, down the stairs, through the corridor, into his study, the bathroom, the sheet metal panel, the screws. Corroded screws.

Blisters were not an impediment. He would have a shower.

The screws turned, marginally, then fully. He pried the panel free. Round things. Not faucets. Not bolts. Round things. Spigots. Spigots that hadn't been turned in years, frozen.

He rifled through the tool box, seized on a wrench, wrestled the spigots open.

He would have a shower.

He stepped back, out of harm's way, opened both faucets. The pipes gurgled, water burped, spurted, sprayed, gushed. Dirty water, rusty with age. Brown, orange, tan. Clear.

He would have a shower.

He stripped naked, felt the temperature. Just right. He stepped under the shower head and immersed himself, allowed the water to cascade upon him, closed his eyes, rejoiced.

Mayim hayim, he thought. Living water. Not really. Not a spring, an ocean, a pond, a lake. But it restored him, brought him back to life. It was resuscitating, a comfort for his soul.

His eyes opened. That was it. *Mivkah. Mayim hayim.* What Moshe was doing with Daniel, naked in the lake. It wasn't abuse. It was mivkah, ritual immersion.

But why? Why?

Arthur closed the faucets, stood dripping, pondering.

Why?

It wasn't abuse. It was mivkah. Purification. But Brenda would never see it that way, could not see it. Not in her anger. Not with her history. She would report it, and Moshe would be indicted. The temple would be indicted. Every boy and girl in the family program, spread and fingered unless he could figure out why. And convince Brenda.

But he didn't know why. And he couldn't convince Brenda.

Arthur dried and dressed, tucked his shirt properly into his pants, returned to his desk. It was nearly two in the morning. He had seven hours to figure out why. There had to be some reason for Moshe's behavior, something simple, something that would make it all go away.

Seven hours to review everything, not the materials on his desk but the materials in his mind.

He returned to the moment of creation in the cul-de-sac by the Garfinkels' house, recalled the families expanding and contracting, the six days in the points of the star, Shabbat in the middle. Daniel was likely standing behind the camera. Andy and the knife. Then the talk of Adam and Eve, sex in the garden of Eden.

Noah. What was the evil in the generation of Noah? Sex with the angels. Sex again. The tower of Babel, children building the tower out of boxes. Hanukkah, Moshe's story of the little girl, so cute, holding the little girl on the roof of the Temple in Jerusalem, lowering her down on a rope to pour more oil into the menorah.

Abraham and Isaac, the sacrifice that did not happen. Moshe said Abraham had been willing to slaughter his son, would have done it, wanted to. The merit was that he was willing not to, to move from human sacrifice, the offering of a child, to the offering of an animal.

That damned bar mitzvah service in the Everglades with a stolen Torah scroll. Jacob running away from home. Jonah running away from home. The business with the angels. Too many angels, too much with angels, as if they were real. Appeasing Esau. Jacob kept his distance from Esau afterward. Moshe never mentioned that. There was a lot Moshe never mentioned, only what he considered important, like Joseph losing his clothes. He dressed the boy in Joseph clothes, removed the clothes, layer by layer. It was getting worse and worse. Queen Esther. Drag queen Esther. She liked Halloween more than Purim. She was too old for Halloween. That was Tamar, not Esther. In Venice, California, where she could see the ocean between the buildings.

Arthur cradled his aching head in his arms and lowered it to his desk.

CHAPTER 21

MONDAY, 4:50 A.M.

Arthur awoke on the couch. He had no memory of moving to it. It was almost five o'clock. He felt a moment of panic—but also of disappointment. On one hand, only four hours were left. On the other, he had hoped it would be later and over. Might as well be done with it. He was empty. He had no why, no reason, no excuse, no obstacle to the charges. He had been through everything, everything again, and had slept on it.

Was there anything more he could do? He could clean up. That was all. There was nothing more to read, to see, to hear.

He cleared the remnants of Chinese food from the coffee table into his wastebasket, tied off the plastic bag, brought it to the outside office, found a new plastic bag in the supply closet, relined his wastebasket. That done, he turned to his desk, the mound of video- and audiotapes. Where could he put those?

He searched the closets, found a cardboard box that had contained a cartridge for the laser printer. It was just large enough. He packed the box with care and placed it in his closet, underneath his robes. The journal he left on his desk. It was quite attractive, the way Brenda had covered it. But that, too, was evidence. He could not forget to include it with the tapes.

He returned the tool chest to the maintenance closet, walked back through the stage curtains, paused to face the darkened auditorium, and stood there, confronting the emptiness before continuing on to his study.

There were still four hours before he would make the call. Whom should he call? Dade county police. Just anyone in the department? Whoever answered the phone? A suspicion of child molestation, that's what it was. There would be an office, someone to take down the information. A suspicion, only a suspicion, but that was like being a little bit pregnant. Once the suspicion was attached, there was the presumption of guilt.

Why did he feel guilty? What had he done?

He sat at his desk and turned the pages of Brenda's journal, looking at the pictures the way he used to in grammar school. The more pictures, the less the text, the easier the reading assignment. Symbols, doodles, portraits. Moshe and Daniel on the bench on Ocean Drive, one sitting this way, one the other. Like a Victorian love seat, he thought. He didn't like his thoughts and closed the book.

Not quite six o'clock. How long had it been since he had witnessed a sunrise?

He walked through the parking lot toward the playing field, toward the pale illumination in the east. He singled out one light above the horizon many times brighter than the surrounding stars. Venus, probably. Maybe Jupiter. Another month and the heat and humidity would be uncomfortable, even so early in the morning, but in late May the sea breeze was still refreshing. Arthur sat in the bleachers. No soccer game, no softball, but a sunrise, and that was worth cheering.

Where his thoughts had gone, he did not know. He wasn't aware of any as the day grew around him. There was but the sunrise, himself, and no intermediary. His awareness alone became a ripple in the moment of the sublime, enough to move him gently from the field back to the parking lot.

Carpool, he thought, and with that, the pit in his stomach opened and he fell into it. The day was hot, or he had fever and was perspiring. He walked around the buildings to the door the caterers used, let himself back in.

He had no desire and no need to return to his study. He continued down the corridor to the sanctuary and chose a seat in the last row where the friends of the bar mitzvahs sat, talking through the service. They had become so disruptive in recent years, the temple had hired a security guard to chaperone and command silence. Arthur chose one of those seats, as far as he could sit from where he stood in robes. A prayer book was inserted into the wooden sleeve attached to the back of the chair in front of him. The sleeve had been decorated with wads of gum, a circle, a smiley face. How many children had contributed to that mural? How many bar mitzvah services had it taken to complete it? Was it complete? What might it look like in another year? Another ten years?

Arthur removed the prayer book, opened to the morning service. He

266

began to pray. He hadn't davenned the morning service in so long, he wondered if he still knew how. In the seminary, for a short time, he had experimented with morning prayer. In the congregation, he had been busy leading prayer, too busy to bother with prayer for himself. But that morning he began to pray.

He began with the morning blessings, for his sight, for the clothes he was wearing, for free will, for the ability to take a step, one foot in front of the other. He stood up for that blessing, felt his weight press down against the soles of his feet.

He said a blessing for his body, acknowledgment of the collection of holes and spaces that constituted his body, that they remained appropriately open or shut so he could function, so he could breathe.

He said a blessing for his breath, that it came in and out and in again.

He said no psalms, but stood in resonance with the light that poured through the stained glass windows before him.

He whispered the Sh'ma, "Hear O Israel, the Lord our God, the Lord is One."

He took tiny steps forward toward the presence of the Holy One to begin his petition as hundreds of generations had before him. "You are blessed, God of Abraham, God of Isaac, God of Jacob . . ." He finished, "as you were a shield to Abraham, please also be a shield to me."

He stood after completing his prayer, unaware he was standing. When he became aware, he sat and fell into unawareness again.

Something like distant thunder, a distant pounding drew his attention away from nothing in particular. Was it inside him or out? Where was it coming from?

The door. Someone was banging on the door, back behind his study. What time was it? Nearly nine. Something had happened to the passage of time. His watch was moving faster, or he was moving slower.

The distant pounding stopped, then started again. He should attend to it. He stood, found his knees painful, one leg slightly numb. How long had he been sitting without moving? He had not been sleeping. What had he been doing?

He walked down the corridor by the door to his study. His phone was ringing, the door was pounding. Which should he attend to first? He continued on to the door and opened into a blinding sunlight.

"Thank God," Brenda said. She walked in behind him, Daniel in tow.

Arthur followed her to his study. The phone was still ringing. It was Charlotte. "Where have you been?" she asked. "I've been ringing you for the last half hour."

"I think I've been praying," Arthur said.

"Well, Brenda has been trying to get in touch with you. I sent her over to the temple. She should be there already. She should have been there some time ago."

"She's here."

"Are you all right? You'll call me when you're done, okay? Let me know if you want me to come and get you."

Why should she come and get me? Arthur asked himself. He had the Oldsmobile.

Brenda was there, with Daniel. She was dressed in jeans and a man's shirt. No makeup, her hair in a ponytail. He had something to say to her, if he could remember it. "This is for me to do," he said. "I've been through everything. I understand what the situation is. I'll call the police myself and make the report."

"No," she said.

"You don't have to do it," he continued. "I'll do it. Let everything come through me. It will be easier that way."

"No," she said again.

"It's okay," Daniel said.

"What's okay?" Arthur asked, turning toward him, before realizing it was Daniel who had spoken.

"I'm okay," he said. "He didn't do anything to me."

Arthur turned to Brenda. Tears were running down her face in old tracks. She was the one who wasn't able to speak. She could only shake her head.

"Mik-vah," Daniel said. "To bring my soul into this world." His words came slowly, but they formed a sentence.

Brenda spoke. "It wasn't what I thought. I don't know why I thought such a thing. Maybe I do know. It's not important. Stephanie explained it to me, what had happened, what Moshe did. Moshe had called her and asked her to call me, because I wouldn't talk with him. So she called.

"She said Daniel's soul was not completely in this world. We knew that. We just never talked about it that way. It's like he wasn't fully born." She reached out for Daniel's hand.

"Over the year Moshe drew close to Daniel, somehow bound his soul to his, one tied to the other. They became friends. I saw that. But I don't think I really knew what it meant to have a friend. I've never had a friend like that.

"Stephanie said the word for friend in Hebrew comes from the same root as joining. Moshe joined his soul to Daniel's. Bit by bit, he drew Daniel into this world.

"Thursday, I think they must have been together all night." Arthur felt the warning in her aspect, lest he misinterpret. "A breakthrough of some kind. Daniel's soul broke through, became attached, anchored. I can't pretend to know what happened. Maybe someday Daniel will be able to tell me, or Moshe, if he'll still speak to me.

"Morning came. I saw the two of them in the living room, thought nothing of it. I didn't want to disturb them, went to the grocery to get some milk, came back and found them. You know about that."

"I undressed me," Daniel said.

"Mikvah," Brenda said. "Daniel was there when Margolit and Dana did their mikvah, the day before their wedding. The way Moshe explained it, *mayim hayim*, immersion into living water to embrace a soul. Daniel understood that. He wanted that. It was important to him."

"I undressed me," Daniel said again.

"So Daniel walked into the lake and immersed himself. He came back out, and that's when I saw them." She burst into sobs, huge sobs, such that Arthur had no choice but to put his arms around her, to hold her, comfort her. He pressed her to him, hugged her, felt her warmth, her tears. "Moshe was blessing him," she said between sobs. "That's why he kissed him. It was a blessing. A blessing."

Arthur held her, rocked her until she had cried herself out of tears.

"A blessing," Daniel said.

There was a gentle knock at the door. Charlotte was standing in the doorway. "I didn't want to interrupt. I came to take you home. I didn't think you would be able to drive."

CHAPTER 22

SUNDAY, JUNE 11

Sunday morning, June 11, shortly after ten in the morning, Arthur Greenberg parked his Oldsmobile across the street from Brenda's house, out of harm's way. There were already a good many cars, more than thirteen families, Arthur guessed. Charlotte reached over to touch him on the thigh, reassurance.

In the dining room he helped himself to a sesame bagel and cream cheese.

"Hey, Arthur," Leonard Shuk said. "Good to see you."

Arthur nodded, the paper plate close to his mouth to catch the crumbs.

George Lopez looked up from the kitchen. "Coffee?" he asked.

"Black. Thank you."

He found a place to sit on the steps leading down to the family room. Children ran by in both directions. "I'm happy you're doing this," Brenda said. She was dressed in tan microfiber slacks and a white blouse. She sat beside him and began to wire him for sound. He was surprised. "What's wrong?" she asked.

"But Moshe is doing the program. We're only here to observe."

"Moshe suggested we put the mike on you for this one."

"But Moshe is here?" He hadn't seen Moshe and looked around in a bit of panic.

"Moshe is here," she said. "With Daniel. They'll be out shortly."

Brenda left to tend to the kitchen. Charlotte sat beside him, held his hand.

"What's going on?" he asked her. "Are you part of this?"

"Nothing's going on that I know of," she said.

Moshe and Daniel walked by them, down the steps. "Hey, Artie," Moshe said and smiled. He clapped his hands twice and began humming a niggun softly, one Arthur knew well from the tapes. Those close by joined in. Soon all were singing, moving toward the family room. The space became crowded, adults and children occupying all the furniture, covering most of the floor. Charlotte began to sing. Arthur, too.

Moshe took a beanbag from his pocket and threw it casually from one hand to the other.

"The name of this program is 'The Beanbag of the Law.' Brenda and Daniel are going to help me with it. Brenda is going to hand out name tags, and Daniel has a text. Pass them out please."

Brenda distributed the name tags. Daniel walked about with the texts.

Arthur watched Daniel. His steps were deliberate, careful. He handed out the papers one by one.

Daniel had been lost most of the sessions, behind the camera or in a corner, attentive to a world most saw only in their dreams. That's the way Moshe explained it.

Moshe had taken Arthur for a drive in the Porsche, down to Alabama Jack's on Card Sound Road. They sat at a table by the railing and watched the gulls hover for scraps. They talked about the family program, Moshe's plans, but mostly about Daniel.

"Daniel was a challenge," Moshe said. "Lost between worlds, never quite grounded in the World of Action. Do you know the vocabulary of the Kabbalah? *Asiah, Yetzirah* . . . ?"

Arthur did not.

"It's a matter of time, space, and soul. All dimensions exist in all the worlds. Consider what your dreams are like. Space and time exist, but not as we know them in this world. Things change into things, time isn't the same. Daniel was seeing things like that. It's as if his soul hadn't descended all the way to the bottom of space and time."

"What did you do?"

Moshe thought about that, attempted to answer, stopped, and thought again. "I don't know that I can explain it. I went to where he was and got to know him there. He got to know me, trust me. I kept leaving him, to come back to our world. Eventually he came with me. I think that's the best I can do."

Arthur watched Daniel maneuver through the space and time of the family room. He was in the real world, the World of Action, as Moshe called it. Others were beginning to notice it, also following him, knowing something was different, not quite what. The children noticed, more than the adults.

Brenda had saved one of the name tags for Daniel. "You're Hillel," she said. He smiled. Arthur had never seen Daniel smile before.

"Eighteen name tags," Moshe said, "starting with me. I get to be Moses." He tapped the name on his jersey. "From Moses, down through the generations, all the way to Rabban Gamliel. Ready? Here we go." He stood, threw the beanbag high in the air, caught it and read from the text, "'Moses received the law from God at Sinai and passed it to Joshua.' Who's Joshua?"

Marsha Perlman was Joshua. Moshe threw the beanbag across the room. Marsha caught it.

Moshe read from the text, "Joshua passed the law to the Elders. Who's the Elders?"

Gina Cohen, maybe twelve years old, was the Elders. Marsha threw the beanbag to Gina. She caught it.

Moshe continued, "The Elders passed the law to the Prophets."

George Lopez raised his hand. Gina threw him the beanbag.

Moshe read, "The Prophets passed the law to the Great Synagogue. Who's the Great Synagogue?"

Joseph Holstein, maybe eleven years old, was the Great Synagogue. George tossed him the beanbag.

Moshe read, "The people of the Great Synagogue used to say three things." He looked up to Joseph. "Joseph, you have to say three things."

Joseph read, "The people of the Great Synagogue used to say three things: Be careful in making a decision, have a lot of good students, and make a fence around the Torah."

Moshe said, "Simeon the Just was one of the last of the Great Synagogue. Who's Simeon?"

Jessica Garfinkel was Simeon. Joseph threw the beanbag wide, too wide for Jessica. It fell to the floor.

The room was silent. "Too bad," Moshe said. He walked to the fallen beanbag, picked it up, made a show of dusting it off, tossed it into the air, caught it and said, "Moses received the law from God at Sinai and passed it to Joshua."

"From the beginning?" "All over again?" came the protests.

Moshe didn't respond. He threw the beanbag to Marsha Perlman. "Who passed it to the Elders." She tossed it to Gina. "Who passed it to the

Prophets." Gina threw the beanbag overhand across the room to George Lopez, a hard throw, off target. George reached out and caught it with ease. ". . . to the Men of the Great Synagogue." George flipped it to Joseph. "Who used to say three things."

Joseph read, "Be careful in making a decision. Have a lot of good students. And make a fence around the Torah."

"Simeon the Just was one of the last of the Great Synagogue," Moses said.

All eyes were on Jessica Garfinkel. She stood, prepared to receive the beanbag. Joseph threw it wide again, but she caught it with one hand, to sighs of relief.

Moshe said, "Simeon the Just used to say something also."

Jessica consulted her text, "He used to say: 'Three things hold up the world—Torah, offerings to God, and deeds of loving kindness.'"

Moshe said, "Simeon the Just passed the law to Antigonus of Soho." Michael Capstan raised his hands. His father stood behind him. Jessica threw the beanbag underhand.

"What did Antigonus of Soho say?" Moshe asked.

Michael read slowly. "Don't be like one who works for pay, but be like those who work out of love."

The readings were simple but profound. Each pass was made with increasing care. The tenth pass was made. The eleventh, twelfth, thirteenth, fourteenth. The fifteenth was to Abtalion. Stacy Clark was Abtalion. She read, "Be careful not to teach falsehood, because, if you do, your students will be damaged after you."

Moshe said, "Abtalion passed the law to Hillel." Daniel was Hillel.

Stacy walked the beanbag over to Daniel and put it into his hands.

Moshe said, "Hillel used to say three things."

Daniel held the beanbag and said, slowly, one phrase at a time, "If I am not for myself . . . who will be? If I am only for myself . . . what am I? And if not now . . . when?"

Moshe allowed the moment its weight. The astonishment in the room was palpable. Arthur understood Daniel had rehearsed the lines, studied them. Daniel had become a Hillel, a speaking Hillel. The impact required time to settle. Brenda leaned against Arthur, not doing anything about her tears.

"Hillel passed the law to Shammai," Moshe said at last, almost in a whisper.

273

Robert Kantor stepped forward. Arthur wondered what Robert would do, how he might rise to the occasion. Robert took the beanbag from Daniel's hands, put out his arms and drew Daniel into a hug. Daniel hugged him back. They stood like that for a long time.

Several of the children came forward, those who understood what had happened, then those who didn't but wanted to be part of it. All of the children stood around Daniel in a giant hug.

"Thank you," Moshe said. "Daniel thanks you, too. It may be too difficult at the moment for him to say so, but he will."

The hug unraveled.

Moshe said, "Shammai received the law from Hillel. What did Shammai used to say?"

Robert read, "Set a regular time to study Torah. Say little and do much. Greet everybody happily."

"And Shammai passed the law on to Rabban Gamliel. Who is Rabban Gamliel." Brenda took a name tag out of her pocket and stuck it to Arthur's shirt.

"I guess I'm Rabban Gamliel," he said.

Robert walked the beanbag over to him. Arthur took it, turned it over, examined it carefully.

"What did Rabban Gamliel used to say?" Moshe asked.

Arthur read, "Get yourself a good teacher and remove yourself from doubt. That's what Rabban Gamliel used to say."

Moshe nodded toward Arthur. "That's what Rabban Gamliel used to say." He turned to address the families. "Daniel and I are going to take a walk. This has been a lot for him. We're going to go out and relax a little bit. Rabbi Greenberg can finish the session. Help him with it. He's new here. Daniel, do you want to come with me?"

Daniel took Moshe's hand. The two of them walked out toward the lake.

Brenda gave Arthur the instructions for the balance of the program. He had been set up, but he felt no anger. He had faith. If Moshe had put the program in his hands, the program was something he could do. After all, if he wasn't a prophet himself, he was the child of a prophet.

"A niggun," he said, sounding in his own ears like Moshe. "But you don't want to hear me sing. I sing in the key of H. We need someone with a musical ear. Orly, would you begin?"

Orly seemed surprised Arthur knew her name. She began chanting a tune, one he recognized, but he was too busy learning the remainder of the program to sing.

Arthur finished reading what Moshe had written, closed his eyes and smiled. "A question to consider," he began, then opened his eyes to examine the faces, all turned to him. "In small groups, please. Adults and children together, children not with their own parents." Children scurried about the room, laying claim to their favored adults. "Ready?" Arthur asked. "We saw the beanbag passed through the generations eighteen times. The first pass was from God to Moses. The last pass was from Shammai to Rabban Gamliel. Which of the eighteen passes was the most important?"

"The first." "From God to Moses." Instant answers.

"Think about it before you answer." Arthur considered the question himself, saw the simple beauty in it.

Someone was tugging at his shirt. A child. "Do you want to study with us?" she asked. He looked quickly around the room. Everyone was involved in learning, Charlotte in a group across the room.

"Yes," he said. He listened to what each person in the group had to say, afraid to speak himself for fear of stopping the responses.

He looked toward Orly, caught her eye, so she would know to resume the niggun. Talk tapered off.

"What are the possibilities?" Arthur asked. "Which pass is the most important?"

"The first one," was one response.

"The last one," was another.

"That's what it comes down to," Arthur said. "The first or the last. So many people ask me if God really gave the Torah to Moses at Sinai, as if that's the most important thing in the world. I know how to answer them now.

"Think about this." He threw the beanbag up in the air and caught it, did so again, and again. "Moses catching the law from God at Sinai." He let the beanbag fall. "Oops. I have to go all the way back to the beginning." He threw the beanbag up and caught it. "Not so much, one pass, even if it is from God to Moses. We already know Moses dropped it once.

"Now this pass, this next one, is the last one, from Shammai to Rabban Gamliel. If I drop this one, we have to go back and do the whole program again. Nobody seemed upset when I dropped the pass from God to Moses, but this time, I'm serious. If I drop this one, we do it all over again from the beginning."

275

He threw the beanbag into the air, missed it with his right hand, but caught it low to the ground with his left.

"If I had dropped that, we'd have to do all eighteen generations. Now, a question. Were you more apprehensive when I was playing with the beanbag when we were talking about the first pass or the last?"

"The last."

"Maybe that tells us which was more important."

George Lopez said, "So if that's the case, did God really give the law to Moses at Sinai?"

Arthur held the beanbag up, looked at it. "It's been through a lot of generations. I think more important than God giving the law to Moses at Sinai is us giving the law to our children here in Miami. Miami is more important than Sinai."

"But without one, you don't have the other," George continued.

"Drop the first pass, just one generation. But if we drop this pass," Arthur threw the beanbag up, watched it fall, caught it again at the last moment, "if we drop this one, it isn't just eighteen generations we lose. It's all the generations. Forty, sixty, a hundred generations from Sinai up to the present. The most important pass is from us to our children. Three thousand years at risk. We'd better be careful how we make this pass."

Arthur raised the beanbag and threw it with some force toward George. George caught it with a casual grace, examined it, with curiosity, as if some mystery were contained in it, then bent over and placed it into the hands of his youngest child.

"One more thing for us to do," Arthur said. He looked toward Brenda. She took the cue and passed around blank name tags and pencils. "Each of us is now a rabbi, every one of us. You can choose your own name. They had colorful names back then. We can have colorful names, too. They had names like Yosi ben Yo-ezer of Zeredah or Nittai the Arbelite. We can be Happy Harry from Homestead, or Marsha the Marbelite, whatever we choose. So in this part of the program, you choose a name, and along with your name, a wisdom statement. What did you used to say? Each of us has some wisdom, deep inside, even if it's only for this moment, at this point in our lives. This is what we're going to do. Go back into groups. Decide on your name. Write it on your name tag. Write one sentence, a wisdom statement you are willing to share."

Arthur returned to his study group. Susan Cohen, president of the sisterhood, became Suzanne the Mavin. She used to say, "A maybe is better

276

than a no." Jennifer Garfinkel, not quite bat mitzvah age, became Rabbi Jennie by the Sea. She used to say, "A maybe isn't better than a no when it comes to smoking or drugs." Susan began to giggle. Jennifer, too. Arthur realized this woman and pre-teen had become friends, would remain friends throughout the years. Joseph Holstein became Rabbi Joseph with the Colored Coat. Rabbi Joseph was eleven years old. He used to say, "Don't judge a person by his designer jeans." Miriam Capstan became Miriam of the Well. She used to say, "When you're thirsty, the water will be there."

Groups came together, shared names and wisdom, with smiles and laughter. Arthur felt eyes turn now and then to him. He looked down at the blank name tag in his hand.

He was the only one without a name.

"I am Artie," he said. "Artie, from New Jersey. Artie from New Jersey used to say, 'Remember where you came from, know where you are going, and stand tall in between.'"

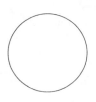

CHAPTER 23

JULY

Tamar and Cindy told them to go, not to worry. They would be happy to have the day to themselves, just to walk through the French Quarter.

That was the problem with a Corvette, Charlotte said. There was room only for two. But New Orleans wasn't a town that demanded a car. Most everything was in walking distance, or on the streetcar line.

Arthur and Charlotte were quiet as they drove out of the city. "It's been a good week," he said. Three days they had driven the back roads through Florida, hugging the coast through the panhandle, on into New Orleans. Tamar and Cindy had flown in, were already in their room at the Royal Orleans when Arthur and Charlotte arrived.

Two days they were together, taking tours, window shopping, jazz and Cajun music in the evenings. Tamar and Cindy danced the two-step. They weren't the only women dancing with each other.

The Corvette navigated back roads through the bayous, shady trees knee-deep in water, into Lafayette. There were wonderful antiques in Lafayette, Charlotte said. They found the recommended district, acres of old things from France to see. That was for Charlotte.

Arthur sat, phonebook in hand, and began calling agencies. Searching for Grace, hoping to find his brother's son.